# The Boss's
## *Christmas*
## Seduction

D1353477

# The Boss's *Christmas* Seduction

## LYNNE GRAHAM
## LUCY MONROE
## CAITLIN CREWS

MILLS & BOON

Published in Great Britain 2015
by Mills & Boon, an imprint of Harlequin (UK) Limited,
Eton House, 18-24 Paradise Road, Richmond, Surrey, TW9 1SR

THE BOSS'S CHRISTMAS SEDUCTION
© 2015 Harlequin Books S.A.

*Unlocking Her Innocence* © 2012 Lynne Graham
*Million Dollar Christmas Proposal* © 2013 Lucy Monroe
*Not Just the Boss's Plaything* © 2013 Caitlin Crews

ISBN: 978-0-263-91567-9

012-1015

Harlequin (UK) Limited's policy is to use papers that are natural, renewable and recyclable products and made from wood grown in sustainable forests. The logging and manufacturing processes conform to the legal environmental regulations of the country of origin.

Printed and bound in Spain
by CPI, Barcelona

# UNLOCKING
# HER INNOCENCE

LYNNE GRAHAM

**Lynne Graham** was born in Northern Ireland and has been a keen Mills & Boon® reader since her teens. She is very happily married, with an understanding husband who has learned to cook since she started to write! Her five children keep her on her toes. She has a very large dog, which knocks everything over, a very small terrier, which barks a lot, and two cats. When time allows, Lynne is a keen gardener.

# CHAPTER ONE

CHRISTMAS. It was *that* time of year again. Not in a jolly mood, Vito Barbieri grimaced, his darkly handsome features hard with impatience. He had no time for it—the silliness of the festive season, the drunken antics and the extravagance, not to mention the lack of concentration, increased absenteeism and reduced productivity from his thousands of staff. January was never a good month for the profit margins.

Nor was he ever likely to forget the Christmas when he had lost his kid brother, Olly. Although three years had passed the tragedy of Olly's horribly wasted life was still etched on his mind. His little brother, so bright and full of promise, had died because a drunk got behind a car wheel after a party, Vito's party, where he and his brother had argued minutes before that fatal car journey. Guilt clouded his happier memories of the boy, ten years his junior, whom he had loved above all else.

But then love always *hurt*. Vito had learned that lesson young when his mother walked out on her husband and son for a much richer man. He never saw her again. His father had neglected him and rushed into a series of fleeting affairs. Olly had been the result of one of those affairs, orphaned at nine years old when his English mother died. Vito had offered him a home. It was probably the only act of generosity Vito had never regretted, for, much as he missed Olly, he was still grateful to have known him. His sibling's sunny outlook had briefly enriched Vito's workaholic existence.

Only now Bolderwood Castle, purchased purely because Olly fancied living in a gothic monstrosity complete with turrets, was no longer a home. Of course he could take a wife and watch her walk away with half his fortune, his castle and his children, a lesson so many of his friends had learned to their cost, a few years down the road. No, there would be no wife, Vito reflected grimly. When a man was as rich as Vito, greedy, ambitious women literally threw themselves at his feet. But tall or short, curvy or skinny, dark or fair, the women who met the needs of his high sex drive were virtually interchangeable. Indeed sex was steadily becoming nothing to get excited about, he acknowledged wryly. At thirty-one years of age, Vito was reviewing the attributes he used to define an attractive woman by.

He knew what he *didn't* like. Airheads irritated him. He was not a patient or tolerant man. Intellectual snobs, party girls and social climbers bored him. Giggly, flirtatious ones reminded him too much of his misspent youth and tough career women rarely knew how to lighten up at the end of the day. Either that or they wanted a four point plan of any relationship laid out in advance. Did he want children? Did he actually know if he was fertile? Did he want to settle down some day? No, he didn't. He wasn't opening himself up to that level of disillusionment; particularly not after losing Olly had taught him how transitory life could be. He would be a very rich and cantankerous and demanding old man instead.

There was a knock on the door and a woman entered the room. Karen Harper, his office manager, Vito recalled after a momentary pause; AeroCarlton, which manufactured aeroplane parts, was a recent acquisition in Vito's business empire and he was only just getting to know the staff.

'I'm sorry to disturb you, Mr Barbieri. I wanted to check that you're happy to continue endorsing the prisoner rehabilitation placement scheme we joined last year? It's run by the charity New Start and they recommend suitable applicants who they fully check out and support. We have an office trainee starting tomorrow. Her name's—'

'I don't need to know the details,' Vito cut in smoothly, 'I have no objection to operating such a scheme but will expect you to keep a close watch on the employee.'

'Of course,' the attractive brunette declared with a bright smile of approval. 'It feels good at this time of year to give someone in difficulty a new chance in life, doesn't it? And the placement does only last three months.'

More goody-goody sentimental drivel, Vito thought in exasperation. He supposed the applicant had paid her debt to society through serving her sentence in prison but he was not particularly enamoured of the prospect of having a potential villain on the premises. 'Did this person's crime involve dishonesty?' he queried suddenly.

'No, we were clear that we wouldn't accept anyone with that kind of record. I doubt if you'll even see her, Mr Barbieri. She'll be the office gopher. She can take care of messages, filing and man reception. At this time of year, there's always room for an extra pair of hands.'

A momentary pang of conscience assailed Vito, for,

astute as he was, he had already noticed that the manager could be a little too tough on her subordinates. Only the day before he had overheard her taking the janitor to task over a very minor infringement of his duties. Karen enjoyed her position of power and used it, but he could only assume that an ex-con would be well equipped to cope.

Ava checked the postbox as she did at least twice every day. Nothing. There was no point trying to avoid the obvious, no point in continuing to hope—her family wanted nothing more to do with her and had decided to ignore her letters. Tears pricked her bright blue eyes and she blinked rapidly, lifting her coppery head high. She had learned to get by on her own in prison and she could do the same in the outside world, even if the outside world was filled with a bewildering array of choices, disappointments and possibilities that made her head swim.

'Don't try to run before you can walk,' her probation officer had advised. Sally was a great believer in platitudes.

Harvey's tail thumped the floor at Ava's feet and she bent down to smooth his soft curly head. A cross between a German shepherd and a poodle, Harvey was a large dog with floppy ears, a thick black curly coat and a long shaggy tail that looked as though it belonged to another breed entirely.

'Time to get you home, boy,' Ava said softly, trying not to think about the fact that the boarding kennels where Harvey lived could not possibly house him for much longer. During the last few months of her sentence Ava worked at the kennels—outside work was encouraged as a means of reintroducing prisoners into the community and independent life—and she was all too well aware that Harvey was living on borrowed time.

She loved Harvey with all her heart and soul. He was the one thing in her life that she dared love now, and on the days she saw him he lifted her heart as nothing else could. But Marge, the kind lady who ran the kennels and took in strays, had limited space and Harvey had already spent months in her care without finding a home. Harvey, however, was his own worst enemy because he barked at the people who might have given him a for-ever home, scaring them off before they could learn about his gentle, loyal character and clean habits. Ava knew how big the gap between appearances and reality could be; she had spent so many years putting on a false front to keep people at arm's length, believing that she didn't need anyone, didn't care about other people's opinions and was proud to be the odd one out. At home, at school, just about everywhere she went, Ava had been alone…

Except for Olly, she thought, and a fierce pang of pain and regret shot through her as sharply as a knife. Oliver Barbieri had been her best friend and she had to live with the knowledge that it was her fault he was dead. She had gone to prison for reckless driving but the memory of the trial was blurred because she had already been living in a mental hell and no court could have punished her more than she had punished herself. It hadn't mattered that her father had thrown her out of the house in disgust or even that she had been advised not to attend Olly's funeral and pay her last respects. She had known she didn't deserve pity or forgiveness. Even so she did not remember the crash. During it she had sustained a head injury and was left with memory loss, meaning she recalled neither her fateful, incomprehensible decision to drive while under the influence of alcohol or the accident itself. Sometimes she thought that amnesia was a blessing, and sometimes that only fear of reliving what she had done lay behind her inability to recall the later stages of that awful night.

She had met Olly at boarding school, a trendy co-ed institution with high fees and a fantastic academic record. No price had been too high for her father to get his least-loved child out from under his roof, she acknowledged sadly. Always made to feel like the cuckoo in the family nest, Ava was the only one of three children to have been sent away from home to receive her education. It had driven yet another wedge between Ava and her sisters, Gina and Bella, and, now that she had truly become the prodigal daughter, there was no sign that anyone wanted to welcome her back to the fold. Of course her mother was dead and there was nobody left to mend fences or at least nobody who cared enough to make the effort. Her sisters had their own lives with husbands and children and careers and their ex-con sister was simply an embarrassment, a stain on the Fitzgerald family name.

Scolding herself for that demoralising flood of negative reflections, Ava strove instead to concentrate on the positives: she was out of prison, she had a job, an actual *job*—she still couldn't believe her good fortune. When she had first been recommended for the New Start programme she had not held out much hope of a placement because, although she had left school with top grades, she had no relevant office work experience or saleable skills. But AeroCarlton had offered her a lifebelt, giving her the chance to rebuild her life, with a reputable firm on her CV she would have a much better chance of getting a permanent job.

Harvey's tail dropped as he stepped through the doors of his foster home. Marge put on the kettle and shooed him out into the garden because he took up too much space indoors. Marooned there, Harvey pressed his nose to the glass of the French windows in the living room, watching Ava's every move.

'Here…pass this around tomorrow when you start your new job,' Marge urged, pressing a paper catalogue on Ava. 'A few orders would be very welcome and I've got to say that the work my lovely ladies have put in so far is exceptional.'

Ava glanced through the booklet of hand-knit and embroidered cushions, bookmarks, hat and scarf sets; spectacle cases, toys and even lavender bags, most of which depicted various cat and dog breeds. In an effort to raise money to fund the stray and abandoned animals currently staying in her kennels, as well as in local foster homes, Marge had set up a little cottage industry of animal-loving neighbours and supporters who knit and sewed. It was an impressive display of merchandise, nicely timed for the Christmas market, but, Ava thought ruefully, the ladies could have broadened their designs a little to appeal more to the younger market.

'I know you walked here for Harvey's benefit but have you got your bus fare home?' Marge pressed anxiously, her friendly face troubled by the tiredness etched in Ava's delicate features.

'Of course I have,' Ava lied, not wanting Marge to put her hand into her own far from deep purse.

'And have you got a decent outfit to wear tomorrow?' Marge checked. 'You'll have to dress smart for a big office.'

'I picked up a trouser suit in a charity shop.' Ava would not have dreamt of admitting that the trousers were a little too tight and the jacket unable to button over her rather too generous bust. Wearing them with a blue shirt, she would look smart enough and nobody was likely to notice that her flat black shoes were too big. She would have liked shoes with a heel but beggars couldn't be choosers and it would take a lot of paydays to build up a working wardrobe. Once she had adored fashion, but she had given up that pursuit along with so many other interests that were no longer appropriate. Now she concentrated on the far more important challenge of simply getting by, which came down to paying rent, feeding and clothing herself as best she could. The adventurous, defiant girl who had sported the Goth look—black lace, leather and dyed black hair cut short as a boy's—had died along with Olly in that car crash, she conceded painfully, barely recognising the very cautious and sensible young woman she had become.

Prison had taught her to seek anonymity. Standing out from the crowd there would have been dangerous. She had learned to keep her head down, follow the rules, help out when she could, keep her mouth shut when she couldn't. Prison had shamed her, just as the judgement of the court had shamed her. Much had been made of her fall in the local newspaper because of her comfortable family background and private school education. At the time she had thought it very unfair that she should be pilloried for what she could not help. Then in prison she had met women who could barely read, write or count and she had worked with them, recognising their more basic problems. For them, getting involved in criminal activities had only been a means of survival, and Ava knew that she had never had that excuse.

So what if your father never liked you? So what if your mother never defended you or hugged you and both parents always favoured your sisters over you? So what if they labelled you a troublemaker in primary school where you got bullied? So what if your mother was an alcoholic and her problems were ignored for years?

There would never be an excuse for what she had done to Olly, whom she had loved like a brother, she thought wretchedly as she walked wearily home to her bedsit. Everything always seemed to come back round to the events of that dreadful night. But somehow she had to learn to live with her massive mistake and move on from it. She would never ever forget her best friend but she knew he would have been the first to tell her to stop tormenting herself. Olly had always been wonderfully practical and great at cutting through all the superficial stuff to the heart of a problem. Had he lived, he would have become a wonderful doctor.

'It's not your fault that your mother drinks…it's not your fault that your parents' marriage is falling apart or that your sisters are spoiled stuck-up little brats! Why do you always take on the blame for everything wrong in your family?' Olly used to demand impatiently.

Full of anticipation, Ava laid out her clothes for the next morning. Having been assured by New Start that her history would remain confidential, she had no fear of being seen as anything other than the new office junior. She had learned to love being busy and useful because that gave her a feeling of achievement, instead of the hollow sense of self-loathing that had haunted her for months after the crash when she had had far too many idle hours in which to dwell on her mistakes.

'You can make the coffee for the meeting. There will be twenty members of staff attending,' Karen Harper pronounced with a steely smile. 'You can make coffee?'

Ava nodded vigorously, willing to do anything to please and already sensing that pleasing Miss Harper, as she had introduced herself, might be a challenge. Shown into the small kitchen, she checked out where everything was and got busy.

At ten forty-five, Ava wheeled the trolley into the conference room where a formidably tall man was speaking to the staff surrounding the long table. There was colossal tension in the room and nobody else spoke at all. He was talking about change being inevitable but…it would not be happening overnight and redundancies looked unlikely. His voice had a mellifluous accent that was instantly recognisable and familiar to her ears: Italian. As his audience shifted in their seats with collective relief at the forecast, Ava poured the boss's coffee with a shaking hand. Black, two sugars, according to the list. It could *not* be Vito, her dazed mind was telling her, it could not possibly be Vito. Fate could not have served her up a job in a company run by the man whom she had most injured. And yet she *knew* Vito's voice, the deep drawl laced with a lilt over certain vowel sounds that used to make her tummy flip as if she were on a roller coaster. She did not dare look, would not allow herself to look, as she walked down the side of the room to serve the boss first and slipped right out of her too large shoes so that by the time she reached the top of the table she was barefoot!

Vito had glanced at the girl bent over the coffee trolley, noting the fiery hair glinting with gold and copper highlights wound into a knot on the top of her head, the delicacy of her profile, the elegance of her slender white hands and the tight fit of her trousers over the small curvy behind that segued down into long slim legs. There was something about her, something that captured his attention, something maddeningly familiar but what it was he could not have said until she straightened and he saw an elfin face dominated by pansy blue eyes. His breath caught in his lungs and he stopped breathing, unable to believe that it could be *her*. The last time he had seen her she had had black hair cropped short and the blank look of trauma in her gaze as if she couldn't see or hear anything happening around her. Ferocious tension etched harsh lines into the almost feral beauty of his strong handsome face.

Oh dear heaven, it was Vito Barbieri! Feeling sick from shock, Ava froze with his cup of coffee rattling in her trembling hand.

'Thank you,' Vito breathed with no expression at all, his dark golden eyes skimming her pale shaken visage as he accepted the coffee from her.

'Mr Barbieri, this is Ava Fitzgerald who joined the staff today,' Karen Harper advanced helpfully.

'We've already met,' Vito pronounced with icy bite. 'Come back when the meeting is over, Ava. I'd like to speak to you.'

Ava managed to step smoothly back into her shoes on her way back to the tea trolley. With the rigorous self-discipline she had picked up in prison, she served the rest of the coffee without mishap although her skin was clammy with perspiration and she breathed in and out rapidly to get a grip on herself.

Vito Barbieri—it was a horrible coincidence that her job opportunity should turn out to be in his business. But what on earth was he doing at AeroCarlton? She had read the company website and there had been no reference to Vito, yet he was obviously the boss. So much for her big break! Vito wouldn't want her anywhere near him: he despised her. When she returned to that room he would tell her that she was sacked. Of course he would. What else could she expect him to do? It was her fault that Olly was dead so why would he employ her? He had been shocked to see her. The grim tightness of those lean, bronzed features had been unusually revealing. Had he known who she was in advance he would have withdrawn her placement before she'd even arrived at AeroCarlton.

Vito, the bane of her life from the age of sixteen. She clamped an uneasy hand to the tattoo seared over her left hip where it seemed to burn like a brand. She had been such a stupid and impulsive teenager, she acknowledged wretchedly, deeply shaken by the encounter that had just taken place. None of the boys at school had attracted her. She had had to go home with Olly for the weekend to see her dream guy. Ten years her senior and a fully grown adult male with the killer instincts of a business shark, her dream guy had barely noticed she was alive, let alone sitting up and begging for his attention. True, he had seemed a little taken aback by his brother's choice of companion, taking in Ava in her Goth getup with her dyed black hair and mutinous expression. She had never stayed in a castle before and had been trying very hard to act as if she were cool with the intimidating experience.

'Ava?' Ava wheeled round and found Karen Harper studying her. 'You didn't mention that you knew Mr Barbieri…'

'My father works for him and we lived near his home,' Ava admitted awkwardly.

The brunette pursed her lips. 'Well, don't expect that to cut you any slack,' she warned. 'Mr Barbieri's waiting for you. Clear the coffee cups while you're in there.'

'Yes. I didn't know he…er…worked here.'

'Mr Barbieri took over AeroCarlton last week. He's your employer.'

'Right…' With a polite smile that was wasted on the disgruntled woman frowning at her, Ava beat a swift retreat, nausea bubbling in the pit of her stomach. Serious bad luck seemed to follow her round like a nasty shadow! Here she was trying to adjust to being back in the world again and the one man who probably wished that the authorities had kept her locked up turned out to be her new boss.

Vito was resting back against the edge of the table and talking on the phone in fast fluid Italian when she reappeared. Nervous as a cat facing a lion, Ava used the time to quietly load the china back onto the trolley but the image of him remained welded onto her eyelids: the tailored black business suit cut to precision on his very tall, broad shouldered and lean-hipped frame, the white shirt so crisp against his bronzed skin, the gold silk tie that echoed his eyes in sunlight. He was breathtakingly good-looking and exotic from the bold thrust of his high cheekbones and strong nose to his slashing dark brows and beautifully moulded sensual mouth.

He hadn't changed. He still exuded an aura of authority and crackling energy that whipped up a tension all of its own. Olly's big brother, she thought painfully, and if only she had listened to Olly her best friend might still have been alive.

'Stop trying to flirt with Vito, stop throwing yourself at him!' Olly had warned her in exasperation the night of that fatal party. 'You're not his type and you're too young for him and even if you weren't, Vito would eat you for breakfast. He's a predator with women.'

Back then Vito's type had been sleek, blonde, elegant and sophisticated, everything Ava was not, and the comparison had torn her up. He had been out of reach; so far above her it had broken her heart. She had become obsessed by Vito Barbieri, wildly infatuated as only a stubborn lovelorn teenager could be, cherishing every little scrap of information she could find out about him. He took sugar in his coffee and he liked chocolate. He supported several children's charities that dispensed medical aid in developing countries. He had suffered a challenging childhood when his parents broke up and his father took to alcohol and other women to assuage his grief. He loved to drive fast and collected cars. Although he had perfect teeth he hated going to the dentist. The recollection of all those once very much prized little facts sank Ava dangerously deep into the clinging tentacles of the past she had buried.

'We'll talk in my office next door,' Vito decreed, having come off the phone. He moved away from the table and opened a door on the other side of the room. 'Leave the damn trolley!'

That impatient exclamation made her hand shoot back from the handle she had automatically been reaching for. Colour ran like a rising flag up her slender throat into her heart-shaped face, flushing her cheeks with discomfiture.

Stunning eyes narrowed, Vito studied her, his attention descending from the multicoloured topknot that was so unfamiliar to him, down over her pale perfect face with those big blue eyes, that dainty little nose and lush, incredibly tempting mouth and straight away he felt like loosening his collar because he felt too warm. Memory was pelting him with images he had put away a long time ago. Ava in a little silver shimmery slip of a dress, lithe curves only hinted at, legs that went on for ever. He breathed in slow and deep. The *taste* of Ava's mouth, her hands running up beneath his jacket over his shirt in an incredibly arousing way. Sex personified and prohibited, absolutely not to be touched under any circumstances. And he had broken the rules, he who never broke such rules, who prided himself on his self-control and decency. True, it had only been a kiss but it had been a kiss that should never have happened and the fallout from it had destroyed his family.

Emerging from that disturbing flash of recollection, Vito was tense as a steel rod. He would sack her, of course he would. Having her in the same office when he would not be moving on until the reorganisation was complete was inappropriate. *Utterly inappropriate*, just like his thoughts. He would not keep the young woman who was responsible for his brother's death in one of his businesses. Nobody would expect him to, nobody would condemn his reasoning. But quick as a flash he knew someone who would have done... Olly, caring, compassionate Olly, who had once acted as the voice of Vito's unacknowledged conscience.

Ava moved unsteadily past him, bright head high, refusing to show weakness or concern. Vito was tough, hard, ruthless and brutally successful in a business environment, willing to take a risk and fly in the face of adversity, everything Olly had never been. And yet that had not been the whole story either, Ava conceded painfully, for, macho as Vito undoubtedly was he had been so supportive of the news that Olly was gay, admitting that he had already guessed. Vito had suspected why, like Ava, Olly was the odd one out at school.

And she still remembered Olly laughing and joking in enormous relief at his brother's wholehearted acceptance.

A prickling wash of tears burned below Ava's lowered lids and a flood of anguished grief gripped her for the voice she would never hear again, for the supportive friend she had grown to love.

# CHAPTER TWO

THE film of dampness in her eyes only slowly receding, Ava shook her bright head as though to clear it and glanced around herself. The office was massive with an ocean of wooden flooring surrounding a contemporary desk and one corner filled with relaxed seating and a coffee table. Everything was tidy, not one thing out of place, and it exactly depicted Vito's organised, stripped-back style, the desk marred only by a laptop and a single sheaf of documents.

'I couldn't believe it when I recognised you,' Vito admitted flatly.

'It was just as much of a shock for me. I didn't know you owned this business.' Ava's strained eyes darted over him, absorbing the strong angle of his cheekbones, the stubborn jut of his chin and then falling helpless into the melted honey of his beautiful eyes. Eyes the shade of old gold, fringed by outrageously long and luxuriant black lashes. Her heart started to pound as if he had pressed a button somewhere in her body and her mouth ran dry as a bone.

'What are you doing here?' he demanded sardonically. 'I assumed you'd reapply to medical school once you were released.'

Ava froze, her facial muscles tightening. 'No—'

Vito frowned. 'Why not? I'll agree you couldn't expect the university to hold open your place until you got out of prison but you were a brilliant student and I'm sure they would be willing to reconsider you.'

Ava stared steadily back at him but she wasn't really focusing on him any longer. 'That time's gone. I can't go back there...' She hesitated, reluctantly recalling how excited she and Olly had been when they had both received offers to study medicine at the same university. It was unthinkable to her that she could now try to reclaim what Olly had for ever lost because of her. 'I'm here because I needed a job, a way of supporting myself.'

An enquiring ebony brow quirked in surprise. 'Your family?'

Ava raised her chin. 'They don't bother with me now. I haven't heard from any of them since I was sentenced.'

'They are taking a very tough line,' Vito commented, suppressing a stab of pity for her that he felt was inapt.

'They can't forgive me for letting them down.'

'People forgive much worse. You were still a foolish teenager.'

Ava snatched in a shuddering breath, her hands knotting into fists by her sides. 'Have *you* forgiven me?'

Vito went very still, his body rigid with sudden screaming tension, his face hard beneath his bronzed skin. His cloaked eyes lashed back to her with a hint of flaring gold, bright as an eagle hunting for prey. 'I can't.'

Ava felt as sick as if he had punched her and she didn't know how she had dared to ask that crazy question or even why she had asked it. What other answer could she have expected from Olly's brother?

'He was the only family I had,' Vito breathed in curt continuation, his handsome mouth compressing into a harsh line.

Ava was trembling. 'He was pretty much irreplaceable. So what now?' she asked baldly, forcing herself to move away from the topic of Olly before she lost control and embarrassed herself even more. 'You can't want me working here even temporarily.'

'I don't,' Vito admitted grimly, for he had far too many unsettling memories attached to her and his brother and he hated such reminders. He swung away from her with surprising grace for so large a man and moved behind his desk. She *needed* the job, the chance to take up her life again. He recognised that: he just didn't want her doing it around him. She had stolen Olly's life and now she had her own back. Or did she? Her entire family had cut her loose. She had also given up her dream of becoming a doctor. Where was his sense of fair play? Did he usually kick people when they were already down and out? She was struggling: he could see it in the shaky set of that luscious mouth, in the fierce tension of her slim body. Given the opportunity his little brother would, he knew, have urged him not to punish Ava for what had happened. Typical Olly, always the peacemaker, Vito reflected broodingly, his even white teeth gritting as he searched inside himself for some similar strain of compassion and found only the yawning emptiness that the loss of his brother had created.

'So do you want me to leave immediately?' Ava enquired flatly, fighting to keep the unsteadiness out of her voice.

Vito didn't want to look at her because she was making him feel like a bully and, whatever he was, he was not that. He glanced down at his desk and inspiration struck him in the form of the Christmas list lying there. That would be perfect: it would get her out of the office and she revelled in all that Christmas bull so it could not be viewed as a punishment either. From what he could see she had already had her punishment.

'No, you can stay for the moment,' he breathed harshly, thinking that he could shift her elsewhere after the festive season was over and it would cause a lot less comment. 'I have a task I want you to take care of for me...'

Shocked by that sudden turnaround when she had been so sure he was going to sack her, Ava moved quickly forward, too quickly for her ill-fitting shoes. She stepped out of one shoe, having forgotten to clench her toes in it for staying power. 'What is it?'

'What is wrong with your shoes?' Vito demanded impatiently as she lurched to an uneven halt to thrust her foot back into the item.

'They don't fit.'

'Why not?'

Ava reddened. 'Everything I'm wearing is second hand.'

Distaste filled Vito at the mere idea of wearing someone else's clothing.

Recognising his reaction, Ava turned pale with chagrin. 'Look, the last time I was free I was eighteen and wearing Goth clothes. I've grown out of that and I couldn't turn up here to work in a pair of old jeans.'

Vito pulled his wallet out, withdrew a wad of banknotes and extended it to her. 'Buy yourself some shoes,' he told her drily.

Ava was aghast at the gesture. 'I can't take *your* money.'

'You're planning to refuse your salary?'

'No, but that's different,' she argued. 'It's not personal.'

'This isn't personal either. You might try to sue us if you have an accident and you're not much use to anyone round here when you can't walk properly,' Vito fielded without hesitation as he reached for the document, eager to get her back out of his office. 'And you'll probably be doing a lot of walking.'

'What are you talking about?'

He handed her the sheet of paper and the money together. She was close enough to pick up on the spicy scent of his cologne and note the flexing of lean strong muscle below his shirt as he leant forward, compensating for the height difference between them. At over six feet tall, he towered over her five feet four inches. All too readily, however, she remembered the warm, solid feel of his muscular chest below her palms and she stiffened defensively. When he came close, she still wanted to touch him; it was that simple. Guilt assailed her when she thought about the way she had once behaved in his radius.

'It's my Christmas list for the associates we give presents to. Karen Harper will issue you with a company credit card and you will follow the suggestions and go out and gather them all up. OK?' Vito spelt out shortly, his smouldering gaze pinned to the damp pink pout of her mouth.

What was it about her that ensnared him? Vito wondered in frustration, feeling the tight heaviness and drag of response at his groin. While she seemed naively unaware of her own sexual power he was all too aware that he found everything about her, from that peachy mouth to the tightness of her blouse over her full round breasts and the fit of her trousers, ridiculously tempting. He wanted her. He wanted to bed her so badly it almost hurt to think that he could never have her and the very thought of that shocked him afresh. It had been so long since a woman affected him on a visceral level. The last time had been with her, in fact, and that bothered him, bothered him in a way he didn't appreciate being bothered. No, he definitely didn't want her under his feet during his working day.

Ava looked up at him in surprise and clashed involuntarily with scorching dark golden eyes of such stormy beauty she could hardly breathe. A tingling sensation ran through her, tightening her nipples like a sudden blast of cold air, although there was nothing chilly about the well of heat building low in her pelvis.

'You want me to go shopping?' she queried disbelievingly. 'But I'm not a girly girl.'

'Nevertheless if you want to retain employment here you will do as you are told,' Vito countered drily.

Ava flushed and nibbled at the soft underside of her lower lip, the tip of her tongue slicking out to ease the dryness there, while she swallowed back the spark of temper he had ignited. His innate dominance and self-assurance had always set her teeth on edge. His way or the highway, she got that message loud and clear and it was nothing new to her. She was used to rules now, accustomed to respecting the pecking order to stay safe. That she should have to do the same thing to stay employed should not be a surprise.

'Don't do that with your mouth…and don't look at me like that,' Vito chastised.

Look at him in what way? If the look had been inappropriate, she had been unaware of the fact and her chin came up at a mutinous angle. 'I don't know what you're talking about.'

He dealt her an unimpressed scrutiny, dark eyes brilliant and shielded by his lush lashes. 'Don't play the temptress with me. Been there, done that.'

In the state of tension she was in that insolent warning was the tipping point. Lashed by memories of the humiliation he had once inflicted on her, Ava flushed as incandescent rage lit her up like an internal fireworks display. 'Let's get this straight now, Vito,' she bit out furiously. 'I'm no longer that silly infatuated girl you once called a tease! I'm a whole lot wiser than I used to be. You're like a lot of other men—you don't take responsibility for your own behaviour.'

'And what's that supposed to mean?' Vito shot back at her rawly, unprepared for that sudden attack.

'I'm not some fatally seductive Eve, whom no poor male can resist. What happened that night wasn't entirely my fault. You came on to me, you kissed me because you *wanted* to, not because I somehow *made* you do it!' Ava shot back with angry emphasis, blue eyes star-bright with condemnation. 'Deal with your own share of the blame and don't try to foist it on me!'

Wrath blasted through Vito like a cleansing flame, wiping away every other complex reaction that she stirred. That fast he wanted to kill her and it was not the first time she had done that to him. He had dealt with the blame a long time ago but that did not alter the fact that she had used her body around him like a lethal weapon, deliberately stoking the kind of desire that no principled adult wanted to experience in a teenager's radius. It had been a recipe for disaster and had it not been for the car crash that had followed he would have remained satisfied by the outcome of their confrontation. But while he had tried to nip the situation in the bud Ava's fiery temperament had ensured that it had blown up in his face instead.

'I have no intention of discussing the past with you,' Vito delivered crushingly. 'Go buy the shoes and start on the Christmas list, Ava.'

It was a direct order and she was tempted to ignore it when every fibre in her body was still primed for battle. She wanted to defend herself, she had never got the chance to defend herself against his cutting allegations because Olly had interrupted them. But as she had reminded him she was no longer the teenager who had once found it almost impossible to control her emotions. She breathed in slow and deep and, giving him a look that would have daunted a lesser man, she turned round and headed for the door.

'Yes, you have grown up,' Vito remarked silkily, having the last word.

Her teeth clenched, her slender hands curling into tight fists but her spine stayed straight and her mouth firmly closed. Deep down inside she might want to scream at him, shake him...*kiss* him? The shock of that stray thought cooled her temper as nothing else could have done. Although she had got over her crush on him a long time ago, she had also spent the last three years in an all-female environment, forced to repress every sexual instinct, she reasoned impatiently. It was hardly surprising that exposure to a male of Vito's stunning good looks and high-powered sexuality, not to mention the memory of how she had once felt about him, could now make her vulnerable. So, take a chill pill, she urged herself impatiently, you're only human and he's the equivalent of toxic bait to a rat. He might have spectacular packaging but he also had a brain like a computer in which actual emotion had very little input. Even at eighteen she had appreciated that Vito's fondness for his little brother was the sole Achilles' heel in his tough and ruthlessly maintained emotional armour. She had not required Olly's warning to appreciate that she and Vito were chalk and cheese in every way that mattered. Money and success mattered way more to Vito than people. He kept other human beings at a distance and rarely allowed anyone into his inner circle or his private life. She did not count his affairs in that category for, according to what she had witnessed on the sidelines of his life, more sex than feeling was involved in those relationships.

Karen Harper was just replacing the phone when Ava entered her office and she wore an expression like a cat facing a saucer of sour cream. 'Company credit card, right?' she checked icily.

Ava nodded and presented the Christmas list. The brunette gave it a cursory glance. 'You appreciate that I will be checking your purchases very closely,' she spelt out warningly. 'I also advise you to stay strictly within budget. In fact your main objective should be to *save* money rather than spend it.'

'Of course.'

'Obviously Mr Barbieri believes you're up to the challenge because he knows your family,' Karen commented curtly, making her own poor opinion of the decision crystal clear. 'But unfortunately shopping is not work.'

'I just do what I'm told to do,' Ava fielded and turned on her heel, hoping that being at an enjoyable distance from Karen for a couple of days would ultimately do her no harm.

Ava returned to her allotted desk to go over the list and make plans. Saving money? When it came to the question of saving money she was, without a doubt, the go-to girl for she had never had enough cash to get by comfortably. Even though her family had always lived well, Ava had rarely been given money and had survived during term time at school through a series of part-time holiday jobs waiting tables and stacking shelves. Studying the list, she dug out Marge's catalogue to see if any suitable substitutes could be found within those pages. Surely charitable gifts would be more acceptable during a period of economic austerity when most people were feeling the pinch? She did a little homework on the computer to find out what she could about the interests of the recipients and hit pay dirt several times on that score, making helpful notes beside those names. That achieved, she paused only to pin a picture of Harvey to the office noticeboard in the forlorn hope that the dog might take someone's fancy. Marge had said Harvey could stay only two more weeks in her home as she was expecting the usual influx of abandoned and surrendered animals that followed the festive season. Ava tried to picture Harvey with a bow in his hair as a much-wanted gift and frowned: he just wasn't cute and fluffy enough to attract that kind of owner. But he was such a *loving* animal, Ava reflected painfully, knowing that the dog would have to be put to sleep at the vets' surgery if she could not find him a home. How could she have been so irresponsible as to let herself get attached to him?

When she left AeroCarlton, Ava went straight to buy a pair of shoes because the muscles in her feet were aching at the effort it took to keep the second-hand ones on. As soon as she could she would pay Vito back. Although she then made a start on the Christmas list unfortunate images continued to bombard her brain at awkward moments, scattering her thoughts and disturbing her. She didn't want to think about the night of the party but suddenly she couldn't think of anything else.

Every year Vito held a Christmas party for his senior staff, estate employees, tenants and neighbours. It was the equivalent of the local squire of Victorian times throwing open his grand doors to the public. That last year Ava had become so obsessed by Vito that she wouldn't even go out on a date with anyone else.

'It's unhealthy to be so intense,' Olly had told her in frustration that winter. 'You can't have Vito. He's not into teenagers and never will be. In his eyes you're only one step removed from a child.'

'I'll be nineteen in April and I'm mature for my age,' she had protested.

'Says who?' Olly had parried unimpressed, his blond blue-eyed and open face as far removed from his half-brother's as day is to night for he had inherited his English mother's looks rather than his Italian father's. 'A mature woman would never have got that tattoo on her hip!'

And, of course, Olly had been correct on that score, Ava acknowledged ruefully. An alcohol-induced decision on a sixth form holiday abroad had resulted in that piece of nonsense. She had marked herself for life over a teenage infatuation and needed no-one to tell her how foolish that was. When she eventually worked up the courage to get naked with a guy she knew she would cringe if there was any need to make an explanation.

In the present her mind careened back to that disastrous party when, for a change, she had gone all out to look sophisticated and had abandoned her Goth attire for the evening. Not that she wasn't fully aware at the time that her regular appearances in short black leather skirts and boots attracted Vito's attention! Did that make her a tease? She had seen girls out on the town wearing much more provocative clothing. Admittedly Vito's frighteningly elegant girlfriends had never appeared in such apparel. But just for once at the Christmas party Vito had been single with no eager possessive beauty clinging to his arm like a limpet and laughing and smiling at his every word.

From the first moment when Ava had met Vito Barbieri when she was sixteen there had been a buzz when their eyes met. It had taken her more than a year to reach the conclusion that he felt that buzz too but that he was fighting it tooth and nail. He had never said a word out of place and had been careful to stay out of reach and treat her more than ever like a little girl. But more than once she had been conscious of his eyes on her and the burn of satisfaction that minor triumph had given her had merely encouraged her to visit the castle when Vito was in residence. That he could be attracted to her and *never* do anything about it had not once crossed her mind as a possibility. It didn't matter how often Olly warned her that she was wasting her time dreaming about Vito. As long as Ava was aware that the attraction was mutual she had cherished the hope that eventually he would succumb.

With hindsight that insouciant confidence of hers made Ava recoil in mortification. How could she ever have truly believed that Vito might date her? The daughter of one of his employees, whose father lived with his family near Bolderwood Castle? His little brother's best friend? An eighteen-year-old still at school studying for her final exams with no experience and no decent clothes? Unfortunately, the depth of her obsession with him had ensured she ignored all common sense when he was around.

Her whole family had attended that party. Ava had worn a silver shift dress, cut down from a maxi that her sister, Gina, had put out for recycling. Somehow there had never been money to buy new clothes for Ava. The dress had been simple, even modest, and she had been careful with her make-up and her hair, keen neither to shock nor repel. She had seen Vito watching her from the doorway while she was dancing with the children she was helping to look after at their separate party in another room. Needing to stoke her confidence, she had been drinking, something she was usually more careful *not* to do, always fearful that her mother's weakness might some day turn out to be hers as well.

Ava no longer remembered when she had first appreciated that her mother was different from other mothers. She had often come home from primary school and found her mother out for the count on her bed. But then Ava's had never been a happy home because her parents fought like cat and dog. Furthermore, her mother had always been distant with her. And with a father who called her 'Ginger' if he called her anything, even though he knew how much it hurt her feelings to suffer that hated nickname in her own home, she had never suffered from the illusion that she was a much-wanted child. A full ten years younger than her eldest sister, Bella, Ava had often wondered if she was an unplanned accident resented by both her parents for neither of them had ever had any time for her.

But for all that she had loved her mother, Gemma Fitzgerald's death while Ava was in prison had been a severe shock and source of grief for she had long hoped that as she got older she might finally forge a closer relationship with her parent. In her teens she had realised that her mother had a serious problem with alcohol and was sober only in the morning, getting progressively drunker throughout the day on her hidden stashes of booze round the house until she was usually slumped comatose on the sofa by early evening. Ava's father and sisters had studiously ignored Gemma's alcoholism and done everything they could to cover it up. Divorce had been mentioned but never rehabilitation until the night her mother was caught driving while under the influence by the police and her father's punitive rage had known no bounds when the incident was reported in the local paper. Gemma had lost her licence and gone into rehab, returning home from the experience pale, quiet and mercifully sober.

Having noticed Vito watching her the night of the Christmas party, Ava had decided to take the bull by the horns, a decision that she would live to regret. She had tracked Vito down to the quiet of the library where he was standing by the fire with a drink in his hand. Tall, darkly beautiful and powerful, he had riveted her from the minute she walked through the door.

'What do you want?' he had demanded edgily.

Ava had perched on the side of the desk in a way that best displayed her long shapely legs and put her directly in front of him. As she had carefully adjusted the hem to a decent length she had felt his eyes on her as hot as the flames in the fire and excitement had filled her like a dangerous drug urging her on. 'I want you,' she told him boldly, no longer content to only offer lingering looks and encouraging smiles in invitation.

Vito treated her to a brooding look of derision that dented her pride right where it hurt most. 'You couldn't handle me,' he countered drily. 'Go and find some boy your own age to practise your wiles on.'

'You want me too,' Ava responded doggedly for, having started, she found it quite impossible to retreat with dignity and she stabbed on regardless with her suicidal mission to make him finally acknowledge what she believed already lay between them. 'Did you think I wouldn't notice?'

'It's time you went home and sobered up,' Vito retorted with scorn. 'This conversation is likely to embarrass you tomorrow.'

Ava continued to stare at him with unconcealed longing, her blue eyes languorous, her soft pink mouth pouting in reproach at his refusal to match her honesty. 'I don't embarrass that easily and I am well over the age of consent.'

'Your body might be but your brain is way behind,' Vito riposted, shifting closer in a fluid step that made her heart race. 'Go home, Ava. I don't want this nonsense.'

'I would be much more fun than any of those women

I've seen you bring back here!' she challenged. 'I'm not the clingy type.'

Vito stopped dead right in front of her. 'I'm not looking for fun. You've got nothing I want…and a little word of warning. Most men prefer to do their own chasing. Your in-my-face approach is a complete turn-off.'

Colour flamed into Ava's cheeks at his blunt rejection of what she had to offer. She snaked off the desktop in a surge of temper and wrapped her arms round his neck to prevent him from backing away from her. 'I do not turn you off,' she argued vehemently, gazing up into his dark golden eyes, which were spectacular in the firelight. 'That's a total lie! Why won't you tell the truth for once?'

'Ava…' Vito groaned in frustration, reaching up to detach her hands from his neck.

But before he could do so she stretched up and kissed him with every atom of craving she possessed. The muscles in his lean, strong body turned rigid and then he suddenly crushed her lips under his, his tongue spearing hungrily down into the tender interior of her mouth to make her literally shudder with excitement and a blissful sense of coming home. That single kiss was like dynamite to her self-control. With an eager gasp of response she melted into him, bones turning to mush under the onslaught of the piercing hunger gathering low in her pelvis. A door opened but she didn't hear it, reacting only when it slammed shut again.

'Vito…for heaven's sake, what are you doing?' Olly yelled in dismay. 'Let her go!'

Vito thrust Ava away roughly from him, the distaste on his face unmistakable. 'You're a calculating little tease…and you won't take no for an answer.'

'I'm not a t—'

Olly closed his hand round her forearm. 'Time to go home, Ava. I'll drive you.'

Ava's head swivelled, her furious eyes pinned to Vito's shuttered face in condemnation. 'How dare you call me a tease?' she launched at him as a sense of humiliation engulfed her, for she had made her last desperate move and he was still rebuffing her, resolutely refusing to acknowledge the sense of connection between them.

For the very first time in the immediate aftermath of that encounter Ava worried that her feelings were entirely one-sided. Was it possible that a man could be attracted to a woman without actually wanting to act on it? The same way people could admire a painting in a museum without needing to own it? That humiliating realisation came crashing down on Ava like a big black storm cloud. Her last recollection of that evening was of rushing down the steps of the castle in floods of tears with Olly chasing after her, urging her to calm down. The image that came next in her memory was waking up in hospital with a mind that was a terrifying blank, the events of the previous evening only returning slowly over the following days in jagged bits and pieces. But she had never been able to fully recall that car journey or the crash. Her defence had made much of the yawning gaps in her memory during her trial.

But ignorance had not protected her even from her own painful questions. How could she have got behind a steering wheel in the state she had been in? She had never been able to answer that question to her own satisfaction. Even more saliently, the car had belonged to Olly and he had been sober so why on earth had he allowed her to drive when she wasn't insured to drive his car?

Shoulders bowing beneath the stress of recalling her stupid selfishness that evening, Ava focused her swimming eyes on the Christmas list and resolved to get on with the task at hand. Revisiting the past, she decided, was a very bad idea when her mistakes had resulted in indefensible behaviour and tragic consequences.

# CHAPTER THREE

'COMPLETE junk!' Karen Harper pronounced triumphantly, laying a cushion woven with an image of a dog down on Vito's desk. 'Ava has made a complete pig's ear of the Christmas list and bought ridiculous gifts! She'll have to return the stuff and someone else will have to take charge of the list.'

An expression of exasperation crossed Vito's face for he did not appreciate having his busy morning interrupted by inconsequential dramas. He had only given Ava the list to get her out of the office and was in no mood for fallout from that decision. He swept up the phone. 'Ask Ava Fitzgerald to join us,' he told his PA.

Ava was sheltering in the cloakroom, cheeks still burning after a mortifyingly public scene with the dissatisfied office manager. Having done what she had been asked to the best of her ability, Ava had been furious when Karen Harper looked over her carefully chosen purchases and labelled her 'an idiot' in front of her co-workers. She accepted that she was just a junior but felt that even a junior employee deserved a certain modicum of respect and consideration. Her pale heart-shaped face tight, she finished renewing her lip gloss and moved away from the mirror.

'Mr Barbieri wants to speak to you,' Vito's PA, a glamorous blonde in her early thirties, informed Ava in the corridor.

Ava walked stoically back into Vito's office. Twenty-four hours had passed since their last encounter and after the restless night she had suffered while she fretted over what could not be changed she wished it had been longer. Getting out of bed to face another day had been a challenge. Having to deal with a man who despised her was salt in an already open wound. That he was the same guy she had once loved hammered her pride to smithereens.

Vito, a devastatingly elegant figure in a charcoal grey suit expertly tailored to his tall, powerful physique, viewed her with cool precision, the sooty lashes that ringed his remarkable eyes visible even at a distance. He indicated the cushion. 'Ava...care to explain this?'

'Matt Aiken and his wife breed Labradors and show them at Crufts. I thought the cushions were the perfect gift.'

'What about that ugly pottery vase?' Karen Harper broke in.

'Made by a charity in Mumbai that supports homeless widows,' Ava explained. 'Ruhina Dutta is very forthright about the needs of minorities in India. I thought she would appreciate the vase and a charitable donation more than she would appreciate perfume,' Ava continued levelly, encountering an unreadable look from Vito that made her even tenser. She could not tell whether he approved of her outlook or not, but that lingering scrutiny sent high-wire energy shooting through her like lightning rods.

'And that silly chain from Tiffany's?' Karen was in

no mood to back down. 'It doesn't even have a proper catch—'

'Because it's a spectacles chain. Mrs Fox complained in a recent interview that she is always mislaying her glasses.'

Vito released a short laugh, his impatience with the subject unconcealed. Ava went pink, noting that he was now avoiding looking directly at her and feeling ignored even though she told herself that it was stupid to feel that way. Surely she no longer wanted his attention?And if he wanted to treat her like the office junior she was supposed to be, she would have to get used to receiving as much attention as the paint on the wall.

'What about all that animal-orientated stuff you've bought?' Karen demanded sharply. 'It's unacceptable for you to only buy gifts from your favourite charity.'

'A lot of people on that list have pets. You told me to save money if I could.'

'I certainly didn't tell you to buy junk!' Karen Harper snapped.

'Some of the proposed gifts on the list were incredibly expensive and at a time when so many people are cutting back, those suggestions struck me as OTT,' Ava admitted in a rueful undertone. 'But, of course, anything I've bought can be changed if required.'

'That won't be necessary. Finish the job—you've obviously done your homework on the recipients,' Vito conceded, his strong jaw line squaring as he skimmed a detached glance at Ava and extended the cushion to her. 'But I don't like to waste my time on trivia. Please remove this difference of opinion from my office.'

The office manager stiffened. 'Of course, Mr Barbieri. I'm sorry I interrupted you.'

The other woman insisted on checking the remainder of the list with Ava before she went out shopping again. Ava was embarrassed when a couple of co-workers chose that same moment to return Marge's catalogue with orders and cash attached.

'You're here to work, not to sell stuff for your pet charity,' Karen said icily. 'When you get back this afternoon I have several jobs for you to take care of, so be as quick as you can.'

When Ava returned, footsore and laden with carrier bags, Karen took her straight down to the filing cabinets in the basement and gave her enough work to keep her busy into at least the middle of the following week. Ava knew it was a punishment for stepping out of line and accepted it as such without resentment. True the basement was lonely, dull and filled with artificial light but it was a relief to know that she need no longer fear running into Vito. Earlier he had behaved unnervingly like a stranger and she didn't know why that should have surprised her or left her feeling ridiculously resentful. After all, he was the last man in the world from whom she could expect special treatment.

A week later, Vito was studying his companion over lunch in a famous restaurant. By any standards Laura was beautiful with her long blonde fall of hair and almond-shaped brown eyes. She didn't ring his bells though: he thought her mouth was too thin, her voice too sharp and she was painfully fond of bitching about the models she worked with. Was he simply bored? There had to be some reason why his mind constantly wandered, why it had suddenly become a challenge for him to sit still even long enough to eat a meal. The unease that had been nibbling bites out of his self-discipline for days returned in full force.

His day had had an unfortunate start with a call from his estate manager, Damien Keel. Damien, keen to get his festive calendar organised, had asked him if there would be a Christmas party this year at the castle. Ironically it was the first time that Vito had been asked that question since his brother's death but Damien, a relatively new employee, had never been part of that loop. The first year, nobody had asked or expected a party and since then Vito had just quietly ignored that custom. Now, suddenly, he felt guilty about that break with tradition. His staff deserved the treat. Three years was long enough to make a public display of grief. He decided there and then that it was past time he rein-stated normality. He glanced at Laura, happily engaged in a very long drawn-out story about yet another rival in the modelling world, and he suppressed his growing impatience. He knew he would be moving on from Laura as well.

Striding back into AeroCarlton, he glanced at Reception. There was no sign of Ava in the general office either. For a gopher she was keeping an exceptionally low profile. It was not that he *wanted* to see her, more that he was steeling himself to accept her presence. But it was a week since he had last laid eyes on her and he was getting curious.

'Is Ava Fitzgerald still working here?' he asked his PA.

'I don't know, sir...'

'Find out,' he instructed.

Ava was in the basement, the layout of which she now knew like the back of her hand. She had filed away entire boxes of documents, and when she had completed that task Karen had introduced her to her shiny new and fiendishly complex filing system and put her to work on it. In the distance she heard the lift clanging as the doors opened and she did not have long to wait for her visitor.

'Since you won't go out to lunch, I've brought lunch to you,' a familiar voice announced.

Suppressing a groan, Ava spun round from the cabinet of files she was reorganising and smoothed down her skirt in a movement that came as naturally as breathing to her in Pete Langford's radius. Of medium height and lanky build, Pete looked over her slender figure in a way that made her feel vaguely unclean. It was a few days since he had made his first call down to the basement to chat to her and even her display of indifference had failed to daunt him. Now he extended a panini and a soft drink to her while he lounged back against the bare table in the centre of the room.

'Take a break,' he urged, setting the items down on the table.

'You shouldn't have bought those.' Her stomach growled because her tiny budget didn't run to lunches. 'Give them to someone else—I have some shopping to do.'

'Do it after work. I'm here now,' he pointed out as if she ought to drop everything to give him some attention.

Ava hated being railroaded and valued her freedom of choice. She didn't fancy an impromptu lunch with Pete in the solitude of the basement and had no desire to drift into a situation where she would have to fight him off. He was the sort of guy who thought he was

God's gift and who believed persistence would pay off. One of her co-workers had already warned her that he went after all the new girls. 'I'm going to take a break upstairs,' she told him.

Pete sighed. 'What's your problem?'

'I don't have one. I'm just not interested,' Ava told him baldly.

'Are you gay?' Pete demanded abruptly. 'I mean, all that time in prison, I suppose you didn't have much choice...'

Ava lost colour and stiffened. 'Who told you I was in prison?'

'Was it meant to be hush-hush? Everybody knows.'

'It's not something I talk about,' Ava retorted curtly, trying not to react to the news that her past was an open secret amongst her co-workers, some of whom had proved quite reluctant to speak to her. The bite of humiliation, the pain of being the oddity and distrusted while people speculated about her crime, cut deep.

'Who told *you?*' another, harsher male voice enquired from the doorway. 'That was supposed to be confidential information.'

Ava levelled her stunned gaze on Vito. He must have used the stairs because she hadn't heard the lift. He stood at the door, his gorgeous eyes a brilliant scorching gold, his lean strong face hard as granite as he awaited Pete Langford's response. Having heard that last crack about Ava being gay, Vito was taut with outrage and simmering fury. He did not understand why he was so furious to find Ava with another man until it occurred to him that after her prison sentence she was probably a sitting duck for such an approach and that as her employer it surely behoved him to ensure that nobody took advantage of her vulnerability. Not that at that precise moment Ava actually looked vulnerable, he conceded abstractedly. Her eyes were sparkling with angry resentment and her slim but undeniably curvy figure was beautifully sculpted in the black pencil skirt and tight-fitting red shirt she wore. Without any warning, another image was superimposed over her: Ava, amazingly elfin cute in a lace corset top, short black leather skirt and clunky boots. Startled, he blinked, but the damage had been done and he was left willing back a surge of arousal.

Pete Langford had turned shaken eyes onto his employer. 'I don't remember who first mentioned Ava's background,' he mumbled evasively, his former attitude of relaxation evaporating fast below Vito's intimidating stare. 'Look, I'd better get back upstairs.'

'What a good idea,' Vito pronounced deadpan, his big powerful body taut with silent menace.

As the lift doors closed on Pete's hurried departure Ava frowned uncertainly. 'What was that all about?'

'How long have you been working down here?' Vito demanded, ignoring the question.

'Since I finished the Christmas list that day I was in your office,' Ava admitted.

'You've been working down here a full week? *Every* day, *all* day?'

In silence, Ava nodded, entrapped by the aura of vibrant energy he emanated. Her gaze locked to his face, scanning the sinful cheekbones, the bold nose and sensual mouth. Suddenly she didn't blame herself any more for having a crush on him at the age of sixteen. After all, he turned female heads wherever he went.

'It must feel like you're back in a cell!' Vito ground

out grimly, scanning the bare comfortless lines of the big room with angry dissatisfaction.

'It's work and I'm grateful to have a job,' Ava countered quietly. 'And if you think this place reminds me of prison, you have no concept of what prison life is like.'

'Putting you down here was not my idea,' Vito informed her grimly.

'I didn't think it was. You're not petty but you did want me out from under your feet and I am literally fulfilling that function here,' she pointed out, dimples appearing as she shot him an irreverent grin.

And that grin lit up her heart-shaped face like the dawn light. She was beautiful. Why had he never realised that before? The fine-boned fragility of her features allied with that transparent complexion and the contrast of that fiery hair was stunning. He didn't like red hair, he reminded himself, at least he had never had a redhead in his bed. Not that he wanted her there either, he told himself fiercely, fighting the heat and tension at his groin to the last ditch of denial. He didn't want her, he had never wanted her, he had just kissed her once because she gave him no other choice. Or was that the excuse she had labelled it? He studied that ripe pink mouth, bare as it was of lipstick, and remembered the taste of her, heady, sweet and unbearably sexy...

Ava's bright blue eyes had widened and darkened. The sparks in the atmosphere were whirling round her faster and faster. It was like standing in the eye of a storm. She moved forward, unconsciously reacting to a sexual tension she could not withstand. Her clothes felt shrink-wrapped to her skin and she was insanely conscious of the swell of her breasts and the tingling tightness of her nipples while the heat between her thighs made her press those offending limbs tightly together.

In the humming silence, Vito stared back. It was all right to look now, he reminded himself sardonically. She was no longer jailbait. The thought cut a chain somewhere inside him, slicing him free of the past. He coiled a hand round her wrist and pulled her into his arms, dark golden eyes volatile, ferocious energy leaping through him in a wild surge of lust.

His other hand lifted slowly and his forefinger traced the fullness of her lower lip, his touch light as a butterfly's wings. Ava almost bit his finger in frustration, her breath escaping her in an audible gasp. Kiss me, kiss me, *kiss me*, she willed him. Her craving was so great at that moment that there was no room for any other thought. He lowered his handsome dark head and drove her lips apart with a passionate kiss, driven by all the hunger pent up in his powerful body. And it was just what she wanted, what thrilled her most, desire leaping through her slight body like a blinding light as his tongue delved into the sensitive interior of her mouth and the world spun in ever faster circles round her. Her knees wobbled and she kissed him back with the same passion, her tongue twinning with his, her breasts crushed to the wall of his hard muscular torso, all awareness centred on sensation and satisfaction. He eased her back from him, long fingers skating up over her taut ribcage to close round one breast, teasing the prominent peak with an expertise that drew a moan from her throat. He set her back from him, took a slow step away, smouldering eyes locked to her like precision lasers.

'This is not the place, *belleza mia*.'

Ava snatched in a gigantic gulp of oxygen to regain control of her treacherous body and the searing disappointment of his withdrawal. But she knew it had cost him, had felt him hard and ready and awesomely male against her, and the awareness soothed her tumultuous emotions as nothing else could have done. *This* time she was not the only one in the grip of that savage wanting.

'I will have you moved from the basement immediately,' Vito told her flatly, not a bit of expression in his deep drawl, his shrewd gaze veiled and closed to her.

'That's not necessary,' Ava declared.

'It is. I hope I deal fairly with all my employees and isolating you in the basement with only boring repetitive work to carry out is not acceptable.'

A little devil danced in her eyes. 'Do you kiss them as well?'

Vito stilled at the door, strong jaw line squaring. 'You're the first,' he confessed darkly.

'Aren't you about to tell me that it won't ever happen again?' Ava prompted, heart in her mouth at the thought.

Vito dealt her a thunderous glance and she went pink, registering in some surprise that she had been teasing him, set on provocation. He headed back to the stairs, still buzzing with aftershocks and the agony of sexual restraint. She could set him on fire with one look, one kiss. He could have quite happily lifted her onto the table, spread those long slim thighs and satisfied them both, but Vito was always distrustful of the new and enticing and preferred to hold back and stay in control. If he could stay in control, he was willing to admit that he wanted Ava Fitzgerald. In fact he wanted her a whole lot more than he had wanted a woman in a long time. Perhaps it was because she had once been forbidden fruit. He examined that possibility but the how and the why couldn't hold his attention. He was free, she was free and she was an adult now. As long as he kept those realities in mind there was nothing more complex at play.

*She killed Olly.*

Vito stamped on that unwelcome thought and buried it deep. Sex was straightforward. Sex he could handle. He didn't need to think about it or question the authenticity of a basic human urge to mate. She was beautiful and she excited him. And that excitement was rare enough in his life to wipe out every other consideration and finer feeling and take precedence. Of recent, life had been desperately dull apart from the occasional energising business deal. It was the season of goodwill and suddenly he was willing to flow with it.

An hour later, Karen Harper called Ava upstairs to cover the reception desk. She then made coffee for a meeting, tidied the stationery cupboard and ran various errands. The end of the day came much faster than usual and she went straight to Marge's house to collect Harvey for the evening. Marge, delighted at the orders the catalogue had received from various AeroCarlton employees, gave her an evening meal. Afterwards, Ava took Harvey for a long walk and sat on a bench for a while, patting the curly head resting against her thigh and talking to him. Sometimes she could still hardly believe that she was once again living a life that was no longer controlled by strict regulations and ringing bells. Having spent hour after hour locked in a cell, she appreciated the freedom of physical activity. In prison the only exercise she'd had was pacing doggedly round the exercise yard. The open prison, of course, had not been as restrictive and there she had had access to a gym.

When her mobile phone rang she did not initially realise that it was hers and finally wrenched it out of her pocket, believing that it had to be one of her family as she answered it.

'It's Vito. I need your address. I want to speak to you.'

Surprise gripped Ava. She was already on her feet. She reluctantly gave her address, telling herself that it was foolish to be embarrassed about her humble accommodation. He would scarcely expect to find her inhabiting a penthouse apartment. As there wasn't time to return Harvey to Marge's and get back in time to meet Vito, she walked the dog back fast with her. Her mind was working even more actively than her feet.

Vito would want to tell her that the kiss had meant nothing. As if she didn't know that! As if she hadn't got old enough and wise enough yet to appreciate that workaholic billionaires of his calibre didn't come on to the office junior, particularly not when she was a former offender, guilty of causing a tragic car crash that had cost his closest relative his life. Vito, she assumed, had succumbed to a lusty impulse as she had heard even the best of men did occasionally. Was that her fault? she asked herself anxiously. Had her shockingly physical awareness of Vito Barbieri somehow put out the vibes that had lured him into that kiss? It was a lowering suspicion and her chin came up. He had better not try to tell her that she had tempted him again!

# CHAPTER FOUR

A SLEEK silver limo with a driver was parked outside the building where Ava lived. As she hurried down the street lined with weathered and grimy brick-fronted houses Vito emerged from the back seat, looking every bit as immaculate in his dark cashmere overcoat and suit as he had earlier. Her hair was wind-tousled, her make-up long since worn off, and her shabby jeans and fleece jacket far from flattering but she told herself that she didn't care. How could you even begin to impress a guy who had everything and dated international models and celebrities?

'Ava...'

'This is Harvey. Be nice,' Ava urged as Harvey growled. 'Show me your paw.'

Somewhat taken aback, Vito watched the hairy dog sit and raise a paw, round doggy eyes pinned to him with suspicion. 'You have a pet?'

'No, actually. Harvey's a stray who needs a home. I'm not allowed to keep a dog here. I live on the third floor.'

'This isn't a good area for a woman living alone,' Vito remarked following her up the stairs.

'Did you think I hadn't noticed?' Ava asked, unlock-

ing her door and stepping inside before bending down
to free Harvey from his lead.

Disconcerted by that mocking reply, Vito watched
the worn denim flex over her curvy derriere. The more
he saw of the sleek elegant lines of her body, the more
he liked it. His fingers curled into loose fists. 'I don't
like to think of you living round here...although at least
you have a watchdog.'

'I can't keep Harvey here overnight. I'll have to take
him back to Marge's later.'

'Who's Marge?'

'She runs a small boarding kennels and takes in
strays. I worked there for a few months while I was in
an open prison. I still help out when I can. She has a
whole network of volunteers, who provide foster homes
for strays and try to rehome them. The same people also
make those dog cushions and the like to sell for funds,'
she explained.

Vito had already lost interest. As Harvey settled on
the rug by the single bed Vito paced deeper into the
small room to take a considering look at the shabby
furniture and the severe lack of personal effects and
comforts. The rug on the linoleum floor was the sole
luxury. 'I can't believe your family are leaving you to
live like this.'

'Look, living here is a lot more comfortable and private than a hostel dormitory would be,' Ava replied with
spirit. 'Would you like coffee?'

'I've just had a meal. I'm fine,' Vito responded with
a polite nod, stationing himself by the dirty window.
He noticed that his breath was misting in the air; there
was no heating. He was appalled to find her living in

such surroundings and no longer marvelled at the fact that she had been wearing second-hand shoes.

'You can take your coat off—I promise not to steal it!'

'It's too cold in here.'

Ava crouched down to switch on the gas fire. She used it for an hour every evening to heat the room before she went to bed. She smiled to herself. Vito might be tough but he loved heat. If there was no sunlight he had to have a fire on. Olly used to tease him about it. At the thought her smile died away as quickly as it had come and she wondered if she would ever be in Vito's company without remembering the awful loss she had inflicted on him.

'You said you wanted to speak to me,' she reminded him, turning to face him.

His eyes glittered like black diamonds in the light from the lamp by the bed. 'I have a suggestion to put to you.'

Ava rested her head to one side, copper-red hair glinting like fire across her dark jacket, strands of honey gold lightening the overall effect.

'You look like a robin when you do that.'

Ava didn't want to be compared to a bird. Since when was a robin stylish or sexy? It was more of a perky, cheeky bird, she reasoned, and then flushed at the way her mind was working, seeking a compliment, approval, anything other than his indifference, that was her and it was pathetic at her age to still be so needy!

'I want to hold the Christmas party again this year,' Vito continued doggedly. 'Well, I don't really *want* to but I believe it's time.'

'You mean you haven't had one…*since*?' Ava completed, her voice cracking a little on that final emphatic word, which encompassed so much.

A haunted darkness filled Vito's stunning eyes, revealing a clear glimpse of pain, and it tore up something inside her. 'No, not for three years,' he responded flatly.

'OK...' Recognising that further enquiry would be unwelcome, Ava strove to match his detached attitude and ram down the pained feelings swelling inside her that sometimes felt too big and powerful to hold in. 'So?' she prompted jerkily, wondering what the subject could possibly have to do with her.

'I want you to organise it—the party, the decoration of the house, the whole festive parade,' Vito extended, a sardonic look on his handsome face.

'*Me?* You want *me* to organise it?' Ava was incredulous at the idea, utterly filled with disbelief.

'You and Olly always took care of it for me before,' Vito reminded her, noting how very white she had become, the subject no easier for her than it was for him. 'I want you to do it again, deal with the caterers and all the fuss. I won't be involved but I think my staff and neighbours should feel free to enjoy the event again.'

Finally, Ava accepted that he was making a genuine request but it did not remove her astonishment. 'You can't have thought this through. Me? Have you any idea what people would think and say about me doing the arrangements for the party again?'

Vito raised an incredulous brow. 'I have never in my life stopped to worry about what other people think,' he countered with resounding assurance. 'It strikes me as the perfect solution. You will recreate Christmas in the same spirit as Olly did. The two of you revelled in all that traditional nonsense.'

Ava dragged in a ragged breath and had to literally swallow down the unnecessary reminder that Olly was gone. Nonsense, yes, she recalled helplessly, Vito had always believed the seasonal festivities were nonsense, only excepting those of a religious persuasion from his censure. Even so, he had tolerated her and Olly's efforts to capture the magic of Christmas with the same long-suffering indulgence that an adult awarded childish passions.

'I suggest you stay at AeroCarlton for what remains of the week and move into the castle at the weekend.'

'M-move into the castle?' Ava stammered, shaken at the suggestion.

'You can hardly do the work from here,' Vito pointed out, his measured drawl as cool as ice on her skin.

Christmas at Bolderwood, the stuff of dreams, Ava conceded abstractedly and familiar images washed through her mind: gathering holly and ivy from the forest, choosing the tree and dressing it, eating mince pies by the fire in the Great Hall. Even as she felt sick with longing at the recollection of happier times something snapped shut as tight as a padlock inside her brain. Christmas *without* Olly in what had once been Olly's happy home: it was unthinkable. She didn't deserve it, couldn't even consider such an undertaking when she had for ever destroyed Christmas for Vito.

'I couldn't do it. It would be a frightful mistake to use me. It would offend people.'

'If it does not offend me, why should it offend anyone else?' Vito enquired with arrogant conviction. 'You're over-sensitive, Ava. You can't live in the past for ever.'

'You can't forgive me!' Ava suddenly cried in jagged protest. 'How do you expect me to forgive myself?'

Vito cursed her emotional turbulence. Everything he controlled she expressed, but he saw her attitude as another sign that he was taking the right path. 'It's three years. It might feel like it only happened yesterday but it's been three years,' he pointed out harshly. 'Life has to go on. Make this Christmas a proper tribute to Olly's memory.'

Ava was struggling to suppress such a giant surge of emotion that her legs trembled under her and she braced her hand on the back of a chair, her eyes stinging with a rush of tears. Olly's memory. It always hurt too much to examine her memories of him and then be forced to accept the reality of his death again.

'Do you really think that my brother would have wanted to see you living like this?' Face taut, eyes ablaze with impatience, Vito lifted both arms in an unusually dramatic gesture of derision.

Ava's chin came up at that question and her spine straightened. 'No, I know he wouldn't have wanted this,' she admitted grudgingly, blinking back the tears that had almost shamed her. 'But I can't help it.'

'*Che cosa hai!* What's the matter with you?' Vito reproved, his dark deep voice growling over the vowel sounds. 'You're a fighter—I expected more from you.'

Mortified colour sprang up over her cheekbones, flooding her porcelain pale skin like the dawn on his Tuscan estate. That stray thought, far too colourful for a man who considered himself imaginative only in business, set his even white teeth on edge. He looked at her, grimly appraising her appearance in shabby clothes. Hair like molten copper in an unflattering ponytail, face dominated by bright blue eyes and that luscious mouth, garments too shapeless and poorly fitting to compliment even her slender figure. Nothing there to fascinate or tit-illate, he reasoned impatiently, but his attention roamed back to her delicate features and lingered. A split second later he was hard as a rock, his blood drumming through the most sensitive part of his body as he imagined that succulent mouth pleasuring him.

'Yes, I'm a fighter,' Ava breathed shakily, gazing back at him, feeling the change in the atmosphere and finding it quite impossible to ignore it. How could he make her feel this way without even trying? All right, he was very good-looking but surely she should have outgrown her teenaged sensitivity to his attraction? The pulse low in her pelvis was a nagging ache and she spun away restively, determined to get a grip on her physical reactions. After all, he had just challenged her pride, her belief in herself, and she could not let that stand unanswered. She might be afraid of other people's reactions to her, but she was not prepared to admit the fact that rejection still hurt her way more than it should have done. 'If you really want me to, I'll do it…Christmas for you but don't blame me if people think you're crazy.'

Vito had fixed his brilliant eyes to Harvey, who had practically merged with the hearth rug in his relaxation. 'I've already told you how much I care about that.'

'Yes, but—'

'I prefer women who agree with me.'

'No, you do not!' Ava snapped back. 'You just get bored and walk all over them!'

Vito felt that even walking over her might be fun and his black lashes dropped low on his reflective eyes. He was still in an odd mood, he acknowledged in exasperation, a mood of unease where random thoughts clouded his usually crystal-clear brain. He wondered if it was the season or talking about Olly that had disturbed him and settled for that obvious explanation with relief. 'Staying at the castle may give you the opportunity to see your family again.'

'It will shock them, annoy them, as they've made it quite clear they don't want me back in their lives,' she pointed out heavily. 'But that's their right and I have to accept it.'

Vito made no comment, still taken aback by what he had done. A spur of the moment idea had fired him up with an almost missionary zeal to make changes. Putting Ava in charge of Christmas was as much for her benefit as his own. It would toughen him up, banish the atrocious vulnerability that afflicted and destabilised him whenever he thought about his little brother. That was a weakness that Vito could not accept and he could no longer live with it and the necessity of constantly suppressing negative responses. He thought of all the people who had recommended therapy to deal with his grief and his beautifully moulded mouth took on a derisive slant. Therapy wasn't his style. He didn't discuss such things with strangers, nor would he ever have sought professional help for a loss he deemed to be a perfectly normal, if traumatic, life experience. He was *totally* capable of dealing with his own problem and by the end of the Christmas party, when Ava Fitzgerald departed from his life again, he would have finally made an important step in the recovery process. Avoiding her, acting all touchy-feely sensitive as he saw it, would have been the wrong thing to do, he acknowledged fiercely. He would deal with her in the present and move on, all the stronger for the experience.

'Can I bring Harvey with me to the castle?' Ava

asked abruptly, realising that that would remove the dog from Marge's small overcrowded house.

Dark brows drawing together, Vito frowned, for his antipathy to indoor animals had only allowed him to stretch as far as a guinea pig and goldfish even for Olly.

'Honestly he won't be any trouble!' Ava promised feverishly, eager to persuade Vito round to her point of view. 'It's just Harvey will be put down if I can't find a home for him because Marge hasn't the room to keep him any longer. It'll buy him a little more time, that's all, and who knows? Someone may take a fancy to him on your estate.'

Vito surveyed Harvey, who was snoring loudly, remarkably relaxed for an animal apparently facing a sentence of death. He did not think he had ever seen a less prepossessing dog. 'Is he some peculiar breed?'

'No, he's a mongrel. He was a stray but he's young and healthy.' Ava gave him a tremulous, optimistic smile. 'He loves children too. He would be a great addition to the party if I put a Santa hat on him…or maybe I could dress him up like a reindeer?'

Vito groaned out loud at the thought of more festive absurdity. 'Bring him with you if you like but don't get the idea that I'll keep him.'

'Oh, I would never expect that.' Ava laughed, released from tension and weak with relief on Harvey's behalf. 'I'll keep him away from you. I know you're no good with dogs. Olly told me you were bitten when you were a child!'

Annoyance coursed through Vito and his eyes veiled, his jaw line hardening. He was an extremely private man. He wondered what other inappropriate revelations his little brother had made and once again he reflected that the sooner Ava was out of his workplace, the better.

'I'll have to get permission from my probation officer to leave London,' Ava told him suddenly, her expression anxious. 'I see her every month.'

'You'll only be away a couple of weeks—why bother mentioning it?'

'I'm out on parole, Vito. I have to follow the rules if I don't want to end up back inside,' she replied tightly.

Vito compressed his lips and gave an imperious nod of his handsome dark head in acknowledgement. 'I'll send a car to pick you up late Sunday afternoon.'

And then he was gone and the room felt cold and empty as if the sun had gone in. She sat down by the fire, all of a sudden cold on the inside as well and very shaky. What had she done? What madness had possessed her to agree to his proposition? The same madness that had made Vito Barbieri voice the suggestion? He wanted closure. She understood that, felt worse than ever when she thought about how hard it must have been for so reserved a male to deal with such a colossal tragedy. But on one level he was right—life went on whether you wanted it to or not and, just as he had done, she had to learn how to adapt to survive.

'I understand you'll only be here until Friday,' Karen Harper remarked sweetly the following morning as she checked over the typing that Ava had completed and sent her out to cover Reception over lunch. 'I had no idea just how friendly you were with the boss—'

'Friendly would be the wrong word,' Ava fielded awkwardly. 'Vito's still my boss.'

But the atmosphere around her for the rest of the

week was strained and she was in receipt of more nosy questions than she wanted to answer. It was a relief to leave early on Friday to keep her regular appointment with Sally, her probation officer.

'You'll be staying in a *real* castle?' Sally queried, goggle-eyed, as she made a note of the address.

'Not a medieval one—Bolderwood is a Victorian house,' Ava explained.

'And owned by Oliver Barbieri's brother,' Sally slotted in, smiling widely at Ava. 'He must be a very forgiving person.'

'No, he'll never forgive and forget where his brother's concerned and I don't blame him for that,' Ava replied tautly, her expression sober beneath the older woman's curious gaze. 'But he thinks we both need to get back to normal and he sees this as the best way of achieving that.'

'It's still a remarkably generous gesture.'

Travelling down to Bolderwood Castle two days later in the opulent luxury of a limousine with Harvey asleep at her feet and her holdall packed in the boot, Ava was thinking that she had never known that Vito possessed such a streak of generosity. But she should have done, she reasoned ruefully. Hadn't he given Olly a home when his kid brother was left alone in the world? A little boy he had only met a couple of times, a half-brother some adults might have thoroughly resented? Yet on the outside Vito Barbieri was as tough and inflexible as granite. In business he was as much feared as respected by competitors and at work—if AeroCarlton was anything to go by—his very high expectations and ruthless efficiency intimidated his employees.

As the familiar countryside passed the windows Ava grew increasingly tense. She was both terrified and exhilarated to be heading back to her childhood stomping grounds. Would she dare to visit her father or her sisters? She thought not, best not to push herself in rudely where she wasn't wanted. Her father and sisters would only resent her for turning up uninvited on their doorsteps and putting them on the spot. Her eyes awash with moisture, she blinked back tears. She had to put her life back together alone but at least she still *had* her life.

'You have a very negative attitude,' Olly had once scolded her with his easy smile.

But then aside of his mother dying and his father having been an absentee parent, Olly had received a level of security, love and support from adults that Ava had never known. She knew that that was why she was prickly, suspicious of people's motives and always prepared for the worst. As the limo waited for the giant electric gates to open at the foot of the castle drive Ava's heart was in her mouth and she felt like scrambling out of the car and running away. *Of course* people were going to think she was utterly shameless and insensitive to come and stay at Bolderwood after what she had done!

The car headlights illuminated the rambling Victorian mansion in the distance. Complete with four turrets and a forest of Elizabethan-esque chimneys, the original architect had recklessly borrowed the style of almost every previous age to embellish his creation. Ava had always thought it was a madly romantic house built in the days when owners had loads of staff and constantly entertained guests. Vito had a very large staff but kept the entertaining to the minimum. Throwing open the doors of his private home for the Christmas party was a major challenge for a male who happily lived behind locked gates and electric fences the rest of the year.

Eleanor Dobbs, the slim brunette housekeeper in her thirties, greeted Ava at the imposing front door. 'Miss Fitzgerald,' she said without an ounce of discomfiture. 'I'll show you straight up to your room so that you can get unpacked.'

'Just make it Ava,' Ava urged, her cheeks flushed with intense self-consciousness. 'How have you been?'

'It's been quiet here since your last visit,' the older woman remarked on her efficient passage up the sweeping staircase. 'We're all very pleased that the Christmas party is to be held again.'

A fixed smile on her taut face as she made determined small talk, Ava found herself standing in the principal guest room without quite knowing how she had arrived there. It was a massive room with a charming en suite bathroom in the turret complete with window seat. A fire burned in the grate of the marble fireplace, flickering shadows across warm brocaded walls and antique mahogany furniture. She stared in astonishment at the imposing four-poster bed draped in embroidered gold silk.

'Why have you brought me in here?' Ava whispered.

'Mr Barbieri asked me to prepare this room for you,' Eleanor advanced.

Ava froze. 'Where *is* Mr Barbieri?' she asked tightly.

'I believe he's in his bedroom.'

The housekeeper departed and Ava expelled her pent-up breath in a hiss while she scanned the opulence of the room. Totally unsuitable, she reflected incredulously. Vito could not put her in the main bedroom reserved for only the most honoured VIPs. My goodness, there was even a fire burning in the grate! Harvey, no slowcoach at spotting the most warm and comfy place in the room, settled down on the rug and lowered his shaggy head down on his paws.

'Don't bother getting comfortable,' Ava warned him ruefully. 'We're not staying in the five-star accommodation!'

Leaving Harvey, she crossed the landing at a smart pace to knock on Vito's bedroom door while she waited outside with folded arms. When there was no answer she knocked again and waited with mounting impatience. Finally she just opened the door and went in, only to stop dead on the threshold at the sight of Vito emerging from his en suite clad in only a pair of black briefs.

For a split second she simply stared, eyes wide, mouth dropping open in shock and awkwardness. He had an incredible body because he worked out and swam regularly in the basement fitness suite. Vibrant skin the colour of honey glowed in the lamplight, drawing attention to his powerful shoulders, truly remarkable abs and a stomach as flat as a washboard. Short black curls accentuated his pectorals while a silky dark furrow of hair ran down over his concave belly and disappeared below the waistband of his briefs. With her attention lingering in that most private area, embarrassment bit deep into Ava and she spun around, rejecting the view and presenting him with her back. 'I'm so sorry...I didn't mean to interrupt you—'

'At least close the door,' Vito said drily.

She shoved the door shut, her face so hot she thought eggs could have fried on it. What on earth had she been doing staring at him like that? As if she'd never seen a half-naked man before—she *hadn't*, though, apart from on the beach. Her lack of experience at almost twenty-two years of age affronted her pride. She was a case of arrested development, imposed by her years locked away in prison. Obsessed with Vito before she lost her freedom she had missed out entirely on the phase of youthful experimentation.

'*Che cosa a successo*...what has happened?' Vito drawled, cool as ice water with an edge of mockery.

Ava spun back to him, catching the sardonic hint of amusement written on his face as though on some level he relished her discomfiture. 'I came straight to find you because you simply can't plonk me in the main guest room!' she shot at him. 'It's a very bad idea.'

Engaged in drawing up the zip on a pair of close-fitting designer chinos, his magnificent torso providing a stunning display as his hips arched back and the ropes of muscle across his abdomen flexed, Vito had never looked more assured or calm. Being half naked in her presence clearly did not trouble him in the slightest. 'Let me decide what is appropriate,' he advised.

'Well, that's just it, isn't it?' Ava snapped back at him heatedly, inflamed by his refusal to take the subject seriously. 'Obviously I can't trust you to *do* what is appropriate!'

His black brows were level above his spectacular dark deep-set eyes. 'This is my house and I am the best judge of that. What I say goes here.'

His arrogant unconcern infuriated Ava. 'How can you completely ignore how other people will feel about me staying here?'

An ebony brow lifted. 'It's none of their business.'

'You have a hell of an attitude problem, Vito!' Ava hurled.

'Agreed,' Vito fielded softly as he reached for the shirt draped over the back of a chair. 'I never could stand being told what to do.'

The crack was not lost on Ava. She reddened, her lush mouth compressing. 'I'm not trying to tell you what to do—'

Vito studied her with interest, noting that she had chosen to travel in her office skirt and shirt, the violin curves above and below her tiny waist pronounced in the outfit. He wanted to rip the restrained garments off her, clothe her in excessively feminine silk and lace lingerie so that he could picture her lying on his bed without even stretching his imagination. Seeing her in his bedroom, he decided, was a disturbingly intimate experience.

'*Sì*, you are. You're a real little bossy-boots—you always were,' he riposted, watching her succulent lips part in surprise at the comeback, recognising the flare in her bright blue eyes with wicked anticipation.

Ava threw her head high, thick silky hair shimmering like a fall of molten copper round her cheekbones, eyes huge and fiery with defiance. 'I am *not* a bossy-boots!'

'Olly always did as he was told,' Vito murmured silkily. 'But be warned—I *don't*. You're in the main guest room purely because it was my decision to put you there.'

'Then put me somewhere a little more humble!' Ava cut in angrily.

In the strained silence that stretched in the wake of

her demand, the atmosphere hissed and buzzed like a crackling fire.

'No,' Vito responded, sliding a long arm smoothly into his shirt, his mind still engaged in imagining her on his bed seductively clad in little frilly bits of nothing. The pulse of urgency at his groin made him clench his teeth together. Desire, he recognised in exasperation, levelled all boundaries and defences.

'But I'm not an honoured guest here, I'm an employee!' Ava pointed out furiously. 'I should be staying in the staff quarters—'

'No,' Vito said again very quietly. 'I stand by my decision.'

'But it looks bad—'

Vito pulled on the shirt. 'You're a bright girl, Ava. Work it out for yourself.'

'Work what out?' Ava flung back at him in frustration. 'It's obvious that you can't treat me like a special guest without causing talk.'

Vito moved forward, the open shirt fluttering back from his strong muscled torso. 'Correct me if I'm wrong but didn't you spend three years in prison in punishment for your crime?'

Ava lost colour and her gaze dropped uneasily from his. 'Obviously I did.'

'So, you were tried and sentenced and you paid the price society demands. Where does it say that you have to go on paying?' he enquired impatiently. 'I put you in the principal guest room because if I treat you with respect everyone else will take their lead from me and award you the same level of respect.'

'It's not that simple,' she protested in a gruff undertone.

'It is,' Vito contradicted with serene confidence. 'Don't allow your insecurities to make it seem more complicated.'

A tempest of rage roared through Ava like a dam breaking its banks and she flung her head back, coppery hair dancing round her slim shoulders. 'I don't have insecurities!' she slammed back at him, defending the pride that was all she had left.

'Ava,' Vito countered very drily, 'you've always been a seething mass of insecurities.'

'That is not true…that is *so* totally untrue!' Ava hurled back at him tempestuously.

'*Madonna diavolo*…tell the truth and shame the devil,' Vito urged, lifting a hand and trailing a long finger mesmerically slowly along the length of her full lower lip.

Ava jerked her head back, startled by the tingle of awareness his touch ignited, which was already travelling straight to the heart of her body. 'Don't touch me…'

'You don't mean it,' Vito husked, shifting closer still to angle his handsome dark head down and lower his mouth to hers. 'You and I both know you don't mean it.'

# CHAPTER FIVE

Vito settled a hand on the shallow indentation at the base of Ava's spine and tilted her forward into potent contact with his lean, powerful body. The heat and the ferociously physical feel of him against her shrivelled her defences, even before the hungry urgency of his mouth on hers blew them away completely. Locked to him, she swayed, knowing she had never dreamt that a kiss could make her feel so much. His pure passion called out to her and awakened a desperate craving for more.

She kissed him back eagerly, too worked up even to worry that her kissing might be of the amateur variety, too afraid that he might back off again as he had done twice before. As that subconscious fear penetrated she closed her arms round him, inviting, encouraging, no rational thought involved in the action. The piercing invasion of his tongue inside her mouth sent the blood racing like crazy through her veins and accelerated her heartbeat. Nothing had ever felt that necessary to her, nothing had ever felt that *right*.

'Per l'amor di Dio, Ava,' Vito growled against her mouth. 'You drive me crazy.'

'Is that bad?' Ava queried, stretching up on legs that

suddenly felt too short to plant a kiss against the un-smiling corner of his handsome mouth.

Vito twisted his head to capture her lips again with a deep groan that vibrated inside his powerful chest, big hands cupping her hips to force her closer so that she was sensually aware of his arousal. Involuntarily she rejoiced in his affirmation of her feminine power. The musky designer scent of him flared her nostrils and she shivered as he suckled her lower lip and the moist sweep of his tongue tangled with her own, other sensations that were yet more seductive taking charge of her as she pressed the tingling heaviness of her breasts into the hard wall of his chest.

She didn't feel the zip of her skirt going down, only registered its fall round her ankles a split second before he lifted her clear of its folds and brought her down on the bed. Boy, was that a smooth move, she thought help-lessly, just a little unnerved by such active proof of his experience and the fact that she was already on the bed without having decided to let him take her there. So, stop this now, stop acting like you can't control this, a dry little voice pronounced inside her confused head. A few kisses were one thing, more than that something else entirely. And although when she was younger she had often fantasised about occupying a bed with Vito in it, reality was a great deal more daunting. She could not forget Olly calling his big brother a predator with women. As Vito flipped off her shoes she sat up against the pillows and drew her knees up in a nervous gesture. Discarding his shirt, he came down on the foot of the bed and that fast, her troubled eyes drawn to his gleaming honey-coloured torso, she was lost to all common sense.

Her fingers spread across his warm flesh but he had his own ideas. He smoothed her slim legs flat and embarked on her shirt buttons, kissing her every time he released one. Air rushed in and out of her lungs and caught in her throat. She braced her hands on his satin-smooth shoulders. Her shirt vanished and with it her sensible cotton bra. He caressed the soft ripe swell of her breasts with appreciative hands, long fingers expertly teasing the throbbing peaks until a little moan escaped low in her throat. He took that as an invitation to dip his dark head and continue the delicious torment with his tongue. As he caressed her the tide of sensations rippled down her body and she felt an urgent heat building between her thighs.

'Don't stop touching me, *gioia mia*,' Vito urged, golden eyes smouldering with hungry appreciation as he looked down at her.

Colour flushed her cheeks and her fingers slid down over the tense muscles of his stomach and over the smooth cotton of his trousers to the hard bulge below. With a roughened exclamation, Vito released the button on his chinos and ran the zip down, his eagerness exciting her. Skimming the briefs out of her way with an unsteady hand, she ran an exploratory fingertip over his erection. He was velvet on steel, smooth and hard. While he lifted his hips every time she touched him it did not seem the right moment to consider the fact that there was a good deal more of him in that department than she had dimly expected. Ignorance pushed aside, because she was ready to learn from discovery, she bent her coppery head to take him in her mouth.

'No, I want you now,' Vito protested, drawing her up

to his level again to crush her generous mouth under his with erotic force. 'Is this what you want?'

Ava blinked, languorous blue eyes momentarily bemused. What *she* wanted? No problem answering that question and no hesitation for she suffered not a shade of doubt: him, absolutely only him. 'Yes…'

His fingers drifted down the long line of her slim thigh and she trembled, wanting, needing almost more than she could bear, wondering wildly if everyone felt every tiny caress so strongly and craved as much as she did. Or had the years she had spent shut away from the world made her rather more desperate? The thought shamed her, somehow forcing her to think of the caution she was abandoning. But then just once she wanted to go with the flow, experience rather than pre-plan. She gazed up at him, outwardly tranquil until she collided with the hot glitter of desire in his eyes. He was gorgeous. He was everything she wanted. How could she fight or deny what she was feeling?

'I love your body, *cara mia*,' he told her huskily. 'You're beautiful.'

In that moment he truly made her feel beautiful and she smiled dreamily, not believing but willing to credit that in the heat of passion she had magically acquired a special lustre in his eyes. As she watched him wrench off his chinos her heart began to beat very fast again. She didn't want to think and she tuned out her anxious thoughts but they broke through to the surface of her mind regardless, insisting on being heard. This was sex, nothing more to Vito, she reasoned reluctantly. She knew that, had to accept it. It never was anything more to him and she wasn't naïve enough to think that anything more than intimacy might come from it. The exhilarating spark of attraction that had always leapt between them was finally finding expression and it felt inevitable, something that would have happened no matter what she did.

Her panties seemed to melt away during another bout of heated kissing. She loved the taste and fire and strength of him. He stroked her soft, needy flesh below and she trembled as he slid a finger into her, while his thumb rubbed the madly sensitive little bead of her clitoris, making her tremble with delight.

'You're so wet...' he told her fiercely.

Shame engulfed Ava but she quivered as sensation drowned out everything in sweet waves she could hardly withstand in silence. Little whimpers escaped her throat in spite of her attempt to hold them back. She twisted as if she were in a fever, all control wrenched from her by the pleasure and the tormenting anticipation. He shifted away from her, leaving her body throbbing and pulsing with need and impatience. She heard the sound of foil tearing, knew he was donning protection and then he returned to her, rearranging her limbs with indisputable expertise. In one sure deep thrust he entered her and a choked cry of pain parted her lips, the sharp jab of discomfort unexpected and unwelcome.

Vito froze above her in shock, shaken dark golden eyes clinging to her hectically flushed face. 'I am the first?' he demanded in disbelief.

'Don't make a production out of it,' Ava urged, so embarrassed that she could not even meet his eyes. It hadn't occurred to her that it might hurt the first time. She hadn't thought about that aspect, had just lain back and expected nature to take its course, but possibly he was a little too passionate and well endowed for so relaxed an approach.

'How did you expect me to react?' Vito bit out, wildly disconcerted by what he had just learned about her. Ava, the teenager he had once deemed to be a seasoned little sexual temptress, was actually a virgin? That prospect had never crossed his mind once and he was not a man who liked surprises. Indeed he had an engrained distrust of surprises that came in a feminine package, life having taught him far too much about their hidden agendas.

'Well, it's done now,' Ava said baldly, refusing to cringe in mortification and mustering every ounce of her pride to her rescue. Evidently she wasn't the veteran of the sheets that he had assumed that she was and if he was disappointed he would just have to live with it.

'But why...*me*?' Vito growled suspiciously.

Ava angled up her hips to distract him and his broad shoulders tautened as he attempted to withdraw from the hot, tight embrace of her body. A second such movement from her became his undoing. He sank back into her enticing honeyed heat with a splintering groan of tortured desire and rage burned like a banked-down fire in his accusing gaze.

Ava evaded that look and shut her eyes. She had signed up for the whole experience, hadn't she? She wasn't about to allow him to wreck everything. Although did she really have any influence over Vito? Given the chance, it seemed he would have stopped, *rejected* her. Was virginity such a turn-off? Or was he afraid that her inexperience would prompt her to demand more from him than he was prepared to give? She had heard the old cliché that suggested virgins were more likely to become too attached to their lovers, seeking ties that went beyond the physical. That, she immediately sensed, was most likely what he feared. Well, he would soon discover that she cherished no such illusions where he was concerned.

'This isn't what I wanted,' Vito ground out.

'We don't always get what we want,' Ava pronounced woodenly, shifting her hips as a wonderful little tremor of devouring hunger and excitement shimmied up from her pelvis again like a storm warning. 'Don't spoil this….'

Torn between wanting to strangle her and wanting to keep her in bed for a week, Vito swore in his own language even as the natural promptings of his powerful libido took over. He had never wanted a woman as much as he wanted her at that moment but she felt like a guilty forbidden pleasure again. He didn't screw virgins, he didn't take advantage of inexperienced or vulnerable women.

Ava gave herself up to the pleasure, arching up in welcome to the enthralling glide of his body into hers. The ravenous excitement grew and grew as he thrust with simmering heat and strength and her body clenched and tightened round him, sending waves of exquisite sensation rolling through her body. His insistent rhythm quickened and her heart slammed inside her chest, the driving force of desire controlling her until at last she reached a quivering peak of spellbinding joy that spilled through her like an injection of happiness. Spasms of ecstasy were still rocking her when he shuddered over her in his own climax and she held him close, knowing she never wanted to let him go again but that she had to hide the fact.

'That was…different, *mia bella*,' Vito pronounced raggedly, pressing a slow measured kiss to her brow and then vaulting out of the bed to stride into the bathroom.

Ava breathed in slow and deep. She had revelled in that brief moment of togetherness but he had instantly shied away from that cosiness and she was not surprised; she was forewarned. *Different?* Not exactly a compliment she would queue up to receive, she acknowledged unhappily. As Vito reappeared she sat up, the sheet tucked beneath her arms, and said with deliberate carelessness, 'Different? It was just a bit of fun.'

An arrested expression froze his features, drawing her attention to the black shadow of stubble outlining his chiselled jaw and strong sensual lips. His eyes were as hard and bright as black diamonds between his screening lashes. '*Come ha detto?*...I beg your pardon?' he said levelly.

'The sex,' Ava murmured glibly. 'It was just a bit of fun, nothing you need to get worked up about.'

'You were a virgin!' Vito slammed back at her censoriously.

'And next week I'll be twenty-two-years old,' Ava informed him. 'How many twenty-two-year-old virgins do you know? It was past time I took the plunge.'

Already struggling with the turbulence of his emotions and a savage sense of guilt, Vito was inflamed by her reckless defiant attitude. Had he really believed her to be vulnerable? She talked as though she were coated in armour and she made it sound as though she had deliberately chosen him to deflower her. Furthermore she had reduced what they had shared to a basic meeting of bodies and, although on one level he accepted that that was what it had been, he could not subdue his angry sense of resentment. He had not meant to injure her in any way but he had made the crucial mistake of letting his high-voltage sex drive override his intelligence.

'I didn't look for the honour of becoming your first lover,' Vito spelt out with grim forbearance. 'In fact if I'd known I would never have touched you. I *assumed* you were experienced.'

Ava propped her chin on the heel of her hand, bright blue eyes misleadingly wide and calm, all anxiety and despondency suppressed for she refused to parade her true feelings in his presence. 'I am now,' she pointed out, high colour blooming over her delicate cheekbones as she made that claim.

'Casual sex is definitely not what you need right now,' Vito informed her with harsh biting conviction.

Her eyes veiled while she wondered how anything she did with him could be considered casual. Certainly not on her terms but on *his*? That was a very different matter. For Vito, sex could never have been anything else but casual with her. 'You don't know what I need— how could you? Look, give me something to wear so that I can return to my own room…'

Vito strode into the bathroom and emerged again to toss a black towelling robe on the bed. Her generous mouth arranged in a tight line of restraint, Ava dug her arms into the over-large garment and pulled it carefully round her to conceal her body before sliding out of the bed and knotting the sash at her waist. With fast-shredding dignity she stooped to pick up her discarded clothes and shoes, her heart like a crushed rock inside her weighing her down intolerably.

Ava shed the robe and stepped straight into the shower in her room. She was shell-shocked by what

had happened between her and Vito Barbieri. Somehow,
heaven knew how, her teenaged self had taken over her
all-grown-up self and triumphed. Feeling the ache at the
heart of her body, she grimaced and washed her body as
roughly as someone trying to scrub their sins away with
soap and water. When she was dry she pulled on jeans
and a tee, fed the dwindling fire with a log and sat down
beside it with Harvey. So, she had finally had sex and
he had made it amazing but her emotions were in total
turmoil. Idiot, she castigated herself as she smoothed
Harvey's shaggy head and he rested back against her,
brown eyes lovingly pinned to her tearstained face. I
will not cry over Vito Barbieri, Ava told herself furiously. I made a mistake but *he* made a mistake as well.

She would act as if it had never happened, she decided in desperation. That was the only way to behave:
as if it had been an inconsequential and meaningless
episode she was keen to forget. She should never have
gone to his bedroom, never have stood there shouting
at him, challenging and provoking him. Just then the
question of which room she occupied seemed unutter-
ably trivial and not worth the fuss she had kicked up
over it. Vito wasn't used to being challenged, she reminded herself ruefully. Vito dug in like a rock bed-
ding down when you crossed him.

The knock on the door interrupted her thoughts. It
was a maid with a tray.

'Mr Barbieri thought you might be hungry,' she explained, setting the tray down on an occasional table
by the window and whisking the insulated cover off
the plate.

'I could have come downstairs for it,' Ava said guiltily, looking down at the beautifully cooked chicken

meal, her taste buds watering in spite of herself. As a
teenager she had been downright uncomfortable at being
served by the staff while she stayed at Bolderwood but
now she was rather more practical in her outlook. Jobs
at the castle were highly sought after because Vito paid
well and offered good working conditions as well as ap-
prenticeships in the key country skills still in demand
on the estate.

'No need with a big staff and only two people to look
after.' The girl laughed, clearly unfamiliar with Ava's
past history with the Barbieri family.

Ava ate because she was indeed hungry and then she
dug out a notebook and began to draw up a to-do list.
Obviously calling the caterers came first and she would
have to visit the garden centre that usually supplied the
wreaths and garlands for the house. For the first time
she wondered how she would get around because she
had been banned from driving for the foreseeable future. Deeming that a problem better dealt with in daylight, she unpacked her holdall, which took all of five
minutes. She took Harvey downstairs and, as directed
by the housekeeper, she fed the dog in a rear hall before
clipping on his lead and setting off through the solar-
lit wintry gardens to take him for a brisk walk. The
dim light was eerie, casting flickering shadows in the
breeze with only the sound of her own feet crunching
on the gravel paths in her ears. The whole place was
just crammed with memories for her, she acknowledged
painfully, for she could still remember sunbathing on
the lawn and larking about with Olly while they studied for their final exams…the exams her friend had
never actually got to sit. Ava had sat hers because her
case had taken months to come to court. For most of

that period she had been away at school where she was shunned like a leper for the tragedy she had caused and when she had finally come home her welcome there had proved even colder.

That night she slept in her comfortable bed, too exhausted to be kept awake by her mental turmoil. When she rose she was shocked to discover that it was almost nine, that she still felt tender in a certain place and was in no mood to celebrate the loss of her virginity. Clad in her jeans, her trusty notebook in her back pocket, she clattered downstairs with Harvey to take care of his needs first. Eleanor Dobbs was waiting for her when she came back indoors to direct her into the dining room for breakfast.

'Could I have a word with you after you've eaten?' she asked.

'Of course. Is Vito here?' Ava enquired stiffly, guessing that Eleanor wanted to discuss arrangements for the party.

'The helicopter picks him up at seven most mornings,' the older woman explained.

So, Vito was still locked into very early morning starts, Ava reflected without surprise while she tucked into cereal, fruit and coffee for breakfast. Work motivated him as nothing else could and he didn't work because he needed more money either. Fabulously wealthy though he was, Vito still worked virtually every day of the week because he had once been the child of a spendthrift bankrupt and had lived through periods of great insecurity. He had only put down permanent roots at Bolderwood for Olly's benefit, recognising that the little boy had needed a place he could call home.

Digging out her notebook before she even left the

dining room, Ava called the local caterers, who had provided the food and refreshments at the last party. She arranged a meeting for the following day and was heading up the stairs when the housekeeper appeared again.

'There's something I want to show you,' Eleanor told her uncomfortably. 'I thought maybe you could help.'

Ava lifted a fine brow. 'In any way I can,' she said evenly, wondering why the other woman was so tense.

Ava's tension mounted, however, when Eleanor Dobbs took her upstairs to what had once been Olly's room. She unlocked the door and spread it wide. Ava stood on the threshold in shock, for the room was untouched and looked as though it was just waiting for Olly to walk back in and occupy it. 'Why hasn't it been cleared?'

'I offered to do that soon after the funeral but Mr Barbieri said no. He used to come in here then but as far as I'm aware it's a couple of years since he did that.' The older woman grimaced. 'After all this time it just doesn't seem right to leave the room like this…'

Ava breathed in deep and straightened her shoulders. 'I'll sort it out,' she announced. 'Just bring me some boxes and bags and I'll go through all this stuff and decide what should be kept and stored. Then you can clear the room.'

'I'm very grateful,' Eleanor said ruefully. 'I didn't like to approach Mr Barbieri about it again. It's a sensitive subject.'

Alone again, Ava touched one of Olly's fossil specimens and tears swam in her eyes. Time had stood still within these walls, transforming the room into Vito's version of a shrine. That wasn't healthy, she thought painfully, recalling his speech to her about life going on.

The housekeeper helped her sort through Olly's possessions. Ava bagged his clothes for charity and put his Harry Potter first editions, the fossil collection and his photo albums into boxes. Leafing through the particular album that captured her two-year friendship with Vito's brother, she laughed and smiled through her tears as warmer less painful memories flooded back to her. It was the first time she had allowed herself to recall the good times they had had together and afterwards, although she felt drained, she also felt curiously lighter of heart.

When the job was complete she took Harvey out to the garden where roses were still blooming in the mild winter temperature and as she looked at those beautiful blooms an idea came to her and she went back indoors to get scissors. She had never got to say an official goodbye to Olly, but she could now visit his grave and pay her last respects without fear of offending anyone as her appearance at his funeral would have done. Her battered fake leather jacket zipped up against the breeze, she left Harvey in Eleanor's care and walked out onto the road, turning towards the small stone church little more than a hundred yards away. It had once been part of the Bolderwood estate, having been built and maintained by the original owners of the castle, but to maintain his privacy Vito had provided separate access for the church.

A blonde woman climbing out of a sporty car parked outside an elegant house opposite the church stared at Ava with a frown as she opened the gate of the cemetery, which was surrounded by a low wall. Ava laid her flowers down on Olly's grave, noting with a quivering mouth that a stone angel presided over his final resting place: Olly had had great faith in angels.

'It *is* you, isn't it?' a sharp female voice exclaimed abruptly.

Ava spun round and recognised the blonde she had seen at the house across the road. She was very attractive, beautifully dressed in the sort of garments that shrieked their designer labels, and Ava felt very much at a disadvantage with her wan face and shabby clothing. A faint spark of familiarity tugged at the back of Ava's brain though and she surmised that she had seen the woman before. 'I'm sorry, I don't know you.'

'Why would you know me? I'm Katrina Orpington but we've never moved in the same social circles,' the blonde informed her scornfully. 'But I still know you—you're that Fitzgerald girl, the one who killed Vito's little brother! What on earth are you doing here at Oliver's grave?'

Chalk white though she was, Ava stood her ground. Her picture had been in the local paper a lot at the time of the court case and evidently she had been recognised. 'I just wanted to see where he was buried... It may be my fault that he died but he was my best friend,' she pointed out unhappily.

The blonde's lip curled with contempt. 'Well, I think your presence here is in very bad taste. Crocodile tears won't wipe out what you did. I'll never forget Vito's face that night—he was devastated!'

'Yes...I'm sure he was.' Ava's voice had shrunk to a mere whisper. 'But I can't change that and I didn't mean to offend anyone by coming here.'

'You have a thick skin and a lot of nerve, I'll give

you that!' the blonde pronounced, turning away to stalk back out of the cemetery.

Moisture stinging on her cheeks in the steadily cooling afternoon air, Ava went into the church and sat down on a rear pew, using the silence and sense of peace that churches always gave her to get a grip on her see-sawing emotions. There was no escaping what she had done but she had to live with it, trust that she'd learned from it, hope that people would eventually stop seeing her as a killer and give her the opportunity to prove that she could be more than the sum total of her past sins. She thought of the previous night and cringed, deciding that she had sunk to slut level with Vito Barbieri, an unwelcome reading of the situation at a time when her spirits were already low. Feeling deeply vulnerable and alone, she said a prayer and then walked quickly back to the castle.

The afternoon flew by as Ava checked the rooms that would be used for the party and talked to the housekeeper about which pieces of furniture would need to be moved. Having made endless detailed lists and another couple of appointments, she was satisfied with her day's work. Apprehensive about being around when Vito came home, she took Harvey out for a long walk on the estate. A muddy Land Rover stopped beside her on one of the lanes and a tall blond man in his early thirties climbed out to introduce himself as the estate manager, Damien Skeel. It was wonderful to give her name to someone and see no awareness of her past in their response. Damien kept right on smiling at her, told her that his staff were delighted that the Christmas party was going ahead and urged her to contact him if she needed assistance with anything.

By then it was getting dark and Ava hastened home. She used the castle's rear entrance and straight away took care of feeding Harvey. She was about to head upstairs to freshen up when Eleanor Dobbs rushed through the green beige door that separated the main house from the kitchen wing, her face flushed and tense.

'Mr Barbieri is very angry that his brother's room was empty. It's my fault that it was done...I mean, I asked you to help. I told him that but I don't think he was listening,' she explained unhappily.

Ava stiffened. 'Oh, dear,' she muttered regretfully, suddenly wishing that she had never got involved.

'What the hell were you thinking of?' Vito roared at her as she crossed the hall a minute later and looked up to see him framed in the doorway of the library.

# CHAPTER SIX

VITO was an intimidating sight. Still clad in a dark business suit teamed with a gold silk tie, he strode forward, his big broad shoulders blocking out the wall lights behind him. Ava had never quite appreciated how much taller he was than her until he stood in front of her, towering over her by a good nine inches, his face racked with condemnation.

Her breath rattled in her dry throat, a flush highlighting her pale complexion because it was the first time she had seen him since they had parted in his bedroom the previous evening and at that moment she was more conscious of that earlier intimacy than of her apparent offence. As she clashed with his hard gaze an utterly inappropriate tingle of erotic awareness spread through her body like poison. Vito grabbed her wrist and pulled her into the library, where he shut the door behind them.

'*Per meraviglia!* What were you thinking of?' he demanded a second time, his Italian accent giving every word with a growling edge. 'I came home, noticed the door was open…saw the room stripped. I couldn't believe my eyes! Who, I wondered, could possibly have the colossal nerve and insensitivity to go against my wishes in my own home?'

While he spoke, his breath fracturing audibly with the force of his wrath, his eyes hot and bright with outrage, Ava hastily thought of, and discarded, several possible responses in favour of simple honesty. 'I thought it was for the best—'

'*You* thought?' Vito erupted with incredulous bite. 'What the hell has it got to do with you?'

'Obviously I should have asked you about what you wanted done first,' Ava declared shakily, for she had never dreamt that her intervention might rouse such a reaction.

'It was none of your business!' Vito glowered at her in a tempestuous fury she had not known he was capable of experiencing. He was in such a rage that he could hardly get the words out and she knew that he was finding it a struggle to voice his feelings in English rather than Italian.

'I thought I understood how you felt. Obviously I was mistaken but I honestly believed that clearing the room would make you feel better,' Ava protested tautly.

'How the hell could a bare room make me feel better? It's simply another reminder that Olly's gone!' Vito ground out bitterly while treating her to a burning look of fierce rage.

Was that rage directed at her as the driver of the car that awful night? As she couldn't blame him if that was the underlying source powering him, her shoulders slumped. 'I didn't get rid of the personal stuff. His collections and photos and books and letters were all boxed up and kept,' Ava told him eagerly.

Vito snatched in a ragged breath, his mouth settled into a tough, contemptuous line. 'I want it all put back… exactly as it was!'

Ava straightened her slim shoulders, her bright blue eyes deeply troubled by that instruction. 'I don't think that's a good idea—'

'*You* don't think?' Vito's deep drawl scissored over the words like a slashing knife. 'What has it got to do with you? Did seeing that room empty of Olly make you feel guilty? Is that what your invasion of my privacy is really all about?'

'Yes, seeing his room again made me feel guilty and very sad. But then even being in this house makes me feel guilty. But I'm used to feeling like that and it didn't influence my decision.'

'Your decision?' Vito derided with positive savagery, his voice raw with aggrieved bitterness. 'You *killed* my brother. Was that not enough for you? What gave you the insane idea that desecrating his room and my memory of him would make me feel better?'

At that lethal reminder, spoken to her by him for the first time, Ava flinched as though he had struck her. The blood slid away from below her skin, leaving only sick pallor in its wake. He had the right to hate and revile her: who could deny him that outlet when he had never before confronted her on that score? Her tummy filled with nausea and an appalling sense of shame and guilt that she knew she could do nothing to assuage.

'I was unforgivably high-handed...I can see that now,' Ava admitted jerkily, pained regret slicing through her that she could have been that thoughtless and inconsiderate. Unfortunately she had always been quick to act on a gut reaction and think about consequences later and this time it had gone badly wrong for her. 'But I honestly wasn't thinking about how *I* felt when I cleared the room. I was thinking about you.'

'I don't want you thinking about me!' Vito roared as he strode across to the decanter set on the sofa table and poured himself a shot of whiskey. 'My thoughts and feelings about my brother's death are entirely my affair and not something I intend to discuss.'

'Yes, I have got that message but that locked-up untouched room didn't strike me as a healthy approach to grief,' Ava dared to argue, her attention resting on the rigid angles and hollows of his strong face and the force of control he was clearly utilising to hide his feelings. He was as locked up inside as that blasted room, she thought in sudden frustration, but it was a revelation to her that he possessed the depth that fostered such powerful emotions.

'What would you know about it?' Vito slashed back at her rudely, for once making no attempt to hide how upset he was, which she found oddly touching.

'I've been through something similar and talking about it or even writing about it for purely your own benefit helps,' she murmured ruefully. 'Grief can devour you alive if you get stuck in it.'

He skimmed her with cutting emphasis. 'Spare me the platitudes! And don't ever interfere in my life again!'

'I won't, but remember that it was *you* who told me that you can't live in the past for ever and that life has to go on,' Ava reminded him wretchedly. 'I'm sorry if I misinterpreted what you meant by that. I thought I was helping.'

'I don't need or want your help!' Vito slammed at her in a wrathful fury as he wrenched open the library door again. 'Tell Eleanor I'm eating out tonight!'

And Ava was left standing there in the pool of light by the desk. She gritted her teeth. She was hurting, Vito was hurting but he didn't want anyone, least of all her, to recognise the fact. That wounded her but she had no right to feel wounded because she *had* been insensitive not to broach the topic of clearing Olly's room with him personally.

A soft knock sounded on the door and Ava moved forward to open it. 'Vito said—'

'Don't worry, I heard him,' Eleanor confided with a grimace and she winced as the sound of a powerful car tearing down the drive carried indoors. 'I hope you told the boss that clearing that room was *my* idea.'

'I encouraged you and I got stuck in first. I thought it was the right thing to do as well. Forget about it,' Ava advised.

Eleanor frowned. 'I've never seen Mr Barbieri lose his temper like that. Should I start putting the room back the way it was?'

'I would wait and see how he feels about it tomorrow...but maybe listening to my opinion isn't the right way to go,' Ava pointed out heavily, reaching down to fondle Harvey's ears as he bumped against her knee.

'Harvey's got a lovely nature,' the housekeeper remarked in the awkward silence. 'I'll spread the word about him needing a home but, if you ask me, he's already happy to have found a home with you.'

'But pets aren't allowed where I live in London,' Ava muttered, struggling to concentrate when all she could hear, over and over again in her buzzing head, was Vito saying, 'You killed my brother.' And she *had*, not deliberately but through recklessness and bad judgement. That was a truth she had to live with, but just then acknowledging it wounded her as much as it had the day in hospital when she had first learned that Olly had died in the crash.

Ava had no appetite for the delicious evening meal brought to her in the solitary splendour of the dining room. After rooting through Vito's library to find a Jane Austen novel she hadn't read in several years, she went for a swim in the basement, desperate to escape her unhappy thoughts. Afterwards, the warmth and privacy in her bedroom along with Harvey's relaxing presence enclosed her. Momentarily she remembered how noisy prison had been and how comfortless, with metal furniture fixed to the wall and a tiny floor space with only a view of another prison block out of the small window. Bells had rung sounding out meal times and exercise periods, barred gates had clanged and sometimes alarms had gone off as well. Pounding music had been an almost constant backdrop while other inmates shouted from cell to cell, bored silly at being locked up for so many hours a day. She shivered. The first two years she had had to struggle to get through every day but she had eventually settled into a routine. She had found work helping others to read and write and had learned to appreciate tiny things like the right to buy a hot chocolate drink or a snack with her meagre earnings. She had also learned very fast to stop feeling sorry for herself because there were so many others dealing with much worse stuff than she had on her plate.

Recalling that stark reality, Ava decided to run a bath in the opulent turret room en suite and luxuriate in the selection of bathing products available. Staying at the castle was very much like staying at a five-star hotel. It was a luxury holiday and she ought to make the most of it because reality would soon be back loudly knocking at her door again, she reminded herself impatiently. But she felt so horribly guilty about having wounded Vito by forcing him to face up to his half-brother's death all over again. She had trod in hobnail boots all over his sensibilities by foolishly underestimating his attachment to the picture of the past that could still flourish in that locked room. He was right. Who was she to say it was healthy or otherwise to leave that room as though time had stopped dead?

Ava wasted a lot of time lounging in the decadent bath, topping up the water to warm it when she got cold, fighting with all her might to escape her unhappy thoughts. She had screwed up again and she clenched her teeth hard and tried again to blank her mind. She donned her pyjamas, blew dry her hair and set her mobile phone alarm to wake her up early. But *not* early enough to run into Vito as she was convinced that he wouldn't want to share the breakfast table with her. She took Harvey out for a last run before clambering into her comfortable bed to read until she got sleepy.

When the door opened rather abruptly, Harvey leapt up and barked and Ava sat up with a start. Just about the very last person she was expecting walked in, leaning back against the door to close it. Harvey barked again, tense with suspicion at the interruption. Ava leant out of bed to soothe him into silence and he subsided and slunk back to his favourite spot by the dying fire.

'I saw the light from outside and realised you were still awake,' Vito informed her as she glanced at her watch to note that it was after eleven. 'Damien gave me a lift home from the village pub.'

Absolutely flummoxed by his appearance in her bedroom wearing nothing more than his boxer shorts—his towelling robe was, after all, still lying in a heap on her floor—with his hair still tousled and damp from the shower, Ava was as tense as a bowstring but trying against all the odds to act normally. 'Oh, yes, I met Damien when I was out walking today and he introduced himself. He's very friendly.'

His face tensed, his eyes narrowing with laser precision. 'Was he flirting with you?'

'Possibly,' Ava responded tactfully, because Damien had been flirting like mad with her during their brief conversation, even confessing to her that young single women were scarcer than hens' teeth in the neighbourhood and that he had started attending the church services in the hope of meeting more people, only to discover that the greater part of the congregation was as old as the hills.

'I'll warn him off...I don't share,' Vito delivered darkly.

Ava blinked. 'You really don't need to warn him off.'

'I don't do one-night stands either,' Vito continued with lashings of assurance.

In the act of dragging her eyes from his truly magnificent physique, Ava blushed like a tongue-tied adolescent and could think of absolutely nothing to say to that when he was clearly, in spite of their earlier difference of opinion, planning to spend the night with her.

'But I think, right now, I could be very much into fun, *bella mia*,' he confided raggedly, the tough front lurching slightly.

'I don't know how to do casual,' Ava told him jerkily, her nerves getting the better of her vocal cords but the sting of his reproof about casual sex unforgotten.

'I don't either,' Vito murmured silkily, tossing something down on the bedside cabinet and throwing the duvet back and climbing into the bed beside her as though he slept with her every night and it were the most normal thing he could do.

'Vito…' Ava began in a troubled voice.

Vito ran a finger caressingly down the length of her slender throat to rest where a tiny pulse was beating out her tension below her collarbone. Hot golden eyes looked levelly into hers. 'I don't want to sleep alone tonight.'

'Oh,' Ava said stupidly, but in truth she was transfixed by the admission from such a source. Vito, who needed no one, listened to no one and who never confessed to human weakness was telling her something she had never expected to hear from him. He wanted— no, *needed*—to be with her and he could not have said anything more calculated to appeal to her.

He brushed his lips very gently across hers, his breath fanning her cheek. 'Do you want me to leave?'

Ava froze at the offer. 'Er, no—'

'But hopefully you don't want me to stay because you wanted me at eighteen and couldn't have me?' he pressed, evidently concerned that that might be the case.

He was asking her to divorce the past from the present and she wasn't sure she could do that. 'I just want you,' Ava said gruffly, shorn of her usual cool. 'But I assure you that I got over my obsession with you at eighteen.'

'I don't like the idea that I'm taking advantage of you,' Vito admitted grimly. 'Here I am, I'm not drunk but I'm not sober either, and I'm not even thinking about what I'm doing.'

'That's OK, no big deal,' Ava soothed softly, patently

unaware of how rare it was for Vito to do anything without thinking it through first. 'It's not important.'

'I'm not about to fall in love with you and marry you or anything like that!' Vito warned her, derision at the idea giving his mouth a sardonic twist. 'This is an affair, nothing more complex. Don't overthink it.'

'I never thought I would say it but you talk too much,' Ava told him with sudden amusement. 'I'm not that daft dreaming teenager you remember—I grew up and I'm not even twenty-two yet. I don't want to get married for years and years and years!'

'I don't *ever* want to get married,' Vito traded, throwing himself back against the pillows while wondering how he could possibly be irritated by her total lack of interest in marrying him. Naturally that was good news and she was blessedly free of the carefully presented hypocrisies with which his more usual style of lover sought to set him at his ease. Of course she was ten years younger than he was and that was a fair gap, he acknowledged, tension filtering through his momentary relaxation. In fact it was almost cradle-snatching.

Ava leant over him, her hair brushing a big shoulder while she marvelled at the conversation they were having. 'I don't want to marry you. I want to play the field and have fun first.'

'If Damien Skeel comes on to you, you tell me,' Vito spelt out rawly in a knee-jerk reaction that shook him because it seemed to come from some strange place inside him he didn't recognise. 'And you're not going to be playing the field and having fun with anyone but me until we're over. Is that understood?'

A pang pierced Ava. She didn't like to hear him talk of their affair being over before it had even really begun.

It hurt, just as breaking up would hurt, she reminded herself impatiently. She wasn't a kid any more. She didn't cherish a little soap bubble fantasy of Vito falling madly in love with her and sweeping her down the aisle to an altar. Even as a teenager she had not been that naïve.

'Do you always lay down the law in bed like you're in the boardroom?' Ava teased.

'I need to with you. You're a new and very original box of tricks, *cara mia*,' Vito contended, pushing her playfully flat against the pillows to extract a long, drugging kiss that sent her heartbeat into overdrive.

She felt tiny beneath him, crushed by his broad chest and the hair-roughened thigh that had slid between hers. She was madly aware of her nipples tightening into tingling buds and of the hard press of his arousal against her. He wanted her. For a split second she simply luxuriated in that sweet wonderful knowledge. She wanted him and he wanted her. Finally, the time was right. And then in dismay she recalled the rather childish tattoo on her hip and resolved to buy some large plasters as soon as she could to conceal that revealing marking before he could see it. He wouldn't think of her as an adult for long if he caught a glimpse of that.

Vito sat up and tossed back the duvet. 'What on earth are you wearing?' he demanded.

'My PJs.'

'Gingham just isn't sexy,' Vito pronounced with authority and embarked on the buttons.

Ava lay there stiff with embarrassment while he stripped off her pyjamas and reminded herself that he had seen it all before and that it was silly to feel so self-conscious. 'Put the light out,' she still urged him.

'No...you're a work of art and I want to savour you,' Vito countered without hesitation, studying the long svelte line of her pale body. 'I was in far too much of a hurry yesterday.'

'I'm cold,' she told him, hauling up the duvet at speed again.

'No, you're shy and I never realised that before. Ava Fitzgerald...*shy*,' Vito commented with rich amusement. 'Wow...you've turned as pink as a lobster.'

'If you refer to lobsters and me in the same sentence again you can go back to your own room!' Ava hissed vitriolically, blue eyes sparkling like sapphires in her elfin face.

'It's not happening.' With a sudden laugh, Vito crushed her mouth beneath his again, his tongue delving deep in a devouring kiss that sent erotic thrills coursing through her all too ready body. When he discarded his rigid self-discipline and reserve, there was so much passion pent-up inside him, Ava thought, thrilled by his approach.

His mouth closed over the swollen peak of her breast and she shivered as he tasted and teased her with his tongue. The glide of his teeth followed and she moaned, startled and aroused, the heat at the heart of her beginning to build. Her hips arched and he stilled her.

'We're going to do this right this time, *bella mia*,' Vito informed her, his exotically handsome features taut with determination.

'*Right?*' Ava repeated in disbelief. 'Keep the control freakiness for the office.'

'I am not a control freak,' Vito growled.

He *so* was. Ava cupped his face and connected with smouldering golden eyes that made her heartbeat hammer. He was beautiful. She just loved looking at him, and then he kissed her again with that sensual full mouth and the ability to think fell away. As he began to lick and kiss his way down over her body her hands dug into his shoulders and suddenly it was a challenge to breathe. She thought he might be going to do...*that*, not something she could imagine doing with anyone, not even him. She tried to urge him back up again but either he failed to take the hint or he deliberately put himself out of reach.

'Vito...I don't think I want that,' Ava muttered tightly.

'Give me a one-minute trial,' Vito purred, settling hot, hungry eyes on her. 'While you think about it.'

Already pink, Ava could feel herself turn hot red and she just closed her eyes, not wanting to be inhibited and a turn-off. His hands smoothed over her thighs and eased them apart. I'm not going to like this but I'll put up with it, she decided, and then he touched her with his tongue on the most super-sensitive part of her body and she almost leapt in the air at the sensation. He made a soothing sound deep in his throat that she found incredibly sexy. Slow-burning pleasure turned to raw ecstasy incredibly fast and she went wild, gasping and rising off the bed as an explosive climax engulfed her. Dazed by it, she felt limp as he shifted over her and sank into her hard and fast. Nothing had ever felt as intense. Her body had discovered a new level of sensitivity and in its already heightened state, his rapid powerful movements swiftly awakened the throbbing heat and hunger of need again.

'*Porca miseria!* You make me wild!' Vito panted.

Her every sense was on hyper alert and excitement

as she had never known was clawing at her. She didn't have the breath to respond. Her fingers raked down his back over his flexing muscles as she reacted to sensations as close to pleasure as torment, wanting more, *wanting*, her entire body reaching as her back arched and the glorious splintering high peak of blinding pleasure engulfed her again as a shrill cry was wrenched from her.

'On a scale of one to ten that was a twenty,' Vito husked in her ear. 'I'm sorry, I was rough—'

'I liked it,' Ava mumbled in a forgiving mood, both arms wrapped round him, happiness dancing and leaping through her limp, satiated body like sunlight on a dull wintry day.

'You're miraculous, *gioia mia*,' Vito said thickly, an almost bemused look in his stunning dark eyes as he bent down awkwardly and dropped a kiss on her nose. But he then freed her from his weight and proximity so fast that her hands literally trailed off him and she half sat up in surprise as he strode into the bathroom. He had used contraception, she reminded herself dizzily. Miraculous? Was that good? Her mind was full of words like, 'astonishing, magnificent, unbelievable'. Even so, she wished he hadn't left her so suddenly. As that thought occurred to her Vito reappeared and swept up his robe to put it on. Ava blinked. He wasn't coming back to bed? Perhaps he was hungry.

Vito had got halfway to the door before Ava spoke. 'Where are you going?'

'To bed.' Vito half turned back to her, a brow slightly quirked as though he wondered why she was asking such an obvious question of him.

Such fury shot through Ava that she felt light-headed

with it. 'Oh, so that's it for tonight, is it? Having got what you wanted, you just walk out on me?'

Vito swung all the way round and levelled stunned dark eyes on her. 'I always sleep in my own bed…it is not meant as an insult or any kind of statement.'

'You mean you *never* spend the night with anyone?' Ava prompted, utterly disconcerted by the news.

'I like my privacy,' Vito admitted a shade curtly, unable to understand why she was complaining when no other woman ever had.

'Well, you can have all the privacy you want from me,' Ava snapped back at him. 'But let me make one thing clear—if you walk through that door you don't get back in again on any pretext!'

His eyes shimmered and narrowed, his face tensing with the surprise and considerable hauteur of a male unaccustomed to any form of rejection from a woman. 'You can't be serious.'

'That's the way it is, Vito. Take it or leave it. I thought the practice of *droit de seigneur* went out with the Crusades and you're not going to treat me like a late-night snack and get away with it!' Ava slung tempestuously as she punched a pillow, doused the light to leave him poised in darkness and lay down again.

Vito opened the door, hesitated—*fatally*, he later realised. He thought of waking up beside Ava. He shed his robe where he stood.

As Ava felt the mattress give beneath his weight she thought about the power of 'miraculous' sex over a male and it made her want to punch him more than ever. He was spoilt by too much money and too many eager-to-please women.

'Am I expected to cuddle as well?' Vito enquired with sardonic bite.

'If you value your life, stay on your own side of the bed,' Ava advised bluntly.

Silence fell, a silence laden with nerve-racking undertones. Ava grimaced in the darkness and wished she had kept quiet. You could lead a horse to water but you couldn't make it drink, she reminded herself wryly, a situation not improved by the fact that he was stubborn as a mule. He didn't do the cuddly sleeping-together stuff but she didn't think she could do an affair without affection at the very least. Who are you kidding? she asked herself. She was only at the castle for another two weeks and the minute the party was done, she would be history. She needed to learn how to take each day as it came just the way she had done in prison, but there was no way on earth that she would live according to *his* rules alone.

'I shouldn't have lost my temper with you about Olly's room,' Vito mused very quietly.

'I shouldn't have gone ahead and touched it without speaking to you about it first,' Ava traded, her stiffness receding a little.

'I used to go in there and sit in the months after the funeral,' Vito volunteered curtly. 'Fortunately I managed to wean myself off that habit, so there was no reason to leave the room the way it was while he was alive.'

Ava gritted her teeth and bit back hasty words because Vito was a stiff-upper-lip kind of male. 'Why should you have had to wean yourself off going in there?' she finally asked. 'There was no harm in it if it gave you comfort.'

'It was a weird thing to do,' Vito asserted in a tone

that warned her that he expected her to agree with him on that score.

Ava suffered a truly appalling desire to hug him but she imagined him shaking her off and didn't move a muscle in his direction. 'No, it wasn't weird. It was completely natural. He was on your mind. You didn't need to fight off the urge as if it was wrong. You're just terrified of feeling emotion, aren't you? But all you did was make it harder for yourself.'

'I am not terrified of feeling emotion!' Vito grated in disbelief.

Ava begged to disagree in silence. Macho man had not been able to cope with the threatening desire to sit in his kid brother's room occasionally and quite typically he had walled his grief up inside himself, convinced that that was the best way.

'I'm *not*,' Vito repeated doggedly, wondering why he had conversations with her that he never had with anyone else while trying to recall emotional moments without success.

Ava smiled and went to sleep.

# CHAPTER SEVEN

FLOWERS would be old-fashioned, Vito reasoned five days later, during a boardroom meeting at his London headquarters that he was finding unbelievably tedious. He had another five hours to put in before he could call it a day. Impatient, he glanced at the wall clock again while his mind wandered to picture Ava clad in sexy lingerie reclining on his bed and then immediately discarded the fantasy. Unlike most of his past lovers, she would hit the roof if he gave her a gift like that. *What am I? Your little sex toy?* So attuned had he become to Ava's feisty take on life, he could actually *hear* her saying it. No, definitely not the lingerie. What did you give a woman who acted as if your millions didn't exist? Chocolate? Boring, predictable. Exasperation sizzled through his tall, powerful physique. He could not recall ever expending this much mental energy on anything so trivial. What did she need? Clothes. Ava was the proud possessor of the very barest of necessities. But she wouldn't like him buying her clothes either. His big shoulders squared, his strong jaw line clenched. *Dio mio*, she would just have to put up with it.

'Mr Barbieri…?'

Vito focused on the speaker with a blankness of mind

he had no prior experience of in a business setting. He wondered if he was ill. Maybe he had the flu, maybe he had allowed himself to get too tired. Yes, that was it, too much sex, not enough rest, he decided, relieved by the explanation but acknowledging that he was not about to change his ways…not with Ava under his roof. He stood up lithely and offered his apologies for his sudden departure while explaining that he had somewhere else to be.

That same day, Ava made her decision over breakfast: she would go and see her father. It was a Saturday and the older man always liked to stay home and read the papers in the morning.

Fear of rejection, nerves and guilt had kept her from the door of her former family home, she acknowledged ruefully. Her court case and prison sentence along with the newspaper articles written about her fall from grace had seriously embarrassed her family and her father, who worked as a member of Vito's accounting team, had been convinced that her role in Olly's death had ensured that he was passed over for promotion. For those reasons, she was certainly not expecting a red carpet rolled out for her but she wanted to say sorry and discover if there was any way of restoring some kind of bond with her relations. If it crossed her mind that there never had seemed to be much of a bond between her and them, she suppressed the thought and concentrated on thinking positively.

The past week had proved incredibly busy but all the party arrangements were running smoothly and she had begun to decorate the house. She tried not to think too much about Vito while she was working. After all, in less than a week's time she would be leaving and the affair would be over. That was *not* going to break her heart, she told herself firmly, but the hand in which she held her cup of coffee trembled. Hastily she set the cup down again. If she gave way to stupid feelings, started fancying that she was in love and all that nonsense she would be digging her own descent into despair by the time it ended. And no man was allowed to have that much power over Ava because in her experience, with the single exception of Olly, the people she loved had always hurt her badly. No, just as Vito didn't do marriage, Ava didn't do love.

Admittedly she was attached to him in some ways, she acknowledged grudgingly. He kept on trying to take her out to dinner and places which she hadn't expected, having assumed he would be as keen as her to keep their involvement with each other under wraps. Certainly the staff must have guessed but by the time such rumours spread further afield Ava would be long gone. She had told Vito she had nothing to wear that wouldn't embarrass them both in public but it was just an excuse to hide the fact that she didn't want people to know they were involved. Much wiser to stay under the radar, she reflected ruefully, having no desire to attract controversy or see Vito outraged or upset by people who would be appalled that he could have fallen into bed with the woman responsible for his brother's death. That was life and Ava had learned not to fight it.

Vito and her? It was just sex, she told herself every time he was with her. He couldn't keep his hands off her but, to be honest, she couldn't keep her hands off him either and the awareness that they had such a short time together had simply pushed the intensity to a whole new level. He was with her every minute he was at home and, although he was characteristically working on a Saturday, he had gradually started finishing earlier and earlier. They argued at least once a day, being both very strong-willed people. But they never let the sun go down on a row either and he stayed with her every night, dragging her up to breakfast with him at an unforgivably early hour while striding through the castle shouting for her if she wasn't immediately available when he arrived home. She knew he liked her and that he cared about what happened to her. She respected his fair-mindedness, was even fond of him. But aside of the wild bouts of sex that took place every time they got within touching distance, that was the height of it, she told herself staunchly. With six days of the affair to go, she believed she was handling the upcoming prospect of their separation with logic and restraint rather than with the obsessive depth and despondency that would once have threatened her composure. After all, hadn't that obsessional passion of hers for Vito once sent her running out of control into that car with tragic consequences? She knew better now.

The neat detached home that Ava's parents had brought her up in sat behind tall clipped hedges on the outskirts of the village. Even though it was two miles from the castle, Ava walked there. Damien Skeel had been instructed to put a car and driver at her disposal to facilitate the party arrangements but Ava didn't want an audience to witness her being turned away from her father's front door. As smartly dressed as she could contrive, she braced herself and rang the doorbell.

She was bewildered when a stranger answered the door and wondered in dismay if her father had moved house after her mother's death. 'I'm looking for Thomas Fitzgerald,' she said to the middle-aged blonde woman. 'Has he moved?'

'I'm his wife. Who should I tell him is here?' the woman responded.

Ava's eyes widened as she tried to hide her shock that her father had remarried. 'I'm his youngest daughter, Ava.'

'Oh.' The polite smile dropped away and the older woman turned her head hurriedly and called out, 'It's… *Ava*!'

Her father appeared from the direction of the kitchen, a tall thin man with grey hair and rather cold blue eyes. 'I'll deal with this, Janet. Ava…you'd better come in,' he said without any sign of warmth.

But an invite to enter her former home was still more than Ava had expected after having her existence ignored for three long years, and her tension eased a tiny bit. True, it was a shock that her father had already taken a second wife but she had no resentment of the fact because her parents had never been happy together. The older man showed her into the dining room and positioned himself at the far side of the table, distancing tactics she was accustomed to and which felt dauntingly familiar.

'I suppose you want to know what I'm doing here.' Ava spoke first, used to the older man's power play of always putting her in that position.

'If you're hoping for a handout you've come to the wrong place,' Thomas Fitzgerald informed her coldly.

'That's not why I came, Dad. I've served my sentence—that's all behind me now and, although I know I caused a lot of trouble for the family, I…' Ava paled and struggled to find the words to express her feelings in the face of the look of icy distaste that her father wore.

'I suppose you were sure to turn up like the proverbial bad penny sooner or later,' he pronounced drily. 'I'll keep this short for both our sakes. I'm not your father and I have no obligation towards you.'

Ava felt as if the floor had dropped away below her feet. '*Not*...my father?' she repeated thickly, incredulous at the statement. 'What are you talking about?'

'While your mother was alive it was a secret but thankfully there's no need for that nonsense now,' he told her with satisfaction. 'My wife and your half-sisters are aware of the fact that you're not a real member of this family. Your mother, Gemma, picked up a man one night and fell pregnant by him. And *no*, I know nothing about who he was or is and neither did your mother, who was...as usual...drunk.'

'Picked up a man?' Ava echoed, her pallor pronounced and a sick feeling curdling in her stomach.

'Yes, it's sordid but that's nothing to do with me. I'm telling you the truth as your mother finally told it to me,' Thomas Fitzgerald continued with open distaste. 'You were DNA tested when you were seven years old and my suspicions were proven correct. You are *not* my child.'

'But nobody ever said anything, even suggested that...' Ava began jerkily, trying and failing to get her freefalling thoughts into some kind of order and comprehend the nightmare that seemed to be engulfing her. 'Why didn't you divorce my mother?'

'What would have been the point of a divorce?' the older man asked with unhidden bitterness. 'She was an alcoholic and I had two daughters, whom I couldn't have trusted her to raise alone, *and* I had my career. I didn't want people sniggering about me behind my back either. I tried to make a go of the marriage in spite of you. I was a decent man. I fed and clothed you, educated you, did everything a father is expected to do...'

Momentarily, it was as though a veil had fallen from Ava's perceptive powers as she looked back at her childhood and adolescence. 'No, you didn't. You never liked me.'

'How was I supposed to like you?' he shouted at her in a sudden eruption of rage. 'Some stranger's bastard masquerading as my own daughter? It was intolerable that I should be forced to pretend but I was responsible for your mother because I married her. There was no one else to take care of her and I had to think of Gina and Bella's needs. I did my duty by you all but it was a lot more than your wretched mother deserved!'

The door behind Ava opened. 'Thomas, I think you've said enough,' the female voice said quietly. 'It's not the girl's fault that you had to put up with so much.'

It was his wife, Janet, *her* stepmother...no, not her stepmother. These two people were actually no relation to her at all. The shock of that realisation punched through Ava and left a big hole where she felt her brain should be. She turned in a clumsy circle. 'I should leave.'

'I think that would be best, dear. You remind Thomas of a very unhappy time in his life,' Janet informed Ava in a reproachful tone.

Ava walked straight back out onto the road, feeling as if she had concussion because she couldn't think straight. The secret was out: she finally knew why her father had never liked her and her mother had always preferred her sisters. Evidently she was 'some stranger's bastard', not a legitimate child of Thomas Fitzgerald's first marriage, not to mention being a constant galling reminder of his wife's infidelity. No longer did she need to wonder why the man had persisted in calling her 'Ginger', why she had been sent off to school, shunned and excluded from the family when she messed up: she wasn't a part of the family and was barely entitled to call herself by the name Fitzgerald. All her life she had been a cuckoo in the nest and now she knew why and there was absolutely nothing she could do about it. No amends that she could make, no bridges she could possibly build. The family reunion she had prayed for was nothing more than a silly girlish pipe dream.

Vito flew back to the castle in his helicopter, warned the pilot he would be returning to London within the hour and strode from the helipad towards the front door. There he spotted Damien Skeel lounging up against the bonnet of his four-wheel estate vehicle and he frowned.

'I suppose you don't happen to know where Ava is?' Damien asked hopefully. 'I was supposed to pick her up at one but apparently she went out and she must have forgotten about the arrangement.'

'Where were you taking her?' Vito was relieved that he was neither insecure nor possessive when it came to women. Growing up with an emotionally unstable father had taught him to despise such behaviour.

'To choose the Christmas tree for the castle from the estate plantation,' his estate manager informed him with a smile. 'And I hoped to fit in lunch.'

Ava was still keeping their affair a big dark secret, Vito registered, and his dark golden eyes smouldered at the realisation. He breathed in slow and deep. 'I'll

choose the tree with her tomorrow,' he heard himself
declare.

The blond man frowned in surprise but nodded
coolly. 'If you see her, tell her I was sorry to miss her.'

Not as sorry as you might have been had you not
missed her, Vito reflected with gritted teeth. There were
times when Ava infuriated him and this was one of
those occasions. Was she attracted to Skeel? Was that
why she refused to acknowledge her relationship with
Vito? His lovers usually went out of their way to boast
about sharing his bed. Given the smallest opportunity
they showed him off like a prize and proudly posed by
his side for photos. But *not* Ava. Ava attached no strings
and imposed strict boundaries. He was, in retrospect,
amazed that he had been invited to share her bed. She
never, ever asked him what time he would get back
home. And she wouldn't phone him, didn't even text.
He walked out of the castle in the morning and, for all
she knew, he might have been dead five minutes later.
But then all that made her one hundred per cent perfect
for a guy like him, he reminded himself staunchly. No
demands, no avaricious streak, no hidden agenda. What
you saw was what you got with Ava and Vito knew how
rare a quality that was.

His keen gaze tracked a sudden glimpse of movement on the drive and he registered that it was Ava. On
foot and dressed like a bag lady in her jeans and horrible jacket, but even at a distance nothing could out-
shine her grace of movement or the delicate beauty of
her features against her coppery hair. He supposed they
were about to have the mother and father of all rows and
felt surprisingly insouciant about the fact. He was very

focused and persistent when he wanted something, he would wear her down.

'Ava…' Vito greeted her from the wide shallow run of steps at the castle entrance.

Lost in a reverie, Ava glanced up and blinked in surprise. Was it that time already? Surely he shouldn't be home in broad daylight? Like a vampire he was usually only available during the hours of darkness. For a brief moment, she was snatched from her hopeless thoughts by Vito's sheer charismatic appeal. He was truly stunning from his cropped black-as-night hair to his hand-stitched shoes and designer suit. The minute she saw him she wanted to touch him but always quenched the urge, determined not to feed his ego. If he could be cool, she could be even cooler.

Vito threw his big shoulders back and gave her a blinding smile that in a normal mood would have made her suspicious. 'We're going shopping…'

Her lashes fluttered because she didn't know what he was talking about and really couldn't be bothered asking for clarification. Everything felt so far removed from her that a glass wall might as well have separated them.

'And since you're here, let's leave right now,' Vito proposed, descending the steps and closing a hand over hers.

It was second nature to Ava to yank her hand free and say in dismay, 'No—someone might see—'

'It's not like I'm trying to shag you on the front lawn!' Vito flamed back.

'Don't be crude,' Ava told him.

Vito expelled his breath in a furious hiss. He thought of all the years he had spent with *normal* women, greedy, vain, untrustworthy women, who would never have dreamt of pushing him away. And then there was Ava. He stopped dead and closed his arms round her like a prison.

'What you...doing?' she mumbled, all at sea again, an odd distracted air about her.

Vito took advantage. He never failed to take advantage when the right opportunity offered because Ava didn't drop her defences very often. He scooped her up against him so that her feet parted company with the ground and brought his mouth crashing down on hers with devouring eroticism, and that explosion of high-voltage sensation broke through her barriers and she blinked in bewilderment, suddenly depth-charged out of her state of shock. His tongue snaked against hers and a helpless shiver ran through her. He was *so* incredibly sexy, she thought dimly, swept away by the throbbing swelling of her breasts and the hot dart of pulsing warmth between her thighs. He just touched her and she wanted to chain him to the bed. He rocked against her, letting her know that he was equally aroused, and that was when she recalled that they were still in full view of the castle windows and she shimmied down the length of him like a fleeing cat.

'No! I don't want to be seen doing this with you!'

They were already more than halfway to the helicopter. Vito decided not to make an issue of it, although where had not making an issue of Harvey got him? Harvey kept on giving him a paw and nudging him expectantly. Harvey was pushy, desperate to be noticed now that he was sentenced to sleeping downstairs at night, and he stalked Vito round the castle when he was at home. 'He *likes* you,' Ava had said appreciatively but it was not an honour that Vito had sought.

'Where are we going?' Ava prompted suddenly.

'London…shopping,' Vito proffered casually, wondering why she wasn't putting up a fight about the prospect.

'In a helicopter?' Her head ached with the force of the self-discipline she was utilising to hold her flailing emotions in check.

'It'll give us more time.'

'I'm not really in the mood.'

'It's your birthday tomorrow. This is my treat,' Vito pronounced.

Presumably he wanted to buy her a present and if he had organised the trip for her benefit she didn't want to be difficult about it.

'Is there anything wrong? You're very quiet,' Vito commented, leaning down to do up her seat belt for her when she ignored the necessity.

'Thanks.' Ava forced a smile, striving to behave normally. 'No, there's nothing wrong.'

The helicopter rose noisily into the air. Nothing short of physical force would have dragged the truth from Ava about what she had learned from Thomas Fitzgerald earlier that day, she conceded painfully. Apart from the embarrassing reality that the older man still worked for Vito, such a private and wounding revelation had no place in a casual relationship. That was not what she and Vito were about and she would adapt to the sordid discovery that she would never know who her birth father was without anyone's help. But a shopping trip…? Strange, she reflected wearily. She had always assumed that most men didn't like shopping, but at least the pastime would provide a useful distraction from the burden of her unhappy thoughts.

Vito had requested that a personal shopper meet them at Harrods. He cast a questioning glance at Ava as the woman tried to engage her in a discussion about her likes and dislikes but Ava's responses were few and her lack of interest patent. Determined to make the most of the occasion, Vito got involved, chose his favourite colours, nodded and shook his handsome head when outfits were displayed on hangers and freed from the threat of Ava's interference, announced that *everything* was required. With all the animation of a shop window dummy, Ava tried on several garments. That achieved, the outfits began to pile up because Vito shopped as fast as he worked. The personal shopper called in two co-workers to help while Ava continued to hover in an apparent world of her own. Vito stifled his exasperation and decided that unlike most women she had little interest in what she wore. Handbags and shoes joined the pile, along with a beautiful green velvet designer gown, which Vito knew at a glance would be perfect for the party. In the lingerie department, determined to see the back of the gingham pyjamas, he looked to Ava to finally take part in the proceedings because he could not credit that she would let him do the choosing, and he was stunned to see that silent tears were rolling down her cheeks. She seemed totally unaware that she was crying in a public place...

# CHAPTER EIGHT

At Vito's request they were shown into a room with seating and the concerned team assisting them promised to rustle up a cup of tea.

His hands on her slim shoulders, Vito settled Ava down into an armchair as if she were a sleepwalker. He lifted a handful of tissues from a box on the table and pushed them down into her tautly clenched hands. '*Per l'amor di Dio*...what has happened?' he demanded, gazing down at her.

Ava pressed a tissue to her face to dab it dry and wiped her eyes. 'Nothing,' she said gruffly. 'I'm sorry—'

'No, I'm sorry I dragged you out when there's obviously something very wrong. I should have *seen* that you were acting strangely,' he ground out rawly. 'This was supposed to be a treat, not an endurance test that distresses you, *bella mia*—'

Ava stared woodenly down at her knotted hands. 'I'm really sorry...how embarrassing for you to have me behaving like that in public. I'm surprised you didn't walk off and leave me.'

Vito crouched down in front of her and tilted up her chin so that he could better see her reddened blue eyes and the pink tip of her nose. 'Am I that much of a bastard? I will admit to a split second of very masculine panic but that's all.'

Ava encountered beautiful dark golden eyes fever bright with frustration. He hated being out of the loop: she knew that much about him. 'It's not something I can talk about, I'm afraid. I'm all right now, though. The pressure inside me just built up too high and I didn't even realise I was crying.'

'Are you pregnant?' Vito demanded with staggering abruptness.

Ara was taken aback by the question, an involuntary laugh was dredged from her tight throat. Evidently that was *his* biggest fear. 'Of course I'm not and as we've only been together a week, how could I possibly be pregnant?' she whispered just as a knock sounded on the door. 'Or even know that I was?'

'It happens,' Vito said darkly, thinking of Olly, whom his father had sworn had been conceived after a single night. He vaulted upright to open the door and accept the cup of tea that had arrived, settling it down on the table by her side.

'We've been too careful. That's not the problem,' Ava told him dully as she sipped gratefully at the refreshing brew.

'But what *is* the problem?' Vito growled.

'It's nothing to do with you or our relationship and I'm getting over it already,' Ava insisted staunchly, wiping her eyes with determination and blowing her nose, still wincing at the embarrassment of having lost control to such an extent in front of him. 'You see? I'm absolutely fine.'

'You're anything but fine,' Vito contradicted without hesitation. 'You're not yourself at all. Let's finish up and get out of here, but don't think you've heard the last of this. I need to know what's wrong.'

Her face tightened. 'We don't have that kind of relationship.'

'What kind of a relationship do we have?' Vito shot back as she set down the tea and stood up, composed again.

'Fun, casual,' she declared.

Dark colour highlighted his strong cheekbones. 'I can handle problems.'

'You couldn't handle this one and why would you want to anyway?' Ava asked frankly. 'It's not like this is the romance of the century or serious or anything!'

Vito went rigid, his hard jawline clenching, his wide sensual mouth compressing into a surprisingly thin line.

'And now you're offended because I'm not supposed to be that blunt, and maybe you'd just like to say goodbye to me here right this minute!' Ava completed on a rising note of anger.

At that invitation, Vito's eyes flamed burning gold. '*Che cosa hai?* What's the matter with you?'

'I'm giving you an escape route.'

'Shut up,' Vito told her in a seethingly forceful undertone.

Ava drew herself up to her full five feet four inches. 'What did you just say to me?' she demanded.

'Zip it!' Vito bit out with unmistakable savagery. 'Let me tell you what we are going to do. We will complete the shopping trip and leave.'

Ava parted her lips, ready to let loose another volley of the angry aggression that had come out of nowhere to power her mood. Without warning, a rush of screaming anxiety engulfed her next, when she belatedly appreciated that she was actually trying to talk herself out of staying with him for what remained of the week. To her horror, she couldn't accept that prospect, couldn't face the idea of saying goodbye there and then. That acknowledgement shocked her sufficiently into clamping her mouth shut on her dangerously provocative tongue. What the heck was wrong with her? What difference this week or next week? But the threat of separation from Vito managed to flood her with such appalling fear that she couldn't answer her own question.

'I'll take you straight back to the castle when we're finished,' Vito pronounced.

She caught a glimpse of them together in a tall mirror and reddened, thinking that she looked more like a messy teenager than a grown woman in her jeans and jacket. He had to be mortified to be seen out and about with a female that badly dressed and all of a sudden, in spite of the emotions still bubbling inside her like a witch's cauldron, she was ready to make concessions. Her birthday treat? She had thrown his generosity back in his face and wrecked the outing.

Concealing his surprise, Vito watched from a discreet distance as Ava selected lingerie, unwilling to give her an excuse to lose her temper again. What the hell was going on with her? He wondered if he would ever understand her, wondered why he should even want to when he was usually up and out at the first sign of complications in an affair. But she had never been moody with him before. She vanished into a changing room with a bundle of garments.

Ava stripped, glanced in dismay at a couple of tags marked with eye-watering prices and wondered if he was insane to be spending so much money on her when they only had another week together. But it could be a good week just like the first if she could only stop thinking about the ending that would come with it. Her mouth down curved at the lowering thought that she was certainly in the mood to please as she put on a dress: *he* liked dresses, dropped hints like bricks around her about feminine clothes, loved her legs. And her bottom and her breasts. Just not *her*! Her eyes prickled. She couldn't even blame him. His brother was dead because of what she had done. What she had now with Vito was the most she could ever have because he would never be able to surmount that barrier between them.

Vito's was not the only male head to turn in the vicinity when Ava reappeared, a slim chic beauty in a form-fitting dress, jacket and high heels.

'Am I allowed to jump you in the limo?' Vito growled, hot golden eyes pinned to her face.

Ava laughed. She knew she looked good, hadn't frankly known she could look that good in a new outfit and was very aware that she had him and the helpful saleswomen to thank for it because she had virtually no experience of either choosing or wearing more decorative formal clothes.

'No,' she told him, suppressing the memories of Thomas Fitzgerald, her late mother and her wretched childhood. She would get over it, adapt to the new knowledge about herself, much as she had adapted to other things.

Having emerged from the shop, a procession of bags and boxes already piled into the limousine awaiting them, Vito closed an arm round her spine. Suddenly a man called out Vito's name and he halted in surprise. A blinding flash lit them up and a man with a camera shot them a cheeky smile before taking off into the depths of the milling crowds on the pavement.

'My word, why did he want to take a picture of us?' Ava asked as Vito tucked her into the car.

'He's probably paparazzi.' But the incident sent a vague sense of unease filtering through Vito because he was not accustomed to that kind of press intrusion in his life. 'I can't imagine why he wanted a photo of us.'

'He knew your name. You must get a lot of that sort of attention,' Ava assumed.

'Usually only in the business papers and if I have a celebrity on my arm, which is rare these days,' Vito confided, a frown drawing his fine ebony brows together. 'I'm a very private person. I don't know what the source of his interest might have been.'

'I hardly think it was me.'

'You do look stunning,' Vito countered reflectively.

Self-conscious colour lit her fair complexion. In her fancy feathers, she felt ridiculously vulnerable. 'Where are we going now?'

'You look stunning. I shall keep on saying it until you acknowledge it, *bella mia*.'

Ava ignored him. She had earned very few compliments in her life and never knew how to handle them. Deep down inside she thought he only said such things because he believed all women expected it and she despised insincerity.

'I originally planned for us to spend the night in my city apartment.'

'Didn't know you had one.'

'It's handy when I'm flying in late from abroad or working through the night. But you're not in the mood for dining and clubbing, are you?' Vito murmured lazily.

'I'm in full party-pooper mode,' Ava admitted with a grimace. 'Sorry. I'd just like to go—'

'Home,' Vito slotted in. 'When situations change, I adapt quickly.'

Her fingernails curled in silent protest into the wool jacket on her lap. His home, not hers. The locality had nothing to offer her now. She no longer had a home base. So what had changed? she asked herself irritably, angry that she still felt so bruised and alone. The people she had believed were her family until earlier that day had long since made it clear that they wanted nothing to do with her anyway, consequently it was over-sensitive to still be feeling so gutted about it. Suck it up, she told herself irritably.

Studying the tension etched in her delicate profile, Vito wanted to shake Ava like a money box the way you do to extract the last stubborn coin. What was wrong with the rational approach of telling him what the problem was so that he could sort it out? That would settle things and she would return to normal and stop being so polite and silent. Maybe he should have let her dump him. He had never been dumped. Was that why he was still with her even though she was being an absolute pain? She was screwing with his head. He knew she was doing it but had yet to work out how.

Dusk was falling by the time Ava mounted the steps to the entrance of Bolderwood Castle. She walked in the big front door and was instantly enfolded in a ridiculously soothing sense of security. A log fire was crackling in the huge hall grate, flickering warm inviting shadows over the ornamented garlands and the tall ivy-draped glass candle vases on the mantelpiece. It looked beautiful and painfully familiar at one and the same time. She could remember roasting chestnuts by the fire with Olly, laughing when he sang a Christmas song off-key. While she was thinking, Harvey hurtled past her and bounced up to greet Vito first with fawning enthusiasm. Ava looked on without comment, having already accepted that Harvey was, at heart it seemed, a man's dog, for as soon as Vito had become a regular fixture in Harvey's life Harvey had firmly attached himself to him.

'Don't put hair on me,' Vito warned the dog, patting his head to make him go away again, but Harvey was a needy dog and he kept on pushing for more.

'He doesn't shed hair—we think it's the poodle in him.'

'Poodle?' Vito repeated in disbelief, surveying Harvey, who was a large animal by any standards and very disreputable in appearance with his floppy ears and messy curly coat. 'Aren't poodles little and fluffy?'

'There are big ones too but…Harvey is a mongrel.'

Harvey looked up at Vito with round brown pleading eyes and nudged his thigh again. Vito sighed heavily. 'All right. He can stay.'

Shaken, Ava stared up at him. 'For good…*here?* Are you serious?'

'I wouldn't have said it if I wasn't,' Vito imparted wryly.

Ava gave a yelp of delight, hurled herself at Vito and locked her arms round his neck in a display of natural exuberance. 'You won't regret it, Vito. He's very loyal and loving and he'll protect you if anyone ever threatens you.'

Vito stared down at the animated triangle of her face, transfixed by the complete transformation that had taken place. 'Nobody has ever threatened me.'

'He'll want to sleep beside your bed.'

'That's an undesirable trait, Ava.' But he locked his arms round her slim supple body and drew her up to his level to extract a passionate kiss, noting that her bright blue eyes were almost laughably disconcerted by his sudden unexpected assault. 'Of course you can sleep beside my bed any time you like…but I'd prefer you *in* it, *gioia mia.*'

In that instant being wanted felt unbelievably wonderful to Ava's battered emotions and in response her own hunger consumed her in a great greedy flood. As Vito toyed with her soft full lower lip, teasing, stroking the delicate interior, she angled her head back, shamelessly inviting more. With an appreciative growl, he curved his strong hands round her bottom and hoisted her up against him, making her violently aware of the fullness of his erection.

'Bed…*now,*' Vito husked against her lush mouth as he carried her upstairs. 'I can't wait…'

And secure in his arms, Ava wondered when the attraction between them had become so powerful that her body simply reacted without her awareness, the peaks of her breasts straining full and tight with arousal, the secret place at the heart of her intensely hot. She could no longer control the desperate urgency and need eating her alive from inside out. He set her down on the bed, where she peeled off her jacket, kicked off her high heels and shimmied out of her dress like a shameless hussy eager to meet her fate. He stood in front of her, stripping, and he didn't stop until he was naked, a lithe bronzed vision of muscular male perfection, uninhibited in his urgent arousal. He leant over her, crushing and tasting her luscious mouth, his tongue dallying, delving deep to ramp up her yearning. And throughout that exercise he was undressing her with deft hands, peeling away her new and delicate floral underwear. Long fingers playing with the protruding pink buds of her breasts, he made her gasp and part her slender thighs, hips digging into the mattress beneath her.

'You're so sexy,' he groaned against her swollen mouth when he lifted her up against him, the long thick column of his erection hot against her stomach. 'I've never wanted a woman like this…I'm burning up.'

He brought her down on her knees on the bed in front of him, reaching down to stimulate the tiny, unbearably sensitive nub at her core. An almost anguished whimper of sound was wrenched from her tight throat. Her breath was coming in shallow pants, her whole body poised on the edge of an anticipation so intense it hurt. He stroked her and she flinched, aching and hypersensitive to the caress.

'You're so ready for me, *bella mia*. That really fires me up,' Vito growled in her ear as he nudged her thighs further apart, his hands running up and down her slender spine and dropping lower to touch the swollen buds of her breasts.

*'Please…'* she moaned, wild with impatience, twisting her head round, catching a glimpse of the smouldering dark golden eyes fixed to her.

His hands firm on her hips Vito thrust into her hard and deep and groaned with earthy satisfaction. Her inner muscles gripped him as a shockwave of amazing sensation engulfed her. She threw back her head

and moaned. As he sank into her raw excitement made
her heartbeat race. She quivered, insanely receptive to
his dominance, and then sobbed as the melting waves
of delirious pleasure engulfing her swept her up higher
and higher until she reached the ultimate peak. While
Vito thrust into her with a final forceful twist of his hips
and a savage shout of release, Ava was shattered by the
power of her own climax. An ecstatic cry tore from her
lips and she slid forward onto her stomach, all strength
drained from her satiated limbs.

'Your passion is the perfect match for mine,' Vito
breathed with satisfaction, kissing the nape of her neck
with lingering appreciation and slowly pulling back to
release her from his weight. Just as suddenly he fell
still again.

Recognising the change in the atmosphere, Ava
turned over to stare up into his stunned dark eyes.
'What?' she pressed with a frown.

In answer, Vito used his strong hands to turn her
back over onto her stomach again. 'You finally took
the plaster off...I had no idea it was hiding a tattoo.' A
wondering forefinger traced the pattern of the ink marking on her left hip. It was a heart pierced by an arrow
with a name in the centre. *His* name.

Aghast at the news that she had lost the plaster,
guessing it must have come off in the shower that
morning, Ava turned over again so fast that she was
breathless. 'You *saw* it?' she gasped strickenly, swift
hot colour washing up beneath her fair skin as extreme
mortification gripped her.

Vito nodded slowly, thoughtfully. 'As a rule I'm not
into tattoos but I think I can live with you having my
name branded on one hip,' he breathed tautly, wicked

amusement fighting to pull at the corners of his firmly controlled mouth. 'When did you get that done?'

Her face still burning with the intensity of her embarrassment, Ava sat up, hugging her knees defensively, her eyes shielded by her lashes. 'I was eighteen on a girlie holiday in Spain. It was a drunken dare and I went for it because some of the other girls were getting stuff done and it seemed like a good idea at the time…but it was very stupid.'

'Eighteen?' Vito grimaced. 'No, it wasn't a good idea to have a name put on your body at that age.'

'I've regretted it ever since.'

Vito closed his arms round her small tense figure, a wolfish smile suddenly slashing his handsome mouth. 'I like it. It appeals to something primitive in me, *bella mia.*'

'I'll probably save up and get it removed some day,' Ava muttered, ignoring his comment.

'You were so young in those days,' Vito remarked ruefully.

'But I'm all grown up now,' Ava reminded him, keen to drop the subject, that place on her hip still burning as though she had been touched by a naked flame. As she turned to glance at the clock by the bed she froze and exclaimed, 'Oh, no, I was supposed to meet Damien at lunchtime and I totally forgot about him!'

'I'll take you to choose a tree tomorrow.'

Ava's mouth fell wide in shock. '*You*…will?'

A fine ebony brow elevated. 'Why not me?'

'Crashing about in the undergrowth looking at trees isn't really your thing,' Ava challenged.

Never having been a fan of the great outdoors, Vito

didn't argue with that assessment. He stretched out beside her in the tumbled sheets and folded her to him with determined hands. 'I have no choice. Damien's trying too hard to get with you.'

Her bright blue eyes sparkled with amusement. 'I can handle Damien. You can be very possessive.'

'I'm not the possessive type. Easy come, easy go, that's me,' Vito told her with unassailable assurance and then he frowned, his black brows pleating as he suddenly sat up again to stare down at her in consternation. 'I didn't use a condom!'

Ava winced, unable to hide her dismay or her surprise that he could have been so careless. 'I wasn't thinking either,' she sighed in grudging acknowledgement of their mutual passion, already engaged in mentally working out where she was in her cycle. 'We should be all right, though. It was the wrong time.'

'*Any* time can be dangerous when it comes to conception,' Vito countered, his face taut with disquiet. '*Accidenti!* I was so excited I forgot—that's never happened to me before.'

'There's always a first time. I think we'll get away with it,' Ava reassured.

Too shaken by his oversight, Vito said nothing. He could not believe that even in the heat of passion he had overlooked the need for precautions. He had never made that mistake before. There was something about Ava that destroyed his usual innate caution. Unlike her, however, he wasn't an eternal optimist and he was already thinking, What if she's pregnant? If it happened, he would deal with it. After all, he was not a panic-stricken teenaged boy.

* * *

The next morning, Ava looked in growing wonderment at the vast collection of clothes that filled the boxes, garment bags and carriers in one corner of her bedroom. What on earth had come over Vito? She was only with him another week and he had bought her more clothes than she could wear out in several years of sustained use! While she stowed away the garments she selected a pair of jeans, woollen sweater and a quilted jacket to wear and quickly got dressed to go down for breakfast.

'Happy birthday,' Vito declared from his stance by the fireplace, where a crackling fire took the chill from the room. 'Are you sure you want to choose the tree today? It's exceptionally cold.'

'The party schedule is tight. It has to be today so that I can dress the tree tomorrow.' Ava tried very hard not to stare at him. After all, it was barely forty minutes since they had parted in her room to shower and dress. Now, just like her, Vito was casually clad, a powerfully masculine figure who dominated the room with his presence. The strong hard bones of his face allied to the deep-set brilliance of his spectacular dark eyes gave him a sizzling charismatic appeal that ignited every cell in her body. He lit her fire, he floated her boat, he turned her on, she acknowledged abstractedly, instinctively struggling to fight free of the sexual charge he put out, wishing she were less of a pushover in that category. She badly needed distance, rational thought and a cool head…but terrifyingly none of those necessities were at her disposal.

Vito tugged out a chair by the table for her in an effortless display of courtesy that made her tense. He treated her as though she required his care and protection and, although his attitude often jarred with her staunchly independent spirit, she was also aware that on some level he was satisfying a secret craving deep down inside her. 'We're having pancakes this morning—my housekeeper tells me they're your favourite,' he announced.

A wash of over-emotional tears momentarily stung Ava's eyes. Nobody had ever made a fuss about her birthday before. Indeed on several occasions that special date had been entirely overlooked. Equipped as she now was with the true facts of her background, Ava could understand why her mother had sometimes found it easier to simply ignore her youngest daughter's birthday. In many ways, Ava conceded ruefully, she had been a neglected child, who was neither properly fed nor clothed, while her teenaged sisters had often stayed at friends' houses to avoid coming home, leaving Ava alone with her alcoholic and often insensible mother.

Wary of the surge of her unstable emotions and distressing memories, Ava tucked into the pancakes with determined appetite. A small, square jewellery box sat beside her plate and she rigorously ignored it, scared of what it might contain. My goodness, hadn't he spent enough money on her during the shopping trip? What else might he have given her?

'Aren't you going to open it?' Vito finally prompted.

'It embarrasses me when you spend money on me.'

'It didn't cost me anything.'

Intrigued, Ava reached for it and opened it. Her heart jolted to a sudden halt and she swallowed with difficulty because the box contained Olly's gold St Christopher medal. 'You can't give me this.'

In answer, Vito sprang upright, hooked the chain onto his fingers and nudged her hair out of the way to place it round her neck. 'You should have something to remember him by, *cara mia*,' he said flatly.

'Thank you...' Ava said shakily as the cool metal settled against her skin. She was painfully touched by the gift. It could surely only mean that Vito had moved beyond thinking of her solely as his brother's killer to recall instead her once close and loving friendship with his sibling. For that piece of undeserved good fortune she was eternally grateful.

'It once belonged to my father and Olly cherished it. Come on,' Vito urged hurriedly as her mouth trembled. 'It's time to pick the tree...'

Ava hastily swallowed back the thickness of tears clogging her vocal cords and clattered down the steps in his wake with Harvey to climb into the waiting four-wheel drive. Vito drove down rutted tracks to the conifer plantation at the back of the estate and vaulted out to retrieve a paint tin and brush with which to mark the chosen tree. The icy breeze stung her damp cheeks. Her hand stole up to brush the St Christopher at her throat. St Christopher, the patron saint of safe journeys. Olly hadn't been wearing it the night of the crash because the chain had broken.

She trudged into the great stand of trees, banishing recollections of long-gone Christmases with rigorous self-discipline. In the mood she was in the last thing she needed to be doing was wallowing in the past, she conceded humbly. She paused in front of a fifteen-foot-tall conifer with a model shape and dense branches that skirted it almost to the ground. 'That's definitely the one.'

Vito marked it with the paint and set down the tin to ram his chilled hands into the pockets of his jacket, standing tall and braced into the wind clawing his black hair back from his darkly handsome features. 'That was quick.'

'It's a classic…oh my goodness, it's snowing!' Ava carolled, hurrying into the clearing open to the sky to raise her hands to the fat white flakes floating slowly down.

Vito watched her chase snowflakes, her bright blue eyes intent against her breeze-stung complexion, her vibrant copper hair anchored below a cream woollen hat. She had no thought of what she might look like, no concern that he might laugh at her. She was as uninhibited in her enjoyment as a child, her enchantment etched in her face with an innocence she had yet to lose. Seeing that vulnerability disturbed him, put him in mind of the fact that even her family had rejected her. It was the belated acknowledgement that her family lived only down the road that prompted him to say, 'I think it's time you visited your family.'

Ava froze. 'Been there, done that,' she declared stiffly without looking at him as she stooped to lift up the paint tin. 'I'm freezing…let's get back to the car—'

'When did you visit them?'

'Yesterday,' she extended reluctantly.

Vito frowned and made the connection, shrewd dark eyes bronzing with sudden intensity. 'What the hell happened?'

'I found out that I'm not Thomas Fitzgerald's daughter, after all. I'm a bastard, father unknown,' she confided doggedly between gritted teeth as she stalked ahead of him towards the car.

'You're…a *what*?' Vito closed a strong hand round

her slim shoulder to force her to turn her head to look back at him again.

Ava explained what she had learned in as few words as she could manage. 'So, you see, you really couldn't expect any of them to have visited me while I was in prison or to bother with me now—I'm not and never have been part of their family and they finally feel that they can be open about that.'

Appalled, Vito swore under his breath in Italian. 'You should have been told a long time ago and never in such a cruel manner.'

'Nobody was cruel!' Ava interrupted in heated disagreement. 'Thomas Fitzgerald was fed up with having to live a lie and you can't blame him for that.'

'I—'

Her eyes flashed with anger. 'It's none of your blasted business!'

Silenced by that forthright declaration, Vito drove back to the castle with a fiercely tense atmosphere between them. Ava breathed in slow and deep, fighting to control her distress. She hadn't wanted to tell him but he had virtually forced her to speak. Now he had to be embarrassed for her but the last thing she wanted or needed was his pity. Every atom of her being reared up in a rage at that humiliating prospect.

Eleanor Dobbs was waiting for them in the big hall. The housekeeper's expression was grave and anxiety infiltrated Ava as the older woman extended a folded newspaper to her employer.

Vito glanced at the headline, *'Barbieri with bro's slayer,'* and the accompanying photographs, one of Ava at the time of the accident, the other of her by his side in London the day before. His handsome mouth compressed into a tough line while Ava peered over his arm to study the same article and turned white as the snow beginning to lie on the ground outside.

## CHAPTER NINE

PRESSED into the library, Ava filched the newspaper from Vito to get a proper look at the article. She spread it out on his desk and poured over it to read every word while he remained poised by the fire to defrost, his expression forbidding and stormy.

'This is horrible,' she muttered in disgust.

'It is what it is,' Vito responded stonily. 'The truth we can't change. I can't sue anyone for telling the truth but I wish I'd chosen to be more discreet in your company yesterday. What I *do* want to know is where they got the tip-off from. I will be questioning my staff. Nobody else knew you were here.'

*The truth we can't change.* That statement rang like the crack of doom in Ava's ears and her heart sank to the soles of her feet. It *was* the truth, the elephant in the room whenever they were together. Serving a prison sentence hadn't cleared her name, rehabilitated her reputation or made her one less jot guilty as charged of reckless endangerment of Olly's life. She stilled on that thought, cold inside and outside, her skin turning clammy. Maybe this was the real punishment for what she had done, she conceded, never ever being able to forget for longer than a moment in time.

Vito strode to the door. 'I'll talk to the staff.'

'Wait…at least one other person knew I was here,' Ava volunteered abruptly. 'I was visiting Olly's grave and she recognised me. I thought I'd seen her before somewhere but I didn't *know* her—Katrina Orpington?'

Halfway out of the door, Vito came to a sudden halt. 'Katrina? The vicar's stepdaughter?'

'Is she? Blonde? Looks a bit like a model? She called me a killer, thought it was offensive that I should be in the cemetery,' Ava advanced woodenly.

Vito's gaze flared hot gold. 'And you didn't warn me? *Dio mio,* is there anything you're willing to tell me?'

Her troubled eyes veiled and her soft lips firmed. 'You don't need to hear that kind of stuff.'

'I don't need to be shielded from it either!' Vito growled, his anger unhidden.

In the simmering silence Ava perused the newspaper again. No, on one score Vito had proved correct: the item contained no lies, simply the facts inviting people to make their own judgement of how appropriate it was for Vito to be entertaining his brother's killer. In the photo taken yesterday, having taken fright at the sudden appearance of the photographer, she was clinging to Vito, leaving little room for doubt that theirs was an intimate relationship. The article would certainly raise brows and rouse condemnation. Her face burned, guilt and regret assailing her. Vito had been good to her. He did not deserve public embarrassment on her behalf. She should never have come to Bolderwood: returning to the scene of her crime had been asking for trouble. It hurt that she had made the mistake but that Vito was being asked to pay the price.

All she could do was leave: the solution was that

simple. Gossiping tongues would fall silent once people realised she was no longer around. She hurried upstairs to her room, dug her rucksack out from between the wardrobe and the wall and proceeded to pack it with her original collection of sparse clothing. She discarded the outfit he had bought her but kept on the underwear. She wondered if someone would give her a lift to the local railway station, checked her purse to see if she had enough for the fare: she *didn't*. She would ask Vito for a sub on her salary although she cringed at the prospect of directly approaching him for money and accepting it from him. It would feel downright sleazy.

Without warning the door opened. Vito scanned the small pile of clothing on the bed, the open rucksack, and shot a gleaming, cutting look at her that would have withered a weaker woman. '*Madre di Dio!* What the hell are you doing?'

Ava ducked the direct question. 'I should never have come here in the first place—it was asking for trouble! I did try to warn you about that.'

Vito shifted a silencing hand. 'Enough with the lie-down-and-die mentality,' he derided. 'You're tougher than that.'

'Maybe I thought I was but I've just realised that you can't beat social expectations, you can't flout the system and then complain when you become a target.'

'No, you can't if you're a coward.'

Blue eyes darkening with fury, Ava pushed her chin up. 'I'm not a coward.'

'You're getting ready to scuttle out of here like a rat leaving a sinking ship,' Vito contradicted without hesitation. 'What else is that but cowardice?'

'I'm not a coward!' Ava proclaimed, inflamed by the charge. 'I can take the heat.'

'Then take it and stay.'

Ava snatched in an uneasy breath. 'It's not that simple. You don't need this…er…trouble right now.'

Vito squared his big broad shoulders. 'I thrive on trouble.'

Ava tore her strained gaze from the bold challenge in his features, her heartbeat quickening. She wondered how long it would be before she could picture that darkly beautiful face without that happening. Here she was, twenty-two years old, and she was as infatuated as a teenager with a man who could only hurt her. That was not a record to boast about and the best thing she could do for both of them was sever the connection in a quick, clean cut that would cause the least possible damage. Vito was a stubborn guy. The very idea that he should conform to social mores was anathema to him. Vito was always ready to fight to the death to defend his own right to do as he liked. A textbook knee-jerk reaction from an arrogant, aggressive male.

'Look,' Ava breathed on a more measured note, 'all the party arrangements are in place. I'll leave clear notes and contact details for all the outside help I engaged—'

'I don't give a flying…*damn*…' he selected between gritted white teeth '…about the party! You know how I feel about Christmas.'

'Can Harvey still stay?' Ava prompted anxiously.

The animal concerned voiced a little whine and pushed his muzzle anxiously against Vito's thigh, his need for reassurance in the tense atmosphere pronounced.

Vito groaned out loud at the question. 'I think you'd have to kidnap him to take him away.'

Ava nodded woodenly because she knew she was going to miss Harvey's easy companionship and affection. Of course she would miss Vito too but that would be *good* for her, character-building, she told herself urgently. She had let herself get too dependent on Vito and that was dangerous. It was better to get out now on her terms at a time of her choosing rather than wait for his inevitable rejection. 'I have to leave.'

'You're not going anywhere,' Vito decreed harshly.

'Be reasonable,' Ava urged. 'I can't stay after that story was published in the papers…as if people around here even need reminding of what I did!'

'It doesn't bother me,' Vito fired back without scruple.

'Well, it bothers me!' Ava flared back at him out of all patience, her hands planted on her slim hips for emphasis. 'And what difference does it make anyway? So, we part a few days earlier? This was only ever going to last two weeks.'

Eyes smouldering between thick black lashes over that assessment, Vito shifted closer with silent fluid grace. 'Says who?'

'Says me!' Ava thumped her chest in emphasis with a loosely coiled fist. 'Do you think I'm stupid, Vito? Did you think I wouldn't appreciate that once the party was over, we were too?'

His face set even harder. 'I never said that.'

'Yeah, like you were planning to come calling at my humble bedsit on a regular basis!' Ava scoffed in disbelief. 'Why can't you at least be honest about what we have here?'

'Do you think that could be because when I dare to disagree with you, you immediately accuse me of subterfuge?' Vito queried smooth as silk, a sardonic ebony brow raised.

Ava was getting more and more worked up over her inability to get through to him. He was dancing around words, refusing to match her candour, selfishly complicating things when she wanted it all done and dusted, neat and tidy and over while she still had the strength to deal with it. Before she even realised what she was doing, both her hands lifted in frustration and thumped his broad hard chest instead. 'It's *over,* Vito! Fun while it lasted but now the writing's on the wall.'

'Not on my wall,' Vito fielded, closing strong hands round her waist and lifting her right off her startled feet to lay her down on the well-sprung bed.

'What the heck are you talking about?' Ava snapped back at him in bewilderment, scrambling breathlessly back against the headboard to stay out of his reach.

'*My* agenda, rather than yours…sorry about that,' Vito delivered rawly, dark golden eyes glittering like starlight in his lean taut features as he came down on his knees at the foot of the big bed and began to move closer again. 'It's not over for me yet. Sorry, if that disrupts your rigid timetable. But I still want you…'

Sentenced to involuntary stillness by his extraordinary behaviour, Ava stared fixedly at him. He was stalking her like a predatory jungle cat ready to pounce. 'Now just you stop right there!' she warned him shrilly.

She drove him insane, Vito acknowledged darkly. Somehow every time they clashed she brought emotion into it, the emotion he shunned and she unleashed like a tidal wave. 'I'm not stopping,' Vito almost purred with assurance. 'And you know I don't back down...'

That dark sensual voice of his was compelling, sending a deeply responsive echo strumming right through her taut length. 'You know I'm right, Vito.'

'You always think you're right,' Vito husked. 'But on this occasion, you're wrong. I want you.'

A jolt of desire shot through her, making her achingly aware of the heat at her feminine core. Her cheeks burned with mortification. 'We only got out of bed a couple of hours ago!' she slung.

'And I'm still hungry, *bella mia*,' Vito growled deep in his chest, drawing level with her to bend his head. 'Doesn't that disprove your theory that I'm ready to let you go?'

'You don't *let* me do anything!' Ava launched back at him in a rage. 'And I know you well enough to know that you won't be ready to let me go until *you* make that decision.'

His fingers feathered slowly through her tousled coppery hair and curved to her taut jaw. 'You're a lot of hard work but I still burn for you.'

Ava flung back her head in defiance. 'Well, my flame's gone out. Common sense snuffed it,' she traded.

'What the hell does common sense have to do with this?' Vito demanded thickly, crushing her stubbornly compressed mouth beneath his and revelling in the way her soft full lips opened for him as the tip of his tongue scored that sealed seam.

His mouth devoured her and she wanted to eat him alive, powered by a frantic desire that terrified her when she was trying so hard to make him see sense. But there was no sense in that all-encompassing overwhelming hunger that gripped her. Her hands came up of their own volition to cup his high cheekbones and then threaded into his thick silky hair. The spicy scent and taste of him only made her want more...*always* more. When did she reach satiation level? When would that terrible craving ease enough to allow her to hold it at bay?

'I'm packed, I'm leaving,' she mumbled obstinately when he freed her swollen mouth long enough to let her breathe again.

'I could chain you to the headboard to keep you here,' Vito told her silkily as he closed a possessive hand round a full breast below her sweater, a thumb massaging the already swollen peak. 'Now doesn't that open an interesting field of possibilities?'

Ava trembled, sexual frissons of sensation running through her like liquid lightning. 'Only if you're a perv,' she told him doggedly.

'You like it when I'm dominant in bed,' Vito traded with fiery erotic assurance in his stunning eyes.

Ava planted her hands to his shoulders and pushed forward, off balancing him back against the pillows. A wolfish grin split his bronzed features and he laughed with rich appreciation, hauling her down on top of him with shocking strength to take her mouth again with ravishing force. She shivered violently, insanely aware of the male arousal resting like a red-hot brand against her and the hand sliding down over her quivering stomach below her unfastened jeans to tease her with knowing expertise.

'Don't forget that I'm an equal opportunities employer,' Vito reminded her raggedly, lifting her out of her jeans with more haste than finesse.

'I'm in the middle of packing!' Ava raked at him in

a frustration steadily becoming more laced with self-loathing.

'But you're not going anywhere now,' Vito pointed out, shedding his jeans with positive violence and drawing her back up against him, all hot and ready and hard.

'We should have discussed this like civilised adults—'

'You talk too much,' Vito told her, delicately tracing her lush opening with carnal skill and then, having established her readiness from the whimper of anguished sound that exited her straining lungs, he shifted over her and sank into her with a raw primal sound of satisfaction that she found insanely arousing.

That fast the moment to stand her ground was lost and her body took over, her hips angling up to accept more of him…and then more and then, heavens, the pulsing, driving fullness of him was pushing her closer and closer to the edge she had never thought to visit again with him.

In the aftermath, his heart still thundering over hers, she held him close, adoring the weight and intimacy of him that close, wanting and barely resisting the urge to cover him in kisses. But while her body was satisfied, her brain was not and with every minute that passed she was seeing deeper into herself. She wanted to run away because she was scared of getting hurt. Why was she likely to get hurt? Solely because she felt too much for him. She was hopelessly, deeply and irretrievably attached to Vito Barbieri, indeed as much in love as a woman could be with a man. For too long she had denied her true feelings, suppressed them and refused out of fear to examine them.

'And now you're thinking too much…for a sensible adult,' Vito reproved, noting her evasively lowered lashes and mutinously closed lips before he lowered his handsome head to rub a stubbled cheek against the soft slope of her breast and drink in the familiar scent of her with a sense of bone-deep satisfaction. 'This isn't complex. We're in a good place right now...don't spoil it, *gioia mia*.'

'I need a shower,' she said stubbornly, whipping her clinging arms off him again.

'You are *so* obstinate,' Vito grated, rolling off her with sudden alacrity and viewing her with forbidding cool from the other side of the bed.

'Whatever turns you on,' Ava replied glibly.

And she did, any time of day, every time, *all* the time, Vito mused grudgingly, watching the lithe swing of her slim curvy hips and spotting the tattoo of his name inked onto her pale skin as she vanished into the bathroom. Ava had taught him what a weekend was, how to walk away from work, daydream in important meetings. She was like an express train to a side of life he had never known before and sometimes it spooked him. He should have let her leave, a little voice intoned deep in the back of his mind, get his work focus back on track, return to...*normal*? Yet being with Ava felt astonishingly normal even when her backchat was ricocheting off the walls around him. The phone by the bed buzzed and he flipped over to answer it.

In the shower, Ava was scrubbing the wanton evidence of her weakness from her skin when Vito appeared in the doorway, a towering bronzed figure with a physique to die for.

She rammed the shower door back. 'Don't I get peace anywhere?' she sniped.

'That was Eleanor on the phone. Your sisters have arrived for a visit—she put them in the drawing room.'

Ava froze in stark shock and equally sudden pleasure. 'Gina and Bella have come here to see me?'

'Obviously they read that newspaper article…or your ex-father figure talked. Dress up,' Vito advised. 'You don't want them feeling sorry for you.'

'Or thinking that you would consort with a poorly dressed woman,' Ava completed cheekily.

'I'd consort with you no matter what you wore,' Vito imparted with a lazy sardonic smile.

'But you probably prefer me in nothing,' Ava pointed out drily.

Her mind awash with speculation, Ava dug in haste through her extensive collection of new clothes. Gina and Bella, both in their thirties, were always well groomed. Vito's comment had struck a raw nerve. Ava didn't want to look like an object of pity, particularly after the humble letters she had sent in hope of renewed contact with her siblings had been ignored. So, why on earth were they coming to see her now? Her generous mouth down curved as she wondered if her sisters were planning to ask her to leave the neighbourhood to protect them from embarrassment. Gina, married to an engineer, and Bella, married to a solicitor, had always seemed very conscious of what their friends and neighbours might think of their mother and her drink problems. Elegant in a soft dove-grey dress teamed with a pale lavender cardigan, her revealingly tumbled hair carefully secured to the back of her head, Ava slid her feet into heels and went downstairs.

Nerves were eating her alive by the time she opened the drawing-room door. Vito was not there. Gina and

Bella were small, blonde and curvy like their late mother and both women swiftly stood up to look at her. Recognising the pronounced lack of physical similarity between her sisters and herself, Ava marvelled that it had not previously occurred to her to wonder if they had had different parentage.

'I hope you don't mind us calling in for a chat,' Gina said awkwardly. 'We came on impulse after seeing that photo of you in the paper with Vito Barbieri. Dad didn't realise that you were staying here at the castle when you visited him and Janet yesterday.'

'I don't think he would have cared had I come down on a rocket from the moon,' Ava declared wryly as she sat down opposite the other two women. 'I was only in their home for about five minutes and once he'd said his piece there didn't seem to be anything more to say.'

'Well, actually there is more,' Bella spoke up tensely. 'Dad might still feel that he has an axe to grind over the fact that he chose to pretend that you were his child all those years but, no matter what Mum did, you're *still* our sister, Ava.'

'Half-sister,' Ava qualified stiffly, unable to forget her unanswered letters. 'And let's face it, we've never been close.'

'We may have grown up in a very dysfunctional family,' Gina acknowledged, compressing her lips. 'But we don't agree with the way Dad is behaving now. He's made everything more difficult for the three of us. He demanded that we keep you out of our lives. He prefers to act like you don't exist.'

'And for too long we played along with Dad for the sake of family peace,' Bella admitted unhappily.

'And sometimes we used his attitude to you as an

excuse as well,' Gina added guiltily. 'Like us not coming to see you while you were in prison. To be frank, I didn't *want* to go into a prison and be vetted and then searched like a criminal just for the privilege of visiting you.'

'We did once get as close as the prison gates,' Bella volunteered with a wince of embarrassed uneasiness.

'*Prison*-visiting…it just seemed so sordid,' Gina confided more frankly. 'And the gates and the guards were intimidating.'

'I can understand that,' Ava said and she did.

Eleanor Dobbs entered with a laden tray of coffee and cakes, providing a welcome distraction from the tension stretching between the three women.

'Mum wrote a letter to you just before she died,' Gina volunteered once the door had closed behind the housekeeper again.

Ava sat up straight and almost spilt her cup of coffee in the process. 'A…*letter*?'

'That's *why* we tried to work ourselves up to come and visit you—to give you the letter,' Bella confessed.

'Why didn't you just post it to me?' Ava demanded angrily. 'Why didn't anyone ask if I could visit her before she died? I didn't even know she was ill.'

'Mum passed away very quickly,' Gina told the younger woman heavily. 'Her liver was wrecked. Dad didn't want you informed and Mum insisted that she couldn't face seeing you again, so we couldn't see the point of telling you that she was dying.'

Ava absorbed those wounding facts without comment. News of her mother's death had come as a shocking bolt from the blue while she was in prison. She had been excluded from the entire process. Now she had to accept the even harsher truth that, even dying, her mother had rejected a chance for a last meeting with her. 'The letter...' she began again tightly.

Bella grimaced. 'We didn't post it because we know prisons go over everything offenders get in the post and the idea of that happening to Mum's last words didn't feel right. But we've brought it with us...not that it's likely to be of much comfort to you.'

'Towards the end Mum's mind was wandering. The letter's more of a note and it makes no sense.' Gina withdrew an envelope from her handsome leather bag and passed it across the coffee table.

'So, you've read it, then,' Ava gathered.

'I had to write it for her, Ava. She was too weak to hold a pen,' Bella explained uncomfortably. 'It's obvious that she was feeling very guilty about you and she did want you to know that.'

Ava's hand trembled and tightened its grip on the crumpled envelope. She still felt that her sisters could have made more of an effort to ensure that the letter came to her sooner but she said nothing.

'We all loved her but she wasn't a normal mum,' Gina remarked awkwardly. 'Or even a decent wife and we all suffered for that.'

Her attention resting on Ava's pinched profile, Bella grimaced and murmured, 'Let's leave this subject alone for the moment. Are we allowed to satisfy our crazy curiosity and ask what you're doing living in Bolderwood Castle?'

'I'm organising the Christmas party for Vito,' Ava advanced. 'Everything else just sort of happened.'

'Everything else?' Gina probed delicately. 'You used to be besotted with him.'

'I got over that,' Ava declared, privately reflecting that proximity to Vito and a closer understanding with him had merely made her reach a whole new level of besottedness.

'Come on, Ava. The whole countryside is talking and you're killing us here,' Bella complained. 'Spill the beans, for goodness' sake!'

As the door opened Ava was rolling her eyes in receipt of Bella's pleading look and saying, 'Vito's not my partner or my boyfriend, nor are we involved in anything serious…he's just my lover.'

'Outside the bedroom door I rarely know where I am with your sister!' Vito quipped without batting a single magnificent eyelash while he strolled fluidly across the room to greet her sisters as if it were the most natural thing in the world.

Registering that Vito had heard that unplanned statement, Ava turned a painful beetroot shade, her discomfiture intense. But she hadn't wanted her siblings to get any ambitious ideas about where her relationship with Vito might be heading and a dose of plain speaking had seemed the best approach to take. Ava watched as her siblings reacted predictably to Vito's stunning good looks and white-hot sex appeal. Gina stared at him transfixed while Bella giggled ingratiatingly at almost everything he said. Vito, in comparison, was smooth as silk as he invited her sisters to the Christmas party and asked them about their children. As distanced as though she were on another planet while she had that all-important letter still clutched in her hand, Ava learned that Bella had given birth to a baby boy the previous year, a brother to round out her trio of daughters. Gina, of course, never as child-orientated, still had only one child, a ten-year-old son, and a successful career as a photo-journalist.

Ava was stunned to hear Vito invite her sisters and their husbands to attend the private lunch that was always staged for his closest friends before the party kicked off in the afternoon.

'Why did you do that?' she demanded accusingly when her siblings had gone.

'It seemed polite and you do want your sisters back in your life again, don't you?' Vito asked levelly.

'Sort of…' Too much had happened too fast for Ava to be sure of what she wanted, aside of Vito. He was the one constant she did not need to measure in terms of importance and that hurt as well. How could she have been stupid enough to let her guard down and fall for him again?

'What's wrong?' Vito prompted, watching troubled expressions skim across her expressive face like fast-moving clouds.

Ava explained about the letter.

'Why haven't you opened it yet?'

'I'm afraid to,' she admitted tightly, her blue eyes dark with strain. 'Bella implied it would be disappointing. It's one thing to imagine, something else to actually *see* her words on paper. If it's unpleasant those words will live with me for ever.'

'Maybe I should open it for you…' Vito suggested.

But such a concession to weakness was more than Ava could bear and she slit open the envelope to extract a single piece of lined notepaper adorned with Bella's copperplate script.

*Ava,*
*I'm so sorry, sorrier than you will ever know. I*
*made such a mess of my life and now I've messed*
*up yours as well. I'm sorry I couldn't face visit-*
*ing you in that place or even seeing you here in*
*hospital—should the authorities have agreed to*
*let you out to visit me. But I couldn't face you.*
*The damage has been done and it's too late for*
*me to do anything about it. I wanted to keep my*
*marriage together—I always put that first and it*
*couldn't have survived what I did at the last. I do*
*love you but even now I'm too scared to tell you*
*the truth—it would make you hate me.*

Eyes wet with tears of regret and disappointment for
she had had high hopes of what she might find in the
letter, Ava pushed the notepaper into Vito's hand. 'It
doesn't make any sense at all. I don't know what's she's
talking about,' she declared in frustration. 'Gina said
Mum was confused and she must have been to dictate
that for Bella to write.'

Frowning down at the incomprehensible letter, Vito
replaced it in the envelope. 'Obviously your mother felt
very guilty about the way she treated you.'

'Did she think I'd hate her when I found out that I
wasn't her husband's child?' Her brow furrowed, Ava
shook her head, conceding that she would never know
for sure what her mother had meant by her words. 'What
else could she have meant?'

Vito rested a soothing hand against the slender rigid-
ity of her spine. 'There's no point getting upset about it
now, *bella mia*. If your sisters are equally bewildered,
there's no way of answering your questions.'

He was always so blasted practical and grounded, Ava reflected ruefully. He didn't suffer from emotional highs or lows or a highly coloured imagination. Reluctant to reveal that she was unable to take such a realistic view of the situation when the woman concerned had been dead for almost eighteen months, Ava said nothing.

His mobile phone rang and he dug it out with an apologetic glance in her direction. That was an improvement, Ava conceded. In the space of little more than a week, Vito had gone from answering constant calls and forgetting her existence while he talked at length to keeping the calls brief and treating them like the interruptions they were. She focused on his bold bronzed profile as he moved restively round the room, another frown drawing his straight black brows together. For once the caller was doing most of the talking, for his responses were brief.

Ava was staring out of the window at the white world of snow-covered trees and lawn stretching into the distance when he finished the call.

'I'm afraid I have to go out,' Vito murmured flatly.

'I'm going to take Harvey for a long walk,' Ava asserted, keen to demonstrate her independence and her lack of need for his presence. It was a downright lie, of course, but it helped to sustain her pride.

# CHAPTER TEN

Boxes of decorations littered the big hall. Ava was using a stepladder to dress the tree and cursing the fact that her carefully laid plans were running behind schedule. It had taken most of the day to have the tree felled, brought to the castle and safely erected in the most suitable spot. A towering specimen of uniform graceful shape, the tree looked magnificent, but she had had to search the attics for two hours before she finally tracked down the lights.

Her generous mouth took on an unhappy tilt. After the tragedy of the last Christmas celebrated at the castle three years earlier, all the festive decorations had been bundled away without the usual care and attention and some items had emerged broken while others appeared to have been mislaid. It saddened her to recall that the last time she had dressed a tree Olly had been by her side and in full perfectionist mode as he argued about where every decoration went, adjusted branches and insisted on tweaking everything to obtain the best possible effect. In truth, Olly had adored the festive season as much as Vito loathed it.

To be fair, though, what happy memories could Vito possibly have of Christmas? When he was a boy, his mother had walked out on his father and him shortly before Christmas and his father had refused to celebrate the season in the years that followed. Olly's demise at the same time of year could only have set the seal on Vito's aversion to seasonal tinsel. Ava did not want to be insensitive towards his feelings.

The night before, Vito had fallen into bed beside her late on and in silence. She did not know where he had been or what he had been doing and even after she made it clear that she was still awake he had not offered any explanation. For the first time as well he hadn't touched her or reached for her in any way and she had felt ridiculously rejected. Her faith in her insuperable sex appeal had dive-bombed overnight. She had started wondering if there was more depth than she knew to his comment that being with her was 'hard work'. She flinched at that disturbing recollection. That tabloid story combined with her distress over her mother's baffling letter and the emotional mood engendered by her reunion with her sisters could not have helped to improve that impression. Vito was not accustomed to complex relationships with women. Perhaps he was getting fed up with all the problems she had brought into his life and forced him to share. He might even have reached the conclusion that he would be quite content to wave goodbye to her after the party. Last night, she thought painfully, she had felt as though he had withdrawn from her again, his reserve kicking back in when it was least welcome.

Her mobile phone rang and she pulled it out of her pocket.

'It's Vito. I can't make it back for a couple of days so I'll stay in my apartment. I should mention though that I've set up a meeting for you with some people for the day after tomorrow. Will you stay home in the morning?'

'What people? Why? What's going on?' Ava prompted, striving to keep the sound of disappointment out of her response. He was a workaholic—she *knew* he was. He might have worked shorter hours the previous week to be with her but it would be unrealistic to expect that sexual heat and impatience to continue. And to start imagining that maybe another woman had caught his eye or that he wanted a break from the woman he had, perhaps unwisely, invited to stay in his home, was equally reasonable.

'I'm bringing a couple of people I want you to meet,' he advanced.

Her brow furrowed, surprise and curiosity assailing her. 'Do I need to dress up?'

'No. What you wear won't matter,' he said flatly.

Who is it? she was tempted to demand, but she restrained her tongue. Vito already sounded tired and tense and she didn't want to remind him that she could be hard work in a relationship. *Relationship,* get you, she mused irritably as she dug her phone back into her pocket and selected a fine glass angel to hang on the tree with careful fingers. A casual affair was a relationship of sorts but not of the lasting, deep kind that led to commitment. She was with a guy who didn't commit and didn't lie about it either. A whole host of far more beautiful and sophisticated ladies had passed through his life before she came along and not one of them had lasted either. He was thirty-one with neither a marriage nor even a broken engagement under his belt and she was the very first woman to live at the castle with him. At that acknowledgement, her mouth quirked. And what was that concession really worth? She had had nowhere else to stay and it was more convenient for her to organise the party while she lived on the premises.

She checked the rooms set aside for the party. The estate joiner had done a fine job with the Santa grotto for the younger children and the nativity set with life-size figures, which she had hired to place in the opposite corner, added a nice touch about the true meaning of Christmas. The room next door was decorated with a dance theme for the teenagers and rejoiced in a portable floor that lit up. On the day there would be a DJ presiding. Across the hall lay the ballroom where the adult event would take place with a manned bar and music. The caterers had already placed seats and tables down one side and the local florist would soon be arriving to install the festive flower arrangements that Ava had selected.

She found it hard to get to sleep that night even with Harvey sleeping at the foot of the bed. Persuading the dog from his station waiting at the front door for Vito's return had been a challenge. That she could have been tempted to join the dog in his vigil bothered her. It was never cool to be so keen on a man and it would not be long before she betrayed herself and he recognised the fact that she had fallen for him. Then he would feel uncomfortable around her and he wouldn't be able to wait to get rid of her. She would leave after the party with dignity and no big departure scene, she told herself fiercely.

A couple of restless nights in succession ensured that Ava slept in the morning that Vito was bringing company back and she had to wash, dress and breakfast at speed. By the time she heard the helicopter flying in over the roof of the castle, she was pacing in the hall. With a woof of excitement and anticipation, Harvey stationed himself back by the entrance again and Ava suppressed a sigh at the sight.

Vito strode into the castle with three other men, a reality that took Ava aback and she hung back from greeting him. Even so her entire focus was on Vito as she drank in his darkly handsome features and the lithe power of his well-built body sheathed in a dark designer suit.

'Miss Fitzgerald?' A stocky man with a tired but familiar face was smiling at her and extending his hand. 'It's been a long time.'

Ava was stunned: he was the solicitor, Roger Barlow, who had represented her when she was on trial three years earlier.

'Possibly longer for her,' the older blond man behind him quipped, catching her now free hand in his. 'David Lloyd, senior partner with Lloyd and Lloyd Law Associates in London.'

'And this is Gregory James,' Vito introduced the final man in the group, a thickly set balding bearded man, with grave courtesy. 'Gregory and his firm were responsible for upgrading the security on the estate after the break-in we suffered here five years ago.'

Ava nodded, while wondering what all these men had to do with her. Was her solicitor's presence a simple coincidence? She glanced at Vito, belatedly noticing the lines of tension grooving his mouth, the shadows below his eyes. Barely forty-eight hours had passed since she had last seen him and he looked vaguely as if he'd been to hell and back, she thought in dismay, suddenly desperate to know what was going on. Why on earth had he brought members of the legal profession home with him?

Vito suggested they all adjourn to the library where everyone but him took a seat. 'I asked Greg to come here and meet you personally, Ava. He'll explain what this is all about.'

'I saw those photos of you in the newspaper on Sunday,' Greg James volunteered, studying her with calm but curious eyes. 'I read the story and I was very shocked by it. I was at the party here that night as well and I had no idea there had been an accident until I read about it. I left the party an hour before midnight to catch my flight to Brazil where I had my next commission.'

'Greg had no idea you'd been tried and sent to prison for reckless driving because he was working abroad for months afterwards,' Vito explained. 'But after he had read that newspaper he phoned me and suggested we meet up.'

'You weren't the driver that night,' Greg James informed Ava with measured force. 'I saw what happened that evening outside the castle. I thought I was seeing a stupid argument between people I didn't know...with the exception of Vito's brother. I had no idea I was witnessing anything that might be relevant to a court case and I thought no more of it until I learned that you had gone to prison over what happened that night.'

Ava's lips had fallen open and her eyes were wide. Her heart was beating so fast she almost pressed a hand against it because she was feeling slightly dizzy. 'What are you talking about? How could I not have been the driver? And what argument did you see?'

David Lloyd leant forward in his armchair. 'Ava...

your defence at the trial was hampered by the fact that you had no memory of the accident. How could you protect yourself when you remembered nothing?'

'As I said, I left the party early,' Greg continued. 'I'd arranged a taxi pickup and while I was waiting for it on the steps outside I saw an argument take place around a car. There were three people there...you, Vito's brother, Olly, and a large woman in a pink dress.'

'*Three* people,' Ava almost whispered with a frown. 'A large woman?'

'The last thing you remembered before the accident was running down the steps towards Olly's car,' her former solicitor reminded her helpfully.

'The large woman followed you outside and a row broke out between you all,' Greg James supplied. 'That's why I noticed the incident. The lady in the pink dress had obviously had too much to drink. She was very angry and she was shouting all sorts at you and the boy.'

Vito spoke up for the first time. 'I'm sorry but I think the lady in the pink dress was your mother. I also saw her leave the castle in a rush. I assumed she'd had another argument with your father. To my everlasting regret I didn't go outside to check on you and Olly.'

'My...*mother?*' Ava was repeating while studying Vito with incredulity. 'Are you trying to suggest that she was driving?'

'Oh, she was definitely driving that night,' Greg James declared with complete confidence. 'I saw her in the driver's seat and I saw her drive off like a bat out of hell as well.'

Nausea stirred in Ava's tense stomach and she dimly registered that it was the result of more shock than she could handle. She skimmed her strained gaze round the room as if in search of someone who could explain things because her brain refused to understand what she was being told.

'With sufficient new evidence we can appeal your conviction,' David Lloyd informed her seriously. 'My firm specialises in such cases and Vito consulted me for advice yesterday. He didn't want to raise false hopes.'

'Mum couldn't have been there…it's not possible,' Ava whispered shakily. 'It couldn't have been her. I mean, she was banned from driving and she'd stopped drinking.'

'She fell off the wagon again at the party,' Vito countered heavily. 'I can confirm that. I called on Thomas Fitzgerald yesterday and your mother's husband confirmed that he caught your mother drinking that night and that they had a colossal row from which she stormed off saying that she was going home. He assumed she was getting a cab and he was simply relieved she'd left without causing a public scene.'

Ava blinked rapidly and studied her linked hands. Her mother *had* worn a pink dress that night but that surely wasn't acceptable evidence. 'If she was in the car what happened to her after the crash?'

'Obviously she wasn't hurt. We can only assume that she panicked and pulled you into the driver's seat before fleeing home. She would have known that Olly was dead.'

'A woman in a pink dress was seen walking down the road towards the village about the time of the crash.' Roger Barlow spoke up, somewhat shyly, for the first time since his arrival. 'The police did appeal for her to come forward but I'm afraid nobody did.'

'Olly wouldn't have let her drive his car. She wasn't

allowed to drive, she wasn't insured,' Ava mumbled in a daze. She was horrified by the suggestion that her mother had not only abandoned her at the crash site while she was unconscious but had also moved her daughter's body to make it look as though she had been the drunk driver who had run the car off the road into a tree.

'You did try to reason with the woman and so did the boy but she wouldn't listen. She kept on saying that she was sick and tired of people trying to tell her what to do and she repeatedly insisted that she was sober. She was determined to drive and she didn't give Vito's brother a choice about it. She pushed him out of her way and just jumped in the driver's seat and slammed the door. He yanked open the rear passenger door and flung himself in the back seat at the last possible moment and the car went off down the drive like a rocket,' Greg James completed with a shake of his head while he studied Ava's pale shocked face. 'You were the front seat passenger. You weren't driving, you definitely *weren't* driving that car that night…'

'Roger drew my attention to the fact that there were other inconsistencies in your case,' David Lloyd informed her helpfully. 'The police found a woman's footprints in the mud by the driver's door although you were still out cold when the ambulance arrived. One of your legs was also still resting in the foot well of the front passenger seat and the injury to your head was on the left side, suggesting that you had been bashed up against the passenger window.'

'When your mother's husband came home later that night, your mother had locked herself in the spare room and was refusing to answer either the phone or the doorbell,' Vito informed her levelly. 'When did your mother finally come to see you in hospital?'

Ava parted bloodless lips. 'She didn't come to the hospital. She came down with the flu and I was home within a few days and receiving outpatient treatment.'

'And how did she behave when she saw you again?'

'She acted like the accident hadn't happened. She got very upset when…er…Thomas lectured me about how I'd killed Olly and ruined my life.'

'She wasn't upset enough to come forward and admit that she was the driver,' Vito breathed, his tone one of harsh condemnation.

'I think we have a very good chance of, at the very least, having Ava's conviction set aside as unsafe,' David Lloyd forecast with assurance. 'I'm happy to take on the case.'

'And obviously I'll take care of the costs involved,' Vito completed on an audible footnote of satisfaction.

The other men were all heading straight back to London again in the helicopter. As the trio stood chatting together Vito approached Ava, who was still frozen in her armchair showing all the animation of a wax dummy. 'I really do have to get back to the office, *bella mia,*' he imparted, searching her blank eyes with a hint of thwarted masculine frustration. 'I pushed a great deal of work aside to deal with this over the last couple of days. I didn't want to bring it to you without checking out the evidence first.'

'I know…you didn't want to raise false hopes,' she said flatly.

'Naturally all this has come as a shock but say the word and I'll stay if that would make you feel better…'

'Why would it make me feel better?' Ava parted stiff

lips to enquire. 'You've already done more than enough for me. I'll be fine.'

Vito remembered tears running down her face that day in Harrods and silently cursed. Amazon woman didn't need anyone, certainly not him for support. He stepped back, anger glimmering in his stunning dark golden eyes, his strong bone structure taut with self-discipline. 'If you need me, if you have any questions, phone me,' he urged, knowing he wouldn't be holding his breath for that call to come.

'Of course.' Ava looked up at him as if she were trying to memorise his features. In truth she was in so much shock and pain, she felt utterly divorced from him and the struggle to maintain her composure was using up what energy she had left.

As soon as she heard the helicopter overhead again, Ava went and got her coat, collected Harvey from the hall and went outside, her feet crunching over the crisp snow that had frozen overnight.

To Ava, it seemed at that moment as though Vito had unleashed another nightmare into her world. In the same week that Ava had lost the man she had believed was her father, she had been confronted with the horrible threatening image of a mother who might have sacrificed her youngest daughter to save her own skin. Was it true? Ava asked herself wretchedly. Was it true that Gemma Fitzgerald could have done such a thing? Was that what her mother's distraught letter was all about? Gemma's *own* guilt, guilt so great she couldn't even face the prospect of seeing Ava again?

Ava's head was starting to ache with the force of her emotions. She tried to imagine how she would feel without the ever-present burden of feeling responsible for her best friend Olly's death. She *couldn't* imagine it, her own guilt had long since become a part of her. But the pain of thinking that her mother might have stood by doing nothing while her daughter was reviled, tried and sentenced to a long prison term in her place was greater than Ava thought she could stand.

Yet Gregory James had been so sure of facts, so certain of what he had witnessed that night. He *said* that Gemma Fitzgerald had been driving. And his description of the scene he had witnessed before the car set off rang more than one familiar bell for Ava. Her mother had been a forceful personality and, under the influence of alcohol, her temper and her determination to have her own way would have been well-nigh unstoppable. Growing up in such a troubled home, Ava had seen many scenes between her parents that bore out that fact. Few people had been strong enough to stand up to her mother, certainly not kind, always reasonable Olly. Olly wouldn't have known how to handle her mother pushing him away and climbing into his car drunk. He wouldn't have wanted to create a scene. He wouldn't have wanted to hurt or embarrass Ava by calling for help to deal with her obstreperous mother. But he wouldn't have wanted to leave Ava alone in that car either at the mercy of a drunk and angry driver... and that would have been *why* he threw himself into the back seat before her mother drove off and, unhappily, also why he had died.

Ava let the tears overflow and sucked in a shuddering breath in an effort to regain control of her turbulent emotions. Harvey licked at her hand and looked up at her worriedly and she crouched down and hugged him for comfort. She felt so weak and helpless.

What had Vito's motivation been in pushing forward the prospect of trying to clear Ava's name with such zeal? Was it for her sake or...*his own*? Was he more interested in cleaning up her image to ensure that his own remained undamaged? Had he resented the charge that he was sleeping with his brother's killer enough to move heaven and earth to prove that that had not, after all, been the case? She reminded herself that had Gregory James not first contacted Vito, the possibility that she had been unjustly imprisoned would never have occurred to Vito. Just like everyone else he had believed Ava guilty and he had never forgiven her for it...

Her phone rang and she answered it. It was her sister, Bella.

'Are you all right?' Bella asked worriedly.

'Not really,' Ava admitted, swallowing one hiccup only to be betrayed by a second audible one.

'I'll come and pick you up,' Bella told her bossily. 'You shouldn't be dealing with this on your own. Where's Vito?'

'He had to go back to London,' Ava explained, feeling a twinge of guilt at that statement when she recalled his offer to stay. But what would he have stayed for? So that she could weep all over him instead? Prove how much very hard work she could be even in what was supposed to be a fun lightweight affair?

Her sister's home was a former farmhouse on the far side of the village, a cosy home filled with scattered toys, a chubby toddler called Stuart with an enchanting smile and a wall covered with photos of children in school uniform and crayon drawings.

'Excuse the mess,' Bella urged. 'Dad came over last night to talk about this. He's appalled by what Vito had to tell him. To be honest we were all just grateful that Mum disappeared that night without making a big scene. You know what she was like…we assumed she'd caught a cab home. All of us were drinking, none of us were driving. We'd arranged a mini cab for midnight to take us back.'

Ava sipped gratefully at the hot cup of tea Bella had made her. 'Do you think it's true?'

'Well, I always had a problem getting my head round the idea that you could be that stupid and I never could work out why Olly was in the back seat without a seat belt when you were supposedly driving. But in the end we all just assumed you'd gone a bit mad for a few minutes and that few minutes was all it took to wreck your life,' Bella remarked in a pained tone. 'I'm so sorry, Ava.'

'You don't need to be. It's done now. I mean, the police thought I was guilty too.'

'I do remember Mum being really weird about it all,' her sister confided with a grimace of discomfiture. 'Now I can understand why. No wonder she felt guilty. It was an incredibly cruel thing for her to do to you… you not being able to remember the crash delivered you straight into her hands.'

Ava hugged the friendly toddler for security, still freaking out at the belief that her own mother could have taken advantage of her like that.

'I know I shouldn't interfere,' the small blonde woman remarked gingerly, 'but I don't think Vito liked being referred to as your lover in that offhand voice you used.'

'Oh.' Ava went pink. 'I didn't know what else to call him.'

'He's very volatile, isn't he?' Bella murmured reflectively. 'I never saw that in him before. In fact I used to think he was a bit frozen and removed from all us lesser mortals, but yesterday it was obvious that he was absolutely raging about what Mum had done to you. I expect he feels horribly guilty—we all do now.'

'I don't want his guilt,' Ava proclaimed and blew her nose. 'After the party I'll be going back to London.'

'Oh, Ava, must you?' Bella pressed. 'Gina and I were looking forward to getting to know you.'

'I would have enjoyed that.' A tremulous smile formed on Ava's lips as her sister gave her a hug on the doorstep. 'But I can't hang on Vito's sleeve much longer—it's getting embarrassing.'

Ava returned to the castle. The caterers phoned with a query and the owner of the firm asked to call out that afternoon to run through the final arrangements for the party one last time. Grateful to be occupied, Ava used her visit as a distraction from her harried thoughts. The bottom line in her relationship with Vito, she had almost told her sister, was that he didn't love her. They didn't *have* a future together. Vito had not once mentioned anything beyond the Christmas party and she wasn't planning to hang around being pathetic in the hope that he suggested she extend her stay. She would get over him, it wouldn't be easy but she would manage it. But the very prospect of a life shorn of Vito tore at her like a vision of death by a thousand cuts.

Vito phoned at supper time and asked in a worried tone how she was. His tone set her teeth on edge and she assured him that she was perfectly all right. He said he'd probably spend the night at his apartment and she didn't blame him. He was fed up with all the hassle and drama she created around her, she decided painfully. She went to bed early, longing for the bliss of sleep, which would settle her tired, troubled mind.

At what point she started dreaming, she later had no clear idea. In her dream she was running down the steps of the castle the night of the crash and she was doing it over and over again. Olly was behind her, telling her he would run her home, and then without the slightest warning the picture in her head changed and her mother erupted into Olly's lecture about Ava's provocative behaviour with Vito.

'I'll drive!' Gemma proclaimed, ignoring Olly before telling him that she was perfectly capable of driving them all home and refused to be driven by a teenager.

As the argument got more heated voices were raised. Ava shouted across the bonnet of the car that Gemma wasn't allowed to drive when she had been drinking and her mother took that as a challenge, thrusting Olly furiously out of her path and jumping into the car to rev the engine like a boy racer. Ava leant across Gemma to try and steal the car keys and the car skidded with squealing tyres on the drive while Olly tried to reason with the older woman and persuade her to stop. The car careened through the gates at the foot of the drive onto the road with Ava screaming at her mother to stop while Olly urged everyone to be calm and think about what they were doing. And a split second later, it seemed, Ava saw the tree trunk looming up through the windscreen, heard Olly cry out her name…and then everything just blanked out.

Ava woke up with a frantic start, her heart hammering, anguish enclosing her like a suffocating cocoon as she realised that she had relived the accident. She was disconcerted to discover that the light was on and Vito, naked but for a pair of jeans, was on his knees beside her. 'You were dreaming and you let out a shriek that would have wakened the dead!' he exclaimed.

But it would never wake Olly, Ava thought foolishly, a sob catching in her throat as she hugged her knees and rocked back and forth. 'I relived the crash…I remember what happened but why now? Why couldn't I remember before?'

'Why would you have wanted to remember it when you thought you were guilty? Was your mother driving?'

Ava nodded jerkily and told him what she had recalled, trembling as she spoke, the images so fresh and frightening she almost felt as though she were trapped back in that car again. In silence, Vito held her close. 'I didn't want you to relive that,' he confessed. 'I didn't really think all this through when I listened to what Greg James had to tell me. I saw what I thought was the chance to fix it all for you and I went and saw David Lloyd and your solicitor and your father to check out all the facts.' His strong profile was tense. 'I was very pleased with myself.'

'Yes,' Ava whispered shakily, glad the tears had stopped, relaxing back into the warmth and security of his arms.

'And then I saw your face this morning and I…I hadn't a clue how to make it better for you,' Vito admitted grudgingly, his frustration over that fact palpable. 'It was only then I saw that you were devastated that your mother could have stood by and hurt you like that.'

'She watched me take her punishment and she never breathed a word,' Ava conceded strickenly. 'Even if she gave way to an impulse to let me take the blame for the crash, she could have thought better of it. She could have made a statement to the police once she realised how ill she was…but even then she didn't think better of what she had done.'

'Let it go. That crash has already ruled your life for far too long,' Vito murmured tautly as he released her and sprang off the bed.

'You weren't sleeping in here with me,' Ava registered with a frown. 'In fact I thought you weren't coming back tonight.'

'I thought better of that but I returned very late and I didn't want to disturb you, *cara mia.*'

'So where are you going now?'

'I left some stuff in my room. I assumed you'd still be up when I got back,' Vito admitted, compressing his lips.

A little less tense, Ava rested back against the pillows. She pushed the jagged images of the crash back out of her mind, still shaken that those mislaid memories had finally broken through to the surface. Her mother had been driving, not her. A sense of relief finally flowed through her but she felt guilty about it, as if somewhere in her mind she still couldn't quite believe that she was entitled to feel that way.

Vito strode back from the door, still bare-chested, his remarkable abs flexing as he settled the items he carried down on the bed in front of her, for all the world like a caveman dragging a dead deer into the cave for his woman.

'Er…you went shopping?' Ava prompted in astonishment, lifting the wilting red roses. 'You should've put these in water to keep them fresh.'

'I haven't physically bought flowers before,' Vito gritted. 'I usually order them on the phone to be delivered.'

'That does cut out the practical aspect,' Ava conceded in an understanding tone, pleased he had chosen her flowers personally. 'Nobody's ever given me flowers before. They're lovely.'

'If they weren't half dead already,' Vito quipped, settling the box of chocolates on her lap.

Ava wasted no time in opening the chocolates while covertly eying the third and final package.

'I'm sorry I didn't appreciate how you would feel about what your mother did to you,' Vito volunteered. 'I couldn't see the wood for the trees.'

'You always think you can fix things.' Ava comfort ate a couple of chocolates and offered them to him before reaching for the final box. It was very light and she peeled off the wrapping and extracted a bubble-wrapped bauble. 'My goodness, it's a tree ornament,' she said, astonished at him having purchased such a festive item.

The hand-decorated bauble twinkled in the light. It was marked with the year. 'Is the date significant?' she asked.

'*Dio mio,* of course it is. It's the year you brought Christmas back to life at Bolderwood. The castle looks fantastic,' Vito informed her, sliding lithely into bed beside her. 'Do you like it?'

'I love it,' she confessed, ensnared by smouldering dark golden eyes and registering that comfort sex was as much on offer as comfort eating.

He removed the tree ornament from her hand and set the chocolates down. But Ava evaded him by scrambling out of bed with the roses. 'I'm just going to soak these in the basin!' she told him, hurrying into the bathroom.

'They're half dead!' Vito growled. 'I'll buy you more tomorrow.'

Ava ran water into the washbasin and caressed a silky petal with an appreciative finger. They were still the very first flowers he'd ever given her and in her opinion, worthy of conservation.

'Thanks for the pressies,' she told him, climbing back into bed. 'I wish I'd got something for you.'

'You're my present,' Vito proclaimed, circling her soft mouth and then ravishing her generous lips with his own with a hunger that made her every sense sizzle with reaction and joy. 'But there's one more I'd like to give you first. It's downstairs below the tree.'

'Oh…downstairs,' Ava responded without enthusiasm, her attention locked to his wide sensual mouth and only slowly skimming up to meet his smouldering dark golden gaze.

'I want you to open it.'

*'Now?'* Ava pressed in disbelief. 'It's two o'clock in the morning and it's the party tomorrow!'

Vito vaulted off the bed and extended the silk wrap he had bought for her. 'It's important, *bella mia,*' he urged.

With a sigh, Ava got up and slid her arms into the sleeves. 'You can be very demanding.'

'It's not a deal-breaker, is it?' Vito studied her with his shrewd gaze, his innate cunning never more obvious to her and she flushed, wondering how much he had guessed about how she felt about him.

'You let Harvey into your bedroom,' she registered,

hearing the dog whining behind the door at the sound of their voices and letting him out.

Vito seized the opportunity to grab a shirt and put it on. 'He cried at the door.'

They descended the stairs, where the dying fire in the grate was flickering enormous eerie shadows over the walls and the decorations. Ava bent down and switched on the sparkling tree lights before spying the large gift-wrapped box below the huge tree. 'What on earth is it?'

'Your Christmas present.'

'But I wasn't going to *be* here at Christmas!' Ava protested.

'I wouldn't have let you go,' Vito countered stubbornly.

'I was planning to leave the morning after the party,' she reminded him.

His handsome mouth quirked. 'The best-laid plans...' he said.

Ava hauled out the box and began to rip the shimmering golden wrapping paper off it, only to expose another differently wrapped box inside. 'What is this? Pass the parcel?' she teased in surprise.

The pile of discarded wrapping grew larger as the boxes got smaller until finally Ava emerged with one tiny box and paled. 'What is it?'

Vito dropped down on one knee in front of her and asked levelly, 'Will you marry me?'

Ava sucked in air like a drowning swimmer and stared at him with bright blue eyes filled with astonishment. Shock was snaking through her in dizzy waves. 'Where did this idea come from? Are you insane?'

'That's not how you're supposed to respond to a proposal!' Vito pronounced, springing back upright again to gaze down at her with a frown.

Ava opened the box and stared at the gorgeous diamond ring inside, the jewels of which shone with blinding brilliance when the flickering tree lights caught them. She blinked, her throat closing over all tight. 'You don't mean this…you're not thinking about what you're doing. You know you don't want a wife. You know you think that if you get married your wife will divorce you and take your castle and your kids and at least half your money—'

'It's a risk I'm prepared to take to have you in my life,' Vito admitted tautly.

Ava looked up at him with drowning eyes. 'You know, I think that's probably the nicest thing you ever said to me but I *can't* marry you. You're only asking me because you know that I wasn't driving that night, after all,' she condemned painfully. 'And that wouldn't feel right.'

'I bought the ring the day *before* Greg James phoned me,' Vito traded. 'And I can prove it.'

'Before?' Ava pressed, startled by the claim. 'But I thought you couldn't forgive me?'

'And I thought it too until I tried to imagine my life without you,' Vito admitted, crouching down so that they were on the same level, his eyes filled with grave honesty as they met hers. 'The forgiveness was there all along. I just didn't realise that I'd already achieved it. We both loved Olly. He loved you and I love you as well. It's a link we will never lose.'

'You *love* me?' Ava gasped, suddenly out of breath as her heart began to hammer inside her chest.

'Why else do you think I'm asking you to marry me?'

Vito demanded with some impatience. 'I didn't think I would ever fall for anyone but I started falling for you the moment you came back into my life.'

'Oh…' Ava said again, sharply disconcerted. 'I love you too but I thought this was just a casual affair?'

'That was my fault. I'm so used to laying down limits and then you came along and washed them all away. Very quickly, I just wanted you, *amata mia.*' Vito reached for her hand, tugged the ring from the box and threaded it onto her engagement finger. 'And tomorrow, when you're acting as hostess at the party, I want that ring on your finger so that everyone appreciates that you're the woman I intend to marry.'

Ava looked down at the ring sparkling on her finger in wonderment and then back at him to take in the tenderness in his gaze with a leaping joyful sense of recognition. 'You really do love me…even though I'm hard work?'

'You made me think, you made me try to be something more than I was. No woman ever affected me that way before,' Vito confided. 'You're not hard work… you're the best thing that ever happened to me. Only one thing about you bothers me…'

Concern assailed Ava. 'What?'

'You don't confide in me. You spent three years in prison and you never ever talk about it.'

'It's not something you want to accidentally refer to in the wrong company. It was a different world with its own set of rules,' Ava told him uncomfortably. 'I had some very low moments in prison. I was scared a lot of the time. I got bullied for having a posh accent. I was strip-searched once because my cellmate was caught with drugs. At the beginning I was on suicide watch under constant surveillance for weeks—'

Troubled, Vito gripped her hand. 'You were suicidal?'

'No, I never was. Unfortunately the psychologist thought I was more at risk. But I was down because I got a six-year sentence for drunk driving. I had no visitors, nothing to do, it took me a long time to adapt and learn how to keep myself occupied.'

'How did you adapt?'

She told him about the reading and writing programme she had eventually participated in and how feeling useful had lifted her mood. The move to an open prison where she had fewer restrictions had also provided a tremendous boost.

'When my parole was granted, when I knew I was getting out, I decided to put the whole experience behind me,' she admitted. 'I didn't want it colouring my life for ever. I just wanted to forget it...can you understand that? Remembering those years just made me feel bad about myself.'

'I do understand,' Vito murmured tautly, closing his hand over hers in reassurance.

Ava shivered. 'It's cold. Let's go back to bed.'

Vito bent down and scooped her up in his arms.

'You can't carry me up the stairs!' Ava told him.

But he did, although he was noticeably relieved to settle her down on the bed again.

Ava dealt him a teasing smile. 'You're wrecked. You'll not be fit for anything now.'

Vito laughed appreciatively as he unzipped his jeans. '*Dio mio,* I love you! Do you realise I've never said those words to anyone before?'

'Not even when you were a teenager?'

'I was a very cynical teenager. Watching my father screw up after my mother left him made a big impression on me. My father thought he was in love with every new woman who came into his life and then, five minutes later, it would all be over again,' he explained with a curled lip. 'I didn't think I had what it took to fall in love and then you came along and lit up everything for me like the sun on a dull day.'

'You do realise that marrying me will commit you to celebrating Christmas every year?' Ava warned him.

'I'll share it with you. I'll always remember that Christmas first brought us together. We'll make new memories. I feel I can be myself with you.'

'Domineering, arrogant, impatient, stubborn,' Ava slotted in, spreading her fingers across his hair-roughened chest and gazing into black-fringed dark golden eyes that made her heart quicken its pace. 'But I do love you very very much. You are also generous and kind and surprisingly thoughtful.'

Vito lifted his tousled dark head in apparent wonderment. 'Is that a compliment from you?'

'I'll give you the occasional one,' Ava promised, running possessive fingers through his black silky hair and studying him. 'You always felt like mine and now you are finally...'

He kissed her and her head swam. She muttered something about needing all her sleep with the party ahead: he ignored it. In the end she kissed him back and the excitement sizzling between them took over to send them soaring with the passion their deep emotions had generated. Afterwards, Ava could never recall feeling happier or more secure and she could feel the past sliding back into its proper place. She had learned lessons from that past but she wanted her future fresh and free of regrets.

The next day the party was an amazing success. Ava wore the green velvet dress under protest, thinking it was far too fancy. Many of the guests arrived on coaches laid on by their employer. She presided as hostess over a select lunch and her ring was very much admired. Vito talked of a winter wedding, Ava gave him a look and talked of a summer one and asked her sisters to be bridesmaids.

'You might be pregnant,' Vito breathed when he got her alone again.

'Of course I'm not. Is that why you asked me to marry you?' Ava asked worriedly.

'Of course not. I'm marrying you because I can't live without you, you little minx,' Vito groaned. 'I suppose I could wait until Easter?'

'No, I'll be a summer bride. We've got to be engaged at least six months to prove that we can live together,' she told him seriously.

'Of course we can. The summer's too far away.'

They got married at Easter and she wasn't pregnant. Vito admitted to being disappointed by that discovery and the idea of a baby took root. The idea of making a family gave Ava a warm, secure feeling inside.

'I don't think it's possible to love anyone more than I love you,' Vito told her on their wedding night in Hawaii.

And Ava knew she felt the same way and rejoiced in the fact that they could agree on some things.

# EPILOGUE

OLIVIA Barbieri was born after a short labour two years later, forcing her mother to ask for her recently won place at medical school to be deferred. She had her mother's eyes and her father's hair and even as a baby proved to be rather fond of getting her own way.

Vito grew accustomed to being engulfed by dogs, child and wife when he came home and discovered much to his own surprise that he loved it. His castle had finally become a home. Harvey had been joined by Freda, a cross terrier puppy tied up with string to the gates and abandoned one evening. Vito had put up less of a fight to that development than expected but the dogs slept downstairs in what used to be the boot room. From an early age Olivia displayed every sign of wanting to sleep there as well and had to be strenuously reclaimed from her doggy companions. Ava had also become fast friends with her sisters and the three families regularly met up together.

Three years after their marriage, Ava commenced studying medicine. She had thought long and hard before reapplying to medical school but had come to the conclusion that she needed a strong career to focus on for the future. She knew it would be difficult to study and do work placements in hospitals at the same time as she had a young child but Vito was prepared to reduce his hours and work more from home so that he could be around to step into the breach. That same year, Ava had her conviction for drunk driving set aside as unsafe and she was content with that judgement.

On their fourth anniversary, Vito treated Ava to a second honeymoon in Tuscany although this time their daughter and her nanny came as well. Long lazy days in the sunlight provided a welcome break from their mutually busy schedules. Even before they flew home, Ava suspected that she was pregnant again and she was pleased for she wanted her children to be close enough in age to play together.

'I'm delighted but I had assumed we were only having one child, *bella mia,*' Vito confided, wondering if he would ever get over the suspicion that he had put a wedding ring on a whirlwind.

'But you're pleased?' Ava wrapped her arms round him, thinking that he was still the most gorgeous guy she had ever met.

'Of course I am. I love you, I love Olivia and I'll love the new baby as well,' Vito forecast with a grin. 'My life just keeps on getting better and better.'

'Do you think another dog would enrich your life too?' Ava asked, quick as a flash to take advantage of the right moment. 'Marge has a nice little—'

'I'll think about it. Don't force my hand,' Vito warned his wife.

'Of course not.'

'And don't look so sad. You know I can't stand it when you look sad,' Vito groaned in despair.

'I love you so much, Vito,' Ava confided. 'I knew you wouldn't say no!'

* * * * *

# MILLION DOLLAR CHRISTMAS PROPOSAL

LUCY MONROE

**Lucy Monroe** started reading at the age of four. After going through the childrens' books at home, her mother caught her reading adult novels pilfered from the higher shelves on the bookcase... Alas, it was nine years before she got her hands on a Mills & Boon® romance her older sister had brought home. She loves to create the strong alpha males and independent women who people Mills & Boon® books. When she's not immersed in a romance novel (whether reading or writing it), she enjoys travel with her family, having tea with the neighbours, gardening and visits from her numerous nieces and nephews.

Lucy loves to hear from her readers: e-mail LucyMonroe@LucyMonroe.com, or visit www.LucyMonroe.com.

For my niece Hannah, because you are a big part of my holiday magic. Thank you for helping me and Isabelle decorate for Christmas and especially for your patience and creativity in decorating my 'Mr Monk' colour-co-ordinated, every ornament evenly spaced tree each year. Few teenagers would be nearly so accepting of my OCD tendencies. Your parents raised you right and I'm in awe of what a lovely and strong young woman you truly are. Love you!

And with a special hug for all the teens that find themselves scrambling for a place to sleep this holiday season. It is my sincerest hope you find warmth and safety wrapped in holiday joy. That as my husband and I have opened our home to some, so might others open theirs to you. Blessings and love!

# PROLOGUE

EYES DRY, HEART shattered, Audrey Miller sat in the chair beside her baby brother's hospital bed and prayed for him to wake up.

He'd been in a coma since the ambulance brought him in three days ago and she wasn't leaving him. *She wasn't letting go of him.* Not like their parents had done.

Not like their two older siblings had.

How could family act like strangers? Worse than strangers? The rest of the Miller clan had cruelly rejected the incredibly sweet, scary-smart twelve-year-old boy. All because he'd told their parents he was gay.

He was *twelve,* for heaven's sake. What difference did it make?

But when he'd refused to recant his words, had insisted it wasn't some kind of phase or confusion despite his tender years, their parents had kicked him out.

Audrey couldn't even imagine it. She wouldn't have known what do at that age, alone and homeless. Toby had, though.

With nothing more than his saved-up allowance, his laptop, and a backpack full of clothes, he'd made his way south the two hundred miles from Boston to New York.

He hadn't called ahead, hadn't questioned. He'd just come to Audrey. He'd trusted her to be there for him when the rest of the family wasn't and she would never betray that trust.

Audrey hadn't thought it could get any worse than her parents kicking Toby out, had been sure that given time to consider their actions they would change their minds and let him move back home. They lived in one of the most progressive cities in the country, for goodness' sake.

But Carol and Randall Miller were not progressive people. She just hadn't realized how very steeped in narrow-minded conservatism they were.

Not until they gave her an ultimatum: remain a member in good standing with the rest of the family or stick by Toby. They'd made it clear that if she stuck by her little brother and supported him in any way they would withdraw all financial support and cut off all contact with Audrey.

Their plan to scare both of their youngest children into compliance with their strict viewpoint of the world had backfired.

Audrey had refused and when Toby had learned what that cost her, he'd tried to kill himself. Toby had used the Swiss Army knife their father had given him for his twelfth birthday to cut his wrists.

It hadn't been a cry for help; it had been a testament to his utter wretchedness at their parents' total rejection. He did it when the house she shared with three other Barnard students was supposed to be empty for several hours.

If Audrey's roommate hadn't forgotten a paper she had to turn in and gone back to the house, if Liz hadn't investigated the running shower when Toby hadn't answered her call, he would have died there, his blood washing down the drain of their old-fashioned porcelain tub.

"I love you, Toby. You have to come back to me. You're a good person." And she would tell him that as many times as it took. "Come back. Please, Toby. I love you."

Toby's eyelids fluttered and then a dazed brown gaze met hers. "Audrey?"

"Yes. Sweetheart. I'm here."

"I…" He looked confused.

She leaned over the bed and kissed his forehead. "You listen to me, Tobias Daniel Miller. You are my family. The only one that counts. Don't you ever try to leave me again."

"If I wasn't here you'd be okay with Mom and Dad."

"I'd rather have you," she promised.

"No, I—"

"Stop. I mean it, Tobe. You're my brother and I love you. You know how much it hurts that Mom and Dad don't love us because we aren't exactly what they want us to be?"

His mouth twisted with pain, his dark eyes haunted. "Yes."

"Times that by a million and then you'll know how much I'd hurt if I lost you. Okay?"

Then she saw something in her little brother's eyes that she would do anything to keep there. A spark of hope amidst the desolation.

"Okay."

It was a promise. Toby wouldn't give up on himself again and neither would Audrey. Not ever.

# CHAPTER ONE

"YOU WANT ME to find you a wife? You cannot be serious!"

Vincenzo Angilu Tomasi waited for his personal administrative assistant to close her mouth and stop making sounds like a dying fish gasping for water. He'd never heard her talk in exclamation points, hadn't been sure she was capable of raising her voice, even.

Fifteen years his senior, and usually unflappably confident, Gloria had been with him since he took over at the NY branch of Tomasi Commercial Bank more than a decade ago.

Enzu had never seen this side of her. Had not believed it existed and would be quite happy to put it behind them now.

When she didn't seem inclined to add anything to her shocked outburst, he corrected, "I will provide these children with a *mama*."

Although he was third generation Sicilian in this country, he still gave the old-world accented pronunciation to the word.

His niece, Franca, was only four years old and his nephew, Angilu, a mere eight months. They needed parents, not uninterested caretakers. They needed a mother.

One who would see them raised in a stable environment unlike what he had known as a child or had been able to provide for his younger brother. Which, yes, would mean the woman would have to become his wife as well, but that was of negligible consideration.

"You can't possibly expect me to find them that. It's impossible." Outrage evident in every line of her body, shock dominated Gloria's usually placid-whatever-the-circumstances expression. "I know my job description is more elastic than most, but this is beyond even my purview."

"I assure you I have never been more serious and I refuse to believe anything is beyond your capabilities."

"What about a nanny?" Gloria demanded, clearly unimpressed with the compliment to her skills. "Wouldn't that be a better solution to this unfortunate situation?"

"I do not consider my custody of my niece and nephew an *unfortunate situation*," Enzu told her, his tone cold.

"No. No. Of course not. I apologize for my wording." But Gloria did not look like she had an alternative description to offer.

In fact, once again, she seemed to be struck entirely speechless.

"I have fired four nannies since I took custody of Franca and Angilu six months ago." And the current caretaker was not looking to last much longer. "They need a *mama*. Someone who will put their welfare ahead of everything else. Someone who will love them."

He had no personal experience with that type of parenting, but he'd spent enough time in Sicily with his family over there. He knew what it was supposed to look like.

"You can't buy love, sir! You just can't."

"I think you will find, Gloria, that indeed *I can*." Bank President and CEO, the driving force behind its expansion from a regional financial institution to a truly international one and founder of his own Tomasi Enterprises, Enzu was one of wealthiest men in the world.

"Mr. Tomasi—"

"She will have to be educated," Enzu said, interrupting

further ranting on his assistant's part. "A bachelor's degree at least, but not a PhD."

He didn't want someone who was driven to excel academically at that level. Her primary focus would not be on the children but her academic pursuits.

"No doctors?" Gloria asked faintly.

"They hardly keep hours conducive to maintaining the role of primary caregiver for the children. Franca is four, but Angilu is less than a year old and far from being school age."

"I see."

"It goes without saying the candidates cannot have any kind of criminal record; I would prefer they be currently employed in an *appropriate* job. Though the woman I choose will give up her current job in order to care for the children full time."

"Naturally." Sarcasm dripped from Gloria's tone.

That, at least, he was used to.

"Yes, well, no candidate should be younger than twenty-five and no older than her mid-thirties." She *would* have to be his wife as well.

"That narrows down the pool significantly."

Enzu chose to ignore his assistant's mocking words. "Previous experience with children would be preferred, but is not absolutely necessary."

He did realize it was unlikely an educated woman in a career now, unless it was one related to children, would have experience with them.

"Oh, and while I will not immediately rule out someone who has been married previously, she cannot have her own children that would compete with Franca and Angilu for attention."

Franca had experienced enough of that sort of neglect and Enzu was determined she never would again.

"The candidates should be passable in the looks department, if not pretty, but definitely no super-model types."

The children had already been subjected to the beautiful but vain and entirely empty-headed Johana as mother and stepmother.

His brother Pinu's taste in women, from his first serious affair, which had resulted in Franca and a mother who had been only too happy to walk away once Enzu met her financial demands, to the wife who had died with him in the crash, had been inarguably abysmal.

This time around Enzu would be choosing the woman and he was confident he could make a far superior decision to the ones Pinu had made in that department.

Gloria did not reply to Enzu's completed list of requirements, so he went on to enumerate the compensation package he'd worked out for the successful candidate.

"There will be both financial and social benefits for the woman taking on this new role. Once both children have reached their majority *without significant critical issues,*" he emphasized, "the *mother* will receive a stipend of ten million dollars. Each year she successfully executes her maternal duties she will receive a salary of $250,000 paid in monthly installments. She will receive an additional monthly allowance to cover all reasonable household and living expenses for her and the children."

"You really are prepared to buy them a mother?" Gloria was back to looking gobsmacked.

*"Sì."* Hadn't he said so?

"Ten million dollars? Really?"

"As I said, the bonus is dependent on both children reaching their majority without going off the rails. It will be paid when Angilu turns eighteen. But if one of the children chooses to follow in my brother's footsteps, she will still receive half for the successful raising of the other one."

He did realize there was a certain amount of self-will in the path a person chose to take in life. He and his brothers couldn't have been more different, though they'd been raised in almost identical circumstances.

"And she will be your wife as well?"

"*Sì*. In name at least." For the sake of Franca and Angilu's sense of family and stability.

Gloria stood, indicating she was ready to return to her work. "I will see what I can do."

"I have every confidence in your success."

She did not look reassured.

Well, that could have gone better.

Audrey brushed impatiently at the tears that wanted to fall. When had crying ever made a difference?

Neither her tears nor those of her then twelve-year-old brother had made a difference to Carol and Randall Miller. Pleading had only been met with disgusted impatience and implacable resolve unhindered by *any* emotion, much less love.

Maybe she should have waited a few weeks until Christmas and asked then. Weren't people supposed to be filled with charity during the Christmas season? Somehow she didn't think it would make any difference to her parents.

Audrey should have known they weren't going to change their minds now. She'd been an idiot to think that Toby being accepted into the prestigious Engineering School's Bachelor of Science program at MIT would make a difference.

But she hadn't even asked for any financial assistance, just a place for Toby to live while he attended school. If her parents didn't want him commuting to the MIT campus in Cambridge from their Boston home they could have provided living accommodation in one of their many real estate holdings throughout the city.

They'd categorically refused. No money. No help in any way.

Wealthy and emotionally distant, Carol and Randall Miller used the carrot and stick approach to parenting, with an unwavering conviction in the rightness of their opinions and beliefs. When that didn't work, they washed their hands of what they considered failure.

Like they had with her and Toby.

It had nearly broken her brother to be rejected so completely by his parents, but he'd come back from the abyss stronger and determined to succeed and be happy. And, at twelve, he'd had more certainty about what he wanted to do with his life than Audrey at twenty-seven.

She had no grand plan for her life. Nothing beyond raising Toby to believe in himself and to be able to realize his dreams. Audrey's own dreams had been decimated six years ago.

She hadn't just lost the rest of her family when she'd taken Toby in. Audrey's fiancé had broken up with her. Thad hadn't been ready for children, he'd said, not even a mostly self-sufficient young boy.

When her parents withdrew their financial support Audrey had been forced to take out student loans to finish her third year at Barnard, but a final year had been well beyond her means. She'd had no choice but to transfer her credits to the State University of New York and complete her degree there.

She'd had to get a full-time job to support herself and her brother. Time and money constraints meant that it had taken her nearly four years of part-time online coursework to finally get her Bachelor of Arts in English Literature.

Her parents had been right about one thing. It was a supremely impractical degree. But she wasn't sure she would have finished university at all if she hadn't been studying something she loved so much. Her coursework had been her one break from the stresses and challenges of her new life.

She and Toby had that in common. They both loved learning. But he was committed to excelling in a way she never had been.

With a determination her parents should have been proud of, Toby had earned top marks in school and worked on gaining both friends and confidence in his new environment. He'd said he was going to be happy and her brother was one of the most genuinely joyous people she knew.

She couldn't stand the thought of him losing that joy once he realized they simply couldn't make MIT happen.

It wasn't fair. He deserved this chance and Audrey just couldn't see any way to give it to him.

Only the best and the brightest even got considered for MIT, and those who truly stood out among this elite group were accepted. The private research university accepted fewer than ten percent of their applicants for incoming freshmen and transferring from another school was almost impossible.

Which made any plan that had Toby attending a less expensive state school to begin with and moving on to MIT such a remote possibility as not to be considered at all.

Toby hadn't just gotten accepted, either. He'd won a partial scholarship. It was a huge deal. His high school administration and counselor were over the moon, but not Carol and Randall Miller.

They hadn't softened their stance toward their son one bit. The one question they'd asked had been if Toby still claimed to be gay. When Audrey had told them he did, they'd made it clear they wanted nothing more to do with their youngest son. Ever.

Worse, they'd offered her both a return to the family fold and an obscene amount of money, more than she would need to help Toby go to MIT, with two caveats.

The money could not be used for Toby and Audrey had to sever all ties with her baby brother.

That so was not going to happen. They were *family* and to Audrey that word meant something.

But all the will in the world wasn't going to pay for Toby to live his dream and attend MIT.

He wasn't eligible for federal financial aid because until the age of twenty-five, their parents' income would be used to determine his *need*. Even if he had been, MIT was a *very* expensive school. Four years of textbooks alone would pretty much wipe out what Audrey had managed to save for his college expenses over the past six years.

The cost of living in Boston or Cambridge was high as well, leaving no wiggle room for Audrey to make up for the tuition not covered by the partial scholarship.

Audrey was still repaying *her* student loans. Her job at Tomasi Enterprises barely covered their living expenses now that her parents had stopped making the child support payments required by the state. Toby had turned eighteen two months ago, and things had gotten lean, but she wasn't pulling any money from his college fund. No matter what.

The New York housing market was ugly. Even outside the city, where she'd moved with Toby when he first came to live with her. And because she wasn't in a city apartment there was no rent control. Each new lease she'd signed had included a bump in their rent. Their current year's lease was going to be up a month before Toby graduated.

Audrey had no idea how she was going to make the new rent without the child support payments. Finding a cheaper apartment in Toby's school district wasn't happening, either. She'd been looking for the past three months, just to get on a waiting list.

She didn't know what she was going to do, but she wasn't giving up.

She might not have any dreams left, but she still had a boatload of stubborn.

Unable to believe what she'd heard, Audrey remained in her stall in the ladies' room for several minutes after the two senior support staff who had been talking in the outer area left.

The bathrooms in the Tomasi Enterprises building were swank, providing an outer sitting area where female employees could take their breaks or breastfeed their babies in onsite daycare. Vincenzo Tomasi was known for his pro-family stance.

While the man himself was an unashamed workaholic, he expected employees with families to actually have a family life. Many of the company's work-life effectiveness policies made that clear.

And what Audrey had just heard would seem to indicate that Mr. Tomasi took his commitment to family even more seriously than anyone could ever imagine. Seriously? Ten million dollars for raising his children acquired through the recent tragic deaths of his brother and sister-in-law? And $250,000 a year in salary besides?

It sounded too good to be true, but it worried her, too. Because Mr. Tomasi clearly believed he really could *buy* a loving mother. What he was a lot more likely to get was a woman with dollar signs in her eyes.

Like the one who had been listening to his personal administrative assistant complain about her new and *impossible* assignment. From the way she'd talked, it was obvious the other senior support staffer was more than interested in trying to become a billionaire's wife. That didn't mean she would make a good mother.

But putting on a show to get the job? Easy.

After all, how many people in Boston believed Carol Miller was an adoring and proud parent? Audrey was only too aware of how easy it was to put on that kind of show.

She'd been taken in herself, once upon a time.

The two women discussing what Audrey considered Mr. Tomasi's very personal business hadn't bothered to make sure no one was using the toilet stalls and could overhear them.

While the stalls had actual interior wooden doors that reached the floors, they were all open air a foot from the ceiling for ventilation purposes.

Sound carried. Words carried. And Audrey had heard an earful.

\* \* \*

Palms sweaty, heart beating faster than a rock drummer's solo, Audrey stood outside Vincenzo Tomasi's office.

Was she really going to do this?

She'd spent the last three nights tossing and turning, her brother's future and Mr. Tomasi's outrageous plan vying for attention in her brain. Somewhere in the wee hours of that morning she'd come up with a pretty brash plan of her own.

Unquestionably risky, nevertheless if it worked she could give her brother the best Christmas gift ever. The realization of the dream he'd worked so hard for.

Going through with it could also result in her immediate dismissal.

But despite the lessons of the past six years, or maybe even because of them, she had hope. She and Toby had made it this far when their parents had been sure they would crash and burn, returning to the family fold repentant and willing to toe the line.

They'd said as much when she'd gone to them to ask for help for Toby's schooling.

So hope burned hot in her heart.

Hope that maybe fate had smiled on her and Toby for once. That maybe destiny had put Audrey in that bathroom stall at just the right time to overhear the conversation between Gloria and the other staff member.

Hope that maybe Audrey could make a difference not only in her own life, and that of her brother, but for two orphaned children. Maybe she could give them the kind of loving upbringing she'd longed for, the kind that their uncle clearly wanted for them.

It was insane, this plan of hers. No arguing that. And probably Mr. Tomasi was going to laugh her out of his office. But Audrey *had* to try.

If for no other reason than to impart to him just how easily his scheme could end up backfiring and hurting the children he was so obviously trying to protect.

Audrey had considered long and hard about whether to approach Gloria first or Mr. Tomasi directly, but eventually she realized she didn't have a choice. Not if she wanted to give her crazy, dangerous plan a chance of succeeding.

Approaching Gloria meant giving the PAA the chance to turn Audrey down before Mr. Tomasi even heard about her. She couldn't let that happen.

Audrey couldn't ignore the semi-public nature of the discussion in the bathroom, either. After that lack of prudence on Gloria's part in keeping her boss' information private, Audrey had no confidence in anything like real discretion on her own behalf.

After all, Gloria's loyalty to her employer was legendary. She had no such allegiance to Audrey and even less impetus to keep Audrey's brazen suggestion to herself.

So Audrey had had to figure out a way to see the CEO without his PAA present. It wasn't as hard for her as it might have been for someone else who hadn't spent the last four years fixated in hopeless fascination on the man who owned the company where she made her living.

She'd seen pictures of him before transferring to the company headquarters from the bank, but the first time Audrey had caught a glimpse of the gorgeous, driven man herself she'd stopped breathing and that part of her that used to dream became captivated.

She'd watched, paid attention to everything she heard about the CEO. And every fantasy between wakefulness and dreaming Audrey had had in the last four years had starred Vincenzo Angilu Tomasi.

Her hand froze on the door handle as she had the sick worry that maybe this plan of hers was just another one of those.

Only she fulfilled every single one of the requirements the PAA had said Mr. Tomasi had for the *job candidates*. Even so, Audrey was fairly certain Mr. Tomasi was in no way expecting an applicant from the lower floor offices of his own building.

While she'd been born into a family that were themselves considered high society, Audrey couldn't begin to lay claim to that now. She'd attended Barnard for three years, but her degree was from SUNY and the only one of her friends from those days who still kept Audrey in her orbit was Liz.

The roommate who had saved Toby's life.

Besides, while Mr. Tomasi might not want a super-model like his late sister-in-law Johana for the position, he probably wasn't interested in a woman as average as Audrey.

Her long hair the color of chestnuts was several shades lighter than his more exotic espresso-brown, and arrow-straight besides. While the drop-dead gorgeous CEO had Mediterranean-blue eyes, an exciting and unexpected combination with his almost black hair color, Audrey's were the same chocolate-brown as her brother's.

And they didn't shine with Toby's zest for life, either. The responsibilities and work of her adulthood had taken that from her.

She was average in height as well, with curves that weren't going to make any man stop and do a double-take. Not like the six-feet-four-inch corporate king, who looked more like an action movie hero than a CEO.

Audrey knew she wasn't the first or last woman to fall for him at first sight.

He didn't need to settle for average.

Oh, crap. All she was doing was psyching herself out and that wasn't going to help. Not at all. Either she was going to do this, or she wasn't.

Okay, so she had a crush on the man. So sue her. She *wasn't* applying for the position because of it.

She was here because she wanted to make life better for three children who deserved something better than the hand dealt to them. Her brother might be eighteen, but he was still her child in every way that counted. Even if he didn't see things that way.

For his sake, and that of the little ones, Audrey had no choice but to take this chance.

Taking a deep breath, she pushed the door open to Mr. Tomasi's office without knocking.

He was sitting behind his desk, reading some papers spread out in front of him.

"I thought you weren't going to be back for another thirty minutes," he said without looking up from the papers, clearly believing the intruder in his office was his PAA.

Just the sound of his voice froze the breath in her chest, making it impossible to speak.

His head came up when his comment was met with silence. At first his eyes widened in surprised confusion and then narrowed. "It is customary to knock before entering the office of your CEO."

Funny he had no doubt she was an employee, not a client or business associate.

"My name..." She had to stop and swallow to wet her very dry throat. "My name is Audrey Miller, Mr. Tomasi, and I'm here to apply for a position with you."

## CHAPTER TWO

ENZU FOUND HIMSELF nonplussed and that never happened.

It had been years since someone had made it past Gloria to importune him for a job or a promotion. In this case promotion it had to be. None but an employee would have made it to this floor in the building without an escort.

It was sheer luck that this woman had come during the one time a week he was in his office and Gloria was not at her desk.

Reading the intelligence in the chocolate-brown eyes gazing at him from lovely, delicate features made him revise that thought. Maybe not luck at all.

This had been planned. He doubted Miss Miller knew about his little-known weakness for chocolate, though. Her beautiful eyes and the determination tinged by vulnerability he saw in them were unexpectedly compelling.

Regardless, he couldn't let this blatant disregard of company policy go unanswered. "There are procedures for applying for a promotion. None of them include importuning your extremely busy CEO."

She flinched at the ice in his voice, but did not let her shoulders slump, or step backward with an apology. "I'm aware. But this particular *job* isn't on the internal promotion and transfer database."

Disappointment coursed through him. It was like *that,* was it? She was hoping to apply for the *job* of his lover. It wasn't the first time this had happened, but it hadn't happened here at work in a very long time.

"I do not keep a mistress on my payroll." He used the insulting word to remind them *both* exactly what kind of calculation had brought Miss Miller here.

Because he found her tempting, and that was shocking enough to make his usually facile brain sluggish.

Besides his love of chocolate, Enzu had a secret passion for old movies. This woman, breaking every company protocol, not to mention good manners, to accost him in his own office, could be the spitting image of his favorite classic movies film star, Audrey Hepburn.

Elegant and refined. Beautiful in an understated way, Audrey Miller had been aptly named.

"I do not want to be your mistress." The quiet vehemence in her voice was hard to mistrust.

He simply raised one brow in question. He could not believe he was prolonging this conversation. He should have sent her packing with a promise to report her actions to her division supervisor already.

"You told Gloria to find you a mother for your children. I'm here to apply for the position."

Shock kept him from speaking for long seconds. "Gloria told you? She thinks you would be an acceptable candidate?" he demanded.

This was not his efficient PAA's style at all. He'd expected a couple of weeks to pass and then a dozen or so dossiers on appropriate candidates to show up on his desk.

This blunt approach to the situation was entirely out of character for Gloria.

"Not precisely, no."

"Then what, precisely?"

"I would prefer not to tell you how I know about the *job* you hope to fill."

That was the second time she'd put an odd, almost disapproving emphasis on the word job. Now he knew what she referred to he could almost understand it, but wasn't she here to apply for the position? If so, she couldn't find his methods as unacceptable as her tone seemed to imply.

"Does Gloria know you are here?"

Miss Miller bit her bottom lip and admitted, "No."

"I see."

"I doubt it."

"You do?"

"If you were that insightful you would realize the very real risk to your children in attempting to buy them a loving mother."

"And yet you are here to apply for the job?" he asked with unmasked cynicism.

"Yes."

"Isn't that hypocritical?"

"No."

Disbelief filled him. "No?"

"I know I am prepared to give them what another woman might only promise for a luxurious lifestyle and multimillion-dollar payoff."

"I assure you I did not build an empire without an ability to read people."

"But you are going about this emotionlessly."

"Which should make me even more capable of making the best decision for Franca and Angilu." And why was he having this discussion with a stranger standing uninvited in his office?

"Not when that decision is about the emotion you are hoping to provide for them."

"A woman does not have to *love* them to be *loving* toward them."

"That you believe that only shows how little you know."

"Excuse me?" Ice laced his tone.

She closed her eyes, as if gathering her thoughts. When she opened them he read frustration, even disappointment, but that determination he'd seen there at first hadn't dimmed. "May I sit down?"

What the hell? "You have fifteen minutes."

Something like anger washed over her features, but she crossed the room and sat in one of the sleek leather armchairs facing his modern, oversized executive desk.

When she didn't speak immediately, he found himself demanding impatiently, "Well?"

"You are looking for someone who will make your children the priority in her life, is that right?"

"You keep calling them my children, but you do realize I have custody of them only because their parents are dead?"

"I know, but your desire to give them a loving mother has made me believe you want to fulfill the role of dedicated father. I guess I shouldn't have assumed." She said the last as if she was talking to herself.

"You are not wrong." He would be a better father than Pinu, who had been borderline indifferent to his two offspring.

"Then they are *your* children?"

"*Sì.*"

She nodded, as if in approval of his admission. He should not care, but he found himself pleased by that.

"So back to my question: you want a woman who will put Franca and Angilu first?"

"Yes."

"And you do not think she has to love them to do that?"

"Financial compensation will ensure it."

"Will it?"

"Of course." He understood money and how to wield it.

"And if something comes into her life that is more important than the money you are paying her to pretend the children are a priority?"

He did not like her description of the job. "She will not be pretending."

"If it is for the sake of the money, how can it be anything but pretense?"

"Regardless, I doubt very much that something will come up that would make someone lose sight of ten million dollars."

"Really? What about a husband who is worth thirty million?"

"I am a billionaire."

"Presuming you are married to this woman, there would be an ironclad prenuptial agreement that only provides her with a yearly stipend and a ten-million-dollar payout nearly two decades down the road."

"You are so certain there would be a prenup?" He hadn't mentioned it to Gloria.

"It only makes sense. A man like you isn't going to offer a woman half of your empire under any circumstances, but particularly if she comes into your life as part of a business proposal, no matter how personal the terms might seem."

He inclined his head in acknowledgment of her insight. "There aren't that many marriage-minded multimillionaires out there."

"But moving in your circles will increase her chances of meeting them exponentially."

"I'm not going to get hoodwinked by a gold digger."

"Maybe. But even if you don't, you must realize that while money can be a very compelling motivator, it isn't always the most important one."

There was something about her tone that made him think she not only believed this, but had personal experience. "Few things trump it."

"You'd be surprised."

Audrey—he found it difficult to think of her as Miss Miller—sighed with the kind of weariness that came from a lot more than a single conversation.

"Tell me, do you think Johana Tomasi married your

brother primarily for the lifestyle she could enjoy as his wife?"

Enzu shocked himself by saying honestly, "Yes."

"And yet, by all accounts, she was not a loving mother."

"You investigated my family?" he asked dangerously.

"Are you kidding?" she asked, with a genuine laugh he found altogether too charming. "I'm a senior specialist in your customer service department; I'm hardly in a financial position to hire a private detective. Johana's exploits were tabloid fodder as much after she became a mother as before."

He could not deny that. "What is your point?"

"She had to know that you would pay her handsomely to be a more involved parent."

Both his brother and sister-in-law had known that, but they'd refused his offers of increases in their allowance in exchange for a quieter lifestyle. "She and Pinu saw no point in having access to money if they couldn't spend it on the lifestyle they enjoyed."

"Exactly."

"Whatever you may think of me, I am not an idiot. I have no intention of bringing a woman like that into the children's lives."

"I do not think you're an idiot at all, just maybe naïve."

"I am far from naïve."

"Oh, you are very worldly and brilliant about money and business…"

"But?" he prompted, knowing that was not all to her assessment of him and inexplicably unable to let it lie.

"But you don't understand emotion."

"Emotion is a weakness I cannot afford."

"That might be true, but do you really want to withhold it from Franca and Angilu?"

"I will give them everything they need."

"You will try. But if you hire them a mother, you are

almost guaranteeing the best they will ever know is kindness born of duty to the *job*."

"You came here to apply for that *job* you are so dispar-
aging of. Are you trying to convince me you wouldn't be
doing it for the money?"

"No."

"Exactly," he said, with much less satisfaction than he
should have felt at her admission.

"But I am also offering to *love* your children, not just
treat them lovingly out of duty."

"You cannot promise to love them."

"Of course I can. They are innocent children, left without their parents. How could I not love them?"

He stared at her, incomprehension washing over him.
She believed what she was saying, and yet... "You claim
another woman would not do the same?"

"I am not other women. I am me. Sure, there are women
out there that would love them, too, but would they be the
women your PAA finds to offer as candidates?" There
could be no question that Audrey didn't believe it.

"Why?"

Audrey's head went back, an impatient sound coming
from her. "I've tried to explain it. You and Gloria, you're
approaching this whole thing without any emotion. That's
almost a guarantee that the women she puts forward and the
one you eventually choose will be every bit as emotionless."

"I still do not see the problem with that." Emotion was
volatile, impossible to predict with consistent accuracy.

"No, I don't suppose you do." She stood. "I shouldn't
have come here."

"On that at least we can agree."

This time Audrey's shoulders slumped and the wince
was more pronounced. Without another word she turned
toward the door and crossed his office, an air of defeat surrounding her as she made the long trek.

She stopped with her hand on the door handle. "Do I need to start looking for another job?"

"No."

She turned the handle.

"Audrey."

"Yes?" She didn't turn.

"I assume you had more reasons for believing you were an appropriate fit for the position than your self-proclaimed affinity for *emotion?*"

She tensed, but nodded. "I meet the requirements."

"Tell me how you know what those requirements are."

She just shook her head, and he got the impression that even if he threatened the job she clearly wanted to keep she wouldn't give in.

Gloria had to have shared her assignment with Audrey in a moment of indiscretion, but the younger woman wasn't about to throw his PAA under a bus. He had to appreciate the loyalty.

"I will not tell anyone about this discussion," he offered.

She had been misguided, but he had no wish to see her pay with her livelihood for what he was certain was an honest attempt to protect his children.

"Thank you." Her voice was flat, lacking the passion that had infused her arguments for her point of view during their conversation.

She went to leave, but he said her name again.

She stopped without replying.

"Look at me," he ordered, unwilling to be ignored.

She turned, her face as blank as a statue. No weakness, no emotion showed there, and he couldn't help but respect that. She had to be disappointed, even a little afraid that he would go back on his word and get her in trouble with her divisional supervisor.

"It was a pleasure to meet you." They might not agree, but he'd found talking with her more invigorating than with any other woman in a very long time.

"Thank you."

She left, with the door closing quietly behind her, as he tried to make sense of the fact he was more than annoyed she hadn't returned the sentiment. He was bothered.

Gloria checked in when she returned a few minutes later. Their afternoon went much as he had planned for it to. Enzu would have been surprised if it didn't.

But throughout his meetings and other work parts of his discussion with Audrey kept popping up to distract him. The way she'd looked when she said she shouldn't have come to his office, like she was disappointed. In him.

It was not a reaction he was used to. That had to be why he couldn't put it out of his mind.

And it had nothing to do with him putting a note with Audrey Miller's name on Gloria's desk before she left for the evening. Audrey had claimed she fit all of his requirements. If that was true, it would be a poor business decision *not* to include her in the pool of eligible candidates.

His PAA looked up at him quizzically. "What's this for?"

"I want her on the list."

"List?" Gloria asked.

"Women who would make a suitable mother to Franca and Angilu."

Comprehension dawned in Gloria's pale grey gaze. "That list. Will do."

"I expect dossiers for a minimum of six women with complete background checks on my desk next Friday."

"That kind of rush on the background investigation is going to cost."

"And?"

"Nothing. I just didn't want you having a fit when you saw the expense report."

"I do not throw fits," he said with great dignity.

"Call it what you like. So long as you don't have one of

them when you see how much this little plan of yours is going to cost."

"Fine."

"If you don't mind me asking…?" Gloria said before he could return to his office for an evening of work.

"Ask."

"Who is Audrey Miller?"

"You do not know?" Suddenly the sinister implications of Audrey knowing what she did were at the forefront in his mind. "She does work here?"

"She might very well. I don't know every employee of Tomasi Enterprises. Even I am not that efficient."

"Look her up in the employee database."

Gloria gave him a strange look, but did as he asked. An employee file popped up on her screen. The picture wasn't all that recent, and there were shadows of fear in the young woman's eyes that he had not seen today, but it was the same one.

He didn't let his relief show.

She'd been hired six years ago by the bank for their call center. That explained how young she looked in the picture. She'd been twenty-one, which made her twenty-seven now. So, she *did* fulfill that particular requirement.

But how she knew about them was still a mystery.

"You don't know her?" he asked Gloria again.

"No. She doesn't even look familiar. But she works on the third floor."

And employees on the top floors rarely interacted with those on the lower floors.

He opened his mouth to demand how Audrey knew about the position if Gloria hadn't told her, but snapped it shut. That question would lead to more and reveal Audrey's visit to his office, which he'd promised not to do.

Enzu didn't consider a security breach. Like all cautious men in his position, he had his office scanned for listening devices on a weekly basis by a security team he trusted implicitly. No business rival was getting sensitive information from Enzu's own lips.

Gloria must have told someone and that someone had to have passed the information on to Audrey. He would look into it further after his search for a wife…and mother to his children…was over. Someone had shown an egregious lack of discretion, but that could be dealt with later.

After he'd made his choice about the woman he would marry.

He ignored the way his mind returned again to Audrey Miller. She would be *one* of several candidates, not *the* candidate.

Even if his libido might demand otherwise.

## CHAPTER THREE

DUMBFOUNDED, AUDREY HUNG up her phone and took off her headset. Someone else could take the next few customer service calls.

Mr. Tomasi's PAA had just made an appointment with Audrey to meet the CEO for an *interview* the following morning.

It had to be for the job of mother to Franca and Angilu. But the way he'd acted he couldn't be interested in her for the position, could he?

Only tomorrow's appointment said otherwise.

Gloria ushered Audrey Miller into Enzu's office.

He flicked a glance to the Rolex on his wrist. Exactly on time.

He mentally marked a tick on this positives column for the customer service specialist who had shown the courage to approach the CEO of her company in an unconventional way in order to apply for an equally unconventional job.

"Ms. Miller, sir," Gloria said.

As if Enzu would forget who the woman was after little more than a week. "Thank you, Gloria."

He eyed Audrey as she crossed the office on unhurried feet, showing more aplomb than most of his upper level managers when called to Enzu's office for a meeting. She wore a knockoff black sheath dress and an open cropped white sweater with black swirls. The pearls around her throat were no doubt *faux,* but they did not look gaudy. Modest heels raised her average height less than two inches.

It was an elegant if inexpensive outfit. Not a sexy one. But Enzu's body reacted like she'd walked into his office wearing nothing at all.

A curse rose to his lips but he bit it back, swallowing the gasp of shock at his immediate physical response just as quickly.

He'd been hard almost the entire time they'd talked last week and it looked like he was going to experience the same phenomenon again. He couldn't remember reacting like this to another woman in years. If ever.

Either he'd allowed too much time to pass since practicing that particular stress-reliever, or this woman was something special. Cynicism directed he lean toward the former.

Audrey moved with an unconscious grace he liked and Enzu allowed himself the minor pleasure of simply watching her finish her journey across his intimidatingly large office. It was one of the many calculated ways he used to establish his dominant role in any meeting that occurred in this room.

Audrey did not appear intimidated.

He found that reaction, or rather lack thereof, intriguing.

She stopped in front of his desk. "Good morning, Mr. Tomasi."

Enzu did not reply immediately, his brain fully engaged with controlling his body's unholy reaction to this woman.

"Thank you for considering me for this position."

Typical, well-used words in an interview, and yet Audrey's sincerity inexplicably touched him.

Her voice was soft, arousing. Not weak.

The subtle strength of a woman. His many summers in Sicily had taught him to appreciate it and never to underestimate the steel that ran through the spine of a woman who had learned to sacrifice for her family.

Unlike most of his Sicily-based family, Enzu had never once heard his great-aunt raise her voice. But there had never been any doubt in his mind who ran the family. His great-uncle could yell with amazing volume, even at eighty. And yet it was the old man's wife whose quiet orders no one in the family dared to disobey.

Enzu's silence must have lasted too long for Audrey's comfort.

Uncertainty glowed in her chocolate gaze as it flicked between him and Gloria, who remained near the door, an assessing look in her pale eyes as she watched the exchange in silence.

Enzu forced himself to speak, allowing none of his response to this interesting woman to show in his voice. "Have a seat, Audrey." He indicated the chair she'd occupied the week prior.

She nodded, silent, and then sat down in a rush as if her legs didn't want to hold her up. The evidence of nervousness on her part surprised him.

"I assume you understand why you are here?"

"You want to interview me for the position of mother to your children?" she asked, her tone implying she found that particular eventuality very difficult to believe.

"Yes."

A sound escaped her. "Oh. Okay." She seemed to relax, though Enzu could not have identified exactly what gave him that impression.

He was as much an expert at reading body language as any psychologist with a PhD. It was a little unnerving to realize he could not pinpoint the change in hers that indicated her more relaxed state.

It occurred to him that this woman would be a challenging adversary across the boardroom table. He would do well not to forget it, either.

"You are still interested in the position?"

"Yes, I am."

"I am glad to hear it."

"You are? I was pretty sure you had no intention of considering me for the position," she offered candidly. "I thought you'd have a stack of files on women you would find a lot more suitable."

"You are not the only candidate, naturally."

"No, of course not." Her perfectly shaped lips twisted wryly.

A sudden inescapable desire to see how they would look swollen from kisses assailed him.

"I'll bring some coffee," Gloria inserted smoothly.

Enzu nodded his approval of that plan, but Audrey turned her head to meet Gloria's eyes. "I'd prefer tea, if it's not too much trouble."

A spark of admiration shone in his PAA's pale gaze. "No trouble at all."

Enzu appreciated Audrey's willingness to assert her own preferences, albeit politely, as well. His years of experience and study of business psychology had taught him that a person who was capable of that combination usually made a reasonable if strong negotiator.

"Thank you." Audrey gave Gloria a small smile before turning back to face Enzu.

The door to his office closed quietly in Gloria's wake.

Enzu glanced down to the interview questions he'd prepared. "Right, then, let's get started."

"Before we do, I have a question for you."

He frowned, irritated. Did she not realize who was doing the interviewing here? Not that he expected her to have no questions of her own, but to insist on having the first one indicated either a lack of understanding of business protocol or significant self-importance.

Curious in spite of himself, he inclined his head.

Serious brown eyes met his. "My brother is gay and he will always be welcome in my home and my life." There was no give in her voice or the square set of her lovely shoulders.

"That is not a question." But it might well explain certain circumstances he had discovered on reading her dossier.

Her hands clenched in her lap. The only indication Audrey was worried about his reaction to her revelation. "Is that a problem for you?"

"Hardly." He might be the controlling and arrogant powerbroker some accused him of being, but Enzu wasn't a bigot.

Her eyes widened, his answer obviously a surprise to her.

"I take it your parents are not as accepting?" That would explain the fact that Audrey had been raising her brother for the past six years despite the fact their very wealthy parents were still living.

"That's putting it mildly."

"So, your brother came to live with you. Why not your older siblings?" She had two, both successful professionals who presumably would have found it much easier to provide for a twelve-year-old boy.

"They share my parents' prejudices."

"That is unfortunate." And unforgivable, in his opinion, but he left that unsaid.

It was the job of parents and older siblings to protect. Enzu had spent a lifetime protecting his younger brother Pinu, but in the end even he could not prevent tragedy.

Audrey shrugged. "It is what it is."

The flat line of her lips and the hardness that briefly masked her features said Audrey was not as insouciant in the face of her family's betrayal of the youngest child as she appeared.

"Is this also the reason your parents cut you off financially halfway through your junior year at uni?" He'd been trying to figure out the dynamics that had led to that set of circumstances.

She'd been attending one of the most prestigious and one of the few remaining female-only institutions of higher learning in the country. Her grades had been good. Her behavior exemplary. Her known associates had all been from good families with no hint of scandal to their names.

There was no record or even hint of inappropriate behavior on Audrey's part that might have caused such a move on the part of her parents.

"Yes."

"You were forced to get a job?" At *his* family's bank. For some reason the fact that his bank had given her the means to support herself and her brother pleased Enzu. "You had to transfer from Barnard to the state university in your final year and pursue your degree part-time?"

"Yes."

"That could not have been easy." In any aspect. "And still you chose to take Tobias in."

For a moment anger burned in her dark gaze. "He would have ended up in foster care or living on the street. Would you have let that happen to your younger brother?"

"No." He'd tried to protect Pinu even from himself. Grief pierced Enzu.

"I'm sorry." Sincerity and honest sympathy infused her tone and demeanor. "I should not have said that."

"It is truth. Tobias is a lucky young man to have you for his sister."

"Toby. He hates Tobias."

No doubt because it was their father's middle name.

Enzu allowed his lips to curve in a half-smile. "Duly noted."

"Toby is my family." Her tone implied an *only* in there.

He could not blame her for the sentiment. "I find your loyalty and tenacity in the face of the many challenges you've faced admirable."

"Just how detailed is that dossier?" she asked with an edge of annoyance.

"Very," Gloria answered for him as she placed tea things on the table beside Audrey. "Tomasi Enterprises employ only the best. The investigative firm we use knows how exacting Mr. Tomasi's standards are."

Far from looking impressed, Audrey was clearly disgruntled. "I don't suppose it occurred to you to simply ask me about my life?"

"You might lie. My investigator has no impetus to do so."

"I guess most men as high up on the corporate ladder as you are cynical." Again, Audrey didn't sound particularly impressed by that observation.

He took his coffee, already prepared to his specifications, from Gloria. "In my experience, that is true."

Audrey opened her mouth to reply and then seemed to think better of her words. She focused on putting sugar and just a dash of milk into her teacup before pouring the hot beverage.

"What were you going to say?" he asked, curious.

If nothing else, he had not yet found himself bored in this woman's company. He could not say that about a great many people he was forced to spend time with in the name of business.

Her brow furrowed in thought. "It's just that I'm not sure I see the point of this interview if you already know all the answers to your questions."

He almost smiled, but held the expression in. She had no idea how much a simple meeting could reveal, even if the only thing discussed was the temperature outside.

"You do not think it is important to establish whether or not there could be a possible rapport between us?"

"Well, if you had the children here, that particular consideration would make more sense."

"You do realize that being their mother mandates also becoming my wife?"

Or hadn't she?

Was it possible that, however she had learned about the position, Audrey had not been made aware of that particular aspect? The stunned expression on her lovely features implied just that.

She jolted, setting the teacup down without taking the sip she'd planned. "What?"

"Surely you can see that you must be my wife in order to actually be their mother?"

"I hadn't thought about that."

"Does the knowledge mean you would like to withdraw your application for the position?" he asked, with no doubt about the answer.

Who would not want to be married to a billionaire?

To his chagrin and grudging appreciation, Audrey took several moments to consider the question.

Finally she said, "Not immediately, no."

He frowned, less than pleased.

"I'm sorry if that offends you. I just hadn't considered..."

Her voice trailed off and he realized Audrey was seriously rattled.

"Yes, well, consider it."

She nodded, still looking a little dazed. "You're not looking for a real wife, though? Right?"

"The woman I choose will share my home, my family and many aspects of my life. In what way is that not real?"

"Oh, I...uh...I just thought..." Her lovely features went an interesting shade of pink before something seemed to occur to her and they paled to an alarming level.

Nonplussed that the idea of becoming his wife was more daunting to her than parenting two small children, he asked, "Are you all right?"

"Y-ye..." She cleared her throat. "I mean, yes."

He watched with interest as she lifted the teacup in trembling hands to take a sip.

Her eyes closed and she took another sip and several

deep breaths before carefully placing the cup down again. "Um…does that mean you're expecting…uh…*conjugal* relations?"

Humor vied with a vicious spike of arousal at the thought of sharing a bed with Audrey and her reaction to the concept.

The prospect did not send most women into stuttering panic. He was surprised she was reacting so gauchely to the idea. Was it possible she did not feel the passion sparking a steadily building electric current between them?

Or was it that she felt it and was overwhelmed by it? She was twenty-seven years old, not some blushing virgin, though.

"Naturally I would expect to have sex with my wife." He did not mention that he'd actually had no intention of any such thing until this very moment.

But he'd had a sudden and inescapable self-revelation. No way could he live in the same house as this woman and not act on the desire she evoked in him.

Shortsighted of him not to realize the efficiency of such an arrangement as well, regardless of who he chose for the role. Enzu wasn't usually a shortsighted man.

"I didn't realize. I'm not… Well, you probably already know." She gave him an appealing look. "I'm sure it's in that invasive report. Your top-notch investigators wouldn't have left something like that out. Right?"

Enzu was unacquainted with the level of confusion he experienced at her disjointed words. "What exactly are you talking about?"

"My… That I'm a…" She didn't finish her thought.

Enzu found himself more intrigued than confused. That she was a *what?*

An idea came to him. One he dismissed almost immediately as impossible. She was twenty-seven, had attended university, and raised her own brother for the past six years.

Still, considering how little information on that front

there was in the report, he could not help wondering. He had thought she was simply more private in this area than anyone he'd ever come across. Even himself.

And Enzu made it a policy *never* to get his name splashed across the tabloids for his sexual liaisons.

There was no evidence of any kind of sex life in the report on Audrey, but that didn't mean she did not have one. An investigator would find it difficult, if not impossible, to name Enzu's sexual partners in the past year.

"Your discretion in that area bodes well for your ability to maintain my confidences."

Enzu had no intention of *telling* his wife sensitive information, but living together in the same house for at least two decades risked her being exposed anyway.

Audrey was back to blushing and looking into her teacup as if it held the secrets of the universe. "I am a very private person."

"I had surmised that."

"But it's not so much a matter of discretion as there being *nothing* to be discreet about," she admitted, almost as if she was embarrassed by that fact.

He was glad to hear she wasn't promiscuous, but he did not want her to think he expected her to have no past sexual experiences. He was not a Neanderthal.

"I find sex a satisfactory stress-reliever but, like you, I do not indulge as often as some might expect." Enzu wasn't celibate by any stretch, but he was not and never had been a player like his brother, either.

He worked sixty-hour weeks, rarely taking days off—even on the weekend; Enzu didn't have time for a lover, or even frequent hook-ups.

Audrey winced, cherry-red washing over her cheeks. "I don't indulge *at all*."

"Not at all?" he asked with some measure of disbelief.

"Not ever," she admitted, as if it was painful to do so. "I'll understand if you want to end the interview right here.

It was a reasonable assumption that I would have at least some experience."

He wasn't sure why she thought he'd want to cut short the interview, but he was a lot more interested in her claim of total inexperience than just *why* she thought he would see it as a strike against her.

Strangely, the urgency of his physical attraction to Audrey only increased at the knowledge of her innocence.

"You're saying you are a virgin?"

*"Yes."*

"But you were engaged." The relationship had ended shortly after Toby moved in with his sister. A formal retraction had even been printed in the paper.

"We were waiting until our wedding night."

"People still do that?" he asked, bemused.

"To hear my parents tell it, anyone with a conscience does."

"They seem to be rather narrow-minded."

"You think?" she asked with some sarcasm. "They're also hypocrites. My oldest sister was born seven months after their wedding day. And she was not a preemie, no matter what my mom claimed later."

Enzu laughed cynically. "While your virginity comes as a surprise, your parents' double standard does not."

Audrey nodded and then rose gracefully to her feet. "Right. I appreciate you considering me. I hope you find someone suited to both you and the children."

He stood, too, coming around his desk and blocking an easy exit from his office. "This interview isn't over."

"It's not?" Her forward momentum had taken her to within inches of him before she stopped.

Her scent, a soft floral fragrance, teased his senses. Arousal spiked through him and he had to control the urge to reach out and touch. "No. Surely you realize that it is *my* responsibility to determine when this interview is over?"

"Yes, of course." She stepped back.

He followed her.

Chocolate-brown eyes widened, but she didn't try moving back again. Perhaps she realized to do so might well trip her backward into her chair in a less than dignified manner.

"I have several more things to discuss with you."

She swallowed, her gaze stuck on his mouth in a gratifying way. The attraction was *not* one-sided. He smiled.

She inhaled sharply and then shook her head, like she was trying to clear it. "But I thought…"

"It would take an insecure man to be intimidated by a lack of experience in his possible future sex partner."

"Oh."

The breathy little sound went straight to his sex. "Do you think I am insecure man, Audrey?"

# CHAPTER FOUR

"Um, no." Her gaze strayed up to his and then back down to his lips, as if she couldn't help herself.

Would it be so bad to include a kiss as part of the initial interview? This position was hardly typical, or covered under usual human resources procedures.

It was only the fact that the interview had already gone so far awry from his prepared agenda that kept him from giving in to further modification to the plan. He was still in control of this meeting. And himself.

"Do I seem intimidated?" he asked, driving the point home.

Audrey licked her lips and gave a small laugh. "Definitely not."

"Then it appears this interview is *not* over." He gently but firmly grasped her shoulders and guided her back to her seat. "I will tell you when we are finished, *sì?*"

"Yes. Okay. That would be good."

Forcing himself to release her, he stepped back. *"Sì."*

"You were born here in the U.S., weren't you?"

"Yes."

"So why do you say *sì* sometimes?"

"I'm not sure. I grew up visiting Sicily every summer and we did not speak English at home."

"Is your mother of Italian descent as well?"

"No. And our family is Sicilian."

"Isn't that the same?"

"Not to a Sicilian."

She grinned. "I see."

*"Bene."* He used the Sicilian for good just to make her smile again.

It worked and he was inexplicably pleased.

"So, your mother learned *Sicilian?*"

"Not well, but then my parents were rarely home."

"Your grandparents raised you?"

"The answer to that question is complicated."

"Do I get to use that reply?"

"No."

She looked at him patiently but with clear purpose.

"You are stubborn, I think."

"Maybe."

There was no maybe about it. "My grandmother was from the Old Country. By the time I was born she spent most of the year *visiting* our family in Palermo. My grandfather ran the bank."

"So, you're saying no one really raised you at all?"

He shrugged. "It was better for Pinu."

"Because you tried to help raise him?"

"For all the good it did. I could not give him a loving mother, or a father…just a bossy big brother."

"You're determined his children will have a better childhood than he did," she said with uncomfortable insight.

She realized he wasn't trying to improve on his own childhood, only on what he'd been able to give Pinu.

*"Sì."*

"I think it's a good thing."

But he saw doubts in her eyes. "You still do not believe I can *hire* a woman to fulfill that role?"

"You're wrong."

"Oh, am I?" he asked, in a tone his senior management would recognize as dangerous.

"Yes. I have no doubt you can entice a woman to marry

you and play the role of mother to Franca and Angilu, especially with the remuneration you are offering—"

"But?"

"But, as I told you last week, I question whether that woman will offer them genuine affection. Children know the difference."

"You are so sure?"

"Yes. Long before my parents played their we-don't-have-a-gay-son card, both Toby and I knew that they didn't feel the same way about us as they did our older siblings, the children they'd planned for."

This was not a conversation he wanted to revisit, so he did not reply with agreement or denial to her implication that Franca and Angilu might suffer the same fate.

Leaning back against his desk, one ankle crossed over the other, Enzu asked, "Are you still determined to wait for marriage before having sex?"

As topic-changers went, it was a resounding success.

Audrey inhaled her sip of tea and had a short coughing fit before demanding, "What? Why would you ask that?"

"Because in addition to having a rapport with the children, my wife and I will have to be sexually compatible."

"You plan on having sex with all the candidates for the position?" Audrey asked with not a little amount of disgust.

He would hazard that not a single other woman on the list of candidates would object to his doing so. However, instead of being annoyed with her for the disapproval set in every line of her body, he found it ridiculously charming.

The truth was, he had no desire to have sex with a bevy of strangers. A man with his wealth and influence could not afford to indulge indiscriminately.

"No, Audrey. Once I have narrowed the candidates down to the most likely hire, she will be introduced to the children in a series of planned meetings. She will also spend time with me, testing our social and sexual compatibility."

"You're talking about choosing a wife like an employee."

"Exactly." He'd always done very well choosing employees.

In the thirteen years since taking over the bank presidency from his father at the tender age of twenty-three Enzu had made exactly four bad hires. He had learned from each mistake.

"You're not normal, you know that?"

"On the contrary, business arrangements for this sort of thing are very common in my world."

"And they're amazingly successful, are they?"

He let Audrey know with a severe look that he did not appreciate her levity.

She frowned back. "What if I don't like the idea of going on a sexual test-drive?"

"I'm afraid it's a non-negotiable." While he had not considered this aspect previously, now that he had he wasn't going to compromise on it.

"But that's not legal. You can't require sex for a job."

"Absolutely, but as much as we are handling this situation like I'm hiring an employee, I am not actually doing so. You won't be working for Tomasi Enterprises or the bank. You will be my wife and the children's mother. Your job here is in no way dependent on what happens in this interview, or later between us, for that matter."

"That's not true."

Shock coursed through him, followed by hot anger he refused to allow to the surface. "You are accusing me of lying?"

"Not exactly. It's just that if I were to be selected as your wife and the children's mother, I believe you would expect me to quit my job."

"That is correct."

"So…"

"Ultimately a successful outcome on your part regarding this position *would* impact your current job, but only in the same way that getting a promotion would do so."

She nodded, still looking a little shell-shocked.

"However, should you withdraw from the application process it will not impact your current or future success with Tomasi Enterprises, or the bank should you transfer back there."

"By 'withdraw' you mean…"

"Refuse the physical aspect." He would not mince words.

"I… This is insane."

"On the contrary; it is efficient."

Her lovely dark eyes narrowed. "You do realize it is illegal to pay for sex in the state of New York?"

Offended, he glared at her, unable to suppress his anger at that particular accusation. "I am not paying for sex."

"It sure sounds like it to me. $250,000 a year."

"That money is to ensure that, as my wife and the children's mother, you would not feel the need to embark on a career to provide an independent income. Many men provide their wives with a significant personal allowance for this very reason."

"Maybe in your tax bracket they do."

Since he had very little experience with life outside his tax bracket, he did not argue the point.

Audrey fiddled with her teacup, but didn't take a drink. "So, this sex thing is a deal-breaker for you?"

*"Sì."*

She went silent for several long seconds, then seemed to come to a decision. He waited with unaccustomed agitation to find out what that was.

"I think you better kiss me."

"What?" Had he heard correctly? "You want me to kiss you?"

"Yes."

"Why?"

"I think that would be obvious."

He was not used to people implying he was thick. "Explain it to me."

"Because if we don't have the chemistry to make it through a single kiss, the rest of this interview is an exercise in futility. Since you're so set on us being physically compatible."

It actually made sense, and he had not considered it because he'd been so intent on *not* giving in to his urge to kiss her.

He nodded and stood up, away from the desk, putting his hand out to her. "That is an excellent point."

She stared at his hand as if she couldn't imagine why it was there, but with only the briefest hesitation she placed her palm against his. The simple touch jolted the underlying buzz of arousal that had not abated since she'd entered the office.

Curling his fingers around her hand, he pulled her to her feet, her body coming within inches of his own.

Their gazes locked, hers filled with trepidation and something else that he had been unsure he would find there: desire.

"You want me."

"I want a kiss," she corrected, but the truth was there.

He wouldn't ignore the fear, though. The knowledge that this kiss was a test for *both* of them made him determined to make it the best she'd ever had. He could not afford to frighten her with overwhelming passion, but he had to show her that the potential to burn up the sheets between them was there.

Not a man who suffered self-doubt, he confidently cupped the back of her head. Using his hold there, and on her hand, he pulled her forward so their bodies touched.

She gasped, her eyes glazing with passion before he even had a chance to bring their mouths together. How had this woman stayed a virgin for so long?

Enzu bent forward and brushed his lips against hers in the gentlest of caresses. Breath escaped her, leaving her mouth parted. That was when he kissed her.

He did not use his tongue, not yet, but concentrated on giving pleasure with chaste lips. Lust rolled through him in inescapable waves, his body going tense with the need to do more than simply kiss.

She made a soft sound of need and he could not help deepening the kiss, pulling her body hard against him. She had to feel his arousal, but she didn't try to back away. She moved against him in an unconscious invitation that took all of his formidable self-control not to accept.

He wanted her naked on the pristine white plush pile carpet of his office.

Knowing that was impossible, and very much afraid he might do it anyway, he forced himself to gentle the kiss and then pull away.

She moaned in protest, her hand coming up to pull his head back down to hers.

He let her have her way and kissed her again, tasting her desire and the English afternoon tea she'd been drinking. He didn't think the sweetness of her mouth had anything to do with the sugar she'd put in it, though.

She hadn't touched him and he was seconds away from coming in his trousers. Enzu *did not* lose control like this. Not even during the earthiest sex with a highly experienced partner.

Alien fear made him push her away, all the way back into her chair.

She looked up at him with passion-clouded eyes, her lips every bit as enticing swollen from his kisses as he'd thought they would be. "I… That was…"

"Yes, it was." He could not help the harshness in his tone.

He was fighting urges that had no place in a work day.

Her gaze slid down to the revealing bulge in trousers tailored too well to hide his need when it was this strong.

"Yes, I want you." He gritted his teeth, refusing to show any embarrassment at the blatant proof of his sexual need.

"You will agree that our chemistry is strong enough to move forward with the interview?"

For a long moment he didn't think she would answer. He wasn't even sure she understood his question.

But finally she nodded. "The interview. Right. Yes, we should continue."

He wasn't running when he returned to his chair behind the oversized executive desk and the privacy it afforded. Enzu did not run. Nor did he grimace at the pain sitting down with a marble-hard erection caused him.

Audrey collapsed on the sofa in the small but welcoming apartment she shared with her brother.

Totally gobsmacked and exhausted by the "interview" she'd had with Vincenzo, she'd begged off the rest of the day from work. She wasn't going to think of him as Mr. Tomasi after that kiss, or while the threat of test-drive sex hung in the air between them.

Wow. That kiss.

She'd never experienced anything like it. She and Thad had been engaged for two years, and come close to breaking their commitment to wait for marriage, but nothing they'd done together had affected her like Vincenzo's kiss.

The man knew what he was doing with his lips. She hadn't wanted it to end. *Audrey had acted with complete wanton abandon.* If it had been up to her they would have still been kissing—and probably doing it without all their clothes on—when Gloria came in to refresh their beverages and remind Vincenzo about his ten-thirty appointment.

He'd told his PAA to reschedule and resumed his exhausting and often invasive questions. All with a dispassionate air that completely belied the ardent kiss they'd shared.

He'd acted like it had been nothing. Maybe for him it had been. He was probably used to getting that worked up.

No doubt he wasn't still suffering from the frustration of unrequited lust.

Her body, on the other hand, was buzzing with physical desires she'd never felt this strongly. Was it because she was a twenty-seven-year-old virgin? Or was it because the man who'd kissed her was Vincenzo Tomasi, the subject of her most secret fantasies?

With no answer she wanted to acknowledge to that question, Audrey tried to go over the rest of the interview in her mind with as little emotion as he'd shown after their kiss.

Thankfully she had several hours to decompress and think about her meeting with the arrogant man.

Toby had football practice after school and wouldn't be home until later. The season was almost over, but Audrey didn't expect to see much more of him than she did now before Christmas break. He had a full and varied social and academic life. She couldn't have been more proud. Audrey had always been a little shy, but Toby wasn't. Not even a little.

He was personable, confident and so intelligent she was in awe of his brain. Considering what he'd gone through, that was pretty much a miracle.

She wasn't entirely sure how her little brother would react to Vincenzo, though. And the idea of them meeting was a much stronger possibility after the morning she'd spent with the CEO.

The kiss had proved their chemistry and the interview had lasted into lunchtime, culminating in his request that she sign a non-disclosure agreement that covered situations beyond that on the papers that she'd signed for her initial employment with his bank. Vincenzo had left his office to give instructions to Gloria for the paperwork.

The PAA had returned only a few minutes after Vincenzo with documents for Audrey to sign.

Rattled from the kiss and the interview that had followed it, Audrey probably hadn't taken as long looking over the documents as she should have. However, after noting that the first few paragraphs were identical to the non-disclosure agreement she'd signed when hired on to his company, she'd found herself skimming the rest when the words blurred together in her brain anyway.

She did note that the agreement forbade her discussing the whole *hiring a mother for his children* thing and she'd had no problem signing it.

By that point she'd just wanted to get out of the office and as far away from the emotions Vincenzo Tomasi provoked in her as she could.

He'd quizzed her on every aspect of his *requirements* for the position, plus a lot more besides.

While he had agreed that on paper Audrey seemed to meet them all, Vincenzo wanted deeper clarification.

She'd expected him to bring up the issue of Toby, since one of the requirements was that she not have any children of her own. When he didn't, she did. But Vincenzo had dismissed the apparent conflict, citing Toby's age and his plans to go off to college the following fall.

He did not deny that for all intents and purposes Audrey was Toby's mom, despite their only having a nine-year age-gap between them. He assured her that he realized Toby was part of the Audrey Miller package.

Vincenzo's concerns seemed weighted toward her willingness to be an "at-home mom" and give up her career.

Since Audrey had never considered her job as anything but a way to support herself and Toby, she felt no qualms about leaving it. If she'd had a career she was passionate about, that would have been something different. For Toby's sake she might have been willing to put even that on hiatus, but as it stood Audrey had no major barriers between her and fulfilling a requirement Vincenzo obviously considered very important.

She wasn't really sure why Vincenzo was so stuck on a dedicated full-time mother for his niece and nephew.

She thought it might be a knee-jerk reaction to losing his brother and sister-in-law.

He'd decided what would mitigate that loss the most for the children and was determined to provide it.

She thought it might be different if any of the grandparents were active participants in the children's lives, but they weren't. Johana's parents lived in Germany and visited the States rarely. They'd never even met their grandson Angilu.

And Vincenzo's parents appeared to be a lot more like his late brother Pinu than Vincenzo, constantly traveling and pursuing fun like it was the elixir of the universe.

Maybe Vincenzo was trying to create the family he had not had growing up, even if the powerful businessman did not realize it.

And that was all well and good. Audrey did not object to being a dedicated full-time parent. In fact she looked forward to it, having lost that personal dream like all the others when Thad walked away.

But the sex…Vincenzo's plan to test out that particular compatibility…had Audrey's stomach tied in knots. Even more so now that she realized how strongly he affected her physically. In a word, it *terrified* her.

She was embarrassingly susceptible where he was concerned.

What happened if she became addicted to his lovemaking and he decided it wasn't good enough with her?

Her deepest fear lay in the possibility that her inexperience and lack of practical knowledge in that area might bore him, if it didn't turn him off completely.

His clinical attitude toward sex between them, or rather him and the most promising candidate, was really offputting, too. Especially after he'd kissed her to within an inch of her life.

What virgin wanted her first time to be some kind of test-drive for compatibility?

# CHAPTER FIVE

ENZU WAS SURPRISED at his own impatience as he waited for the driver to collect Audrey.

In the car parked outside her apartment building, Enzu was ostensibly going through emails on his tablet. He found himself looking out the window instead, watching for her arrival.

It wasn't a new complex, but the buildings were maintained, as were the grounds. A group of teenagers played basketball at the end of the parking lot.

If he was not mistaken, one of those young men was Audrey's brother. The tall, heavily muscled teen matched the pictures in her dossier. Grabbing the ball he was dribbling, he stopped, and his head came around to face the direction of Enzu's car.

The teen waved and yelled something and Enzu realized he'd missed Audrey's arrival. She called out a goodbye to her brother as the driver opened the door nearest her. Audrey paused before getting into the car, her body tense.

At least thirty seconds went by and she did not move, her jean-clad legs showing no indication they would be bending in the imminent future.

Enzu stifled the urge to call her name. There were times for putting a subordinate in place for keeping him waiting. This was not one of them.

His impatience did not stem from his schedule. It was

caused by his desire to see her again. To give in would be to show weakness, a loss of control that would be unacceptable. Enzu was discovering the chocolate depths of Audrey's eyes to be even more addictive than the sweets he indulged in rarely but enjoyed thoroughly.

No, his life was governed by an iron will backed up by careful planning. He did not get surprised; he did not become impatient waiting for something he wanted. Enzu was a rock and everyone around him knew it.

His reputation for being able to wait without urgency for a business rival to slip up, or a meticulously thought-out plan to increase his company's holdings to bear fruit, was legendary.

He could most certainly wait for one rather innocent woman to get into the car.

A moment later Audrey did just that, settling into the seat beside him as the driver closed the door.

"Good morning, Vincenzo," she said, without looking at him as she buckled her seat belt, only the slightest tremble underlying her tone to indicate she wasn't feeling as breezy as she acted. "It's nice and warm in here. I don't think I need this." Audrey tugged on the sleeves of her black peacoat, shrugging it off along with a houndstooth scarf. "I hate wearing a coat for long drives."

"We have that in common." He was in his shirtsleeves and tie.

Enzu had removed his suit jacket before leaving Manhattan and had the driver place it along with his overcoat on the empty front passenger seat.

"Would you like to put your coat in the front?" he asked, when it became clear she meant to put it on the seat between them.

For some reason Enzu did not like the idea of the cloth barrier.

She took far longer to answer than a question so simple

should warrant. Perhaps she was as attached to the buffer as he was bothered by it.

In the end she assented, however. They went through the process of passing the peacoat through the accessibility panel to the driver.

Enzu slid the thickly paneled glass back into place, affording them a measure of privacy. The driver would not hear what was said, and the glass was reflective on his side, though not perfectly opaque. Particularly at night, when a light was on in the backseat for Enzu to work.

They were on their way when Enzu asked carefully, *"Vincenzo?"*

That finally brought her too addictive gaze to his. Instead of looking self-conscious at the familiarity, she frowned. "Really? You are going to suggest I should call you Mr. Tomasi when meeting your children?"

Audrey didn't mention the kiss, earning his respect— even if it was only prompted by the shyness of innocence. Either way, plainly Audrey wasn't trying to trade on their explosive attraction. Most women whom he had shared any sort of intimacy with expected to get something out of it, satisfying orgasms notwithstanding.

Audrey had some other point to make by using his first name that she patently expected him not only to understand but to agree with. He'd found this happening several times during their interview.

It should annoy, but instead her honest and often black-and-white viewpoint fascinated him.

As an international business and power-broker, Enzu found his reality had a lot more shades of gray.

"Their nanny calls me Mr. Tomasi," he pointed out.

"But you aren't hiring a nanny, are you?" She seemed to be trying to read something in his face, with no indication if she'd found what she was seeking. "You're looking for a wife who will be their mother."

"You have a point."

He could feel her mentally rolling her eyes, even though she didn't allow her expression to go there. It suddenly struck him that although Audrey Miller had undeniable trepidation about sex, she wasn't actually afraid of *him*. She hadn't been intimidated the first time she approached him and that hadn't changed.

Even with $250,000 a year and a ten-million-dollar bonus on the line.

This woman was definitely unique.

"I am used to my employees being in awe of me."

She laughed like he was joking. "None of your other employees has the prospect of a sexual compatibility test-drive hanging over their head. Do they?"

"Of course not." And he had no idea what that had to do with the way she approached him as just any other man. "And the prospect should hardly be seen as the Sword of Damocles by you, either."

"Says the man who uses sex as a stress-reliever. You know you could just take up Judo, or something. Join a gym."

Enzu surprised himself with an unfettered laugh. "I'll take the sex, thanks. And I already work out six days a week."

"Six? I let Toby push me into running with him three times a week and that's plenty. What are you? Obsessed?"

"Not hardly." But Enzu's lifestyle had the natural by-product of an excess of adrenaline. A solid cardio and weight regime helped him manage it. Enzu had no intention of having a heart attack before he was forty.

"It's a surprise you have energy left over for sex."

"I promise I do."

She huffed out something he didn't quite catch.

It might have been something about an oversexed throwback, but he wasn't going to ask her to repeat it. "You will enjoy it, I promise you."

"That remains to be seen."

He had a sudden urge to kiss that prim look right off her lovely features. He could not help remembering just how much they would both enjoy that. "I think we proved prospects are good already."

She opened her mouth, shook her head and closed it again.

He waited to see what would come out next.

"How long is the drive to your house?" Audrey asked, clearly ready to put the subject of sex to rest.

"Ninety minutes."

"That can't be convenient."

He shrugged. "I can work in the car. When I am in a hurry I use the helicopter."

"Still, a three-hour commute every day has to be murder."

"I only go to the house on the weekends. The top floor of Tomasi Enterprises is divided into three apartments. Mine takes half of the building space and the two smaller ones are used for business."

"You only see the children on the weekends?" Audrey asked, her tone shocked and not a little disapproving.

"I assure you this is not an uncommon practice in my world." Hell, he would hazard that her own father hadn't made it home to their Boston mansion every night during the work week.

"But who takes care of them during the week?"

"Currently a nanny. But if you will remember the answer to that question is why we are currently in this car together."

"But children need to see *both* of their parents—when they have them—on a much more frequent basis. Especially when they are so young."

"You are suddenly an expert in childhood development?" he asked, with more humor than irritation.

She grinned, the sweet humor coming over her features absolutely arresting. "Research. One thing a degree in English Literature is good for...? Learning how to research."

"You've been studying how to parent small children?" he asked, impressed.

"How else was I supposed to figure it out? I suppose I could take classes. They offer them now pretty commonly."

"Your own mother's example isn't one you want to follow?"

"I don't remember how she parented me as a small child, but, no, I don't think I'd want to leave my children to the nanny and the housekeeper like she did Toby."

"No. That's exactly what I'm hoping to avoid for Franca and Angilu."

Of the six women he'd interviewed he was certain Audrey was the only one who had taken a proactive approach to preparing herself for the actual nature of the job. His decision to single her out for introduction to the children was proving to be the right one.

"It pleases me that you've taken this initiative."

"I'm not in the habit of going into situations blind if I can help it."

"We have that in common as well."

She laughed, the sound wry. "You take the control-slash-prep thing to heights well beyond me."

"I see my reputation precedes me."

"Yes. Your attention to detail and insistence on controlling every aspect of a venture is not exactly a secret." A soft rose washed over her cheeks, but didn't deepen into a full blush.

What was that about? Did she think he would mind that she'd done some of that research she was so adept at on him?

Or did she think he was controlling in the bedroom too? That might disconcert a virgin. However, there could be no denying that his reputation for control in that area was well-earned as well.

Audrey would come to appreciate it, he was sure.

"I hope I'm dressed all right," she said, in a clumsy bid to change the subject. "Mother always said a lady's wardrobe didn't include a pair of jeans, but I live in them outside the office."

Enzu took in Audrey's form-fitting jeans and the tangerine sweater with a scooped neckline that hinted at modest curves. Her trainers weren't brand-new, but they didn't look over-worn, either.

She wore only a small pair of gold earrings, no other jewelry, and had pulled her silky brown hair up into a ponytail.

It was a more casual look than he was used to among the women of his acquaintance, but he couldn't say he found it displeasing. "I do not think the children will care."

"No, I suppose not." She gave him a very serious look from her melting chocolate eyes. "I haven't forgotten what we were talking about."

Funny, he'd thought she wanted to. "Oh?"

"If you live in the city during the week, then the children should also live there."

Okay, *he* had forgotten that discussion.

"You cannot be serious?" He could not imagine two small children in his sleekly modern penthouse.

"I am if you are."

"What does that mean?"

"If you are as committed to being your niece and nephew's *dad* as you expect the woman you hire to be their *mom,* then you'll do whatever is in your power to see them as often as possible."

"Children need a place to play, to be able to go outside."

"So take them to the park. Create a rooftop garden, if the building doesn't have one already. You're a billionaire. You've got options."

He was disconcerted to discover he realized she was

right. He did have options, if he was willing to look outside the box. And apparently Audrey *was*.

He ruthlessly stomped down the urge to reach out and touch this amazing woman. "You didn't have options. Six years ago."

"No. I didn't." Old pain flared in her eyes, then disappeared just as quickly. "But I did my best for Toby with what I had."

"You did an excellent job, by all accounts."

"You investigated Toby too?" she asked, and then shook her head. "Of course you did."

"It's no small thing he's won a scholarship to MIT."

"It's partial."

"Yes."

And dependent on Tobias completing his senior year with a full courseload of advanced classes and a near-perfect grade point average.

Considering how well the young man had done thus far, Enzu had no doubts on that score. Apparently the prestigious university didn't, either.

"He is the reason you want this position, isn't he?" It was the only key issue they hadn't touched on in the interview.

Generally Enzu preferred to draw his own conclusions about people's motivations. If asked, they often lied. However, he found he wanted confirmation of his suppositions in her case.

"Partly, yes."

"Your parents refuse to help with his schooling?" he asked.

"They wouldn't have paid child support if the state hadn't forced them."

"That is criminal." Enzu might have been born in the United States, but his family was Sicilian and he'd spent every summer in the Old Country until he'd started working at the bank.

Even then he'd spent several weeks a year with his extended family.

A Sicilian took care of his children. No exceptions. His father and brother might not have gotten the memo, but Enzu had.

A Sicilian who had the chance to send his child to a good school? He sacrificed whatever was necessary to do so, just as his great-great-grandfather had done for his own son, paving the way for the foundation of their family's current fortune.

The Millers weren't rich like Enzu, but they *were* wealthy and could easily afford to send their son to MIT without the scholarship.

Audrey let out a low, bitter laugh. "I always thought so, but I've learned one thing about my parents. If they can't control their children, that is considered failure, and failure is unacceptable. Better to write it off completely."

"Were they always like that?"

"I didn't notice so much as a child, but then I lived in my own world of books and make-believe." She sighed. "They were always cold, hard to please. I don't remember them ever telling us they loved us, so I should not be surprised it turned out that they didn't."

"And yet they had four children?"

"The first two were planned and exactly to spec. I was Mother's *oops* baby of her thirties and Toby was her *little accident* in her forties."

"No child is an *oops* or an *accident*." Enzu was outraged on her behalf.

His parents were self-serving and allergic to responsibility, but they had never made him feel like they would rather he'd not have been conceived, much less born. Quite the opposite, in fact.

Enzu was certain that his father had been planning for the day he could abdicate his business responsibilities to his son from the day of Enzu's birth.

"I agree, but then as the official *oops* I'm prejudiced in my thinking."

"Franca is not Johana's child." Enzu had not meant to admit that, but eventually he would have to tell Audrey if she turned out to be the successful candidate.

That eventuality was looking more and more likely.

"I know. They didn't even start dating until three years ago."

"You've done your own research."

"Are you surprised?"

"No. More impressed."

"Funny. I find your dossier on me invasive."

"Perhaps I am too used to being the focus of unrelenting interest."

"Your brother and parents spend a lot more time in the forefront of the media."

"It takes a great deal of effort and foresight on my part to keep my own affairs private."

"That explains it."

"Explains what?"

"Why there's all sorts of information about the business exploits of the man who took over his family bank's presidency at twenty-three and became a billionaire by the time he was thirty-five. But no girlfriends. No exploits."

"I do not indulge in girlfriends or exploits worthy of media attention."

"Or if you do you do a very good job of hiding your involvement."

"For instance?"

"Tomasi Enterprises funnels financial resources into a fund that has donated significant amounts to disaster relief ever since the levies broke in New Orleans."

"How did you find that out?"

"I told you, research. The study of English Literature requires a fine ability to follow obscure references and threadbare connections."

"I see. I guess it's a good thing the media sharks that target me weren't English Lit majors."

"Why not let people know about your company's generosity? Wouldn't that be good for the bottom line?"

"We have an official charitable donation fund."

"But it's a lot smaller than the amounts you've given in secret."

"If it weren't, Tomasi Enterprises would be inundated with requests for money. We aren't the Red Cross."

"I think you're a lot of things you pretend not to be."

Audrey's expression worried him a little. "Do not make me into a hero. I am not. If you forget the basic truth that I am at heart a ruthless businessman, you will get hurt."

"And you don't want that?"

"No."

"That's not exactly ruthless."

"I didn't say that if my interests and yours collided I would not hurt you, only that it would be my preference not to."

"I'll try and remember that."

He did not like the humor underlying her tone. "Do."

"Tell me how you ended up the bank's president at twenty-three."

"My father abdicated."

"But didn't he only take over from your grandfather a few years before that?"

She really had done her research. "Yes. Grandfather's heart precluded him continuing in the position. I do not think either of them wanted my father in the chain of command."

"Because your father is more interested in having fun than in making the money that makes that fun possible?"

"You have a way with words."

"That's how I became a customer service specialist."

"I imagine our clients find you a soothing presence on the other end of the phoneline."

Audrey grimaced. "Most of the time, yes. Some people are just plain cranky."

No doubt. "I tend to expect perfection."

"I'm sure you get it."

"Most of the time." He repeated her words.

She smiled. "You didn't really answer my question."

"I did."

"No, you explained the chain of events that led to you being bank president right out of graduate school, but not how you made that work. Most twentysomethings would have ended up sending the bank under."

"I worked summers and weekends at the bank since my fourteenth birthday. And then I interned in management while getting my MBA from Columbia. You could say I was raised in the bank."

"You never acted like you didn't want the responsibility, but it couldn't have been easy watching your brother get to enjoy his youth in a way you never did. Heck, your father was partying up like a twenty-three-year-old when you were busy saving the family fortune."

"Why should I have complained?" Enzu asked in genuine confusion. "I always *wanted* to take over the bank."

"Why?"

Audrey had more insight than most, and Enzu wasn't sure how he felt about that, but he answered her question with candor. "It was painful to watch it languish under my father's leadership. Even my grandfather ignored opportunity after opportunity to grow the business. He was too busy catering to a limited clientele with ties back in Sicily."

The Sicilian branch, Banca Commerciale di Tomasi, had been the beginning of the bank, but that didn't mean it had to continue to be the mainstay institution.

He added, "Tomasi Commercial Bank has always prided itself on being accessible to its Sicilian brethren, but today the American side is far more diversified and international."

"So you had plans to expand the bank from the beginning?" she asked, sounding like she found it hard to imagine someone of his age with those aspirations.

"When I took over, Tomasi Commercial Bank had only three branches on the East Coast. Within three years of me stepping up to the helm we had branches of the bank in all of the biggest U.S. cities."

"Is that when you turned the day-to-day operations for the bank over to a team of senior level managers?"

He was no longer surprised by the depth of her research. "*Sì*. I still guide financial policies and major investments for the bank, but I'm able to keep my involvement down to a once-a-week conference call and the occasional meeting."

"That's kind of incredible."

"It was necessary in order to do what I really wanted."

"Start Tomasi Enterprises?"

"Yes."

The bank provided for his family, keeping them in the lifestyle they were so certain they deserved. But Enzu had wanted more. He'd wanted something that was his alone. So, he'd taken a loan out against his stock in the bank and started Tomasi Enterprises.

"And now you are applying the same brilliant brain that made you a thirty-five-year-old billionaire to finding a loving and attentive mom for Franca and Angilu?"

"That is the hope."

"I think maybe I want you to kiss me again, Vincenzo Tomasi."

"My business acumen turns you on?" She wouldn't be the first woman that had happened to.

His power was more an aphrodisiac than his money for many women.

"Your commitment to putting the same energy into making the children's life a good one that you do your business melts my heart."

"I'm not looking for your heart. You need to understand that."

Audrey didn't look surprised, or particularly worried. "You may just get it anyway."

He shook his head, but bit back the compulsion to argue. She'd offered a kiss and no one could accuse Enzu Tomasi of failing to take advantage of a good thing.

"I think it might be easier if you slid this way."

She unbuckled her seat belt and moved to the center seat, redoing the seat belt before turning to face him, innocent desire darkening her beautiful brown eyes. "Well?"

He was smiling when his lips met hers.

# CHAPTER SIX

It took no time at all for Audrey to simply melt under the caress of Vincenzo's lips.

His expert lovemaking made her own lack of experience a moot point. And it was lovemaking. Regardless of what she'd intended when she asked him for this, it was no simple kiss.

His mouth conquered hers, drawing forth a response that came from the very core of her. Not just her body, though she yearned for a physical intimacy she'd never known, but to the place inside where she'd always believed her soul resided.

How could she feel so hot, so needy and so profoundly *moved* at the same time?

It had never been like this with Thad. They'd been in love, or so she'd believed, but nothing they had done together had blown her away like Vincenzo's kiss.

His hands cradled her head, his lips molded to hers, his tongue only barely brushed the place where they met, and yet her entire body thrummed with a buzz of indescribable pleasure.

The kiss in his office had been amazing, like waking up after years of going through life asleep to her own sensuality. But this? It was beyond that. It was colors coming back into her world she hadn't even realized had faded away.

It was drenching sensation. His high-end cologne

smelled familiar, but it was changed by his own scent enough she could not name the brand. The texture of his lips reminded her that mouths were made for more than talking.

A tantalizing sensation she could not get enough of—the slick glide of his tongue against the seam of her lips, releasing the hint of Vincenzo's unique flavor—taunted her to open her mouth and get more.

And she had thought it could not get better than their last kiss, that maybe she'd even built that kiss up in her memory.

This kiss, so much more powerful than the first, decimated any thoughts in that direction.

Perhaps pleasure built on itself? She didn't remember that happening with Thad, but then it had been six years, and she'd done her best to forget the past so she could live in the present.

Audrey moved restlessly, straining against her seat belt, needing to be closer.

Vincenzo seemed to understand, sliding his arm out from under the shoulder harness to lean over her. His big, warm body pressed hers back into the luxury car's seat.

Her nipples peaked, drawing impossibly tight and pressing against the silky fabric of her bra with pleasure so acute it was almost painful.

Vincenzo's hand slipped down Audrey's body and under the hem of her sweater to caress her stomach. Long masculine fingers spread possessively, causing every centimeter of skin he touched to grow scorchingly hot from each spark that lit her nerve endings.

Her own hands went to his broad shoulders and then slid down and around his back, reveling in the feel of the well-honed muscles bunching under her touch.

She moaned, long and low—no hope of keeping the unmistakably sexual sound inside. A small voice of reason tried to tell Audrey she should be embarrassed by that. She wasn't promiscuous, that voice insisted.

A much stronger voice, the one he'd woken with that first kiss in her office, insisted this felt much too good to be worried about sounding like a woman who couldn't wait for that test-drive Vincenzo had demanded.

His hand drifted up her stomach, over her ribs, stopping only when his thumb rested in the shallow valley between her breasts and his forefinger barely pressed the underside of one curve. That hand just stayed there, tempting, taunting with what it might do next.

Her own fingers clutched the fine fabric of his dress shirt, fisting it in a way that was bound to leave wrinkles.

With a deep groan that rolled through her like a touch, Vincenzo pulled his lips from Audrey.

He tipped his head back, though his upper torso remained pressed against hers, that tormenting hand still resting intimately against her skin. "We have to stop."

She shook her head. No. She did not want to stop. "More kissing." *More touching.*

The sound that came out of him was deeply pained, his gaze flaring with blue fire...the hottest part of the flame.

Unable to stop herself even if she'd wanted to, and she so did not, Audrey strained forward. She could barely reach to match her mouth to his again. Their lips barely touched.

And that was way more arousing than she'd ever thought such barely there intimacy could be.

His head dipped toward hers, and her entire body sighed with relief at the contact.

Only the kiss did not deepen. He did not move his lips against hers. He was warring with himself; the conflict was so intense she could feel it.

As the seconds dragged on the tension emanating from him grew until he was like a perfect sculpture in marble, his breathing the only movement Audrey could discern.

Then, so slowly she felt the withdrawal of his lips in increments, Vincenzo pulled his head back again. "No, *biddùzza*. We cannot continue."

"Why?" How could he want to put the brakes on such amazing pleasure? Unless he was used to that depth of feeling—or, worse…it hadn't been as good for him. "Did I do it wrong?"

His laugh was harsh, his square Sicilian jaw rigid. "If you had done it any more *right,* I would have embarrassed myself."

"Why would you be embarrassed?" That didn't make any sense.

His sardonic expression said she should know exactly what he meant. When she gave no indication that she'd gotten it, because…well…she *hadn't,* his gaze flicked down their bodies.

Hers followed and even she couldn't miss the impressive bulge that had to be pressing painfully against his zipper.

Only then did the implication of his words sink in. "Oh."

*"Sì—oh."*

"But—"

"Your first time will not be in the back of a car with only the illusion of privacy."

"My first time? You thought…you want…?"

*"Sì,* I *want, biddùzza.* Very much."

*"Biddùzza?"*

"Sicilian."

"For?" she prompted.

"There is no precise translation."

"Really?" She wasn't buying it. She'd look it up on the net if he didn't tell her.

He huffed out a breath that could have been irritated or amused. "It means beautiful, but is a more intimate endearment than *bèdda.*"

"Not so hard to translate after all."

He shrugged, giving off an uncomfortable vibe she didn't associate with such a self-possessed man.

What was it about explaining it to her bothered him? Italian men used *bella* all the time. It didn't mean anything.

She was sure it was the same for Sicilian men with *bèdda*. Only he hadn't called her *bèdda,* had he? He'd used a more personal endearment.

She blinked up at him, her mind working. "Do you call other women *biddùzza?*"

"No." Firm. Sure. Even a little scandalized at the idea.

So it was special for her. And unintentional. Which meant the American-born Sicilian tycoon was not as in control as he appeared.

Warmth suffused her being, delight increasing the sexual need thrumming through her. She let her body shift down so his fingers shifted up, covering the underside of her breast. Her nipple ached with the need to be touched as well, but she just stopped herself from slouching into the seat so that could happen.

Vincenzo's breaths were suddenly coming in more rapid gusts between them. "Stop, Audrey."

"I'm not doing anything." Very much. "You're the one with your hand... Well, you know."

He couldn't expect her to ignore that, or the way his big, toned body pressed into hers.

Vincenzo flashed a shark-like grin that was anything but comforting.

"This hand?" he asked, brushing the thumb of his left hand—the one safely cradling her head—down along her neck.

"You know it's not." Though it seemed to be more of a threat to her equilibrium than she'd suspected.

That simple caress revealed the direct line between that tender spot on her neck and the place between her legs clamoring most for his attention.

More than the sensual onslaught, there was something entirely possessive about the way he held her head just where he wanted. Something that said no matter what he might be feeling, regardless of small cracks in his near-impenetrable armor, Vincenzo Tomasi was in control.

Of himself. Of her.

A moment of clarity sent frissons of uncertainty through her. Could she spend the better part of two decades, perhaps even longer, as this man's lawfully wedded wife?

The overwhelming desire to do just that would have taken her legs out from under her if she were standing, it was so powerful.

"You must mean this one?"

He was still playing the sensual game while she'd been having her life-altering internal revelation.

He let one finger slide up to brush over her nipple, bringing Audrey instantly back into their hot, sensual bubble.

This man was lethal. "Y-yes, that one."

He chuckled darkly and moved the overstimulating appendage down her stomach. Slowly. So very slowly. Neither of them made the tiniest sound as he withdrew his hand from under her sweater.

He carefully tugged the hem into place before sitting up. "You are a temptation."

"But you stopped."

"It is for the best."

"According to your plan," she teased.

"It is my habit to follow my plans."

"You never lose patience and just do something because you want to?"

"No."

No room for misinterpretation there. "One thing I've never heard anyone call you is impulsive."

"My cautious nature has served me well."

"You and your company, not to mention Tomasi Commercial Bank."

Vincenzo had pushed the bank to withdraw from high-risk, high-yield bonds before the stockmarket tanked.

His bank and company had suffered minimal damage while the rest of the financial world teetered on the edge of bankruptcy.

"I used to be impulsive." When there had been room in her life for spontaneity.

His expression was tinged with disbelief. *"Used to be?"*

"You think I'm impetuous?"

*"Sì."* One word. No clarification. Absolute certainty.

"I'm not." She couldn't afford to be anymore.

"You do not think coming to my office with no introduction or any idea of how I would react to your initiative to apply for an extremely unorthodox position was impulsive?"

She frowned, unable to actually deny the charge. She *had* had no idea how Vincenzo would react to her. Audrey could have lost her job that day, or at the very least gotten a severe reprimand.

"Desperate times…"

"And was it desperate times that made you ask me to kiss you in my office and again just now?"

"Not desperation, no."

"Did you *plan* to kiss me then or today?"

"No." Today she'd meant to get to know two small children to whom she might well become a mother.

"You see? Impulsive."

"But you kissed me both times."

"While I may not share your impetuous nature, I am a man who knows how to take advantage of a fortuitous circumstance when it arises." He sounded entirely too smug.

"You think an opportunity to kiss is lucky? I would have thought you had plenty of those you turned down all the time."

"In that you would be right, but you have left out the key element to the equation."

"What is that?"

"The opportunity was to kiss *you,* Audrey."

Wow. She didn't know how to respond to that. He'd implied that she was something special, but she wasn't. Just one of several candidates he was considering for a position she was coming to want more and more.

"You're sort of lethally charming, you know?"

"You would be one of only a few who think so."

She just shook her head at such a ridiculous claim.

"I am a workaholic who has spent most of my adult life building a financial empire, not a charming playboy."

Like his brother Pinu. And his father, whose affairs were legendary and legion despite his being married to the same woman for almost four decades.

"If a kiss affects me like this, I'm afraid your *test-drive* is going to kill me," she jokingly admitted.

"I fully intend for you to experience a surfeit of *la petite mort,* I promise you."

The promise of multiple orgasms sent shivers of reaction through her. This man pushed every single one of Audrey's buttons.

Just as she'd warned him, her heart was engaging at light speed, her four-year crush fast becoming something else. No matter that he wasn't interested in her emotions. She had no more choice about that than how quickly her body responded to his kiss.

She wasn't sure she believed in love at first sight, but Audrey would never forget her first glimpse of this powerful man. He'd been to the bank for a meeting. Her heart had ended up in her throat and hadn't dislodged itself until an hour later.

She'd applied for a transfer to Tomasi Enterprises a week later and told herself it was for the bump in pay and responsibilities.

Audrey had spent four years watching him from afar, reading every article that was published in the printed and electronic press about the brilliant business tycoon. She'd saved the link to a rare interview he'd given which had been uploaded to the net in her Favorites.

He'd fascinated her. This man who could take apart a

company with ruthless precision for maximum financial gain, but who had personally driven his own corporate policies that benefitted not only his employees but their families. His charitable contributions were evidence that, no matter how cold and emotionless Vincenzo Angilu Tomasi might appear, his heart was as human as anyone else's.

She only wished it was accessible to her. But that was one miracle she had no hope of.

Audrey didn't know what she would do if Vincenzo chose one of the other candidates to complete his little family. However, there was an undeniable part of her that hoped fervently he did just that.

The fear he would choose her was almost as strong as the fear he wouldn't, and Audrey had the inescapable feeling her heart was going to end up broken either way.

"I should move back to the other seat."

He adjusted his seat belt across his torso. "Don't. It gives me satisfaction to challenge my control."

If she were more confident in her own sensuality it might make her happy to add to that challenge. To spend the rest of the ride teasing him in subtle ways, until maybe that control even broke. Perhaps someday, when she was not a sexual novice.

As it stood, she did her best to bring her own clamoring desires back to manageable levels.

"How did you accomplish the Gatling coup last year?" she asked, pretty sure that the discussion of acquisitions and mergers would be staid enough to help in that endeavor.

What followed was actually both interesting and informative, and not just about that particular financial windfall Vincenzo had engineered. His answer revealed both the power magnate's passion for his work, and a great deal about his personal business philosophy as well.

"So, you try to keep a company active if you can?"

"It depends on the numbers."

"What do you mean?"

"If I can realize a minimum of a ten percent return on investment within a year, or twenty-five percent within three."

"So if you only project a nine-point-seven ROI, you dismantle and sell?"

*"Sì."*

"What if selling for parts wouldn't net you the minimum ten percent either?"

"Then I would not have bought it."

"So, no exceptions?"

"No."

"But you can't be sure about those numbers. I wasn't a business major, but even I know that there has to be a margin for error with any income projection." She worked for a financial institution after all.

She couldn't help picking up a thing or two.

"Naturally. However, that margin is taken into consideration and is far narrower for me than it might be for someone else."

"You don't lack confidence, that's for sure."

"Should I?" he asked, arrogance lacing his tone, and his expression just this side of condescending. "I built a multimillion-dollar investment into a billion-dollar company in less than a decade, during a worldwide financial slump the like of which has not been seen in decades."

"When you put it like that…" She grinned, inviting him to share her self-deprecating acknowledgement of his undeniable financial genius.

He returned the smile, his blue eyes warming in a way that was way too appealing for her peace of mind.

They arrived at his house a few minutes later. Wrought-iron gates swung inward to allow the car through, closing with only a small clang behind them.

The winding drive was so long Audrey did not see the house until they crested a rise after the first curve. A brick mansion that would have made royalty proud rose toward the sky, its windows indicating there were three floors aboveground and no doubt one below as well.

"Full-time mother does not include housekeeping duties?" she asked faintly, entirely daunted by the prospect of keeping up with such a huge property.

"Not at all. There is a full-time housekeeper who oversees a team of maids."

"Sounds like a hotel."

"No. It sounds like a home. My home."

Oh, she'd hit a nerve with that one. She hadn't meant to. "I'm sorry, Vincenzo. I didn't mean to imply it wasn't a lovely place to live."

"Enzu."

"What?"

"My family calls me Enzu."

Audrey didn't point out that she wasn't a member of his family, or that she wasn't even sure she ever would be. She was too busy swallowing down the emotion his invitation to use the nickname engendered in her.

She just nodded.

"The housekeeper does not live in. She and her husband, the groundskeeper, have a small cottage on the property. They are usually in the house from early morning until just before dinner."

"Oh." Audrey wasn't sure what to say to that.

This lifestyle was entirely outside her experience.

Yes, Audrey's mother had a part-time housekeeper who kept her home immaculately clean and running smoothly, as well as a cook. But that wasn't anything like having a bevy of staff charged with keeping this impressive mansion a pleasant home for a billionaire and his newly acquired children.

"Devon serves dinner. Because he likes to." Tolerant affection laced Vincenzo's tone.

"Who is Devon?"

"He is my majordomo."

"You have a majordomo?" She should not be surprised. Vincenzo needed someone with ultimate authority over his domiciles, considering the fact one was a mansion on its own estate and the other a penthouse apartment in the city.

Her research had not revealed other properties, but that didn't mean Vincenzo didn't have any. As that was not of particular interest, Audrey hadn't dug that deep.

"Devon worked for my parents when I was a child and came to oversee my household when I left the family home."

Audrey heard what she wasn't even sure Vincenzo knew he was saying. If she hoped to come into that household and make a place for herself, she'd do well to make a friend of Devon.

"He lives in?" she asked, pretty sure she already knew the answer.

"He, the cook and a night-shift maid are the only ones that do." Vincenzo frowned. "And the nanny, Mrs. Percy."

"You don't like the nanny?"

"She's competent."

"But?"

"She is..." Vincenzo's gorgeous blue eyes narrowed in thought. "Cold. A little emotionless."

It was all Audrey could do to stifle laughter at the irony of Vincenzo Tomasi labeling someone else as emotionless.

# CHAPTER SEVEN

ENZU WATCHED IN pleased amazement as Audrey coaxed his quiet Franca right out of her shell, drawing forth smiles the little girl usually reserved for those she knew well.

He'd been startled when the first thing Audrey had done was to drop to her haunches when she was introduced to Franca, bringing herself down to eye-level.

Enzu often did the same, but that was because he was over six feet tall and did not want to intimidate his diminutive niece. Audrey was hardly a giant for a woman and yet she made the same concession.

She'd put her hand out to shake and waited patiently with an encouraging smile for Franca to shake it. Enzu had been shocked when Franca had done just that.

And the surprises just kept coming.

Audrey was currently sitting on the floor of the playroom, coloring with the four-year-old. Enzu found himself doing what he often did with the children: sitting back as he watched in silence.

He'd taken a seat at the table meant for coloring, but apparently Audrey and Franca preferred the floor.

Audrey laid a new blank piece of paper out between them. "What do you think we should draw now?"

They'd started with people. Franca had drawn a very wobbly stick figure with a square that was supposed to be a computer. She'd said it was Uncle Enzu. Working.

Audrey had praised the picture, but given Enzu a look he didn't want to interpret. He was pretty sure there'd been a component of disapproval and maybe even pity.

"Flowers?" Franca asked uncertainly.

Audrey's enthusiastic agreement had Franca's tense shoulders relaxing and soon they were coloring again. His niece made yellow and pink shapes that vaguely resembled circles with green lines going toward the bottom of the paper. The stems, no doubt.

Audrey drew a single bloom that filled the whole sheet, a big daisy with fat petals and a tiny stem, but exaggerated leaves. She then proceeded to color each fat petal in a truly bizarre fashion.

"Flowers don't have polka dots," Franca whispered in a worried tone to Audrey.

"In our imagination they can be anything we want."

Franca looked askance at Audrey. "Johana said flowers had to be pretty."

Everything inside Enzu froze as he waited for Audrey to respond to Franca's first mention of her dead stepmother since the accident had taken Johana and Pinu from her.

"Did she?" Audrey asked in an offhand manner.

Enzu let out a breath he was just now conscious of holding.

Franca nodded somberly. "She said my flowers weren't pretty enough to keep." Remembered hurt was reflected in the small features. "Johana always threw my pictures away. Percy keeps them. In a special frame."

Enzu's jaw hardened and his less than stellar view of his late sister-in-law dropped another notch, while another tick went in the column of why he had to keep Mrs. Percy on. While the woman always seemed cold toward *him,* it was clear she did not react to her charges the same way.

Audrey stiffened, but her tone remained relaxed. "Maybe she didn't understand art. Some people don't."

"Art?"

"Your pictures are art."

"They are?" Franca asked, eyes the same blue as Enzu's wide with wonder.

"Absolutely. Some people don't realize that art doesn't always look exactly like its inspiration."

"What's inspiration?"

There were an extra couple of syllables in the word that made Enzu smile.

Audrey smiled, too. "Like the flower you're thinking of when you draw one. Or how you remember seeing your uncle working so you drew him."

"Oh. I've got a book about flowers. They're so pretty."

"I'd love to see that book if you want to show it to me."

Franca jumped up. "I'll go get it. It's in the library. Uncle Enzu has shelves just for us."

She was running from the room before Audrey could answer.

Audrey turned troubled eyes to Enzu. "I know I've just met Franca, and I could be jumping to conclusions, but I don't think Johana was the most sympathetic stepmother around."

"My brother had questionable taste in women."

A snort from near the door told Enzu the nanny had returned. "It's not my place to say, I'm sure, but I've been caring for that little tyke for a month now and I'd say your assessment was spot-on, Miss Miller."

Enzu wasn't surprised when the nanny didn't address him directly. She rarely spoke to him. He was pretty sure it wasn't because she was intimidated by his wealth and position, either.

The woman didn't approve of him. He would have fired her after the first week if Franca and Angilu hadn't responded so well to this expatriate Scottish woman of an age to be their grandmother, if a youngish one. Besides, Devon approved of her, and he had shared Enzu's disgust with the other nannies he'd fired.

Audrey just nodded in acknowledgement of the nanny's words. "Has Angilu woken from his nap, Mrs. Percy?"

"You can drop the Mrs., my dear. My families just call me Percy."

She'd never asked Enzu to drop the *Mrs.* and it was news to him that her *families* called her Percy.

He'd thought Franca did so because she found it difficult to remember the *Mrs.,* and Enzu had been unwilling to press the point of manners when the little girl was in such a fragile place.

"Thank you, Percy. And please call me Audrey."

"As you say, my dear."

The nanny actually smiled at Audrey, shocking Enzu even further.

Enzu repeated Audrey's question to the older woman. "Is my nephew awake?"

"He'll nap for another bit, if I know the wee tyke." Mrs. Percy directed her words to Audrey. "We've got him on a schedule that keeps him sweet and sleeping through the night finally, the poor bairn."

"Losing his mother would have been traumatizing for him." Audrey made the words sound almost like a question rather than a statement.

"I take leave to doubt that one saw enough of her bairn for him to even know she was his mum."

The words might well be true, but family loyalty forced Enzu to say coldly, "You are hardly in a position to make such a judgment, Mrs. Percy."

"Am I not, Mr. Tomasi? I am no green girl." The nanny shook her head, like she was disappointed in one of her charges. "Do you think I took this assignment without doing my own research about the family I would be in charge of? Chance would be a fine thing."

He couldn't help it. He looked over at Audrey. The humor sparkling in her delicious chocolate gaze at the mention of research made something in his chest hurt.

He met the nanny's eyes. "I am coming to understand that some employees are as committed to doing background research on me as prudence dictates I on them."

"Employees?" Audrey asked, her voice strained, but not with anger.

The woman was laughing at him and making very little effort to hide that fact.

Mrs. Percy drew herself up in truly imposing manner. "I do not consider my role as that of mere employee, Mr. Tomasi."

"What do you consider yourself, then?" he asked, with more curiosity than annoyance.

"The woman charged with raising your children."

"Surely that is their parents' job?"

"Franca and Angilu have no parents."

"What precisely do you consider me?" he asked, in a tone even Gloria and Devon knew to be wary of.

"An uncle who deigns to visit them once a week for a few hours between your all-important work."

"A billion-dollar company does not run itself."

"And children do not raise themselves. Those wee bairns have a barely-there uncle. No father. No mother. Och, it's a cryin' shame, it is."

"I am working to rectify that," he said, more defensively than he'd intended.

"I'm sure we'll all be pleased to see the results of your efforts."

If Mrs. Percy had spoken in sarcasm he would have fired her on the spot. No matter how impressed with her Devon was. But the nanny had actually sounded sincere.

"We will be seeing more of you around here, then?" she asked Audrey.

"Not exactly, Percy," Audrey interjected.

The disappointed resignation in the Scottish woman's expression made Enzu feel guilty, though he had nothing to feel guilty for. And he did not understand Audrey's reply, either.

They *would* be seeing more of her in future. He wasn't making a decision as important as who would be the children's mother without seeing more than a few hours' worth of interaction.

Audrey patted Mrs. Percy's arm and gave Enzu an implacable look. "You and the children will be joining him in the Manhattan apartment during the week from now on."

Enzu was almost amused to see a look of shock in the nanny's eyes matching the feelings that had momentarily frozen his ability to speak. *Almost* being the key word.

"They will?" he demanded in a tone devoid of emotion.

If he let his voice rise at all he would yell. Enzu did not yell.

Audrey didn't have the sense to back down and her expression said so. "We spoke about it in the car. On the way here."

As if he might not remember when they'd been in the car last when it was less than an hour ago.

"Normally I would oppose such an unsettled lifestyle, but those wee bairns need a parent more than they need to live in the same domicile all of the time." Mrs. Percy ignored the tension thrumming between Enzu and Audrey. "As time goes on they'll come to see both the apartment and this house as their homes. So long as the *people* around them remain constant."

"Yes, well..." For the first time in memory Enzu found himself speechless.

He should be lambasting Audrey for making such a pronouncement and explaining to Mrs. Percy that they weren't going to do any such thing. However, he couldn't make the words come.

Because, as furious as he was with Audrey's highhanded pronouncement, it struck him that she might have been right about the children living with him. He should have thought of it himself.

Which just went to show one more reason they needed a mother.

Before he could say anything, in agreement or denouncement, he realized Franca stood in the doorway of the playroom, her book held against her chest with one small fist.

She looked at him imploringly. "Really? We are coming to live with you for *always*?"

"You do live with me."

Franca's little brows drew together in confusion. "No, we live here."

"This is my house." Even as he said the words he realized the ownership of a house meant nothing to a little girl.

Disappointment began to drain the anticipation from Franca's sweet features.

He could not stand it. Dropping to his knees, he looked into the eyes that could have been his own at that age. "Do you *want* to live with me all of the time, *tesoruccio?*"

"Will you be my daddy? My *real* daddy who loves me like the ones in my stories? The daddies who don't go away?"

Enzu would have said he had no heart to break, but he would have been wrong, because something inside his chest shattered at his niece's questions. The pain was so great he could barely breathe.

There was no answer he could give this child but one. *"Sì."*

"My own true papa? You promise?" She reached out, her small hands cupping his face, her expression so solemn.

He could not even force a word from a throat unaccountably tight. So he nodded.

"Say it. Say you promise. I can believe it then."

"I promise," he croaked out, his own voice weak like he'd never heard it.

How could she believe in him after her own father had let her down so completely? And not in death, but in life.

"My old daddy—the one in Heaven now—he never, ever promised to stay. He liked going away."

God in Heaven. Enzu did not think it could hurt anymore. *He* had let this child down. He'd known Pinu wasn't father material, but had wanted to believe that some of what he had taught his brother had stuck.

He had known Pinu liked the whirlwind of constant fun, but Enzu had never considered he would completely ignore the needs of his own child. Not like their parents had done all too often.

"Can I get a *mama* too?" Franca asked in a tiny voice, as if she thought she should not ask for anything else but could not help herself.

Enzu almost laughed, but it would have come out sounding more bitter than amused so he held it in.

"*Sì.*"

It was a vow.

One he would not break. Even if he had not embarked on the search already he would have promised.

His gaze slid to Audrey, whose eyes glistened wetly. Approval shone in her gaze, and her trembling lips curved in a smile too sweet for the likes of him.

"Well, now, that's something. Maybe I've misjudged you, Mr. Tomasi. Maybe I have." Mrs. Percy looked to Audrey and then back at Enzu. "If your plans are what I've an inkling about, you may just have more common sense than I took you to."

Enzu spent the rest of the day learning how to interact with a four-year-old and a baby from experts. The children had been in his care for six months and this was the first time he'd made baby Angilu smile, or interacted with Franca in any meaningful way.

Because of Audrey.

She hadn't raised any children, but the woman so reminiscent to him of the Hollywood legend who bore her name seemed to instinctively know how to react to both Franca and Angilu. Not to mention the prickly nanny, who unbent enough for the first time in a month of weekend visits to actually invite Enzu into the children's activities.

Audrey even gamely changed Angilu's diaper. Enzu did not take things to that extreme.

He enjoyed his time there more than he ever had, and when the hour came for the car to take Audrey back to the city he informed her that she would be taking the helicopter, so she could stay longer.

She gave him a quiet look he could not interpret.

"You do not think you might have asked?"

"It can make no difference to you, surely?" She would be home at the same time.

"What if I get airsick? Or was looking forward to the car-ride to decompress?"

He opened his mouth, but discovered he had no glib answer to those possibilities. "Would you prefer to take the car?"

"No."

"I do not appreciate games, Audrey."

"And I don't play them. But I won't spend the better part of at least the next two decades being treated like a subordinate."

"You are assuming you will be the chosen candidate?"

"On the contrary. I am making darn sure that if you do choose me you know what I expect in the way of treatment."

It made sense and he had to respect her commitment to honesty. She could have let him choose her and then started making demands after the contracts were signed and the vows spoken.

"I am accustomed to making unilateral decisions." Not having them made for him. "Even with my family."

"I imagine they put up with it because they don't want to give up the lifestyle you provide."

He'd often thought the same thing, had in fact maybe even mentioned it on the few occasions his parents, his brother or his wife might have balked at Enzu's directives.

He did not think admitting to that would stand him in good stead with Audrey, though. Enzu merely nodded agreement.

"I won't live that way."

"What way, exactly?" He needed this particular requirement spelled out to him.

"If it affects me, you discuss it with me. You don't tell me the way things are going to be."

"That is not a natural way for me to be."

"Are you admitting you are controlling?"

"Shouldn't I?"

She laughed. "You really are arrogant, aren't you?"

*"Sì."* He'd never denied it. "I will try to remember to discuss things with you that concern you."

It was a generous concession on his part and he hoped she realized it.

Audrey's expression would indicate that, as Mrs. Percy would say, *chance would be a fine thing.* Nevertheless, she said, "Thank you."

"You will have to remind me when I slip."

"Don't worry, I will." She sounded entirely too pleased with the prospect.

But she'd said she expected to *discuss* his decisions with him, not that she would refuse to adhere to them. He could live with that.

He wondered if she could, once she realized what he had agreed to and what he *hadn't.* That was in the event that he chose *her* for the role of Franca and Angilu's mama.

Not that after today Enzu could imagine deciding on anyone else.

Franca adored Audrey already. Mrs. Percy treated her

like royalty and Devon had given his subtle approval of her as Enzu's friend and guest as well.

"Do you think Devon would be willing to live in Manhattan during the week?" Audrey asked in uncanny synchronicity with Enzu's thoughts.

"I imagine so. He and the cook used to stay with me, but when the children came to live here I put him in charge of the household."

He trusted the older man like he didn't trust anyone else. Enzu was not a man who made friends and his own family had never been on his list of trusted intimates.

"That's wonderful." Audrey beamed at Enzu. "He'll make the weekly transition between homes that much easier on the children."

Speaking of the man himself, Devon came into the family room. "Mrs. Percy has asked me to inform you that the children are ready for their bedtime routine."

"Yes?" Enzu replied.

"I believe she is under the impression you wish to participate. I am quite certain young Miss Franca is expecting you to as well."

"Oh. Yes, we'll be right up." Enzu stood.

Audrey remained seated and was biting her lip.

"Are you coming?"

"Do you think that's wise? The children shouldn't become too attached to me until we've established I'm going to be a permanent fixture in their lives."

He didn't like it, but he grudgingly agreed. "That is a good point."

Enzu didn't understand the look of disappointment that came over her lovely features at his words. Surely she did not expect him to announce right then that he'd chosen her? No, that would not be it. Since he could not decipher it, he chose to ignore it.

"Mr. Enzu?" Devon asked before he could leave the room.

The man refused to call him Enzu, and Enzu was adamant he not be addressed as Mr. Tomasi by a man who had known him since childhood. Mr. Enzu was their compromise.

"Sì?"

"Mrs. Percy has informed me you plan to bring the children with you to the city?"

"Sì."

"I believe extensive preparations at the apartment will have to be made as it is not in any way a child-safe or friendly environment."

"I will not have the children disappointed." He'd said he was taking them with him on Monday and he would. Well, more likely tomorrow, to give them all a chance to settle in. "We will muddle through."

Audrey gave a disbelieving laugh. "Seriously? If you had a building that needed to be ready to host international meetings on a moment's notice and houseguests, what would you do?"

"Find another building. I am not moving." Not only was the apartment his home, but it was the safest place to live for the children, being on top of the well-secured Tomasi Enterprises building.

"And if using another building was not a choice?"

"I would have the necessary preparations seen to."

"Right. Because you are a freaking billionaire, Enzu. You can hire people to childproof your apartment before you take the children down tomorrow afternoon."

"Who said I was leaving tomorrow? I usually return to the City on Monday."

She just rolled her eyes.

"You should not be able to predict my behavior. You barely know me."

"Sheesh, Enzu. Some things are just common sense."

"Like hiring a crew to prep my apartment?"

"Yes."

Devon cleared his throat. "I believe several pieces of furniture will need to be replaced."

Thinking of the glass and chrome theme prevalent throughout the penthouse, Enzu agreed. "I will give instructions for the removal of all furniture deemed dangerous to a four-year-old and crawling infant."

Devon nodded his approval and Audrey smiled hers.

Enzu let out an exasperated sigh. "If that is all? I believe Mrs. Percy is expecting me."

He might have left without getting a response from either his majordomo or Audrey, but Vincenzo had the distinct feeling he had *not* gotten the last word.

# CHAPTER EIGHT

"You were kind of dragging this morning, sis," Toby said as he dug into his full farmer's breakfast.

Audrey shrugged. She'd done pretty well, considering. "I missed my midweek workout."

They'd taken their usual Saturday morning run and followed it with a stop at their favorite diner for their once-a-week indulgence: a traditional breakfast, including eggs, bacon and pancakes in Audrey's case, or very crispy hash-browns in Toby's. Her brother also added buttered toast with jam, but Audrey would never have been able to eat that much.

As it was, she usually left about half of her pancakes.

"I think this new work schedule is kicking your butt." Toby grinned and winked, looking way too knowing for her *little brother*. "And going out on dates almost every night isn't helping."

If only he knew.

"I was home before you were last night," she pointed out, wanting the focus of the conversation off her.

"Yeah, well, I've been dating since freshman year. You haven't been out with a guy since that jerkwad Thad broke your engagement."

Audrey grimaced, but the pain that would have once accompanied her brother's reminder was thankfully absent. Thad's defection on the heels of her parents' rejection had devastated her in a way she'd never shared with anyone. Least of all her baby brother. He'd taken on enough guilt because of the changes in Audrey's life.

Toby chugged down his orange juice and then set the empty glass on the table. "Too bad your work schedule changed right when you met your superhero."

"Superhero?" Vincenzo *was* larger than life, but a superhero?

"Yeah. He's gotta have superpowers of persuasion to have talked *you* into one date, much less three."

She laughed as her brother had intended. "You might be right."

The last week had passed in a blur for Audrey. Having adjusted her work hours to a seven-to-three schedule at Vincenzo's request, she'd spent nearly every afternoon getting to know Franca and Angilu. Some of which had bled into evenings spent with Vincenzo—sometimes in the company of the children, sometimes not.

Audrey didn't feel guilty telling her brother she'd been out on dates, because that was what they'd felt like. Not an extended interview and personality compatibility test for a really different kind of job.

Vincenzo was a charming and urbane companion, treating her like a woman he wanted to spend time with, not an employee or potentially *convenient* wife. Nevertheless, it was a tiring schedule, and restless sleep wasn't helping, but she couldn't do anything about it.

They had shared more scorching kisses and Audrey's dreams were filled with the heated slide of flesh against flesh. She'd woken aching for something she'd never known more times than she wanted to admit.

"I guess when word comes from down on high, you don't have much choice though, huh?"

"Right." If only Toby knew.

To explain the abrupt change in her schedule, she'd told Toby that her boss had requested it, which was not a lie.

No way was Audrey telling Toby the details of Vincenzo's plan, though. If she ended up as Vincenzo's wife and the children's mother, Audrey's brother was never going to know it was anything but a normal marriage.

"So, when am I going to meet this guy?" Toby pressed after they'd finished their breakfast in silence.

*Maybe never.* But she couldn't say that. "We're not at that place yet."

Which, again, was not a lie, but not the entire truth, either. Walking this fine line of honesty with her brother was wearing on Audrey even more than the new work schedule.

Toby did not look impressed by her answer. "What *place* do you have to be in for your brother to meet your date and decide if he's good enough for you?"

"I love you to death, Tobe, but no way are you screening my dates."

"You talk like there have been more than one."

"I'm twenty-seven. Definitely old enough to screen my own men."

Her brother snorted. "Not even close. I may be a teenager, but I've dated more guys than you and I can spot across the length of a football field."

"What are you? Super Spotter?"

Toby flexed impressive biceps. "That's me, teenage superhero."

"Better than a teenage werewolf."

They both cracked up and Audrey sent up a silent prayer of thanks for dodging that particular bullet right now.

"You going to be at the game today?" he asked her as they lingered over coffee, letting their big breakfasts settle.

"Of course." No way would she miss it. Not even for another day spent with Vincenzo and the children at his mansion outside the city. "It's your last one."

"Maybe not. I could play in college, depending."

"At MIT? I didn't even know they had a football team."

"Sure they do. The *Engineers*. Fitting, don't you think?"

"Definitely." She grinned and then turned serious. "But I don't know about you playing. Adjusting to your course-work at MIT is going to be a challenge, even for you."

"About MIT, Audrey—"

"No, Toby. Don't you dare say it," she interrupted. "You got in. You got the scholarship. You have to trust that the rest will come together."

"There's a really big stretch from here to the rest com-ing together. I can get a job, but even I know trying to work full-time and attend MIT isn't going to make it."

"I don't want you working."

"We're not going to have a choice."

"Maybe." She couldn't tell him what she was trying to do to make his dream happen, but she wasn't going to let Toby give up on it, either.

"I applied for more scholarships from independent funds, but the chances of getting a big one is really small, you know?"

She nodded, too choked to speak at first. "Have I told you how proud I am of you?"

"Only like a million times. You're such a *girl,* Au-drey." He tried to sound like he was complaining, but Toby couldn't hide his pleased glow.

"I *am* a woman, Tobe."

"Don't remind me. One who's dating, even." He gave an exaggerated shudder.

She rolled her eyes and threw his words back at him. "Don't remind me."

"Right. You gonna bring him to the game?"

She tried to suppress her horror at the very idea of Vin-cenzo Tomasi at a high school football game, much less meeting Toby before he absolutely had to. "That wasn't my plan, no."

"Yeah, not really convenient, huh?" Toby frowned for just a second. "Wish our last game was a home one."

"There will be plenty of people cheering on your side

of the field. It's not that far away." Only about forty-five minutes north of the city in good traffic.

"Yeah?"

"Yes."

"Maybe you should call your guy and invite him, then, huh?"

Assuming that he was already at the mansion with the children, Audrey did not call Vincenzo.

Not that she would have, regardless. Even if maybe a tiny part of her wished she really was dating Vincenzo and inviting him to watch her brother play football would have been a good idea.

She was making her way around the field to the bleachers for fans of the visiting team when she heard a high-pitched voice yell, "Audrey!"

Stunned, unable to believe she'd heard what she thought, Audrey turned. The sight that met her sent the air exploding from her lungs with the same power of a blow to the chest.

"Franca?" Audrey shook her head, trying to clear her vision.

Obviously she was hearing and seeing things. Maybe the lack of sleep was really getting to her.

But after closing her eyes for a count of five and then opening them again she continued to see the same thing.

Little Franca, bundled up in a pink fur-lined parka and snow boots in deference to New York's chilly November temperatures, stood holding Vincenzo's hand. She looked like a miniature snow bunny.

Audrey couldn't help smiling at the sight.

Highlighting the family resemblance, Vincenzo and Franca wore matching expressions of satisfaction at Audrey's obvious surprise.

"What are you doing here?" Propelled by an irresistible force, she moved toward them. "Where is Angilu?"

"We are here to watch the game with you." Vincenzo's

smile had a predatory edge that was entirely absent in that of his innocent niece.

He was looking stunning in black jeans, ankle boots and a cashmere sweater under a fleece-lined leather jacket. His head was bare and he wore no gloves. Because, unlike normal humans, apparently Vincenzo Tomasi defied even the cold.

"Angi and Percy are at home," Franca informed Audrey. "He's too little to be out in the cold." The small girl was plainly very happy to be considered old enough for the outing.

"Wow. I didn't expect you." Which felt like a huge understatement.

Audrey was completely and totally gobsmacked. She'd been sure that after turning down his invitation to spend the weekend at the mansion she wouldn't see Vincenzo until the following Monday.

"We surprised you," Franca pointed out very happily. "Are you glad?"

Despite Audrey's misgivings about her life with Toby colliding with what was going on between her and Vincenzo, she couldn't say anything but, "Yes, most definitely."

The tiny girl nodded with satisfaction. "Good."

"Shall we find our seats?" Vincenzo asked. "It appears the bleachers are filling quickly."

They were, which would make her brother and the other players on his team very happy.

Bemused, Audrey only nodded.

Somehow she found herself holding Franca's hand. Vincenzo used the arm he rested lightly over Audrey's shoulders to guide them all to a spot near the center of the bleachers about halfway up.

His bodyguards took up positions on either side of the bleachers, another joining them in the stands a little to their left and behind. The security team had made an effort to blend, foregoing their usual dark suits.

It must have worked because no one seemed interested in the three highly trained bodyguards. Vincenzo was another story, however.

Other parents, students and their friends weren't exactly subtle in the avid interest they were showing the gorgeous billionaire.

For his part, Vincenzo seemed oblivious to the scrutiny. Or maybe he was so used to it he took it in his stride.

Audrey wasn't so sanguine. And when the parents of Toby's teammates jockeyed for introductions she was relieved that Vincenzo took care of it himself.

"Vincenzo Tomasi," he said, offering his hand to shake to the men around them. "This is my daughter, Franca."

At that, the little girl positively glowed.

"Are you a friend of Audrey's?" one of the football moms asked.

"Yes," Vincenzo answered simply, showing no compulsion to add details such as Audrey would have felt.

Details that would have tangled her thoughts, not to mention her tongue.

One of the dads asked Vincenzo, "So this is Toby's first game you've seen?"

"It is." Again no further explanation.

The man was good.

"You must be the new guy Audrey's dating," said Brian, Toby's best friend of the non-football-playing variety.

"You are one of Toby's good friends?" Vincenzo asked without answering.

"Best buds since middle school."

"Are you hoping to attend MIT as well?" Vincenzo showed every sign of real interest.

"I wish. Mom and Dad made me apply. I didn't want to waste their application fee, but Dad especially just wouldn't listen. Even if I get scholarships, that's not happening. I'm not letting Mom and Dad go into major debt so I can at-

tend an Ivy League school." The longing in Brian's voice
said just how much he wanted to, though.

His parents were better off financially than Audrey, but
they were still firmly in the middle-class income bracket
and had four kids to put through college, not one.

"That seems to be a recurring theme." Vincenzo's tone
was thoughtful.

"I'm planning to go to UMass Boston. We'll still be
close enough to hang on weekends though, right?"

University of Massachusetts, Boston campus, was
Toby's backup plan, too. It was a good school, but not the
one Audrey knew either her brother or Brian most wanted
to attend.

"Right," Audrey said, giving the teenager an encouraging smile.

She liked Brian. A lot. He'd been a good friend to Toby,
even when her brother came out in high school and some
of his friends dropped him because of it. Brian dated girls,
but he'd joined the Gay-Straight alliance on campus to support his best friend.

Conversation around them settled down once the game
started. Vincenzo's comments and loud team support
showed that not only was he fully aware of which position
Toby played, he had a genuine understanding of the game.

"I didn't realize you were such an enthusiastic fan," she
said to him after a particularly loud shout of approval accompanied by him standing up to give it. "I thought Sicil-
ians were all about European football."

"Soccer has never been my game. There is something
very satisfying to the primitive in me to watch men face
each other in such direct combat."

"It's a game, Enzu."

"Tell that to the young men doing their best to take your
brother out at the knees."

"Don't remind me." Football was a dangerous sport, and

the wide receiver got tackled more often than the quarter-back got sacked.

"He's fast and talented."

"He is."

"He is not interested in playing at university?"

"Maybe."

"But he is not looking for an athletic scholarship?"

"No." She did not want her brother's college education dependent on him being on the football team. "Football is a huge time commitment. Toby can handle it now, but MIT's courseload is terrifyingly heavy."

"Terrifying for him, or for you?" Vincenzo asked with too much insight.

"I just don't want him locked into playing sports when he might need that time to study."

"You're very protective."

"Someone has to be."

Vincenzo didn't reply, going back to watching the game. Very vocally.

When halftime came Audrey suggested getting something warm to drink. Vincenzo sent one of his security guys for hot chocolate, which was not what Audrey had meant. But it did give them the chance to take Franca behind the bleachers to run off some of the amazing amounts of energy stored in the body of a four-year-old.

When the game resumed Franca crawled into Audrey's lap. The third quarter was only half over when the small body went lax in sleep against her.

The look Vincenzo gave Audrey and the sleeping child was odd, almost tender. "Do you want me to take her?"

"No, she's fine. I can't believe she's sleeping through your cheering, though."

"Me neither. It must be a child thing."

"I remember my Danny at that age. He could sleep through an earthquake," a woman in front of them said.

"He did." Her husband turned his head to them and

winked. "We lived in California and he slept right through me carrying him to a doorway and holding him through the after-tremors."

Everyone laughed, but Audrey's heart squeezed. She wanted that. She wanted stories to tell when her children were teenagers; the shared experience of a lifetime spent with another person.

The prospect that Vincenzo might choose someone else for Franca and Angilu's mom grew more painful by the day. Her desire to be the one had never only been about Toby, but Audrey's desire to make a difference in the small children's lives had only been a vague concept before.

Now she knew them. Knew how much Angilu loved his bath time, how important it was to Franca to have her pictures hung on the walls of the nursery. The little girl had been ecstatic when Audrey had showed her a photo on her phone of Franca's latest floral masterpiece, hanging on the cubicle wall in Audrey's workspace.

It had taken less than the week they'd had together for both children to take firm footholds in Audrey's heart. She knew the days to come would only make her attachment to the children stronger.

The probability her heart was going to end up broken at the end of this only grew.

# CHAPTER NINE

ENZU WAITED WITH Audrey outside the athletic building for her brother to come out of the locker room.

She'd tried to get rid of him, saying Franca needed to be taken home and put to bed.

Sending his daughter with one of the bodyguards to the limo took care of that particular argument. Enzu wanted to meet Toby, the young man Audrey had sacrificed so much to protect and raise.

"It could be another hour before he comes out." Audrey tried again.

He doubted it. Particularly after the offer Enzu had made to the team's head coach that afternoon. But he only said mildly, "You think so?"

He was not surprised in the least when a blond youth, easily as tall as Vincenzo, wearing jeans, T-shirt and letterman's jacket came bursting out of the door to the gym building. Eyes the same dark brown as Audrey's scanned the people milling around before landing on Enzu and Audrey.

Toby loped over, his blond hair dark with moisture. "Audrey!"

It said something about how agitated she was that his sister had not noticed the boy's exit until that moment.

She jumped, glared at Enzu and then turned to face her brother. "Hey, Tobe. Great game."

"It was," Enzu agreed with a nod, putting his hand out for the teen to shake. "Vincenzo Tomasi. You are a very talented ball-player, Toby."

The boy's handshake was firm and long enough to indicate confidence, but not so long he gave the impression of trying to prove anything. "Nice to meet you, Mr. Tomasi. Thank you for the party tonight. That's just sick."

"Sick means good in teenspeak," Audrey translated, before demanding, "*What* party?"

"Mr. Tomasi rented a bowling alley for the team and any friends we want to invite to celebrate our last game. Coach told us just now. Free games, shoe rental, food and soda until midnight."

Audrey gasped. "What? I didn't know—"

"Like I didn't know the guy you were dating was the freaking CEO of your whole company?" Toby interrupted.

"We haven't gone public with our association," Enzu inserted smoothly while Audrey looked like she'd swallowed her tongue.

"Why not?" the boy demanded brashly.

Enzu gave Toby a measuring look. "Because a man in my position does not announce who he is dating before he knows if that dating is going to lead somewhere at least somewhat long-term."

"I guess that makes sense." Toby didn't look entirely convinced, though. He turned to Audrey. "So, it's okay?"

"If you go to the party?" she clarified.

"Yeah."

"Yes, but I want you home by one."

"As to that," Enzu said before Toby could reply, "my country home is the same distance in the other direction as your apartment. I would like it very much if you came there instead."

"Why would I come there?" Toby asked in confusion.

"Because you and your sister will be spending the rest of the weekend with me and my children."

"What? You've got kids, man?"

"They're his niece and nephew," Audrey explained. "He got custody when his brother died six months ago."

"Oh." Toby's youthful features reflected honest sympathy. "I'm sorry, man. That blows."

"Yes, it does."

"Text me the address. I'll GPS it on my phone."

Audrey put up one hand in a gesture that meant stop. "Wait, I didn't agree to spend the weekend."

"Would you disappoint Franca and Angilu?" Enzu asked, knowing the answer. "They are looking forward to it."

"Angilu is a baby and you shouldn't have told Franca without asking me first."

"Have you not heard the saying *it is easier to ask for forgiveness than permission?*"

"Oh, how come I didn't know about *that* one?" Toby teased.

Audrey frowned at them both. "We don't have any clothes, pajamas, toiletries… No, it's impossible."

"I took the liberty of having everything necessary procured in your sizes. Including swimsuits. We have an indoor pool," Enzu said to entice the teenager.

Toby looked at Audrey as if to ask if Enzu was for real.

She nodded with clear resignation. "If he says he got us clothes and things, he did. And they probably cost more than I make in a month, too."

"But—"

"As your sister likes to remind me, I am a billionaire and my money can be used for more than making another business acquisition."

Toby looked flummoxed. "Get out of here. A billionaire. Nobody is a billionaire. Well, except maybe one guy I can think of."

So Audrey had told Toby *nothing* about Enzu. Interesting.

Regardless, Enzu found he liked the teen's attitude, so similar to his sister's. Toby treated the CEO of Tomasi Enterprises like any other person. It was refreshing.

"We do not all live in the media spotlight," Enzu said dryly.

"I guess, but, wow…that's just sick."

"I'm glad you think so."

Toby's face took on a serious cast. "We can go to your house, Mr. Tomasi, but my sister gets her own bedroom."

"Toby!" Audrey's cheeks washed a dark rose.

The boy looked at his sister. "Somebody has to watch out for you."

"You are absolutely right, Toby. I give you my word, your sister's room is all hers and not within two corridors of my own." He had his own suite in the mansion, near his niece's and nephew's rooms, but suitably distanced from those used for guests. It was Enzu's sacrosanct place to withdraw in privacy when family came to visit.

"That's okay, then."

"Oh, *is* it?" Audrey asked, voice dripping with sarcasm.

Toby set a direct stare on his sister. "Is he lying?"

"No, I'm sure he's not."

"You don't want to go to a house with a built-in pool?" Toby pushed.

Enzu had thought that would get to the teenager.

"I didn't say that."

"Audrey's not great when plans change unexpectedly," Toby said in an aside to Enzu.

Audrey snapped, "I like it even less when those changes are made on my behalf without my input."

"But I am getting that input now," Enzu argued.

Thinking about the unexpected visitor who had arrived that morning, Enzu was certain that Audrey would have more than his tendency to direct the lives of others to complain about before the end of the weekend.

"You could not have called me earlier?"

"No." She would only have said no.

"Preemptive strike, right?" Toby grinned. "We're study-ing game theory in relation to politics in my advanced gov-ernment class."

Audrey sighed. "I give up. You…" She pointed at Toby. "Be at the mansion by one and not a minute later."

"Woot!" the boy yelled. "Thanks, Audrey. Thank you, Mr. Tomasi."

He hugged his sister and shook Enzu's hand enthusiasti-cally again before running back toward the gym.

Audrey called out, "Toby!"

He stopped and turned around.

She jangled a set of keys. "The car is parked in the front lot."

He jogged back, grabbed the keys and then planted a kiss on his sister's cheek before thanking her again and leaving.

"He's got as much energy as Franca."

"More. He's still awake and will be for hours to come."

Enzu reached out and took Audrey's hand to lead her to the car. "You are not very angry, I hope?"

"More forewarned."

*"Si?"*

"Oh, yes. I'm onto your tricks now, Enzu. You better watch out."

"I am shaking in my boots."

"You don't know how to shake, but I like the boots."

Inexplicably pleased, he smiled. "Thank you. My grand-father always said a man's shoes say a lot about him."

"Yours say you're willing to dress down for a football game, but your clothes are still worth more than my ten-year-old car."

"You need a new car, Audrey."

"No, I do not."

A ten-year-old car could not be reliable. "I am certain you do."

"Well, you aren't buying me one like you bought my

brother's team an after-game party. Thanks for that by the way."

"It was my pleasure." And, strangely enough, it had been.

Audrey shook her head, quiet until they reached the limousine. "No luxury sedan this time?" she asked. "Trying to impress me?"

"We needed room for Franca's carseat." His niece's seat was buckled securely in the safest spot in the limo, in case of an accident. The middle of the seat that backed up to the privacy window, which left the one facing it empty for Enzu and Audrey.

Audrey tilted her head, her delicate brows drawn in thought. "There would have been room in the sedan."

"I did not want to spend the ride home in front with the driver while you were in the back with her," Enzu explained.

Even if they'd taken one of the security SUVs it would have been the same. Unless Enzu drove, and for long distances his security team and insurance underwriters preferred he not do so.

Being CEO of such a successful company had limitations most would never even consider.

"That would be romantic if this wasn't part of an extended interview." Audrey gave him a cheeky grin as she settled into her seat.

He laughed. "But you know the truth."

"I do."

And the truth was he enjoyed every moment of the forty-five-minute drive, talking with Audrey in hushed tones, even though Franca had proved capable of sleeping through much louder noises.

Audrey might have been surprised a week ago when Enzu insisted on carrying Franca inside instead of leaving it to one of the bodyguards. But she'd spent a week witnessing this business genius's very real efforts to fulfill the role of parent.

Yes, he took some things for granted a man with less power, influence and money might not, but Enzu cared.

And Audrey found that genuine desire to be a good father an incredible turn-on. After spending six years in sexual limbo, it was disconcerting to find herself affected so strongly by pretty much *everything* this man did.

They were on the first riser of the grand staircase when a masculine voice spoke from behind them. "Who is this, Enzu?"

Enzu stopped and Audrey followed suit, before turning back to see who had spoken.

The dark-haired man with an insouciant air was unmistakably Vincenzo's father. He made it into the tabloids often enough to be readily recognizable even if Audrey hadn't done her research on the Tomasi family.

Enzu had been slower to turn around, but now he faced his father, who stood in the large foyer as if he belonged there. "Giovannu, this is Audrey Miller. Audrey— Giovannu Tomasi, my father."

"You can call me Papa, Enzu. Using my first name is your mother's affectation, not mine." The older man winked at Audrey. "My wife does not want anyone to know she is old enough to be Enzu's mother. And after all her plastic surgery not even I believe it."

"Don't be snide, Giovannu." Enzu looked down at Audrey. "You may join my father for a drink while I put Franca to bed, if you like."

"I'd prefer to help you with her." No way was he leaving her alone with this social shark downstairs.

The tightness around Enzu's mouth relaxed slightly. "As you wish."

"Surely it does not take two adults to put one child to bed?" Giovannu opined.

"I know you did not think it took either parent when you

were raising *your* children," Enzu said, in a tone that could have cut glass. "We will agree to disagree."

The older man winced and stepped backward, as if needing to create physical distance between them. "Whatever you say, son."

Enzu didn't reply.

He didn't speak again at all until after they had changed Franca into her pajamas and tucked her into bed. Mrs. Percy nodded her approval of their endeavors before disappearing silently into her room.

"Do you know she frightens me more than my old nanny used to do?" Enzu asked with a small smile as they traversed the long hall toward the curved stairway.

"She takes her job and the wellbeing of her charges very seriously."

"*Sì,* but even so she cannot replace a mama who loves them."

The absolute lack of doubt in Enzu's voice came from experience Audrey wasn't about to question. Besides, she agreed. "Oh, so now you admit that to *be loving,* a woman might actually need to love Franca and Angilu?"

"You may have a point in that regard."

"So, your parents are here to visit?" she asked, stopping before they began their descent of the stairs.

Enzu, appearing no more eager to rejoin his father, halted and leaned against the railing. "Giovannu only. My mother is ensconced in their Manhattan townhouse."

"Your parents live in New York City?"

"When they are in the country, yes. Or at least on this coast. They prefer five-star hotels when staying in LA."

"And your father is here without your mother because…?" Audrey prompted, knowing full well Enzu could shut her down at any moment.

"Giovannu ran out of money and reached the limit on his credit cards."

"I didn't know that was possible for a billionaire."

"*My father is no billionaire.* He has no income but the one from our family's bank."

Definitely a touchy subject.

"He wasn't interested in striking out on his own like you did?" she asked carefully.

Enzu gave a bitter laugh. "Not a chance. That would have required the willingness to work. His income from the bank's profits is only a few million a year, which he is required per their prenuptial agreement to split evenly with my mother."

"He's used up this year's dividends?" she guessed.

"And then some."

"So he's here to mooch?"

Enzu laughed, the sound harsh. "He would be severely offended to hear you say so."

"But he *is* looking for a loan?"

Enzu's blue gaze burned with emotions she doubted he realized were there and wouldn't be happy if he did. "I do not extend credit to my father, but he knows he is welcome to stay here."

"And maybe he wants to see you and his grandchildren," she offered gently.

"He wants to avoid my mother after his spectacular breakup with his latest mistress."

"Oh."

"*Sì.*" Enzu let out a frustrated breath. "My parents took no responsibility for their children and take even less for their own lives now."

"You support them?"

"Not directly. His shares at the bank provide Giovannu's income."

"But only because you keep the bank running in the black?"

"*Sì.*"

"You're a good man, Enzu."

He shook his head, but then he didn't see himself the

way she did. He was a driven businessman. No doubt about it. But Enzu was also an adult man who provided financially for his parents even though they never gave him a reason to do so.

He'd taken responsibility for his niece and nephew when other men in his position would have foisted them off on other family. He had an entire cache of cousins, aunts and uncles back in Sicily.

"Will your mother be showing up to cause your father difficulty?"

His weekend at the mansion was seeming less and less like a retreat and more like a war zone by the minute.

"It is a possibility," Enzu admitted.

"Really?" Audrey asked, not sure she wanted to deal with both of the older Tomasis.

"If he does not come crawling home, tail between his legs, soon enough for her you can count on it."

That didn't sound like imminent threat, though. Audrey let her tense shoulders droop in relief. "Will he? Go home, I mean?"

"Oh, *sì*. Frances has income from her parents as well as her half of the bank dividends. She can provide a much more entertaining lifestyle than he will experience here."

*Man.* Audrey had always known money was no panacea, but who said it was easy to be a billionaire with parents like that?

"Want to go for a swim?" she asked on sudden inspiration.

"My father is expecting us to share dinner."

"Are you hungry?" They'd had chili dogs at the game.

"Not particularly."

"You did buy me a swimsuit?"

Blue fire from his gaze licked over her body like she was already wearing it. "*Sì*. It is in your room."

"The one I'm not sharing with you," she teased.

"Your brother is very protective. It is clearly a family trait. I am impressed."

"We watch out for each other, but I have to admit his efforts to play *big* brother can be a little embarrassing."

"Oh? Have you experienced that very often?"

"Not ever before, actually."

Enzu laughed, the sound free of the bitterness that had been hanging over him like a cloud. "Let's go swimming, *biddùzza*. I find I am very keen to see you in swimwear."

"It had better be a one-piece," she warned.

His eyes taunted her. "And if it is not?"

"I'll wear a T-shirt over it."

"That T-shirt?" he asked, referring to the white one she wore under her bright pink sweater.

"Unless you had your personal shopper buy me another one?"

His lips tilted on one side in an enigmatic smile. "Fine."

"What do you know that I don't?"

"Nothing, I am sure."

"Innocent does not look believable on you."

There was that laugh again, and her heart warmed to hear it.

"Come, I will show you to your room and have Devon inform my father we will not be joining him for dinner."

She should feel guilty at the snub to the older man, but Audrey would do almost anything to dispel the pall that had come over Vincenzo after only talking to his father for a couple of short minutes.

The swimsuit turned out to be a bikini.

It wasn't scandalous. The bottoms covered Audrey's butt cheeks, the triangles of the top covered her breasts, and for that she was grateful. However, the smooth expanse of her belly was naked—as was her entire back. She wasn't comfortable with that much skin on display.

So she put the T-shirt on and then donned the bright white thick Turkish robe she'd found on the back of her *en-suite* bathroom's door. Whoever had bought her clothes had even provided a pair of spa shoes in her size.

Audrey slipped them on before leaving her room, only realizing that she didn't know which way to go for the pool when she was in the corridor.

Enzu pushed off from the wall opposite her door, where he'd been leaning and waiting. "I forgot to tell you the pool is on the basement level."

He wore a robe like hers, except his was embroidered with his initials and he had not tied it, revealing his olive-skinned, muscle-layered physique.

Heat flushed up her body, sending urgent electric messages to her core. Audrey had thought her reaction to him was bad before, but right now she just wanted to *jump* him.

Shoving extremely inappropriate thoughts deep into her psyche, she said, "I probably would have figured that out, but I'm glad you didn't make me go searching."

If her voice was a little breathy she could hardly be blamed. Not in the face of provocation like an only partially dressed Vincenzo Tomasi.

"The thought of you stumbling in on my father at his dinner while you are dressed or rather *undressed* as you are is enough to send chills down my spine."

"I'm perfectly covered." *Her robe was tied.*

"How long would you manage to keep that Turkish cotton around your body in his presence, I wonder?"

"You don't think he would try…?" No. Vincenzo could not have meant *that*. She for sure wasn't going to say it.

"Seduce you?" His lips twisted with distaste. "I would guarantee it."

Assuming Vincenzo knew his father best, she didn't deny the possibility. "Trust me, my robe would stay firmly tied."

"You think so? My father can be very charming."

"I may be ridiculously susceptible to you, Enzu, but I'm not usually a pushover with men."

"No, I don't suppose you are."

The fact she was a twenty-seven-year-old virgin did not need to be said out loud.

# CHAPTER TEN

HER FIRST STEP into the basement paradise had Audrey gasping.

Located through a set of sliding glass doors opened with Vincenzo's palm print, the indoor tropical jungle was beyond magical.

Lush foliage flourished under a wall-to-wall ceiling of full-spectrum light panels. The air was warm and humid, but comfortably so. A path of mosaic tiles the colors of sand and earth wound through the tropical plants.

"This is incredible, Enzu," she breathed in awe.

"It is one of my favorite places to retreat."

"I can even hear birds."

"That is the sound system."

The fragrance of exotic flowers teased at her senses. "Don't tell me the flowers aren't real?"

"Most of the plant life is genuine."

It took her a moment to realize the area was untinged by the smell of bleach. "No chlorine in the pool?"

"Salt water and minerals."

The sound of rushing water reached her ears. "Is that a waterfall?"

*"Sì."*

"May I see?"

He smiled, openly pleased by her response to his small

piece of paradise. "I will give you the full tour before we take advantage of the pool."

"I would love that."

The walk to the waterfall was short.

It cascaded over an outcropping of rocks, splashing into a pool that looked at first glance like a natural body of water. Closer inspection revealed the tiled walls and base done in colors to emulate the dark brown silt found in a lake. Muted lighting glowed along the bottom to make swimming safe.

Bamboo loungers covered with thick cushions the color of caramel sat to one side of the pool. One looked like it could be used as a double bed, it was so wide.

"Fantastic," Audrey breathed.

Vincenzo took her hand. "There is more."

He led her along the meandering path to a wild garden of hibiscus, orchids and lilies in vibrant colors. A dining set that complemented the loungers by the pool sat in the center.

Audrey could imagine both very romantic and relaxed family meals shared here. "It's idyllic."

*"Sì."*

"Would it be possible to have lunch down here tomorrow with the children? I think they would enjoy it." The baby's highchair could easily be brought down.

"That is an excellent idea, *biddùzza*. Speak to Devon and he will see to it." Vincenzo tugged on Audrey's hand. "Come. We are not finished with our tour."

What more could there be?

The *more* turned out to be a grotto, its manmade cave walls covered in moss, the ground around the small bubbling pool spongy with it as well. More flowers and abundant foliage grew to either side of the cave opening.

"It's a hot tub?" she asked, tempted to skip the swimming altogether when she saw it.

"Yes, but we keep the temperature at ninety-eight degrees now that the children make use of the pool room."

"Pool paradise, more like."

"Even workaholics have to have their indulgences."

She grinned, looking around at the amazing underground jungle. "This is some indulgence."

"Are you ready for our swim?" Vincenzo asked.

After a last longing look at the hot tub grotto, Audrey nodded. "You bet."

The path looped around to come out on the other side of the pool from where they'd begun.

Vincenzo pressed something on the bark of a tree trunk and a small panel popped open. One of the *not* natural plant life, then. A moment later the bright daylight turned to the gentle orange glow of sunset. The bird sounds grew quieter and were joined by soothing music.

He hung his robe on a hook she hadn't noticed. The sight of the billionaire in European swim trunks was not for the faint of heart. The snug, dark fabric accented his incredible body and did nothing to hide an enviable endowment.

Audrey could not look away. "You're beautiful," she blurted out and wasn't even embarrassed by the proclamation.

There was no shame in such an inescapable truth.

He laughed, the sound strained, his eyes darkened with desire. "Men are not beautiful, *amore*."

"A masterpiece is beautiful, whatever the art form."

"You would compare me to a work of art?"

"What else?"

"A flesh-and-blood man who will not make it to the pool if you do not stop looking at me like that."

"We're going swimming." That was the plan, right?

*"Sì."* He put his hand out. "Now, come here, *biddùzza*. You can hang your robe with mine."

She walked toward him, not conscious of telling her

legs to move, and stopped a foot away, but made no effort to remove the robe.

His hands dropped to the tied sash, olive skin dark against the white, even in the softened light. "May I?"

"Yes." It came out a mere whisper, but he heard.

"You have nothing to fear, Audrey. It is just a swim."

"Is it?" she wondered, not really asking him.

He tugged the belt loose so the robe parted to reveal her T-shirt and swimsuit-clad body. Delighted masculine laughter made her smile.

He pushed the robe off her shoulders. "You decided to wear it?"

"My T-shirt?"

"*Sì*, your cotton armor."

She shrugged. "I don't wear bikinis. I never did. Not even when I was a teenager."

Humor continued to glow in his gaze, like he had a joke he wasn't sharing, but he didn't say anything more as he dealt with the robe. Her gaze skimmed his body—she could not help it—and snagged on the growing bulge in Vincenzo's trunks.

Whatever amused him was also turning him on.

In an unexpected explosion of movement Vincenzo ran and dove into the pool, barely making a splash on entry.

His head broke the surface, dark hair slicked to his skull with water, rivulets of it running down his face, neck and broad shoulders. He grinned at her, his expression less guarded than she'd ever seen it. "Are you coming in, Audrey?"

"Not *biddùzza?*" she teased, moving closer to the side of the pool, one small step at a time.

"Always you are beautiful. No more so than you will be in the pool in your T-shirt, I think."

She did not know what he found so eternally funny about her top. "Is it warm enough?"

"It is a very comfortable ninety-two degrees."

Warm enough for the children to swim comfortably. "Too warm for laps?"

"The heating system is on a schedule. The temperature begins dropping at midnight and is cool enough for exercise at five-thirty in the morning. The heater goes to a higher temperature at eight and it's comfortable enough for play by lunchtime."

"That's nice."

His mouth curved in a knowing smile. "*Sì*, but it will be even nicer when you are *in* the water."

She nodded, but made no move to slide out of her spa shoes and join him.

"Audrey?"

"Uh-huh?"

"Are you coming in?"

"I want to."

"So...?"

"What am I doing here?" she asked him.

"Swimming?"

"I mean, why me...not one of the other candidates?"

"No more meaningful discussions, *amore,* not right now. We are going to *play*."

She sighed. "Why do I think you don't mean Marco Polo?"

"We could play that if you like," he said, dark promise in his voice.

The image of Vincenzo reaching out to *find* Audrey after she called *Polo* burned into her brain. "Uh...maybe not."

"As you wish." But there was laughter lacing his tone.

And she liked that. Too much.

"Are there steps?" She looked around the pool and spied a handrail on the far side, near the waterfall, the top obscured by drooping vegetation.

Vincenzo moved toward the side where she stood and put his arms out in unmistakable invitation. "Jump, *amore,* I will catch you."

"I don't think that's a good idea." But she was slipping out of her shoes, wasn't she?

"You know you want to. You are not the cautious one."

No, she really wasn't. No matter how hard she tried to be "the responsible parent" for Toby's sake.

She jumped.

Vincenzo caught her with a carefree laugh that lodged in her heart, bringing their bodies together in the water.

She laid her hands on his wet shoulders, reveling in the feeling of powerful muscle beneath her fingers. "It *is* warm."

"I told you."

"You did."

"I will not lie to you, Audrey." His expression and tone said this wasn't part of the lighthearted play.

Or maybe it had not been play all along. Leaping into his arms had taken trust. Something Audrey did not easily extend to others. Not after her parents and Thad's betrayals.

"I know, Enzu."

"You trust too easily."

She laughed. "That just proves you can't read my mind. Believe me, I *don't*."

"Then I am honored."

"And I am wet."

*"Sì."* He looked down her body, the air around them suddenly, inexplicably crackling with sensual electricity. "Very much so. You are extremely tempting, *biddùzza.*"

"No more tempting than you." She didn't have to be experienced to know she wanted to do things with this man that did not include paddling through the water.

"I am very glad to hear you say so."

"Are you?"

*"Sì.* While my ardor is unmistakable and easy to see, I cannot be certain the tempting peaks of your nipples have drawn into tight buds from desire or the water."

"My…?" She glanced down between them and realized suddenly why he found her wearing the white T-shirt so amusing.

Neither it nor the bikini top hid her tingling nipples, but the T-shirt itself didn't hide anything else, either.

"White fabric goes transparent in the water," he pointed out unnecessarily.

"I knew that."

"But you forgot?"

"I wasn't thinking."

"I take it you never entered a wet T-shirt contest at university?"

"No! Barnard wasn't co-ed." And she never would have entered such a thing with her no more than average curves anyway.

"There is no competition now, just a very alluring woman in an extremely provocative swimming costume."

"I didn't mean to make it provocative."

"I think that might be what makes it even more so. Your innocence, the hidden body no longer hidden, wet fabric that keeps me from feeling silken skin." His words were a husky whisper against her ear and ended with his tongue flicking out to tease her.

Chills of sensation washed over her from that tiny touch.

"Do you like that?" he asked in a hushed tone.

"I don't know."

"Let's give it another test, then." This time he teased the shell of her ear before tugging on her lobe with gentle teeth and then placing hot, wet kisses to the super-sensitive spot behind it.

She groaned. "I like it."

A small huff of laughter sent air across the sensitized skin and left goosebumps in its wake. "You are very responsive, *amore.*"

"You are very practiced."

"No lover is exactly like another, believe me."

"You're trying to say it's different with me?" she asked in disbelief.

"*Sì.*"

She shook her head.

"Did we not just establish I would not lie to you?"

"But—"

"When I touch you, you are the only woman in my arms, the only one in my mind."

Her throat constricted with emotion and she could find no words to reply, so she did the one thing she knew that to this point she'd been good at.

She kissed him.

He allowed it for scant seconds before taking over the meshing of their mouths, claiming hers with his tongue. His taste melded with hers, creating an addictive flavor.

They moved through the water, but she could not be bothered to lift her head and see in what direction they went. She trusted her body to his care as she melted into the kiss.

Water receded against her skin, indicating that they were moving into the shallow end of the pool. And then he shifted and she felt a solid sloped surface against her back. The pool steps were flanked by foot-wide ramps that could be used for a steadying hand to enter the water and he must have laid her down on one.

He broke the kiss to lean up, away from her. "Let me have your T-shirt."

She didn't think about denying him. It wasn't as if the garment kept her modesty anyway. According to him, it was more exciting than if she'd simply left it off.

But he wanted it off now, and so did she. She craved the sensation of wet, naked skin against skin.

She took hold of her hem and began to peel the wet T-shirt from her body. He helped, his hands sliding against her skin. Whether by accident or design, she didn't care. Every little touch excited, making her need more.

He did something with her T-shirt and then put it down behind her.

"I want to touch you." His voice was thick with desire.

Unable to speak, she nodded.

His gaze burning into hers, he reached around behind her and undid the clasps on her bikini.

Her hands went of their own volition to her chest, holding the triangles of cloth in place. "What about your father? Will he come down here?"

"No."

"You're sure?"

"He does not have access."

"What about—?"

"*No one* will interrupt us."

"What if—?"

He placed one masculine finger against her lips. "Shhh. This is my sanctuary. No one will bother us, unless there is an emergency even Devon cannot handle."

"Is that your standing order for your time down here?"

"*Sì,* though I have a light on the access panel I can turn to green if I am merely looking to relax, not get away completely."

"It's not green right now."

"No, *amore,* it is most definitely red."

"Good." Mustering her courage, she let her hands fall away from her bikini top.

The wet fabric clung to her breasts.

Vincenzo's hands raised to hover a hair's breadth from touching. "May I?"

"Yes," she breathed.

He pulled the fabric away and tossed her top to the side of the pool, the blue fire of his gaze never breaking from hers. *"Molto bèdda."*

"You aren't looking." Air rushed over her wet skin, making her already tight nipples tingle and sending arrows of pleasures directly to her core.

"Aren't I?" he asked as his mouth drew closer to her own.

There was a message here, but she could not decipher it. Rather than trying to figure it out, she shifted her head so their lips met.

Vincenzo hummed in masculine approval as his arms came around her, his hands settling on her naked back. Her excited peaks brushed his hair-covered chest and she shivered in reaction to the cascade of sensation that caused.

He pressed their lips together more harshly than he'd ever done, his mouth possessive and insistent. The kiss was different than any they'd shared so far, and it required a response unlike any she'd given.

As demanding as the kiss was, there was also an element of seeking. Vincenzo wanted something from her and his sensual persistence indicated he was intent on getting it.

She didn't know what he needed. Permission? Sexual submission? The release of the reins she held so tightly on her own passion? For the first time in her life Audrey wanted to give him all of it.

Winding her arms around his neck, she melted into Vincenzo, determined to hold nothing back.

His growl of approval sent pleasure zinging through her. Trusting him completely in this, she didn't tense up as he tilted her back again.

Her nape settled against her T-shirt, her head comfortably held away from the hard slope she rested on. She vaguely realized in that small part of her brain still capable of logical thought that he'd rolled the wet cotton into a neck pillow.

The thoughtful provision for her comfort warmed her heart even as her body thrummed with sexual energy.

Vincenzo moved his mouth along her jaw, placing arousing kisses over her face and down her neck. Each caress of his lips felt like a brand, marking her as his.

A moment of chilling clarity washed over her. This

would change her forever. Vincenzo's lovemaking would ruin her for other men.

As if sensing the weight of her thoughts, he lifted his head, his handsome face set in stark lines of desire. "What is it, Audrey?"

No endearments. He wanted truth.

She couldn't have dissembled if she'd wanted to. "I won't be the same after tonight."

"No, *biddùzza,* you will not."

"No other man will touch me like you do." She didn't mean technique; she meant in her soul.

"No other men."

The harshness of his tone did not bother her. Though he didn't mean it as a long-term declaration, she still wallowed in the possessiveness of the words.

"There is only us."

"Yes," she agreed.

Without another word he lowered his head again, his tongue flicking out to trace her collarbone.

Audrey's entire body shuddered.

He slid his mouth down, kissing the top of her breast with suction that she knew would leave a mark. The thought of having proof of his touch on her body tomorrow made the flesh between her legs throb with pleasure and need.

The water lapped against her breasts, the waves caused by the movement of his body sending it over her nipples. Impossible to anticipate, each occasional caress of water over the highly sensitized flesh sent jolts of bliss through her.

Her hands scrabbled against the slick tile under her, but she couldn't find any purchase to ground herself.

Vincenzo leaned back, a dark smile curving his lips. "Will you trust me, Audrey?"

"I do." More than made sense.

The smile turned into something predatory, but there

was also an unexpected vulnerability in the depths of his blue eyes.

He took both her arms and pressed them over her head, wrapping his own fingers around hers so that one hand clasped her other wrist. "Keep them there."

Instead of anxiety, like she would have expected, peace settled over Audrey. Vincenzo expected nothing from her but her honest response to his touch. She did not have to wonder how to touch him, how to excite him.

His actions took the stress of her lack of experience away, leaving only desire behind. Unfettered by distress, her excitement broke over her in devastating waves.

He released her hands, clearly trusting her to keep them above her head. His fingers trailed down her arm and continued across her skin, leaving goosebumps of delight in their wake.

His hand stopped, fingers resting on her breast so lightly she shouldn't be able to feel them.

But the barely-there touch felt like each fingertip kissed her skin with fire, licks of pure sensation radiating around her aureole. He drew his fingers together, converging on her nipple.

A moan of pleasure snaked out of her throat.

"You are very sensitive to my touch." His fingers pressed more tightly on her peaked flesh, twisting gently. "I wonder how you will respond to my mouth."

Heat flushed her body at his words.

His head lowered tormentingly slowly toward her breast. Their gazes locked.

The sight of him touching her so intimately mixed with the physical sensation, increasing her pleasure nearly beyond what she could stand.

She arched toward him, but he laid his other hand on her stomach, gently pressing down. Audrey let her body relax.

Vincenzo smiled. "*Bene*. Good." His mouth finally covered her other nipple, his tongue flicking the tip before his teeth carefully worried it.

Audrey cried out, the sensation so intense it had to have an outlet.

His hand slid from her breast down her body until his fingertips rested against the top seam of her bikini bottoms. Vincenzo brushed his hand side to side, his fingertips slipping beneath the fabric.

"Enzu. Please..." She didn't know what exactly she was asking for.

Thad had touched her down there, but she'd never felt so desperate for *something*.

He lifted his head, catching her gaze. "You will trust me to take care of you."

"I will." She did.

Her body reverberated with need and something deep inside her told her he was the only one who could meet it.

His gaze warmed with approval that increased her desire as much as the touch of his hand on her body.

She licked her lips, tasting Vincenzo and the slightly salty water of the pool. He made a primitive sound of arousal and his mouth descended on hers, his kiss just as primal.

She responded with all of the sexual and emotional need surging through her, allowing him access, but using every technique of tongue-play she'd learned kissing this master of sensuality.

He touched her clitoris, a swipe and circle of his middle finger against swollen flesh that he repeated over and over again.

She squirmed, her body moving restlessly in the water, her thighs parting of their own volition, but somehow her hands never came down from above her head. Dark delight coiled inside her, tighter and tighter, until it was a compressed ball of energy in her womb. It sent little electric shocks directly to her core, making her most intimate place pulse.

She couldn't breathe, but she didn't want the kiss to end. Her heart was beating so fast she was getting lightheaded and she didn't care.

With a final swipe of his tongue, Vincenzo broke the kiss. He nuzzled her, placing open-mouthed kisses on her face.

His tongue drew a line up from first one temple to the corner of her eye and then the next.

"You cry with your pleasure," he whispered into her ear.

She didn't feel the tears, had none of the other indicators of crying, just drops of moisture leaking from her eyes. She hadn't even known they were there. "I'm sorry."

"No. You will not apologize for being so perfect. It is a rare woman who allows herself to feel so deeply when making love."

"How could anyone hold back from you?" Least of all a twenty-seven-year-old virgin.

"All that matters is that *you* do not."

"I can't."

"Then give your pleasure to me, *amore*. Come for me, now." The demand was whispered against her ear as a second finger joined the first against her clitoris, the double stimulation on either side of the bundle of nerves too much to deny.

She climaxed with a scream, her entire body arching against him, the sensual joy too intense too contain. He lightened his touch, but did not remove his fingers, pulling her through aftershocks that made her cry out and finally whimper with the surfeit of pleasure.

The whole time he whispered into her ear.

"*Bene*. Sweet Audrey, you did *so* well." And, as she floated on the euphoria following the cataclysm of her soul, "*Molto bèdda*. So very, very beautiful, my precious innocent."

She let her eyelids flutter closed, floating on a cloud of exultation, at peace in a way she had not been in all her adult life.

Vincenzo tugged her bikini bottoms off and Audrey let him without a murmur of protest. The sound of the wet fabric hitting the floor beside the pool told her he'd tossed the bottoms to join the top.

Strong arms slid under her back and knees and then water cascaded off her naked body as he lifted her from the water to rest against his solid chest.

His heartbeat was heavy and fast, his breathing rapid like he'd been for a run. Because he wasn't done yet. Not with her and not with his own pleasure.

A small secret smile curved her lips. *They were not done.*

He carried her to an extra-large lounger, laying her down on it before standing up.

She watched in sated expectation as he took off his trunks. His erection was dark with blood and so rigid the tip pointed upward.

Maybe it was her virgin sensibilities talking, but it looked like he had a loaded cannon between his legs. Thick and long, ready for action. The sight of him naked stole what was left of her breath.

Lassitude left her as excitement began thrumming through her blood again.

# CHAPTER ELEVEN

"YOU'RE BIG." SHE licked her lips, the tiniest flicker of worry lighting inside her. "Maybe I should have had my first time with someone less impressive."

"No," he growled out, his expression going from lustful to saturnine.

Oh, he did not like that idea. Not one bit.

"I didn't." She pointed out the obvious.

His jaw hardened, a slight tick indicating her comment had not tamed the savage beast. At all.

"You gave me your trust?"

"Yes."

"You will trust me not to hurt you?"

"First times hurt, Enzu." She wouldn't let him make a promise he could not keep.

"There are ways to mitigate that pain."

"A lot of experience dealing with a woman's virginity, have you?" she asked, irritation pricking the haze of pleasure in a way her anxiety had not.

"None, in fact."

"Then how would you know?"

"Really? *You* must ask this?"

Once again she felt he was laughing at something she did not understand.

"Yes, I must."

"Research."

Speechless, she stared at him with all the undeniable hero-worship she felt. *He'd researched how to make her first time best for her.*

She narrowed her eyes, an idea coming to her. "Recent research?"

"*Sì.* I had no reason in the past to concern myself with such things."

"Oh. That's really sweet."

His smile was as delicious as dessert, but without a bit of sugar in it. "*Sweet* is not a word to describe me, *amore,* believe me."

"I believe you." And she had no desire to have him feel the need to prove how *not sweet* he was.

The man was already overwhelming in his sensual mastery; she did not think she would survive him if he felt he had something to prove.

"Did you enjoy our time in the pool?" he asked, with every evidence of actually wanting her to answer.

"It wasn't beyond obvious?"

"I prefer a direct answer, *biddùzza.*"

"You have control issues. You know that, right?"

"I run a *Fortune 500* company and an international commercial bank. I would not get far if I was indecisive."

"It's more than that. You like having *major* control in the bedroom."

"Are you complaining?"

"No." How could she after the mind-blowing orgasm and its extended aftershocks he'd given her in the pool?

"So you enjoyed it?"

"Yes."

He nodded. "Good."

It occurred to her that maybe the control thing was part of him making her first time good for her. She blurted out the thought as soon as it was fully formed in her mind.

Vincenzo joined her on the double-wide lounger before replying to it. "That is a real consideration, yes."

"But it's not all of it, is it?"

"No. I am most satisfied when my partner cedes control to me during sex."

"You've had a lot of partners who did that for you?" she asked with irrational jealousy.

The man was thirty-six and had never claimed to be a monk.

"None who have given themselves so beautifully to me. You are something special, Audrey."

She liked hearing that a little too much.

Unsure if she really cared, but wanting to move away from the dangerous thoughts and emotions trying to form in her mind, she asked, "Do you ever allow your partners to take control?"

"I never have."

"Hmm." That was an interesting way to put it.

If he never wanted to, wouldn't he have just said *no?*

If intimacy could be this good all the time, she didn't think it mattered to her who appeared to be in charge. Because there was no question in her mind that Audrey's pleasure had driven every moment in the pool.

So, ultimately she had been the one in control. Not that she felt the need to point that out to him.

"It is possible I would be willing to explore things with you that I have not in the past," he said, shocking her into silence. "But I can make no promises."

"What about making love when no one is in charge?"

"Someone is always in control, Audrey, whether the participants acknowledge it or not."

"But some couples share that control."

He shrugged. "It is possible."

"You don't want to, though?"

"Not tonight." He pushed her back onto the lounger, kissing her swollen lips softly. "Tonight you have put yourself in my hands."

"Yes, I have."

"No regrets?"

She almost asked him again how he could possibly doubt that, but stopped herself. He wanted a direct answer. No chance for any misunderstanding between them. "None."

*"Bene."* He began to draw lines down her body with his fingertips. "I am going to touch you."

"Okay."

He smiled. "Close your eyes and feel, *amore*."

She did and he touched her. *Everywhere.* Alternating between soft skimming caresses and pressure that massaged muscles she hadn't realized were sore in her post-orgasmic bliss, he mapped every centimeter of her skin.

From the top of her head, which he massaged with adept, masculine fingers, making her moan in pleasure, to her toes, which he sucked one by one, sending carnal delight zinging up her legs directly to that place in between, to all spots in between, Vincenzo claimed her body with his fingers, lips and tongue.

She was vibrating with the need to climax again when he was done. The leaking tip of his sex said he was feeling the same ache for completion, but he did not move between her legs.

Instead he lay back, his blue gaze holding hers hostage. "Do you want to touch me?"

*"Yes."* Even more than she wanted that ultimate pleasure.

"You have ten minutes. You may touch me anywhere, any way you like." He waited a beat. "But you cannot make me come."

She nodded her understanding, reaching out immediately to caress his chest. She didn't worry that she should start somewhere else. He wanted her hands on his body and that was all that mattered.

He'd taken the pressure off needing to bring him to climax by ordering her not to do so. And he'd shown her that every inch of skin could be an erogenous zone.

All she had to do was follow her own desires and he would like it. She wasn't sure how she knew that, but it was an absolute certainty within her.

Maybe she was just too close to the edge sexually to stress about knowing *how* to do this right, but her lack of practical experience simply didn't matter right then.

She traced the lines of his face, letting her fingertips trail down his neck. "You are so handsome."

"Thank you, *bèdda*."

She shook her head. How could he thank her for the truth? She used her whole hands on his chest, rubbing her palms over the small brown disks with tiny hardened nubs in the center before mapping each line of his six-pack.

If she let herself touch his arousal she wouldn't touch anything else, so she skipped his pelvic area altogether and moved down his legs. She wanted to see if she could bring goosebumps to his flesh like he'd done with hers.

His olive skin did not pimple with sensation, but he shivered for her, his muscles jumping. She was pretty sure she was close to time when she bent over his weeping erection and licked the moisture drops right from the tip.

That got her a groan and the restless shifting of his hips.

She laved his entire shaft, returning again and again to the sweet, nearly clear fluid welling in his slit. She bathed him with her tongue, taking in his intimate flavor, breathing deeply of the male musk emanating from the heated skin.

She was so lost in her own pleasure at tasting him she did not register the hand gently pushing her head.

Not toward the masculine treasure, but away. "Your time is up, my Audrey."

She lifted her head, her eyes unfocused so that he was a blur for the seconds it took her pupils to contract. "Another time I want unlimited minutes to taste and touch you."

"Not tonight."

She inclined her head in agreement. She'd promised him her trust tonight. That she would follow his lead.

"Come here." He put his arms out in invitation.

She didn't hesitate, but dove for that embrace, her body landing on top of his. She kept her legs together, the disparity in their heights making his truly impressive erection settle in the seam of her thighs, just brushing the apex.

"You are delightfully sensual," he praised as he traced her lips with his fingertip.

"I'm not like this with anyone else." Never had been with Thad, and no other man had tempted her out of her self-imposed isolation into anything like this.

"Then it is a precious gift I will treasure."

The reminder that this was a test-drive for the job of his convenient wife flickered through her mind, but passion smothered it.

He rolled them, one strong thigh pressing hers apart.

Was it time? She was ready. More than ready. All trepidation at what was to come was drowned in the waves of bliss being touched by and touching him sent crashing through her body.

She allowed her body to soften under him, spreading her thighs to ease his access.

He leaned up, his hand reaching down to her moist intimate flesh and one finger slipping inside her very slick channel.

"You are very wet, *biddùzza*." There was a wealth of satisfaction in his voice.

She just hummed her pleasure at the very intimate touch.

He spread the wetness up over her swollen clitoris until all of the sensitized flesh between her thighs was slippery with the inescapable proof of her pleasure.

He shifted his body, adjusting their positions so the bulbous tip of his erection sat against her clitoris. Then he pressed down with his pelvis and thrust upward, causing his entire length to drag against her slick folds and pleasure center.

"What...? This isn't..." She couldn't finish a thought, not with him stimulating her most sensitive spot the way he was.

"This is exactly what I wish to do right now. I will make it very good for you. *Sì, amore?*"

"Yes." There could be no other answer.

He continued thrusting until she met him, movement for movement, pressing upward, the ball of pleasure building and centering inside her and then just hovering there, on the edge of bliss as he continued the maddening frottage.

"Please, Enzu! I need..." she begged, her body supplicating along with her words.

He thrust three more times, each glide of his hardened flesh against hers slower and conversely more powerful than the last.

Then he reared back, his hand going down, two fingers sliding inside her without warning, pressing deep.

She winced, her body jerking when they hit the barrier inside, but she told him, "Don't stop."

"I will not."

He massaged her inside, pressing inexorably against the thin membrane that protected her sexual innocence. His other hand slid up her thigh and he cupped her mound protectively. "Mine."

She nodded, her throat too tight and dry to speak.

He pressed his thumb against her clitoris, drawing tight circles over her aching nub.

Suddenly the pleasure inside her was acute, the climax that had hovered so close but just out of reach on the verge of exploding. Her body went rigid, every muscle contracting in anticipation of pleasure so big it would have frightened her with anyone else.

"Now, my Audrey. Come for me again," he instructed as his fingers thrust deep inside her.

Ecstasy detonated and fireworks went off inside her, making her womb contract and every nerve-ending in her body explode. This time she screamed so loud and long her throat was raw with it.

His fingers pressed through the barrier of her body. The pain was there, but unable to break through the astonishing pleasure for dominance of her senses.

He had taken her virginity, but kept his promise. Vincenzo had not lost control, his beautiful sex had not breached her body, stretching her and tearing through the fragile membrane with inevitable pain.

He knelt there, between her legs, and took himself in hand. Once, twice and then his face twisted in a rictus of ultimate delight while he ejaculated onto her body.

When he was done, he used the same hand he'd touched himself with to rub his seed into her skin like lotion. The look in his Mediterranean-blue eyes made the act one of primal claim-staking she was not even sure actual intercourse could have rivaled.

For tonight Audrey Miller belonged wholly to Vincenzo Tomasi. Full-stop.

They cuddled together in the warm humid air and she slid into a doze. Not sleeping deeply, but not fully alert, either. Tonight had been nothing like she could have ever expected or even dreamed about.

Maybe Toby had been right. Maybe Vincenzo was a superhero. He was certainly more man than any other she knew.

He woke her from dreams born of memories they'd made only that night with a kiss. "We must shower and return to our rooms to dress. Your brother will be arriving in less than hour."

Nothing else would have convinced her it was a good idea to leave the security of Vincenzo's arms. But at his words she forced herself to sit up, drawing away from him.

She shivered at the cold not touching him sent through her soul, despite their balmy environment.

He seemed to understand, putting his hand out to take hers. "Come, we will shower together."

She wasn't about to argue at the continued opportunity for closeness.

He led her to a shower tucked into an artfully arranged group of oversize leafy green plants between the pool and the grotto with the hot tub.

The hot water felt wonderful on muscles that were not used to the rictus of extended and multiple orgasms. Even more soothing were Vincenzo's hands as they lathered and washed her body, gentle between her legs as he rinsed away the smears of blood left behind by her torn barrier. He let her wash him as well, his semi-erect manhood growing into full hardness even though it had not been her intention to turn him on.

He laughed when she apologized. "Do not worry about it, *biddùzza*. We will arrange a night when I can lose myself in your body until we both pass out from exhaustion."

She gasped, a zing of desire sparking through her in response to his promise.

They donned their robes after they dried off, but Vincenzo tossed both of their suits with the used towels into a laundry bin.

He held her hand as they made their way in companionable silence along the path back to the sliding glass doors.

A happy yowl sounded, before two balls of fur streaked across the path only to collide into one mass of rolling, spotted fur.

Audrey yelped, but Vincenzo merely laughed. "Finally they decide to show themselves."

"What in the world are they?" she asked, her heart still lodged somewhere in her throat.

Vincenzo grinned, his expression more open and relaxed than she'd ever seen it. "They are ocicats—a feline similar in coloring to the ocelot, but smaller and fully domesticated."

"You have pets?" she asked in absolute shock.

"They were both damaged when their breeder's facility was broken into."

"Damaged? In what way?"

"I will show you." Vincenzo whistled like he would to a dog.

Strangely enough the cats stopped their play and came trotting over. One had only three legs; the other had an ear that had been torn and had healed with ragged edges.

Audrey dropped to her knees and put her hands out for the animals. "You poor lovelies. What are your names, hmm?"

"Spot lost his leg to a glass shard. It was either amputate or lose the cat. Rover's ear was either the result of his brethren's stress at the break-in or more glass. The breeders didn't know which."

"How awful. Dog's names, though?" she asked with teasing disbelief.

"Devon insisted." Vincenzo's lips twitched. "The ocicat is known for acting more canine than feline."

"Your majordomo found them?"

"He learned the breeders planned to euthanize them. Spot and Rover cannot be shown competitively and therefore could not be sold for the usual exorbitant rate. They had already been spayed in preparation for transferring ownership, so there was no hope of using them to breed."

"That's terrible."

"Devon agreed."

"You must have, too, to take on pets."

Vincenzo shrugged.

"They live down here?" she asked.

"They will not leave, though they have been given many opportunities to roam the rest of the house. They suffer a version of agoraphobia. The animal psychologist believes it is the result of their trauma during the break-in."

"You took them to an animal psychologist?" she asked, giving up the fight against loving this complicated man to bits.

If there had ever been a question that he would own her heart completely, there wasn't one any longer. She was head over heels.

"Devon had the psychologist come here."

Audrey laughed as she straightened, having made friends with the two ocicats. "Of course he did."

No wonder Vincenzo didn't keep any birds down here. Even a contained aviary wouldn't be safe against these two. "Are the cats the reason you don't allow your family down here?"

"It is not my entire family. Only my parents."

"Why keep this place from them?" Vincenzo gave so much to his family, even if he didn't recognize that fact. "That just seems so out of character for you."

The look he gave her was hooded. "Do not begin to think you know all that I am. At the most basic, I am ruthless and determined to have my own way."

"What does that have to do with your parents coming down here?"

"My mother would insist the temperature, which is perfectly modulated for the plant life, be changed, that the air be dehumidified. My father would use this place as a way to impress his playthings."

"He would bring his other women here? To your *home?*" Never mind just to the jungle paradise. That was sick—and not in the good way.

"His opportunistic gene is highly developed."

"You make me happier and happier that we opted out of dinner with your father."

Vincenzo nodded, but then sighed. "If you become a

permanent part of mine and the children's lives you will
have to learn to deal with my parents."

That tiny little *if* hurt in ways she didn't have the emotional stamina to examine right then. "Are the cats safe
with the children?" Audrey asked, needing to focus on
something other than that two-letter word.

"Spot and Rover are as affectionate as puppies. Devon
informs me that both children adore them, though Angilu
cannot chase them down like Franca."

"Devon informs you? *You* have never brought the children down here?"

Burnished color streaked Vincenzo's sharp cheekbones.
"No."

"Why not?"

"I did not know how." Vincenzo's jaw locked, his tall
body going rigid with tension.

The admission had not come easily.

"Enzu, even brilliant billionaire tycoons are not born
with an instant manual on how to be a parent."

"I had practice."

"How?"

"Pinu. He was ten years younger than me. Frances and
Giovannu had no interest in parenting. His nanny was not
a *warm* person. I held him when he cried, fed him, played
with him, taught him what I knew of family and life."

"You were a good brother." No wonder Vincenzo was
so determined to offer Franca and Angilu something more.

Again with the shrug. "But the world looks very different from the eyes of a thirty-six-year-old man than that
of a ten-year-old boy. What I felt qualified to do as a child
is more daunting than any business venture as an adult."

She reached up to brush a hand along his jaw and
brought her other hand up to his cheek. The familiar touch
drew their surroundings in until it was just the two of them.
"You are doing fine, Enzu. Franca and Angilu are thriving."

"Now they are."

"You cannot change what their life was like with their parents."

"No, I cannot." Pain laced his tone and guilt she did not understand dulled his gorgeous blue eyes.

"Enzu, give yourself a break. Do you have any idea how incredible it is that you turned out so responsible and caring, considering the way you were raised?" Considering just how badly he'd done in the parent gene pool.

He jerked his head away from her, moving back, the openness and relaxation from just moments ago completely gone. "Do not be fooled, Audrey. I do not deserve either accolade."

"How can you say that?"

"I knew. I knew and I did nothing about it."

"What did you know?"

"How like our parents Pinu had become, and still I left Franca in his care."

"She was *his* child."

"But at the very least I could have been a more involved part of her life."

Audrey could not argue that reality, but it wasn't right for Vincenzo to take it all on himself, either. "You trusted your brother to follow your example, not that of your parents."

"Why should I have been so blind? He followed their example in every other way." Vincenzo shook his head, self-disgust lacing every word. "Franca barely knew me when she became my child six months ago. I had only seen Angilu once, right after his birth."

She could have argued that Vincenzo had been busy earning a living for his entire family, his brother included, but Audrey thought it was more than that. "Maybe you stayed away because you couldn't stand to see the truth of how your brother had turned out."

"I am not a child, to hide from the truth."

"You're also not perfect, Enzu. No one is."

"I have no excuse."

"But you do have reasons and you're doing your best to make it right."

"Now that you are here I am making headway."

"What do you mean?"

"I have gotten to know the children more since you have come into their lives than I did in the first six months they lived in my home."

Well, that was because they hadn't actually lived with him. But she didn't say so. She had a feeling Vincenzo would just make that another guilt implement to flog himself with.

"Come. We cannot change the past and talking it to death is of benefit to no one."

"Enzu—"

"Your brother will be here soon," Vincenzo interrupted her. "Do you wish to meet him in your robe, with your hair a tangled mess on your head?"

"No. Definitely not."

"Then we had best hurry."

He did not take her hand again as they left the pool paradise.

# CHAPTER TWELVE

TOBY WAS RIGHT on time.

Audrey barely managed to get her hair brushed into a neat if wet ponytail and to put pajamas on under the robe before he arrived. He teased her about using the pool without him, but was easily placated by the promise they would be indulging the next day.

Toby and the children thoroughly enjoyed their afternoon in the pool paradise. Toby was as impressed by the indoor jungle as Audrey, and he fell in love with the ocicats, but he really shone with Franca and Angilu.

The baby adored the water and decided Toby was his favorite playmate in it.

Vincenzo emulated some of Toby's play with Angilu and seemed surprised but very happy when the baby responded just as well to him. All three of them had a blast together while Audrey and Franca worked on the little girl's ability to float.

Both children were going to have to have age-appropriate swimming lessons if they were going to live even part-time in a house with a pool. They might not have access to the pool room, but children got into places no one thought they could.

Or so the parenting books Audrey had read suggested.

They didn't see Giovannu Tomasi until dinner that evening.

"I do not understand why we are having dinner practically in the afternoon," he complained to Vincenzo.

"It is six-thirty in the evening, hardly the afternoon. I have explained my dinner hour has been shifted to accommodate the children, so we can eat together as a family before their early bedtime."

That had been one of Audrey's suggestions and it made her happy he'd taken it and was clearly so protective of the change in his schedule.

Giovannu frowned. "That can hardly be convenient with your business schedule."

"I make it work," Vincenzo said with thinning patience.

"You cannot neglect your business responsibilities in order to play happy families, Enzu."

Vincenzo grimaced and Audrey wanted to smack his father upside the head. "If you are very concerned, I am sure Enzu would appreciate you taking a more active role in running the bank," she said.

"As his most recent and hardly his last *lady-friend,* you are hardly in a position to have an opinion on the subject, Miss Miller," Giovannu said with a double dose of condescension.

Toby made a sound like steam escaping a boiling kettle, but Audrey shook her head at him. In a very real sense, Giovannu had a point.

"On the contrary. In our time together, Audrey has proved to have a better understanding of myself and my business than you have ever been capable of, Giovannu."

The ice in Vincenzo's tone would have frozen Audrey where she sat if it had been directed at her.

Giovannu simply waved his hand, as if dismissing Vincenzo's words. "I have a vested interest in the continued success of the bank and your company."

Vincenzo sat very erect, the blue gaze he directed at his father glacial. "First, let me be very clear, you have zero interest in *my* company. Neither you nor Frances will benefit financially, now or ever, from Tomasi Enterprises. Second, Audrey is absolutely right. If you are so worried about Tomasi Commercial Bank I will be happy to cede the presidency to you and you can run it into the ground for all I care."

Vincenzo gave his father a chilling star.

"But do not think I will step back in to bail you out. It *will not* happen. Third, you will treat any guest I have invited to my table with the utmost respect, or you will lose the privilege of being a guest in my home at all. Do we understand each other?"

Giovannu stood up, his expression one of affronted pride. "Perhaps it is time I returned to my own home. I expect better treatment from my son than this."

Vincenzo simply inclined his head. "Devon will arrange for someone to help you pack."

His son's agreement clearly shocked the older man. His mouth opened in slack-jawed disbelief.

It occurred to Audrey in that moment that Vincenzo had probably never stood up to his father like this. He'd made it clear that for the most part he practiced a live-and-let-live-with-an-allowance policy toward his parents.

Vincenzo was driven by his obligation and care toward his family. It would take a great deal to force him to show this ruthless side to those he felt responsible for.

She couldn't help the way it touched her heart he was defending her role so mercilessly.

Audrey looked around the table to see how the children and Toby were taking this altercation.

While Franca sent worried glances toward the men, plainly aware of the tension between them, the actual meaning of their discussion had gone over the child's head. She continued to eat her dinner while having a quiet conversation with Percy about the merits of fresh carrots with dip over the cooked ones on her plate.

Toby was busy playing with the baby, ignoring the argument to the point he'd deliberately turned his back toward Giovannu.

Audrey bit back a smile at her brother's silent message of disgust for the older man. She shifted her attention back to Vincenzo. His eyes were on her. His father was standing silent dumbfounded to his right.

She winked at Vincenzo. He jerked back as if startled, but then a smile started at his mouth and spread like sunrise to his oh-so-compelling blue eyes.

"That won't be necessary. There is no point in allowing a little tiff to drive a wedge between father and son," Giovannu said, as if he and Vincenzo were still engaged in active discussion. "However, I do think I will have my dinner later. This early epicurean hour does not agree with me."

Vincenzo just shrugged, his gaze never leaving Audrey. "If that is your wish."

"Yes, well…" Realizing no one was going to ask him to stay, Giovannu left.

Toby sent Vincenzo a look of understanding. "No offence, but I think your dad and mine went to the same school for jerkwads."

Vincenzo's bark of amusement exploded into full-blown laughter and soon the whole room was laughing. Even the baby and Franca, though the confusion on her tiny face said she didn't know *why* she was laughing.

Audrey, however, gasped out Toby's name in admonishment. "Language!" she prompted.

He grinned and nodded, but the look he shared with Vincenzo said neither male was particularly repentant.

She'd just arrived at her desk on Wednesday morning when Audrey's mobile made the sound of keys on a typewriter, indicating she had a text message.

Smiling, she grabbed the phone, and a small laugh fell from her lips as she read what it said.

R U packed? No PJs needed.

She hadn't seen Vincenzo since Sunday night, but he'd been texting her. Early morning "wake-up" messages right after her alarm went off. Quick reminders to eat, or take her breaks.

Apparently Vincenzo and Toby were texting buddies now, too, and Audrey's brother had ratted her out about skipping breakfast with her new early hours.

Vincenzo was a lot more fluent in textspeak than Audrey and sometimes she spent more time deciphering his messages than answering them.

She sent him pictures of Franca and Angilu from her afternoon visits with them. She shared little jokes about her day and was ridiculously pleased when he started doing the same with her.

The sexy texts had started Monday night, right around bedtime. One-word reminders of their time together on Saturday. Oblique promises of what was to come over the holiday.

Vincenzo had invited her and Toby to stay the four-day Thanksgiving weekend with him and the children at the mansion. Amazingly, the workaholic billionaire was taking almost the entire time off.

Hence his packed schedule leading up to it.

Audrey curled in the chair beside the window in her guestroom.

She was reading. Not watching for the arrival of Vincenzo's car in the drive below. Not.

Percy had arrived with the children in the afternoon. Audrey and Toby had driven up after she got off work. If she'd been thinking, she would have put off their arrival until the following morning.

But Toby had been so excited to return to the mansion and Vincenzo's indoor pool, not to mention the state-of-the-art workout facility. And maybe Audrey had hoped she would get to see Vincenzo.

He was supposed to arrive sometime tonight, after a video conference with one of his West Coast subsidiaries.

She'd had some vague idea about waiting up for him downstairs, until they had arrived and discovered that Giovannu Tomasi was still in residence. Not that he had joined her and the children for supper.

Giovannu had, however, asked Audrey to keep him company while he ate. Since she'd already helped Percy put Franca and Angilu to bed, Audrey had not had a ready excuse for turning him down. Mindful of what Vincenzo had said in regard to learning to deal with his parents, Audrey had realized she shouldn't make up one, either.

It had not been a pleasant hour, but Audrey had not walked away bleeding, either. Giovannu had begun by pouring on the charm, apparently genuinely under the impression that he was utterly irresistible to the opposite sex.

She'd shut him down in a way guaranteed to get her point across: by pretending not to even notice the flirting and responding to him as if he was a particularly trying older uncle.

She'd dropped unsubtle hints that she considered him too old to be seen in *that way*. And wasn't he lucky to have a wife of so many years? After all, many men of his advanced years faced a lack of companionship.

As she'd thought they would, her comments had fallen on the fertile ground of the true egoist's latent insecurities.

She'd looked into his break with his last mistress and discovered that the gossips were convinced the much younger woman had dropped him cold for a younger man with a less impressive financial portfolio.

Giovannu had shifted his approach in what Audrey had come to realize was an attempt to eject her from Vincenzo's life, even if she did not understand *why*.

She'd ignored the barbs, insinuations and blatant accusations that she was an unsophisticated nobody who had no place with a man like Vincenzo. Audrey had had twenty-one years of experience dealing with superior attitudes and verbal put-downs before her parents had cut her from their lives.

Giovannu Tomasi was merely a more spoiled example of the breed with a deeper sense of entitlement. Even if she hadn't known her relationship with Vincenzo was based on his plan to provide a loving mother to Franca and Angilu, Audrey would not have given Giovannu Tomasi the satisfaction of letting him get to her.

Infuriated by her unconcerned reaction, he had quit the field.

Audrey had thought she might take a swim to relax before bed, but had discovered quickly that the memories the jungle paradise evoked when she did not have the distraction of the children were going to be anything but calming.

It would have been different if Toby had joined her, but he'd taken his swim earlier and was indulging in a late-evening workout in Vincenzo's gym.

So Audrey had returned to her room, determined to read until she was settled enough to sleep. Now it had hit midnight and she'd read the same paragraph at least a dozen times before giving up on her book. So she simply sat.

Not waiting.

But definitely in no shape to sleep, either.

The sound of an approaching helicopter arrived scant seconds before its lights swept the front of the mansion as it headed to the helipad in the back.

Audrey surged to her feet. *Vincenzo had arrived.*

Uncaring that she wore only her favorite masculine-style black and white striped silk pajamas, she rushed for the door of her bedroom. She grabbed the matching black robe just before she exited the room.

Tugging it on and tying the sash haphazardly, she hurried down the corridor. She realized she'd left her slippers behind when her bare feet slapped against the cold marble of the staircase.

It was only as she reached the bottom of the steps that it occurred to Audrey she had no idea where to go from here.

"If I may, Miss Miller?" the majordomo spoke from Audrey's right.

"Oh, Devon. I'm so glad you're here. I thought I'd meet Mr. Tomasi, but…" She let her voice trail off with a shrug.

"Is he expecting you?"

"Um…no."

"I see."

"You do?"

The majordomo nodded. "You have no plans to meet Mr. Enzu, however, it is likely he is aware of your impulsive nature and may well be expecting you."

Audrey didn't even blush. Much. "Right."

"Come this way." Devon led her to a smaller, more warmly decorated version of the formal living room. "It is Mr. Enzu's habit to indulge in a single-malt whiskey in here before retiring to his suite when he arrives after the dinner hour."

"I'll wait for him here, then."

"That would be best," Devon said with a significant look to her unslippered feet.

Audrey's toes curled instinctively into the rich pile of the carpet. "Yes, well, um…"

Devon didn't seem to expect her to finish her thought as he lit the gas fireplace and poured a finger of amber liquid into a rock glass before placing it on a table by the chair nearest the fire.

"Would you like a nightcap?" he asked her.

"No, thank you." She'd had wine earlier and wasn't much of a drinker.

Devon inclined his head in acknowledgement. "I will leave you, then."

Audrey sat in the wingback chair nearest the door, her

feet tucked under her. The minutes dragged and she wondered if Vincenzo would forgo his drink tonight. Perhaps Devon hadn't thought to tell him she was waiting?

The sound of two masculine voices in tense conversation approached the opened door.

"I am very sorry to have to tell you, Enzu. But you must believe me. You are my son, after all. I care about you," Giovannu was saying, his smarmy voice doing a remarkable job of sounding sincere. "She made a pass at me."

"Did she?" Vincenzo asked, his tone so void of emotion Audrey had no clue what he was thinking.

Who had made a pass at that old letch? One of the maids? Audrey couldn't believe it. Devon wouldn't hire someone so lacking in taste.

"It was very upsetting, Enzu. There's a wild side to that little Miss Butter-Wouldn't-Melt-In-Her-Mouth. I'm ashamed to say I was tempted, Enzu. You know my weakness for aggressive younger women." He sounded ashamed, and so *concerned*.

Audrey wanted to puke. She had no doubts that, whatever poor female Giovannu was talking about, *she* hadn't been the aggressive one.

"Audrey tried to seduce you?" Enzu asked in that same dispassionate tone.

"No!" Audrey said forcefully at the same time Vincenzo's father claimed an affirmative.

That disgusting, deceitful *toad*.

She jumped up from the chair and stormed to the doorway, noting the expressions on both men's faces. Giovannu's showed shock before he quickly masked it with that fake troubled caring.

Vincenzo's gorgeous face showed no more emotion than his voice, his blue eyes entirely shuttered.

"You've got an amazing poker face," she told him.

The facade cracked with the tiniest fissure of barely-there amusement. "Do I?"

"What are you doing here? Dressed like that?" Giovannu indicated her PJs as if Audrey had come downstairs in a see-through negligee. "Do you see what I mean, Enzu? She couldn't have known you would be home. She was lying in wait for me."

Audrey stomped up to the older Tomasi and glared. "You are an ass." She crossed her arms over her chest. "And what's more you're an idiot if you don't think your son knows it."

"How dare you?" Giovannu drew himself up. "I am a Tomasi. You are nothing. A nobody."

"In that you are very wrong, Giovannu." Vincenzo gently pressed Audrey back so he stood between her and his father still in the hallway. "Audrey is my guest and I warned you what would happen if you disrespected my *invited* guests."

"Didn't you hear me? She tried to—"

"Seduce you?" Vincenzo laughed, the sound cold as the Arctic. "I do not think so."

"You are calling me a liar?" his father demanded in what sounded like genuine outrage. "You would take her word over mine?"

"In a heartbeat." Vincenzo lifted his phone to his ear, pressing a button. "Devon, arrange to have Giovannu's things packed. He will be leaving within the hour."

"What? You cannot kick me out of your house, Enzu. You are my son!"

"Keep saying it. Someday I might believe it means something to you." Vincenzo sounded tired.

"Of course it does. Your mother and I care about you. We care about our grandchildren."

"So much that you couldn't be bothered to even check in on Franca or Angilu once since they arrived this afternoon."

"*She* told you that!" Giovannu glared daggers at Audrey.

"Mrs. Percy told me." Vincenzo shook his head, an expression of disgust coming over his features. "Do you honestly believe I would put two innocent children in your care?"

What was he talking about? Giovannu didn't want to take care of his grandchildren. That was patently obvious.

"*If* I believed I could not do an adequate job of raising them," Vincenzo continued, "I would sooner put them in the care of our family in Sicily. You will never take control of Franca and Angilu, or the shares in the bank Pinu left them."

"Enzu—"

"Don't try to deny your plans. I've had my investigator looking into things. You and Frances have decided you want control of Pinu's wealth and you used the breakup of your latest affair to show up on my doorstep."

The disgust in Vincenzo's tone was mirrored in his expression.

"Only you're such a rotten parent model you didn't even know how to ingratiate yourself as potential caregivers. Let me give you a hint. Being on the outs with your wife over an extramarital affair and ignoring your grandchildren completely isn't even in the ballpark."

Audrey understood then. To Giovannu, the children were no more than the key to accessing more money for his profligate lifestyle.

"I am severely offended you would accuse me of wanting to take the children in some effort to control their inheritance. They deserve two parents, not one workaholic uncle who understands making money and nothing of the human condition."

And that explained why the man wanted Audrey gone. The argument held no water if Vincenzo was paying attention to the children, and in Giovannu's mind that was only happening because Audrey was around.

Vincenzo shook his head. "Coming from anyone else,

those words might hurt. From you? They are nothing more than the braying of the ass Audrey called you."

Giovannu made as if to come into the room, but Vincenzo blocked his entry. "Your things and your car will be leaving my property in…" he looked down at his watch. "…fifty-four minutes. If you do not leave with them, you will be walking, but you *will* leave."

Then Vincenzo shut the door on his astonished father before making a beeline for the drink Devon had poured. He tossed it back like a shot.

Audrey winced in sympathy for his throat and nasal passages. Expensive whiskey like that was not meant for shots.

"Do you want another?" she asked, though.

He shook his head and turned to face her. "You waited up for me."

"I wanted to see you."

"Was there something particular you needed?" he asked, in what she'd come to think of as his business voice.

"At the risk of providing fodder for your father's fantasies of my *aggressive sexual behavior,* I was sort of hoping for a kiss good-night."

"Is that *all* you were hoping for, *biddùzza?*"

"Tonight?" She nodded. "Tomorrow is Thanksgiving and I have to be up early to cook."

"I do have a chef on staff."

"Yes, but he doesn't know how to make Toby's favorite sweet potato pecan pie. And I'm not giving up my recipe for stuffing, so that means I make it."

"You are serious about this? You are not teasing me?"

Audrey shook her head. "Some things have to be done out of love. Holiday food is one of them."

"So, stuffing and pie?"

"And maybe a green-bean almond casserole. Danny's mom loves it."

"So they agreed to come for dinner?"

"Yes. Thanks for inviting them." When Toby had told

Vincenzo that he and Audrey had a tradition of sharing Thanksgiving with Danny's family, her billionaire had insisted they be included in tomorrow's festivities as well.

"Danny will be staying the rest of the weekend, too. According to Toby, both boys are *'totally psyched.'*"

"Toby told his friend about the indoor pool?"

"And your gym. Apparently it's *sick*." She grinned.

"I am glad it passes the teenager test of worthiness."

Audrey walked over to Vincenzo and laid her hand on his arm. "I'm sorry about your dad."

"You have nothing to apologize for."

"You never believed him for a moment. About me making a pass at him."

"Even if I had not known how little regard you have for my father after last weekend's visit, I am in the premier position to judge the likelihood of you behaving aggressively sexually."

"Yes? I think I could become aggressive with you."

"That is good to know."

"Is it?"

"*Sì.*"

"What about the control thing?"

Suddenly it was his hands on her arms, and she was standing so close she could feel Vincenzo's heat.

"What *about* the control thing?" he asked in that darkly seductive voice she'd heard so much of on Saturday night.

She tilted her head back, her lips parting as she tried to think of what to say, but she could not remember what they were talking about.

His kiss was full of promise, heated desire and *restraint*. Vincenzo ended it much too quickly. "Any more of that and you won't be leaving my bed until Thanksgiving dinner tomorrow."

She nodded and then shook her head, seriously discombobulated.

He laughed softly, the frustration of dealing with his

father no longer etched so deeply into his expression. "I will walk you to your room." He kissed her again, outside her door, and then smiled down at her. "I like your pajamas, by the way."

"They're not sexy."

"Define sexy."

"You know."

"I do know. You have me hard and seriously tempted to ignore your need to rise early to show your love for your family through cooking. Definitely sexy."

She was smiling when she closed her door with Vincenzo on the other side.

# CHAPTER THIRTEEN

VINCENZO HAD NEVER experienced a family Thanksgiving dinner like the one Audrey orchestrated.

He'd worked this holiday and pretty much every other one each year since taking his first job at the bank. The American branch of the Tomasi family did not *do* traditional holidays.

He'd had to take a call from Europe early that morning, but the rest of the day was clear and Enzu enjoyed it. Audrey and Toby's friends were a warm and boisterous family, the love between parents and children obvious and genuine.

They were all relaxing in the living room now that they'd eaten their feast. Danny's youngest sister and Audrey were playing with Lego on the floor with Franca. The teen's mother cradled a sleeping Angilu in her arms while the remaining children and their father played Monopoly.

Enzu didn't even know he had board games, but Devon had brought a stack of them on Audrey's request.

"She's a natural mom," Toby said as he sidled up to Enzu. "Audrey's got a nurturing streak as wide as the Grand Canyon and just as deep."

*"Sì?"* As if Enzu did not know.

It was one of the things he found most intriguing about Audrey Miller. She was so completely different than any woman of his acquaintance. Even Gloria, while an estimable PAA, could not be accused of being remotely family-centric.

"It's how I knew…" Toby let his voice trail off.

But Enzu thought he knew what the teen meant. "That you could go to her when your parents failed so spectacularly at their job of caring for you?"

"Yes." Toby's shoulders drooped and then he made a conscious effort to straighten them. "You know, I never looked at it as a failure on their part."

"Audrey didn't fail you, but they did."

"You're right. It cost her so much, though."

Vincenzo thought that was something Audrey would never count. "She's made it clear to me that she considers the cost worth it."

Toby shook his head. "I was just a kid, you know? I kept thinking they were going to change their mind and everything was going to be okay again."

"It was a reasonable expectation."

"Was it?" Toby asked.

"Audrey's actions should tell you how reasonable. She is a very good stick by which to measure sincere family behavior."

"She is, isn't she? I never want her to think her sacrifice has been wasted."

"It has not and I know she agrees with me."

"I'm just glad she's found you."

Vincenzo felt an odd sensation in the region of his heart. "Why?"

"I may not be going to MIT, like we dreamed, but I am going away to college." Toby had a very adult, very Audrey-like expression on his youthful face. "I didn't want to leave her alone."

"No?"

"She doesn't know it, but I applied to universities in New York, too. I've been accepted."

"I thought you and your friend planned to go to school in Massachusetts?"

"Not if it means leaving her on her own."

"You are a good man, Toby."

"Thanks. I think you are, too, Mr. Tomasi."

"Enzu."

"You sure? Audrey drilled polite behavior into me even more strictly than Mom and Dad used to."

"*Sì*. One day soon we may be brothers."

"You think?" Toby asked, excitement barely contained in his tone.

"I do, but you will not say anything to Audrey."

Vincenzo's decision was made, but he felt completely alien nerves about informing her of that fact.

"My lips are zipped." Toby made a zipping and locking gesture across his closed mouth.

Enzu grinned. "Good man."

Later that night, after the children were in bed and the extra dinner guests had left for home, Enzu surveyed the scene he had set with a critical eye.

Everything was ready for the final seduction of a very sensual virgin. Except one thing.

There were too many shadows cast by the clusters of candles on the tables on either side of his bed and the large chest of drawers against the wall. Enzu wanted to see more than their flickering radiance would afford when making love to his *biddùzza*.

He turned on the recessed ceiling lighting, adjusting it to a muted glow.

Better.

Audrey wouldn't even realize the luminescence from the multiple small flames had been augmented.

Casting a final glance at the king-sized bed piled high with pillows and covered with fresh crimson rose petals over the royal-blue silk sheet, he went to answer the soft knock on his suite's door.

Audrey stood on the other side, wearing her pajamas and robe from the night before. Her chocolate gaze reflected unmistakable trepidation and anticipation.

"You remembered slippers tonight," he said by way of a greeting as he stood back to allow her entrance to his personal sanctum, this one even more off-limits to others than his jungle paradise.

She nodded, making no move to come inside.

"Are you having second thoughts?"

Audrey shook her head, her lovely brown hair rippling and sliding against her robe.

He reached out and guided her inside, lust spiking in his belly from the simple touch of his hand against her silk-clad shoulder. She didn't balk but came without hesitation, despite her clear inability to take this step of her own volition.

Just as it had in the pool last week, her instinctual compliance intoxicated him more than the champagne waiting in the other room ever could. She gave herself so beautifully and completely to his desires. She ensnared him with bonds he could not hope to break.

And in her innocence she had no idea.

"I would like you to leave your slippers, robe and pajama bottoms here." He waited to see if she would comply, his atavistic instincts certain of her reaction even as logic insisted the connection between the two of them could not be that deep and elemental.

Against all rational expectation of her reaction, his words seemed to relax her as an undeniable air of tension surrounding Audrey bled away.

She toed off the ballet-style black slippers, managing to place them neatly to the side of the rose petals creating a path from his door, through the suite to the bed in the other room. She surprised him by removing the bottoms first, folding them and dropping them on top of the slippers.

When she went to untie her robe he reached out and gently took over the task without any previous plan to do so.

That lack of fore-planning should bother him. He *always* planned every action in the bedroom. His *control thing*, as Audrey called it, didn't just extend to his partners. Enzu demanded total restraint of himself.

Since his very first foray into sex Enzu had never once lost his self-mastery. Until the previous Saturday night, when he had kissed without thought and come within inches of burying himself inside Audrey's untried body.

It had been his knowledge that to do so would cause her unnecessary pain that stopped him, not his own willpower or plan.

"Enzu?" Audrey looked up at him with inquiry, but no mockery.

He'd lost himself in his thoughts and she was not amused by it, did not tease him about losing *control* of the situation.

"You are a very good match for me, *più amato*." The endearment slipped out, but he would not take it back. *Best beloved*.

He also had no intention of telling her what it meant if she asked.

She didn't, only observed, "Not on paper."

"Externals are not important Not here. Not between us."

"You don't think so?"

"No."

"We are almost polar opposites."

He slid her robe from her shoulders and then dropped it over the back of a nearby armchair. "Perhaps that is what we both need."

"Yes." She smiled, a mischievous light shining in her brown eyes. "I don't think you'd find it nearly as much fun with someone as bossy as you are."

He chuckled, but cupped her cheeks, making sure their gazes met and she could read the sincerity and challenge in his. "I do not believe you would enjoy yourself as much with an overly civilized partner, either."

"I'm not even sure I would have ever been open to another sexual partner," she admitted painfully.

"You have not been tempted in the past six years?"

She shook her head. "At first I was too hurt by the betrayal of the most important men in my life to trust anyone else enough to even go on a date."

"You were busy trying to keep a home together for you and Toby while finishing your schooling as well."

"Yes, but…" She swallowed, trying to turn her head from his gentle hold.

He would not let her. He sensed there was something important here he needed to know. "But what?"

"If I'd been open to it, I could have dated."

"You weren't." She'd already said so. "What is it you think is so important you need to hide it from me?"

Her eyes widened as if his insight shocked her. He almost laughed. Did she not realize he expended more effort reading her than he did his strongest business rival?

He thought back over their words, looking for a clue to what Audrey was trying to keep from him. "You said *at first*."

Fear skittered across her expression.

"What came next?" Had she had a bad experience?

"Toby started high school and he did really well, academically, socially—he was well-adjusted all around."

"And he needed you less?"

"Yes, so I thought I should maybe start dating."

His gut clenched. "What happened?"

"I saw you."

It was so far from what he'd expected to hear Enzu dropped his hold on her face. "What?"

"You were visiting the bank. I saw you in the hall." Clear discomfort colored her voice. "You turned to say something to Gloria and I saw your face full-on."

"There is a portrait of me in the lobby of the bank building." She had to have seen his face before that.

"Yes. I'd looked at it a lot. Only not really consciously, you know?"

"No, I do not know."

"No, I don't suppose you would." She turned away and went to one of the huge bouquets of crimson and white roses that he'd had flown in to fill his suite.

"Audrey..." he prompted, his tone letting her know he would not drop this.

She reached out and ran a fingertip over one velvet blossom before leaning over to inhale the fragrance of the perfectly open blooms.

Her action wasn't necessary. The heady perfume permeated the suite from sitting room to bathroom and the bedroom in between.

She was stalling.

"What did catching a glimpse of your employer have to do with your dating?" he asked, thinking a more specific question would get her talking again.

She turned back to face him, the picture she made in the silky pajama top that just brushed her upper thighs nearly making him forget their conversation all together.

"I didn't see my employer in that moment."

"That makes no sense." Even when she'd worked at the bank, as its president Enzu had ultimately been her employer.

"I saw a man."

Not for the first time in this woman's presence, Enzu found himself speechless.

"A man I wanted."

"That was four years ago."

"Yes."

"So you did not date in hopes of one day catching my eye?" he asked in disbelief.

"No. I *never* thought I'd come under your notice. But it didn't matter."

"Why not?"

"I *couldn't* generate interest in other men."

"Even though you knew there was no chance you would have me?"

"It was so stupid, and I was determined to break the pattern once Toby had gone away to university."

As illogical as it might be, Enzu did not like hearing that. "You were going to date?"

"I'd even created a profile on one of those online dating sites."

"That needs to be taken down immediately."

"I deleted it before it ever went public."

"Good." He did not examine the relief he felt at that assurance. "So, what you are saying is that you've had a *celebrity* crush on me for four years."

"You'd think so, wouldn't you?"

"What else could it be?"

"Love."

"What? You cannot love someone you do not know."

"No, you can't be in love with a stranger. But the spark of love can be ignited. You've fanned it into a raging flame since that first day in your office."

He crossed to her, putting both hands on her shoulders, his urge to kiss her strong. "You are saying that you love me?"

"Yes. Isn't it stupid?"

"I have no experience with the emotion, but I do not think it is *stupid*, no."

"You don't?"

"No." Perhaps these feelings she had for him explained how stunningly she gave herself to him.

"You don't mind?"

"That you love me?"

"Or that when I came to you the first time I obviously had ulterior motives for approaching you?"

"If not for Toby, would you have approached me otherwise?"

"No."

"Then your motives were as you described them. Your attraction to me made it possible to act on your desire to help your brother."

"And Franca and Angilu. I thought I could make a difference for them, too."

He nodded, believing that all too easily now he had gotten to know her.

Giving in to the urge that would not go away, he brushed Audrey's lips with his own, knowing he could not afford to deepen the kiss yet. "We are done with this, *sì?*"

Her eyes widened with distress. "With making love?"

"With talking." He shrugged off his own robe, letting it drop into a pile at his feet and giving Audrey an unblocked view of his arousal. "We have plans for tonight."

"You're very attached to your plans," she teased, but her voice was breathy and her gaze kept getting snagged on his erection.

"I am." Putting action to the sentiment, he led her back to the path of rose petals. "Come, we have many hours of pleasure ahead of us."

She licked her lips and then smiled. "No early morning tomorrow?"

"No." Mrs. Percy had already been warned not to expect him or Audrey to come for the children before lunchtime.

With the new game console Enzu had purchased for the game room, the teens had plenty to keep them occupied as well.

Enzu tugged Audrey along, the rose petals beneath their feet velvety soft against the deep plush pile of his suite's wall-to-wall carpeting.

Audrey gasped when they came into the bedroom.

He stopped and let her take in her surroundings before asking, "You like?"

"Very much. It's so…so romantic."

"A woman's first time comes only once."

"Yes, but…"

"You will never forget this night." He mentally shrugged off the arrogance he heard in his own tone.

She looked at him as if he'd lost his mind. "It could have happened in a broom closet and I wouldn't be able to forget it."

"Because you love me?" he found himself asking, when he'd had no intention of doing any such thing.

He clamped his jaw on any further unplanned verbalizations.

"And because you are my first." She didn't deny the love thing.

He poured them each a glass of champagne and handed Audrey hers before offering his glass for a toast.

"To first times."

The crystal clinked quietly, and then they both took a sip.

Audrey's eyes slid shut and she hummed before taking another sip. "This is very good."

"It is an excellent vintage from the South of France."

She laughed softly as her eyes met his again. "Of course."

"I thought a glass of wine would help your nerves." And if they were going to imbibe it would be something worth drinking.

"I'm not nervous."

The honesty of that statement was obvious in the sincerity of her tone, but also the relaxed lines of her body.

"Your trust in me is humbling." And very little made him feel that way.

"It feels right."

"Giving yourself to me?"

"Yes."

Because she loved him.

He let her take another sip of her champagne before removing her glass from unresisting fingers and placing both flutes, still partially full, back on the small table beside the bed.

"After tonight there is no going back. You understand this?" Their futures would be set.

For the first time anxiety flickered in her chocolate gaze. "Yes."

*"Bene."*

His kiss was intentional and deep.

Melting into him, she opened to his questing tongue without even a token resistance. Pleasure coursed through him. This woman was so perfectly matched to him sexually.

He would show her how right she was to trust him with her body so completely.

He let the kiss build until the need to touch her had become acute. What many did not understand in the type of lovemaking that excited Enzu the most was that he got as much satisfaction out of challenging his own control as that of his partner.

But the time to move things to the next step had come.

He allowed himself to caress her body through the silk of her pajama top, mapping her body's curves—the indent of her shoulderblades, the dip of her waist, the smooth outline of her hips, the soft expanse of her stomach, the gentle ridge of her ribcage, the pillowy curves of her breasts. He cupped them, squeezing and releasing until she made a restless movement with her hips.

Enzu moved on to tease her beaded nipples, sliding his fingers over the silky fabric covering them. He pinched them lightly, enjoying the way her pajama top encouraged his skin to slide off, and then repeating the maddeningly short touch again and again.

She moaned against his lips, the sound as exciting as if she had taken his rigid sex into her hand.

He ended the kiss, once again cupping her cheeks and forcing total focus between them. "I am going to take off your top now."

"Yes," she breathed.

He let his eyes warm with approval as he undid the first and second buttons in quick succession, caressing her breasts with the backs of his hands. The satin fell open to reveal smooth, creamy skin.

He leaned down and pressed sensual kisses to each gentle curve of her upper breasts. Letting his tongue flick out, he tasted the silken skin.

She gasped. *"Enzu."*

He undid another button, widening the gap in the fabric. It caught on the hard peaks and he let it stay there, teasing them both with her almost-nudity.

He dropped to his knees and nuzzled the fabric aside so he could take one raspberry bud into his mouth. Suckling, he teased the tip with his tongue while he skimmed his hands up the backs of her thighs to cup her naked buttocks.

Her hands landed on his shoulders, fingernails digging in hard enough that he knew he would have crescent-shaped marks there tomorrow.

"Please, Enzu, don't tease. I need you."

He lifted his head, giving her his most wicked smile. "You have only begun to need."

She shook her head. "No. You don't understand. I've wanted you so long."

"And you will have me, sweet Audrey. But in my time."

He waited until he saw acceptance in her expression. Willing her to remain still with his eyes, he finished taking her top off. It necessitated removing her hands from his shoulders, but he gave up one pleasure for the promise of a greater one.

She stood silent, still, completely exposed before him.

He had never been so turned on, and if he was not careful he would climax before he ever got inside her.

In an explosion of movement that made her cry out in surprise, he surged up and then lifted her into his arms. Showing her trust in him, she did not scramble to hold onto his neck, though both hands touched his chest, fingers splayed as if she sought to maximize the connection.

He laid her against the pile of pillows, stopping to enjoy the way the royal-blue silk set off her milky skin. Her hair fanned out over the pillow under her head in enticing disarray.

*"Molto bèdda,"* he praised.

"The view's not bad from here, either." She smiled up at him, eyes half-mast with sensual appreciation.

She did not resist when he guided her hands to grip the iron bars of his specially designed headboard, stretching her body and arching her back so her breasts were on tempting display.

With careful hands he arranged her legs so they were spread wide and bent at the knees, pillows placed strategically for her ease.

"Are you comfortable?" he asked, his throat tight with intense desire.

She was blushing like the innocent she was, but she nodded.

"Words, *biddùzza*. I need actual words."

"Yes, I'm comfortable."

*"Bene.* If you become uncomfortable you can move, or ask me to move you."

*"Ask* you to move me?" she inquired in a tone laced with confusion.

"There is great pleasure in leaving the responsibility of every element of your comfort and pleasure up to me, *amore."*

"It doesn't seem fair."

"If it is my own preference it is a fair exchange. Trust

for trustworthiness. Ceded control for beneficial restraint. Pleasure for equal pleasure."

"Yes," she breathed out.

As he knew she would.

Goosebumps were forming on his skin at how well they fit. If he'd believed in such things, he would have thought they were connected on a soul-deep level.

"Thank you," he said, breaking his own rule of not saying the words for something that felt so right.

Her expression said she remembered that injunction from Saturday, but she didn't remind him of it. And for the second time in less than a minute he experienced profound gratitude toward the woman in his bed.

This time he was able to hold back the words, though. He leaned to the side and reached out so he could tug a silver tray with four porcelain dipping bowls within easy reach.

"What's that?" she asked.

"I have two weaknesses," he admitted, instead of giving a direct answer.

"I didn't know you had any."

"*Sì*. Even a control freak like me has his vices."

"I bet you have more than two of those."

He was impressed she'd immediately recognized that the two were not mutually inclusive. Not all vices became weaknesses. And he did not consider one of his weaknesses a vice. Audrey was simply Audrey, a woman like no other.

"I won't take that bet."

Her gaze flicked to the tray and then back to him. "What are your weaknesses?"

"These dipping pots are filled with four different kinds of chocolate." Again he forbore from giving her a direct answer, but he was confident she would figure it out.

"You're a chocoholic." The laughter in her tone and merry eyes did not actually spill out.

"I am."

"Good to know."

"Is it?"

"I think so."

"I am going to indulge, but there is one catch."

"Yes?"

"I will indulge myself…and you…so long as you do not move from your current position. Once you move, whether it is letting go of the headboard or shifting your legs, I will know the time has come to press forward in tonight's activities."

"So, I can squirm? I just can't break position?" she asked, to clarify.

"Precisely." Did she understand the rest of what he'd said as well?

"You're giving me the power to decide when we stop playing."

"Mmm…" he said in approval.

"I get to say when the foreplay ends?" she asked, like she couldn't quite believe it.

"*Sì,* but when you are making that decision be aware you are cutting off one kind of pleasure, delight that can lead to many wonderful things, in order to pursue another."

# CHAPTER FOURTEEN

"You're a fiend." She did not sound like she was making a complaint.

He laughed, his amusement tinged with harsh desire. She would never know how close he'd come to forgetting the game and going straight to the copulating.

But she deserved to be seduced, not merely taken. No matter how much they would both enjoy the joining of their bodies when it came.

He dipped his finger in the milk chocolate and then painted her lips with it, grateful she'd washed away her makeup before coming to his room.

"It smells yummy."

"It will taste even better." He leaned down and gave her a chaste kiss, transferring the chocolate to his lips as well.

Then he deepened the kiss, licking chocolate from her and inviting her with his tongue to do the same to him. The kiss lasted until every bit of chocolate was gone and he was wallowing in a flavor that was pure Audrey.

Forcing himself not to get lost in sensation, he withdrew to dip his finger in the white chocolate this time. He painted her nipples, covered the aureoles completely.

He put his fingertip against her slightly parted lips. "Do you want to taste?"

In answer, she opened her mouth and took his finger

in, licking and sucking with a natural sensuality that sent more desire raging through him.

Lowering his head, he showed her he could play that game, too. First he gave each breast a tongue bath, knowing the soft caress would be enough to tantalize, but not enough to satisfy.

She moaned around his finger, the sound part frustration, part pleasure. That was when he set about suckling the rest of the sweetness from her already tasty nipples. When they were clean of the candy he nibbled each nipple in turn, worrying them with his teeth as Audrey started to squirm, her sounds growing increasingly desperate.

He continued to paint her body with the different flavors of chocolate, letting her taste each one, either from his finger or his lips.

She seemed to like the dark chocolate the best, so he used it on her inner thigh, moving steadily closer and closer to her private, enticing musk.

He didn't put any chocolate on her sex before he tasted it. Her feminine essence needed no enhancement to be entirely alluring. He laved her lips and then pressed his tongue inside her, loving the way her entire body went rigid at this most intimate of kisses.

He moved up so that he could tease her clitoris with his tongue, pressing two fingers inside her and curling upward to stimulate her G-spot.

She gave a strangled scream, pressing her pelvis upward and her clitoris harder against the rigid tip of his tongue.

"Enzu, if you don't stop, I'm going to…" She didn't finish the thought.

But he had no trouble understanding what she meant. Did she think her warning was an incentive to actually withdraw?

He already knew she was close because her clitoris had gotten swollen and shifted infinitesimally upward, indicating her body's primal sexual reaction to his ministrations.

Knowing the time had come, he reached up with his free hand to pinch her nipple and roll it between his thumb and forefinger.

She screamed, climaxing with a whole-body convulsion, her inner walls contracting around his fingers, moisture gushing forth to make her so silky-wet he knew he was going to slide into her like melted butter.

He kept licking, but softened his tongue so her pleasure was prolonged, but not amped to the point of pain.

Suddenly her hands came down and pulled on him. "Inside me. Please, I need you inside me, Enzu."

He reared up, triumphant and so very pleased with his *più amato*.

For the first time in his life he resented the need for a condom, but that did not stop him from putting one on.

"Sunday night."

"What?" he asked, with no idea what she meant.

"We can go without a condom Sunday night. I inserted a vaginal ring on Monday afternoon. The information on the ring said we only had to wait seven days for the birth control be effective."

Just the thought of making love to her without a condom almost had him exploding. He didn't bring up the usual tests that should be done before allowing unprotected sex. He knew she was free of anything because she'd never been with anyone else, and Enzu had not had sex since his last physical with blood tests and an all-clear.

"I will eagerly look forward to Sunday night." Even if he had to fly with her back to the city Monday morning in the helicopter and send the others back by car on Sunday night, she would be in his bed.

Placing the head of his erection against her hot, tight and extremely slick opening, he waited for that addictive gaze to meet his.

"Do it," she pleaded.

He pushed inside, going slow, but not stopping. She

stretched around him, her body flushing with the effort of taking him inside her completely.

He took his time with the first few thrusts, spreading her body's natural lubrication until the drag of her body against his sex was not quite so tight.

Calling on a lifetime of self-control, he proceeded to make love to her with long, slow strokes until it was obvious from the way her body moved beneath him and the sounds she was making that she was building back toward another climax.

He pressed first one and then her other leg straight, making her even tighter, making it possible with an adjustment of his hips and swiveling his pelvis on each downward thrust to stimulate her clitoris.

"Oh! Enzu, yes…that's…I can't…"

Her incoherent ramblings drove his lust to heights he'd never experienced and soon he was slamming in and out of her, his mouth claiming hers in a kiss that told her everything about what he was feeling.

If she was listening.

His balls drew tight and he knew he was going to come very soon. He broke the kiss and moved his mouth to her ear to demand, "Come with me, *più amato*. Now."

He swelled, going hard as steel, and then white-hot ecstasy exploded out of him. She turned her head, catching his lips in a desperate kiss as her body convulsed, her second orgasm ripping through them both.

She went completely boneless beneath him, her eyes shuttering closed. "Amazing," she slurred.

"*Sì*. Unlike anything else."

She nodded drunkenly and he smiled, though he barely had the strength to pull out of her and roll to his side. He would deal with the condom in a moment.

She reached out and he met her questing hand with his, lacing their fingers. His concept of life and himself was in a shambles around him, shattered by lovemaking that for the first time in his life had actually been that.

The prospect of having to admit that truth to himself, much less aloud to Audrey, made Enzu break out in a cold sweat right there in his thoroughly debauched bed.

Audrey lay awake in Enzu's arms in the early hours of the morning.

It was more than a month since their first time together, but Enzu had not officially told her she was his *chosen candidate*.

He hadn't mentioned any of the other candidates since before he'd blown her mind that first time in the pool, though. In fact, he hadn't mentioned the whole looking-for-a-wife-slash-mother-for-his-children thing since Thanksgiving.

She wasn't sure how she felt about that. Their lovemaking was hotter than an active volcano, even the times they didn't play any of his control games.

She didn't want to give that side of their lovemaking up, but she liked knowing it wasn't necessary for intense sexual satisfaction. That they could have completely tender sessions that culminated in a pleasure so profound it was a spiritual experience, not just physical and emotional.

She hadn't known sex could be like that, but then she hadn't known it could be so fun and kinky, either.

No, the sex definitely wasn't the problem. There *was* a problem, though. While Enzu and she continued to spend time together with the children daily, they spent almost no time alone that wasn't dedicated to sex.

He shut down any conversation that might actually lead to talking about feelings. And that worried her. Because her feelings just grew stronger and stronger.

She couldn't imagine he was even considering marrying anyone else, but why hadn't he made it official? Was he waiting for Christmas? Did he have plans to propose under the tree Christmas morning, or something?

Enzu did love his plans, but she almost laughed out loud at the idea regardless. She didn't think he had that kind of romance in him.

So, what was he waiting for?

"What has you thinking so hard, *biddùzza?*"

"How can you tell I'm thinking?"

"Your body is not lax as in sleep. You are not initiating sex, or talking. So…thinking."

She looked up at his beloved features, barely discernible in daybreak's shadows. His eyes met hers, but there was a wariness there she thought she'd glimpsed before.

"Have you made your decision?" she asked baldly.

His gaze flared with surprise and then that wariness again, before he pulled the emotionless mask she'd come to hate into place.

"Do we need to talk about this now?"

"I think we do." She pulled out of his arms and sat up.

He followed suit, increasing the distance between them in the bed. It was only inches, but it felt like a great chasm.

"I do not think there can be any question that our test of sexual compatibility has been a success, can there?" he asked, his tone stilted unlike anything she'd heard from him before.

She couldn't think about the oddness of his delivery. Not when the words were so painful to hear. "Is that all the last weeks have been? A test?"

She jumped out of the bed, searching for her robe. Needing the protection of a layer of clothing between them, she yanked it on and tied the belt with jerky movements.

"No, *più amato.* That is not what I meant." He was out of bed, too, but he stood there naked in the predawn light.

He'd called her that before, on rare occasions, and only when their lovemaking was particularly intense. Another time she would ask what it meant, but right now her heart was threatening to shatter.

"How do I believe you?" she demanded, pain bleeding into her voice. "We have amazing sex, but that's all you let us have. We don't spend any time together."

"We are together every day."

She refused to believe in the desperation her heart wanted to tell her was in his tone. "With the children. Not alone."

"We are alone now."

"For sex."

"We are not having sex right now. That I know how to do. This…" He gestured between them. "*Us*. Talking about feelings. I do not know how to do this."

"How can you say that? You're an adult, a brilliant man. You're fluent in two languages."

"But not the language of emotions."

"If you felt them you could talk about them." Tears choked her throat and she went to turn away.

She needed a shower. Something. Anything away from him.

"No!" The word was loud, filled with power and with anguish.

She turned back to him.

"When would I have learned?" he demanded, fury and pain right there for her to see.

"What do you mean? You don't *learn* to love. You just feel it. And you can't teach someone to love you."

If she could have, she would have. Because not having his love when hers all but consumed her hurt more than any other rejection in her life or even all of them combined.

"You once said we are opposites," Enzu replied, with a desperation she could not deny this time.

But neither did she understand it. "Yes."

"I am a tycoon in business."

"And I'm a low-level employee for your company," she

said, unsure where he was going but unable to deny the entreaty in his blue gaze. "Our financial inequality certainly brought us together."

He frowned. "You don't like that."

"I hate it."

"Has it occurred to you that there is very little a billionaire might need he could not buy for himself?"

She'd only finished her Christmas shopping for him the day before. She was well aware of that fact. "Yes," she said with blatant sarcasm. "I do know."

"So you should realize what a gift it is for you to give me someone on whom to spend that money."

Seriously? That was his argument? "You have Franca and Angilu now."

"And you will guide me in how best to use my fortune to make their lives the best they can be."

Was he saying he *had* made his choice?

"It has been my delight to introduce you to the pleasures of the flesh," Vincenzo offered. "Your innocence is another gift my money could not buy."

"I don't understand where you are going with this."

"Indulge me, please."

She couldn't deny him. "Okay."

"You are very impulsive."

"And you're so controlled sometimes I think you could be a robot."

He winced. "With everyone and everything but you. *You make me lose control.*"

"And that's significant?"

"Very much so."

"I love you," she said, realizing that maybe he needed the words as much as she did. She'd said them before, but she felt the need to repeat them now.

"There is where we are most dissimilar."

"Because you don't love me?" she asked, agony exploding inside her.

"Because you are driven by emotion. You understand it. You are conversant in it. Tell me, what do you believe drives me?"

"Success." But that wasn't the whole truth. "Your desire to take care of your family."

"Yes, and in those things I am fluent."

"I know."

"But tell me, *amore,* who in my life has loved me? Who has allowed me to love them?"

She opened her mouth to say the children, but stopped herself. He wasn't talking about right now. He was talking about for his whole life up until now.

"You loved Pinu." She knew he had. "You love your parents. You took care of them. You still do."

"Pinu did not want my protection or affection. Neither do my parents."

"I think you're wrong. I think Pinu was thankful for your love even if you never told him in words. And he loved you, too. He named your nephew after you."

"You really believe that?" The vulnerability in her billionaire's expression was hard to see.

"I do."

"You are certain you love me? It is not just sex? Or the knowledge I can make things easier for Toby?"

She didn't take offence at Vincenzo's words. She couldn't. He *wasn't* fluent in the language of emotion. In fact he was as inept as a first-year language student in a foreign country.

"Yes, I love you. Very much."

"How do you *know?*"

She gave that question the full consideration it deserved. He needed her answer in a way she could never have foreseen.

"Because being with you makes me happier than when we are apart," she said finally. "Because I crave your presence in my life. Your texts make me smile, every single time I get one."

"I like being able to text you."

She nodded. "I can tell. I know I love you because the thought of living the rest of my life without you hurts more than anything else ever has."

Tension drained out of his body like air escaping a balloon and the most beautiful smile came over his face. *"T'amu."*

"What does that mean?" she asked, thinking she knew but needing to be absolutely sure.

"I love you."

She wanted to throw herself at him, but she asked, "Why in Sicilian?" Was he still trying to deny it in some way?

"Because, despite where I was born, my heart is Sicilian. If I am going to speak in the language of my heart it will come out in Sicilian first."

"Oh." Tears very different from the ones before burned her eyes. "What does *più amato* mean?"

"Best beloved. You are *it* for me, Audrey. Now and for all time." He swept her into his arms and kissed her breathless, then whispered against her hair. *"Ti vugghiu bini.* I love you *very* much."

"Me, too, Enzu." She pulled back, taking his face in her hands like he so often did with her. "I love you with everything in me. To me, you are life."

"And to me, you make life worth living. You make it real."

Their lovemaking after that was world-shattering, leaving their separate lives annihilated, nothing left but what they were together.

Christmas morning dawned bright and cold, a layer of snow turning the world around the mansion into a winter wonderland.

Franca could barely decide what she wanted more: to

open gifts or go outside and make snowmen with Toby. Toby, still very much a kid at heart in some ways, convinced the little girl that gifts were definitely more fun.

Vincenzo insisted the children open their gifts first. Audrey wanted to see each of their reactions, though she suspected the baby would enjoy the paper more than what was wrapped in it, so she didn't argue.

Though she was eager to see what Vincenzo thought of his homemade truffles.

Toby's shout of shocked delight after opening a gift from Vincenzo was loud enough to burst eardrums.

"What in the world…?" Audrey asked, unable to imagine this reaction to anything she and Vincenzo had picked out for her brother.

"It's MIT, Audrey." Toby jumped up and hugged the stuffing out of Vincenzo. "Thank you, Enzu. Thank you." He broke away from Vincenzo and waved the paper at Audrey. "Read it!"

With a confused smile, she took the single sheet and started reading. Emotion welled with each word she read.

Vincenzo had started a scholarship fund for bright students who got accepted into top schools but did not have the funds to attend despite their drive and ability. The first recipient would be Toby's best friend Danny.

Toby had got something even more, though. He'd got Vincenzo's solemn promise that no matter what happened between him and Audrey, Vincenzo would send Toby to MIT and whatever graduate school and PhD program he wanted to follow. All schooling and living expenses to be taken care of on two conditions: an above-average grade point and no drug use of any kind.

So like Vincenzo to put stipulations for Toby's benefit on the offer.

Audrey turned to Vincenzo, the paper dropping from her hand, her heart so full it could burst. "Thank you."

"I want you to know that if you wish to attend graduate school for your master's degree you will have my full support as well."

So much for thinking she could not be a loving mother with interests outside the home. Vincenzo had made a sea change in his thinking. But love could do that.

"Thank you," she said again. "Maybe someday."

He dropped to his knees in front of her. "Do not thank me. This is pure self-interest."

Both Audrey and Toby made identical sounds of disbelief.

Vincenzo just smiled. "Believe me. I have a question to ask you, Audrey, but I need your answer to have nothing to do with what is best for Toby."

"Oh." Audrey put her hand to her mouth, the emotion too big to contain.

Vincenzo presented her with a small wrapped box. She peeled the paper away with trembling fingers. Vincenzo helped her open the ring box—not because she needed it, but because it just felt right.

So, his big hands over hers, they opened the small velvet box to reveal a ring set beautifully with a cluster of chocolate diamonds.

"Your favorite," she choked out with a laugh.

"Like your eyes. Chocolate and filled with light."

"Oh, man. You are determined to make me cry."

"More desperate for you to say *yes,* and mean it for the *right* reasons. I love you, Audrey, with the whole of my Sicilian and American heart. Will you do me the utmost honor and marry me?"

"Yes. I love you, too, Enzu. So, so much! Oh, yes. Always, yes, Enzu!"

Then they were kissing, and hers weren't the only tears adding salty moisture to their lips.

Toby was whooping in the background and then so was Franca, and even the baby started his adorable giggling.

They were a family.

# EPILOGUE

THEY WERE MARRIED on New Year's Eve, with Christmas décor still gracing the church, and Audrey carried a bouquet of crimson and white roses mixed with mistletoe and evergreen.

Toby said Vincenzo just wanted an excuse to kiss her whenever he wanted so the billionaire had supplied his own mistletoe. Vincenzo did not deny it, but he did manage to make Toby speechless when he asked the teen to sign the adult adoption papers that would make Toby a Tomasi.

"I'm not calling you Dad," Toby said, clearly overwhelmed with emotion.

"We are brothers, but you will be an official Tomasi and that is what matters. You belong to us."

Toby's grin split his face and he signed the papers with a flourish.

It was Audrey's turn to be speechless when a wedding guest who turned out to be a judge stepped forward to sign adoption papers for Franca and Angilu, officially making both Audrey and Vincenzo Tomasi their parents.

"How did you get the adoption through so fast?" Some legalities could only be expedited so much.

"I started proceedings the afternoon of your initial interview."

"What? How?"

"That non-disclosure agreement you signed?"

"Yes?"

"It may have included a power of attorney."

"You knew then?" she demanded.

He shrugged. "I had Gloria cancel the other candidates' interviews."

"You're a devious man, Enzu Tomasi, and in this case, I love you for it."

"I am so very glad to hear it, *più amato*. And you? You are my Christmas miracle."

She thought maybe that went both ways, but he was kissing her and she didn't get the chance to say so. She thought maybe he knew.

\* \* \* \* \*

# Not Just the Boss's Plaything

## Caitlin Crews

**Caitlin Crews** discovered her first romance novel at the age of twelve. It involved swashbuckling pirates, grand adventures, a heroine with rustling skirts and a mind of her own, and a seriously mouth-watering and masterful hero. The book (the title of which remains lost in the mists of time) made a serious impression. Caitlin was immediately smitten with romances and romance heroes, to the detriment of her middle-school social life. And so began her lifelong love affair with romance novels, many of which she insists on keeping near her at all times.

Caitlin has made her home in places as far-flung as York, England and Atlanta, Georgia. She was raised near New York City, and fell in love with London on her first visit when she was a teenager. She has backpacked in Zimbabwe, been on safari in Botswana and visited tiny villages in Namibia. She has, while visiting the place in question, declared her intention to live in Prague, Dublin, Paris, Athens, Nice, the Greek islands, Rome, Venice and/or any of the Hawaiian islands. Writing about exotic places seems like the next best thing to moving there.

She currently lives in California, with her animator/comic book artist husband and their menagerie of ridiculous animals.

To the fabulous Sharon Kendrick, who sorted out
what was wrong with an early draft of this book
on a long, rainy, Irish drive to and from Sligo
town (and an atmospheric tour of Yeats country)
—both of which amounted to a Master
Class in writing.

And to Abby Green, Heidi Rice, Fiona Harper
and Chantelle Shaw, for our inspiring
days in Delphi.

And to all the readers who wrote me to ask for
Nikolai's story. This is for you most of all!

# CHAPTER ONE

*TORTURE WOULD BE preferable to this.*

Nikolai Korovin moved through the crowd ruthlessly, with a deep distaste for his surroundings he made no effort to hide. The club was one of London's sleekest and hottest, according to his assistants, and was therefore teeming with the famous, the trendy and the stylish.

All of whom appeared to have turned up tonight. In their slick, hectic glory, such as it was. It meant Veronika, with all her aspirations to grandeur, couldn't be far behind.

"Fancy a drink?" a blank-eyed creature with masses of shiny black hair and plumped-up lips lisped at him, slumping against him in a manner he imagined was designed to entice him. It failed. "Or anything else? Anything at all?"

Nikolai waited impatiently for her to stop that insipid giggling, to look away from his chest and find her way to his face—and when she did, as expected, she paled. As if she'd grabbed hold of the devil himself.

She had.

He didn't have to say a word. She dropped her hold on him immediately, and he forgot her the moment she slunk from his sight.

After a circuit or two around the loud and heaving club, his eyes moving from one person to the next as they propped up the shiny bar or clustered around the leather seating areas, cataloging each and dismissing them, Nikolai stood with his back to one of the giant speakers and simply waited. The music, if it could be called that, blasted out a bass line he could feel reverberate low in his spine as if he was under sustained attack by a series of concussion grenades. He almost wished he was.

He muttered something baleful in his native Russian, but it was swept away in the deep, hard thump and roll of that terrible bass. *Torture.*

Nikolai hated this place, and all the places like it he'd visited since he'd started this tiresome little quest of his. He hated the spectacle. He hated the waste. Veronika, of course, would love it—that she'd be *seen* in such a place, in such company.

*Veronika.* His ex-wife's name slithered in his head like the snake she'd always been, reminding him why he was subjecting himself to this.

Nikolai wanted the truth, finally. She was the one loose end he had left, and he wanted nothing more than to cut it off, once and for all. Then she could fall from the face of the planet for all he cared.

"I never loved you," Veronika had said, a long cigarette in her hand, her lips painted red like blood and all of her bags already packed. "I've never been faithful to you except by accident." Then she'd smiled, to remind him that she'd always been the same as him, one way or another: a weapon hidden in plain sight. "Needless to say, Stefan isn't yours. What sane woman would have *your* child?"

Nikolai had eventually sobered up and understood that whatever pain he'd felt had come from the surprise of Veronika's departure, not the content of her farewell speech. Because he knew who he was. He knew *what* he was.

And he knew her.

These days, his avaricious ex-wife's tastes ran to lavish

Eurotrash parties wherever they were thrown, from Berlin to Mauritius, and the well-manicured, smooth-handed rich men who attended such events in droves—but Nikolai knew she was in London now. His time in the Russian Special Forces had taught him many things, much of which remained etched deep into that cold, hard stone where his heart had never been, and finding a woman with high ambitions and very low standards like Veronika? Child's play.

It had taken very little effort to discover that she was shacking up with her usual type in what amounted to a fortress in Mayfair: some dissipated son of a too-wealthy sheikh with an extensive and deeply bored security force, the dismantling of which would no doubt be as easy for Nikolai as it was entertaining—but would also, regrettably, cause an international incident.

Because Nikolai wasn't a soldier any longer. He was no longer the Spetsnaz operative who could do whatever it took to achieve his goals—with a deadly accuracy that had won him a healthy respect that bordered on fear from peers and enemies alike. He'd shed those skins, if not what lay beneath them like sinew fused to steel, seven years ago now.

And yet because his life was nothing but an exercise in irony, he'd since become a philanthropist, an internationally renowned wolf in the ill-fitting clothes of a very soft, very fluffy sheep. He ran the Korovin Foundation, the charity he and his brother, Ivan, had begun after Ivan's retirement from Hollywood action films. Nikolai tended to Ivan's fortune and had amassed one of his own thanks to his innate facility with investment strategies. And he was lauded far and near as a man of great compassion and caring, despite the obvious ruthlessness he did nothing to hide.

People believed what they wanted to believe. Nikolai knew that better than most.

He'd grown up hard in post-Soviet Russia, where brutal

oligarchs were thick on the ground and warlords fought over territory like starving dogs—making him particularly good at targeting excessively wealthy men and the corporations they loved more than their own families, then talking them out of their money. He knew them. He understood them. They called it a kind of magic, his ability to wrest huge donations from the most reluctant and wealthiest of donors, but Nikolai saw it as simply one more form of warfare.

And he had always been so very good at war. It was his one true art.

But his regrettably high profile these days meant he was no longer the kind of man who could break into a sheikh's son's London stronghold and expect that to fly beneath the radar. Billionaire philanthropists with celebrity brothers, it turned out, had to follow rules that elite, highly trained soldiers did not. They were expected to use diplomacy and charm.

And if such things were too much of a reach when it concerned an ex-wife rather than a large donation, they were forced to subject themselves to London's gauntlet of "hot spots" and *wait*.

Nikolai checked an impatient sigh, ignoring the squealing trio of underdressed teenagers who leaped up and down in front of him, their eyes dulled with drink, drugs and their own craven self-importance. Lights flashed frenetically, the awful music howled and he monitored the crowd from his strategic position in the shadows of the dance floor.

He simply had to wait for Veronika to show herself, as he knew she would.

Then he would find out how much of what she'd said seven years ago had been spite, designed to hurt him as much as possible, and how much had been truth. Nikolai knew that on some level, he'd never wanted to know. If he never pressed the issue, then it was always possible that Stefan really *was* his, as Veronika had made him believe for the first five years of the boy's life. That somewhere out there, he had a son. That he had done something right, even if it was by accident.

But such fantasies made him weak, he knew, and he could no longer tolerate it. He wanted a DNA test to prove that Stefan wasn't his. Then he would be done with his weaknesses, once and for all.

"You need to go and fix your life," his brother, Ivan, the only person alive that Nikolai still cared about, the only one who knew what they'd suffered at their uncle's hands in those grim years after their parents had died in a factory fire, had told him just over two years ago. Then he'd stared at Nikolai as if he was a stranger and walked away from him as if he was even less than that.

It was the last time they'd spoken in person, or about anything other than the Korovin Foundation.

Nikolai didn't blame his older brother for this betrayal. He'd watched Ivan's slide into his inevitable madness as it happened. He knew that Ivan was sadly deluded—blinded by sex and emotion, desperate to believe in things that didn't exist because it was far better than the grim alternative of reality. How could he blame Ivan for preferring the delusion? Most people did.

Nikolai didn't have that luxury.

Emotions were liabilities. Lies. Nikolai believed in sex and money. No ties, no temptations. No relationships now his brother had turned his back on him. No possibility that any of the women he took to his bed—always nameless, faceless and only permitted near him if they agreed to adhere to a very strict set of requirements—would ever reach him.

In order to be betrayed, one first had to trust.

And the only person Nikolai had trusted in his life was Ivan and even then, only in a very qualified way once that woman had sunk her claws in him.

But ultimately, this was a gift. It freed him, finally, from his last remaining emotional prison. It made everything simple. Because he had never known how to tell Ivan—who had built a life out of playing the hero in the fighting ring and on the screen, who was able to embody those fights he'd won and the roles he'd played with all the self-righteous fury of the untainted, the unbroken, the *good*—that there were some things that couldn't be fixed.

Nikolai wished he was something so simple as *broken*.

He acted like a man, but was never at risk of becoming one. He'd need flesh and blood, heat and heart for that, and those were the things he'd sold off years ago to make himself into the perfect monster. A killing machine.

Nikolai knew exactly what he was: a bright and shining piece of ice with no hope of warmth, frozen too solid for any sun to penetrate the chill. A hard and deadly weapon, honed to lethal perfection beneath his uncle's fists, then sharpened anew in the bloody Spetsnaz brotherhood. To say nothing of the dark war games he'd learned he could make into his own kind of terrible poetry, despite what it took from him in return.

He was empty where it counted, down to his bones. Empty all the way through. It was why he was so good at what he did.

And it was safer, Nikolai thought now, his eyes on the heedless, hedonistic crowd. There was too much to lose should he relinquish that deep freeze, give up that iron control. What he remembered of his drinking years appalled him—the blurred nights, the scraps and pieces of too much frustrated emotion turned too quickly into violence, making him far too much like the brutal uncle he'd so despised.

*Never again.*

It was better by far to stay empty. Cold. Frozen straight through.

He had never been anything but alone. Nikolai understood that now. The truth was, he preferred it that way. And once he dealt with Veronika, once he confirmed the truth about Stefan's paternity, he would never have to be anything else.

Alicia Teller ran out of patience with a sudden jolt, a wave of exhaustion and irritation nearly taking her from her feet in the midst of the jostling crowd. Or possibly that was the laddish group to her left, all of them obviously deep into the night's drinking and therefore flailing around the dance floor.

*I'm much too old for this,* she told herself as she moved out of their way for the tenth time, feeling ancient and decrepit at her extraordinarily advanced age of twenty-nine.

She couldn't remember the last time she'd spent a Saturday night anywhere more exciting than a quiet restaurant with friends, much less in a slick, pretentious club that had recently been dubbed *the* place to be seen in London. But then again, she also didn't like to look a gift horse in the mouth—said gift horse, in this case, being her ever-exuberant best friend and flatmate Rosie, who'd presented the guest passes to this velvet-roped circus with a grand flourish over dinner.

"It's the coolest place in London right now," she'd confidently assured Alicia over plates of *saag paneer* in their favorite Indian restaurant not far from Brick Lane. "Dripping with celebrities and therefore every attractive man in London."

"I am not cool, Rosie," Alicia had reminded her gently. "You've said so yourself for years. Every single time you try to drag me to yet another club you claim will change my life, if memory serves. It might be time for you to accept the possibility that this is who I am."

"Never!" Rosie had cried at once, feigning shock and outrage. "I remember when you were *fun,* Alicia. I've made a solemn vow to corrupt you, no matter how long it takes!"

"I'm incorruptible," Alicia had assured her. Because she also remembered when she'd been *fun,* and she had no desire to repeat those terrible mistakes, thank you, much less that descent into shame and heartache. "I'm also very likely to embarrass you. Can you handle the shame?"

Rosie had rolled her extravagantly mascaraed and shimmery-purple shadowed eyes while tossing the last of the poppadoms into her mouth.

"I can handle it," she'd said. "Anything to remind you that you're in your twenties, not your sixties. I consider it a public service."

"You say that," Alicia had teased her, "but you should be prepared for me to request 'Dancing Queen' as if we're at a wedding disco. From the no doubt world-renowned and tragically hip DJ who will faint dead away at the insult."

"Trust me, Alicia," Rosie had said then, very seriously. "This is going to be the best night of our lives."

Now Alicia watched her best friend shake her hips in a sultry come-on to the investment banker she'd been flirting with all night, and blamed the jet lag. Nothing else could have made her forget for even a moment that sparkly, dramatic still Rosie viewed it as her sacred obligation to pull on a weekend night, the way they both had when they were younger and infinitely wilder, and that meant the exorbitant taxi fare back home from the wilds of this part of East London to the flat they shared on the outskirts of Hammersmith would be Alicia's to cough up. Alone.

"You know what you need?" Rosie had asked on the

chilly trek over from the Tube, right on cue. "Desperately, I might add?"

"I know what *you* think I need, yes," Alicia had replied dryly. "But for some reason, the fantasy of sloppy and unsatisfying sex with some stranger from a club pales in comparison to the idea of getting a good night's sleep all alone in my own bed. Call me crazy. Or, barring that, *a grown-up.*"

"You're never going to find anyone, you know," Rosie had told her then, frowning. "Not if you keep this up. What's next, a nunnery?"

But Alicia knew exactly what kind of people it was possible to meet in the clubs Rosie preferred. She'd met too many of them. She'd *been* one of them throughout her university years. And she'd vowed that she would never, ever let herself get so out of control again. It wasn't worth the price—and sooner or later, there was always a price. In her case, all the years it had taken her to get her father to look at her again.

Alicia had been every inch a Daddy's girl until that terrible night the summer she'd been twenty-one. She'd been indulged and spoiled and adored beyond measure, the light of his life, and she'd lost that forever on a single night she still couldn't piece together in her head. But she knew the details almost as if she could remember it herself, because she'd had to sit and listen to her own father tell them to her the next morning while her head had pounded and her stomach had heaved: she'd been so drunk she'd been practically paralytic when she'd come home that night, but at some point she'd apparently wandered out into the back garden—which was where her father had found her, having sex with Mr. Reddick from next door.

Married Mr. Reddick, with three kids Alicia had babysat over the years, who'd been good mates with her dad until that night. The shame of it was still scarlet in her, bright and horrid, all these years later. How could she have done such a vile, despicable thing? She still didn't know.

Afterward, she'd decided that she'd had more than enough *fun* for one lifetime.

"Sorry," Alicia had said to Rosie then, smiling the painful memories away. "Are you talking about love? I was certain we were talking about the particular desperation of a Saturday night shag...."

"I have a radical idea, Saint Alicia," Rosie had said then with another roll of her eyes toward the dark sky above. "Why don't you put the halo aside for the night? It won't kill you, I promise. You might even find you like a little debauchery on a Saturday night the way you used to do."

Because Rosie didn't know, of course. Nobody knew. Alicia had been too embarrassed, too ashamed, too *disgusted* with herself to tell her friend—to tell anyone— why she'd abruptly stopped going out at the weekend, why she'd thrown herself into the job she hadn't taken seriously until then and turned it into a career she took a great deal of pride in now. Even her mother and sisters didn't know why there had been that sudden deep chill between Alicia and her dad, that had now, years later, only marginally improved into a polite distance.

"I'm not wearing my halo tonight, actually," Alicia had replied primly, patting at her riot of curls as if feeling for one anyway. "It clashed with these shoes you made me wear."

"Idiot," Rosie had said fondly, and then she'd brandished those guest passes and swept them past the crowd outside on the pavement, straight into the clutches of London's hottest club of the moment.

And Alicia had enjoyed herself—more than she'd expected she would, in fact. She'd missed dancing. She'd missed the excitement in the air, the buzz of such a big crowd. The particular, sensual seduction of a good beat. But Rosie's version of fun went on long into the night, the way it always had, and Alicia grew tired too easily. Especially when she'd only flown back into the country the day before, and her body still believed it was in another time zone altogether.

And more, when she wasn't sure she could trust herself. She didn't know what had made her do what she'd done that terrible night eight years ago; she couldn't remember much of it. So she'd opted to avoid anything and everything that might lead down that road—which was easier to do when she wasn't standing in the midst of so much cheerful abandon. Because she didn't have a halo—God knows, she'd proved that with her whorish behavior—she only wished she did.

*You knew what this would be like,* she thought briskly now, not bothering to fight the banker for Rosie's attention when a text from the backseat of a taxi headed home would do, and would furthermore not cause any interruption to Rosie's obvious plans for the evening. *You could have gone straight home after the curry and sorted out your laundry—*

And then she couldn't help but laugh at herself: Miss Misery Guts acting exactly like the bitter old maid Rosie often darkly intimated she was well on her way to becoming. Rosie was right, clearly. Had she really started thinking about her *laundry?* After midnight on a dance floor in a trendy London club while music even she could tell was fantastic swelled all around her?

Still laughing as she imagined the appalled look Rosie would give her when she told her about this, Alicia turned and began fighting her way out of the wild crowd and off the heaving dance floor. She laughed even harder as she was forced to leap out of the way of a particularly energetic couple flinging themselves here and there.

Alicia overbalanced because she was laughing too hard to pay attention to where she was going, and then, moving too fast to stop herself, she slipped in a puddle of spilled drink on the edge of the dance floor—

And crashed into the dark column of a man that she'd thought, before she hurtled into him, was nothing more than an extension of the speaker behind him. A still, watchful shadow.

He wasn't.

He was hard and male, impossibly muscled, sleek and hot. Alicia's first thought, with her face a scant breath from the most stunning male chest she'd ever beheld in real life and her palms actually *touching* it, was that he smelled like winter—fresh and clean and something deliciously smoky beneath.

She was aware of his hands on her upper arms, holding her fast, and only as she absorbed the fact that he *was* holding her did she also fully comprehend the fact that somehow, despite the press of the crowd and the flashing lights and how quickly she'd been on her way toward taking an undignified header into the floor, he'd managed to catch her at all.

She tilted her head back to thank him for his quick reflexes, still smiling—

And everything stopped.

It simply—*disappeared.*

Alicia felt her heart thud, hard enough to bruise. She felt her mouth drop open.

But she saw nothing at all but his eyes.

Blue like no blue she'd ever seen in another pair of eyes before. Blue like the sky on a crystal cold winter day, so bright it almost hurt to look at him. Blue so intense it seemed to fill her up, expanding inside of her, making her feel swollen with it. As if the slightest thing might make her burst wide-open, and some mad part of her wanted that, desperately.

A touch. A smile. Anything at all.

He was beautiful. Dark and forbidding and still, the most beautiful thing she'd ever seen. Something electric sizzled in the air between them as they gazed at each other, charging through her, making her skin prickle. Making her feel heavy and restless, all at once, as if she was a snow globe he'd picked up and shaken hard, and everything inside of her was still floating drowsily in the air, looking for a place to land.

It scared her, down deep inside in a place she hadn't known was there until this moment—and yet she didn't pull away.

He blinked, as if he felt it too, this terrible, impossible, beautiful thing that crackled between them. She was sure that if she could tear her eyes from his she'd be able to see it there in the air, connecting their bodies, arcing between them and around them and through them, the voltage turned high. The faintest hint of a frown etched between his dark brows, and he moved as if to set her away from him, but then he stopped and all he'd done was shift them both even farther back into the shadows.

And still they stood there, caught. Snared. As if the world around them, the raucous club, the pounding music, the wild and crazy dancing, had simply evaporated the moment they'd touched.

*At last,* Alicia thought, in a rush of chaotic sensation and dizzy emotion she didn't understand at all, all of it falling through her with a certain inevitability, like a heavy stone into a terrifyingly deep well.

"My God," she said, gazing up at him. "You look like a wolf."

Was that a smile? His mouth was lush and grim at once, impossibly fascinating to her, and it tugged in one hard corner. Nothing more, and yet she smiled back at him as if he'd beamed at her.

"Is that why you've dressed in red, like a Shoreditch fairy tale?" he asked, his words touched with the faint, velvet caress of an accent she didn't recognize immediately. "I should warn you, it will end with teeth."

"I think you mean tears." She searched his hard face, looking for more evidence of that smile. "It will end in *tears*, surely."

"That, too." Another small tug in the corner of that mouth. "But the teeth usually come first, and hurt more."

"I'll be very disappointed now if you don't have fangs," she told him, and his hands changed their steely grip on her arms, or perhaps she only then became aware of the heat of his palms and how the way he was holding her was so much like a caress.

Another tug on that austere mouth, and an answering one low in her belly, which should have terrified her, given what she knew about herself and sex. On some level, it did.

But she still didn't move away from him.

"It is, of course, my goal in life to keep strange British women who crash into me in crowded clubs from the jaws of disappointment," he said, a new light in his lovely eyes, and a different, more aware tilt to the way he held his head, the way he angled his big body toward her.

As if he might lean in close and swallow her whole.

Staring back at him then, his strong hands hard and hot on her arms and her palms still pressed flat against his taut chest, Alicia wanted nothing more than for him to do exactly that.

She should have turned away then and bolted for the door. Tried to locate whatever was left of her sanity, wherever she'd misplaced it. But she'd never felt this kind of raw, shimmering excitement before, this blistering heat weighing down her limbs so deliciously, this man so primal and powerful she found it hard to breathe.

"Even if the jaws in question are yours?" she asked, and she didn't recognize that teasing lilt in her voice, the way she tilted her head to look up at him, the liquid sort of feeling that moved in her then.

"Especially if they're mine," he replied, his bright winter gaze on her mouth, though there was a darkness there too, a shadow across his intriguing blade of a face that she nearly got lost in. *Jaws,* she reminded herself. *Fangs. He's telling me what a wolf he is, big and bad.* Surely she should feel more alarmed than she did—surely she shouldn't have the strangest urge to soothe him, instead? "You should know there are none sharper or more dangerous."

"In all of London?" She couldn't seem to keep herself from smiling again, or that sparkling cascade of something like light from rushing in her, making her stomach tighten and her breasts pull tight. *Alive. At last.* "Have you measured them, then? Is there some kind of competition you can enter to prove yours are the longest? The sharpest in all the land?"

Alicia felt completely outside herself. Some part of her wanted to lie down in it, in this mad feeling, in *him*—and exult in it. Bask in it as if it was sunshine. As if *he* was, despite the air of casual menace he wore so easily, like an extra layer of skin. Was that visible to everyone, or only to her? She didn't care. She wanted to roll around in this moment, in him, like it was the first snow of the season and she could make it all into angels.

Her breath caught at the image, and somehow, he heard

it. She felt his reaction in the sudden tension of his powerful frame above her and around her, in the flex of his fingers high on her arms, in the tightening of that connection that wound between them, bright and electric, and made her feel like a stranger in her own body.

His blue eyes lifted to meet hers and gleamed bright. "I don't need to measure them, *solnyshka*." He shifted closer, and his attention returned to her mouth. "I know."

He was an arctic wolf turned man, every inch of him a predator—lean and hard as he stood over her despite the heels Rosie had coerced her into wearing. He wore all black, a tight black T-shirt beneath a perfectly tailored black jacket, dark trousers and boots, and his wide, hard shoulders made her skin feel tight. His dark hair was short and inky black. It made his blue eyes seem like smoke over his sculpted jaw and cheekbones, and yet all of it, all of *him,* was hard and male and so dangerous she could feel it hum beneath her skin, some part of her desperate to fight, to flee. He looked intriguingly uncivilized. Something like feral.

And yet Alicia wasn't afraid, as that still-alarmed, still-vigilant part of her knew she should have been. Not when he was looking at her like that. Not when she followed a half-formed instinct and moved closer to him, pressing her hands flatter against the magnificently formed planes of his chest while his arms went around her to hold her like a lover might. She tilted her head back even farther and watched his eyes turn to arctic fire.

She didn't understand it, but she burned.

*This isn't right*, a small voice cautioned her in the back of her mind. *This isn't you.*

But he was so beautiful she couldn't seem to keep track of who she was supposed to be, and her heart hurt her where it thundered in her chest. She felt something bright and demanding knot into an insistent ache deep in her belly, and she found she couldn't think of a good reason to step away from him.

*In a minute,* she promised herself. *I'll walk away in a minute.*

"You should run," he told her then, his voice dark and low, and she could see he was serious. That he meant it. But one of his hands moved to trace a lazy pattern on her cheek as he said it, his palm a rough velvet against her skin, and she shivered. His blue gaze seemed to sharpen. "As far away from me as you can get."

He looked so grim then, so sure, and it hurt her, somehow. She wanted to see him smile with that hard, dangerous mouth. She wanted that with every single part of her and she didn't even know his name.

None of this made any sense.

Alicia had been so good for so long. She'd paid and paid and paid for that single night eight years ago. She'd been so vigilant, so careful, ever since. She was never spontaneous. She was never reckless. And yet this beautiful shadow of a man had the bluest eyes she'd ever seen, and the saddest mouth, and the way he touched her made her shake and burn and glow.

And she thought that maybe this once, for a moment or two, she could let down her guard. Just the smallest, tiniest bit. It didn't have to mean anything she didn't want it to mean. It didn't have to mean anything at all.

So she ignored that voice inside of her, and she ignored his warning, too.

Alicia leaned her face into his hard palm as if it was the easiest thing in the world, and smiled when he pulled in a breath like it was a fire in him, too. Like he felt the same burn.

She stretched up against his hard, tough body and told herself this was about that grim mouth of his, not the wild, impossible things she knew she shouldn't let herself feel or want or, God help her, *do*. And they were in the shadows of a crowded club where nobody could see her and no one would ever know what she did in the dark. It wasn't as if it counted.

She could go back to her regularly scheduled quiet life in a moment.

It would only be a moment. One small moment outside all the rules she'd made for herself, the rules she'd lived by so carefully for so long, and then she would go straight back home to her neat, orderly, virtuous life.

She would. She had to. *She would*.

But first Alicia obeyed that surge of wild demand inside of her, leaned closer and fitted her mouth to his.

# CHAPTER TWO

HE TASTED LIKE the night. Better even than she'd imagined.

He paused for the barest instant when Alicia's lips touched his. Half a heartbeat. Less.

A scant second while the taste of him seared through her, deep and dark and wild. She thought that was enough, that small taste of his fascinating mouth. That would do, and now she could go back to her quiet—

But then he angled his head to one side, used the hand at her cheek to guide her mouth where he wanted it and took over.

Devouring her like the wolf she understood he was. *He really was,* and the realization swirled inside of her like heat. His mouth was impossibly carnal, opening over hers to taste her, to claim her.

Dark and deep, hot and sure.

Alicia simply…exploded. It was like a long flash of light, shuddering and bright, searing everything away in the white hot burn of it. It was perfect. It was beautiful.

*It was too much.*

She shivered against him, overloaded with his bold taste, the scrape of his jaw, his talented fingers moving her mouth where he wanted it in a silent, searing command she was happy to obey. Then his hands were in her hair, buried in her thick curls. Her arms went around his neck of their own volition, and then she was plastered against the tall, hard length of him. It was like pressing into the surface of the sun and still, she couldn't seem to get close enough.

As if there was no *close enough.*

And he kissed her, again and again, with a ruthless intensity that made her feel weak and beautiful all at once, until she was mindless with need. Until she forgot her own name. Until she forgot she didn't know his. Until she forgot how dangerous *forgetting* was for her.

Until she forgot everything but him.

When he pulled back, she didn't understand. He put an inch, maybe two, between them, and then he muttered something harsh and incomprehensible while he stared at her as if he thought she was some kind of ghost.

It took her a long, confused moment to realize that she couldn't understand him because he wasn't speaking in English, not because she'd forgotten her own language, too.

Alicia blinked, the world rushing back as she did. She was still standing in that club. Music still pounded all around them, lights still flashed, well-dressed patrons still shouted over the din, and somewhere out in the middle of the dance floor, Rosie was no doubt still playing her favorite game with her latest conquest.

Everything was as it had been before she'd stumbled into this man, before he'd caught her. Before she'd kissed him.

Before he'd kissed her back.

Everything was exactly the same. Except Alicia.

He was searching her face as if he was looking for something. He shook his head slightly, then reached down and ran a lazy finger over the ridge of her collarbone, as if testing its shape. Even that made her shudder, that simple slide of skin against skin. Even so innocuous a touch seemed directly connected to that pulsing heat between her legs, the heavy ache in her breasts, the hectic spin inside of her.

She didn't have to speak his language to know whatever he muttered then was a curse.

If she were smart, the way she'd tried to be for years now, she would pull her hand away and run. Just as he'd told her she should. Just as she'd promised herself she would. Everything about this was too extreme, too intense, as if he wasn't only a strange man in a club but the kind of drug that usually went with this kind of rolling, wildly out-of-control feeling. As if she was much too close to being high on *him*.

"Last chance," he said then, as if he could read her mind.

He was giving her a warning. Again.

In her head, she listened. She smiled politely and extricated herself. She marched herself to the nearest exit, hailed a taxi, then headed straight home to the comfort of her bloody laundry. Because she knew she couldn't be trusted outside the confines of the rules she'd made for herself. She'd been living the consequences of having no rules for a long, long time.

But here, now, in this loud place surrounded by so many people and all of that pounding music, she didn't feel like the person she'd been when she'd arrived. Everything she knew about herself had twisted inside out. Turned into something else entirely in that electric blue of his challenging gaze.

As if this really was a Shoreditch fairy tale, after all.

"What big eyes you have," she teased him.

His hard mouth curved then, and she felt it like a burst of heat, like sunlight. She couldn't do anything but smile back at him.

"So be it," he said, as if he despaired of them both.

Alicia laughed, then laughed again at the startled look in his eyes.

"The dourness is a lovely touch," she told him. "You must be beating them off with a stick. A very grim stick."

"No stick," he said, in an odd tone. "A look at me is usually sufficient."

"A wolf," she said, and grinned. "Just as I suspected."

He blinked, and again looked at her in that strange way of his, as if she was an apparition he couldn't quite believe was standing there before him.

Then he moved with the same decisiveness he'd used when he'd taken control of that kiss, tucking her into his side as he navigated his way through the dense crowd. She tried not to think about how well she fitted there, under his heavy arm, tight against the powerful length of his torso as he cut through the crowd. She tried not to drift away in the scent of him, the heat and the power, all of it surrounding her and pouring into that ache already inside of her, making it bloom and stretch and grow.

Until it took over everything.

Maybe she was under some kind of spell, Alicia thought with the small part of her that wasn't consumed with the feel of his tall, lean frame as he guided her so protectively through the crowd. It should have been impossible to move through the club so quickly, so confidently. Not in a place like this at the height of a Saturday night. But he did it.

And then they were outside, in the cold and the damp November night, and he was still moving in that same breathtaking way, like quicksilver. Like he knew exactly where they were headed—away from the club and the people still milling about in front of it. He led her down the dark street, deeper into the shadows, and it was then Alicia's sense of self-preservation finally kicked itself into gear.

*Better late than never*, she thought, annoyed with herself, but it actually *hurt* her to pull away from the magnificent shelter of his body, from all of that intense heat and strength. It felt like she'd ripped her skin off when she stepped away from him, as if they'd been fused together.

He regarded her calmly, making her want to trust him when she knew she shouldn't. She couldn't.

"I'm sorry, but…" She wrapped her arms around her own waist in an attempt to make up for the heat she'd lost when she'd stepped away from him. "I don't know a single thing about you."

"You know several things, I think."

He sounded even more delicious now that they were alone and she could hear him properly. *Russian,* she thought, as pleased as if she'd learned his deepest, darkest secrets.

"Yes," she agreed, thinking of the things she knew. Most of them to do with that insistent ache in her belly, and lower. His mouth. His clever hands. "All lovely things. But none of them worth risking my personal safety for, I'm sure you'll agree."

Something like a smile moved in his eyes, but didn't make it to his hard mouth. Still, it echoed in her, sweet and light, making her feel far more buoyant than she should have on a dark East London street with a strange man even she could see was dangerous, no matter how much she wanted him.

Had she ever wanted anything this much? Had anyone?

"A wolf is never without risk," he told her, that voice of his like whiskey, smooth and scratchy at once, heating her up from the inside out. "That's the point of wolves. Or you'd simply get a dog, pat it on the head." His eyes gleamed. "Teach it tricks."

Alicia wasn't sure she wanted to know the tricks this man had up his sleeve. Or, more to the point, she wasn't sure she'd survive them. She wasn't certain she'd survive this as it was.

"You could be very bad in bed," she said, conversationally, as if she picked up strange men all the time. She hardly recognized her own light, easy, flirtatious tone. She hadn't heard it since before that night in her parents' back garden. "That's a terrible risk to take with any stranger, and awkward besides."

That smile in his eyes intensified, got even bluer. "I'm not."

She believed him.

"You could be the sort who gets very, very drunk and weeps loudly about his broken heart until dawn." She gave a mock shudder. "So tedious, especially if poetry is involved. Or worse, *singing*."

"I don't drink," he countered at once. His dark brows arched over those eyes of his, challenging her. Daring her. "I never sing, I don't write poems and I certainly do not weep." He paused. "More to the point, I don't have a heart."

"Handy, that," she replied easily. She eyed him. "You could be a killer, of course. That would be unfortunate."

She smiled at that. He didn't.

"And if I am?"

"There you go," she said, and nodded sagely. Light, airy. Enchanted, despite herself. "I can't possibly go off into the night with you now, can I?"

But it was terrifying how much she *wanted* to go off with him, wherever he'd take her, and instead of reacting to that as she should, she couldn't stop smiling at him. As if she already knew him, this strange man dressed all in black, his blue eyes the only spot of color on the cold pavement as he stared at her as if she'd stunned him somehow.

"My name is Nikolai," he said, and she had the oddest impression he hadn't meant to speak at all. He shifted, then reached over and traced her lips with his thumb, his expression so fierce, so intent, it made her feel hollowed out inside, everything scraped away except that wild, wondrous heat he stirred in her. "Text someone my name and address. Have them ring every fifteen minutes if you like. Send the police. Whatever you want."

"All those safeguards are very thoughtful," she pointed out, but her eyes felt too wide and her voice sounded insubstantial. Wispy. "Though not exactly wolfish, it has to be said."

His mouth moved into his understated version of a smile

"I want you." His eyes were on fire. Every inch of him that wolf. "What will it take?"

She swayed back into him as if they were magnets and she'd simply succumbed to the pull. And then she had no choice but to put her hand to his abdomen, to feel all that blasting heat right there beneath her palm.

Even that didn't scare her the way it should.

"What big teeth you have," she whispered, too on edge to laugh, too filled with that pulsing ache inside of her to smile.

"The biting part comes later." His eyes gleamed again, with the kind of sheer male confidence that made it difficult to breathe. Alicia stopped trying. "If you ask nicely."

He picked up her hand and lifted it to his mouth, tracing a dark heat over the back of it. He didn't look away.

"If you're sure," she said piously, trying desperately to pretend she wasn't shaking, and that he couldn't feel it. That he didn't know exactly what he was doing to her when she could see full well that he did. "I was promised a wolf, not a dog."

"I eat dogs for breakfast."

She laughed then. "That's not particularly comforting."

"I can't be what I'm not, *solnyshka*." He turned her hand over, then kissed her palm in a way that made her hiss in a sharp breath. His eyes were smiling again, so bright and blue. "But I'm very good at what I am."

And she'd been lost since she'd set eyes on him, hadn't

she? What use was there in pretending otherwise? She wasn't drunk. It wasn't like that terrible night, because she knew what she was doing. Didn't she?

"Note to self," Alicia managed to say, breathless and dizzy and unable to remember why she'd tried to stop this in the first place, when surrendering to it—to him—felt so much like triumph. Like fate. "Never eat breakfast with a wolf. The sausages are likely the family dog."

He shrugged. "Not *your* family dog," he said with that fierce mouth of his, though she was sure his blue eyes laughed. "If that helps."

And this time, when she smiled at him, the negotiation was over.

The address he gave her in his clipped, direct way was in an extraordinarily posh part of town Alicia could hardly afford to visit, much less live in. She dutifully texted it to Rosie, hoping that her friend was far too busy to check it until morning. And then she tucked her phone away and forgot about Rosie altogether.

Because he still moved like magic, tucking her against him again as if there was a crowd he needed to part when there was only the late-night street and what surged between them like heat lightning. As if he liked the way she fitted there as much as she did. And her heart began to pound all over again, excitement and anticipation and a certain astonishment at her own behavior pouring through her with every hard thump.

At the corner, he lifted his free hand almost languidly toward the empty street, and for a second Alicia truly believed that he was so powerful that taxis simply materialized before him at his whim—until a nearby engine turned over and a powerful black SUV slid out of the shadows and pulled to a stop right there before them.

More magic, when she was enchanted already.

*Nikolai,* she whispered to herself as she climbed inside the SUV, as if the name was a song. Or a spell. *His name is Nikolai.*

He swung in behind her on the soft leather backseat, exchanged a few words in curt Russian with the driver and then pressed a button that raised a privacy shield, secluding them. Then he settled back against the seat, near her but not touching her, stretching out his long, lean body and making the spacious vehicle seem tight. Close.

And then he simply looked at her.

As if he was trying to puzzle her out. Or giving her one last chance to bolt.

But Alicia knew she wasn't going to do that.

"More talk of dogs?" he asked mildly, yet all she heard was the hunger beneath. She could see it in his eyes, his face. She could feel the echo of it in her, new and huge and almost more than she could bear. "More clever little character assessments couched as potential objections?"

"I got in your car," she pointed out, hardly recognizing her own voice. The thick heat in it. "I think I'm done."

He smiled. She was sure of it, though his mouth didn't move. But she could see the stamp of satisfaction on his hard face, the flare of a deep male approval.

"Not yet, *solnyshka,*" he murmured, his voice a low rasp. "Not quite yet."

And she melted. It was a shivery thing, hot and desperate, like she couldn't quite catch her breath against the heat of it.

"Come here," he said.

They were cocooned in the darkness, light spilling here and there as the car sped through the city, and still his blue gaze was brilliant. Compelling. And so knowing—so certain of himself, of her, of what was about to happen—it made her blood run hot in her veins.

Alicia didn't move fast enough and he made a low noise. *A growl*—like the wolf he so resembled. The rough sound made her shake apart and then melt down into nothing but need, alive with that crazy heat she couldn't seem to control any longer.

He simply picked her up and pulled her into his lap, his mouth finding hers and claiming her all over again with an impatience that delighted her. She met him with the same urgency. His hands marveled down the length of her back, explored the shape of her hips, and Alicia's mind blanked out into a red-hot burst of that consuming, impossible fire. Into pure and simple *need*.

It had been so long. *So long,* and yet her body knew exactly what to do, thrilling to the taste of him, the feel of his hard, capable hands first over and then underneath her bright red shirt. His hands on her stomach, her waist, her breasts. So perfect she wanted to die. And not nearly enough.

He leaned back to peel off his jacket and the tight black T-shirt beneath, and her eyes glazed over at the sight of all of that raw male beauty. She pressed herself against the hard planes of his perfect chest, tracing the large, colorful tattoos that stretched over his skin with trembling fingers, with her lips and her tongue, tasting art etched across art.

Intense. Hot. Intoxicating.

And that scent of his—of the darkest winter, smoke and ice—surrounded her. Licked into her. Claimed her as surely as he did.

One moment she was fully clothed, the next her shirt and the bra beneath it were swept away, while his hard mouth took hers again and again until she thought she might die if he stopped. Then he did stop, and she moaned out her distress, her desperation. That needy ache so deep in the core of her. But he only laughed softly, before he fastened his hot mouth to the tight peak of one breast and sucked on it, not quite gently, until she thought she really *had* died.

The noises she heard herself making were impossible. Nothing could really feel this good. This perfect. This wild or this *right*.

Nikolai shifted, lifting her, and Alicia helped him peel her trousers down from her hips, kicking one leg free and not caring what happened to the other. She felt outside herself and yet more fully *in* herself than she had been in as long as she could remember. She explored the expanse of his gorgeous shoulders, the distractingly tender spot behind his ear, the play of his stunning muscles, perfectly honed beneath her.

He twisted them both around, coming down over her on the seat and pulling her legs around his hips with an urgency that made her breath desert her. She hadn't even been aware that he'd undressed. It was more magic—and then he was finally naked against her, the steel length of him a hot brand against her belly.

Alicia shuddered and melted, then melted again, and he moved even closer, one of his hands moving to her bottom and lifting her against him with that devastating skill, that easy mastery, that made her belly tighten.

He was muttering in Russian, that same word he'd used before like a curse or a prayer or even both at once, and the sound of it made her moan again. It was harsh like him, and tender, too. It made her feel as if she might come out of her own skin. He teased her breasts, licking his way from one proud nipple to the other as if he might lose himself there, then moved to her neck, making her shiver against him before he took her mouth again in a hard, deep kiss.

As raw as she was. As undone.

He pulled back slightly to press something into her hand, and she blinked at it, taking much longer than she should have to recognize it was the condom she hadn't thought about for even an instant.

A trickle of unease snaked down the back of her neck, but she pushed it away, too far gone for shame. Not when his blue eyes glittered with sensual intent and his long fingers moved between them, feeling her damp heat and then stroking deep into her molten center, making her clench him hard.

"Hurry," he told her.

"I'm hurrying. You're distracting me."

He played his fingers in and out of her, slick and hot, then pressed the heel of his hand into her neediest part, laughing softly when she bucked against him.

"Concentrate, *solnyshka*."

She ripped open the foil packet, then took her time rolling it down his velvety length, until he cursed beneath his breath.

Alicia liked the evidence of his own pressing need. She liked that she could make his breath catch, too. And then he stopped, braced over her, his face close to hers and the hardest part of him poised at her entrance but not *quite*—

He groaned. He sounded as tortured as she felt. She liked that, too.

"Your name."

She blinked at the short command, so gruff and harsh. His arms were hard around her, his big body pressed her back into the soft leather seat, and she felt delicate and powerful all at once.

"Tell me your name," he said, nipping at her jaw, making her head fall back to give him any access he desired, anything he wanted.

*Alive,* she thought again. *At last.*

"Alicia," she whispered.

He muttered it like a fierce prayer, and then he thrust

into her—hot and hard and so perfect, so beautiful, that tears spilled from her eyes even as she shattered around him.

"Again," he said.

It was another command, arrogant and darkly certain. Nikolai was hard and dangerous and between her legs, his eyes bright and hot and much too intense on hers. She turned her head away but he caught her mouth with his, taking her over, conquering her.

"I don't think I can—" she tried to say against his mouth, even while the flames still licked through her, even as she still shuddered helplessly around him, aware of the steel length of him inside her, filling her.

Waiting.

That hard smile like a burst of heat inside her. "You will."

And then he started to move.

It was perfect. More than perfect. It was sleek and hot, impossibly good. He simply claimed her, took her, and Alicia met him. She arched into him, lost in the slide and the heat, the glory of it. Of him.

Slick. Wild.

*Perfect.*

He moved in her, over her, his mouth at her neck and his hands roaming from her bottom to the center of her shuddering need as he set the wild, intense pace. She felt it rage inside her again, this mad fire she'd never felt before and worried would destroy her even as she hungered for more. And more. *And more.*

She met every deep thrust. She gloried in it.

"Say my name," he said, gruff against her ear, his voice washing through her and sending her higher, making her glow. "Now, Alicia. Say it."

When she obeyed he shuddered, then let out another low,

sexy growl that moved over her like a newer, better fire. He reached between them and pressed down hard against the heart of her hunger, hurtling her right over the edge again.

And smiled, she was sure of it, with his warrior's mouth as well as those winter-bright eyes, right before he followed her into bliss.

Nikolai came back to himself with a vicious, jarring thud.

He couldn't move. He wasn't sure he breathed. Alicia quivered sweetly beneath him, his mouth was pressed against the tender junction of her neck and shoulder, and he was still deep inside her lovely body.

*What the hell was* that?

He shifted her carefully into the seat beside him, ignoring the way her long, inky-black lashes looked against the creamy brown of her skin, the way her perfect, lush mouth was so soft now. He ignored the tiny noise she made in the back of her throat, as if distressed to lose contact with him, which made him grit his teeth. But she didn't open her eyes.

He dealt with the condom swiftly, then he found his trousers in the tangle of clothes on the floor of the car and jerked them on. He had no idea what had happened to his T-shirt, and decided it didn't matter. And then he simply sat there as if he was winded.

He, Nikolai Korovin, *winded*. By a woman.

By *this* woman.

What moved in him then was like a rush of too many colors, brilliant and wild, when he knew the only safety lay in gray. It surged in his veins, it pounded in his temples, it scraped along his sex. He told himself it was temper, but he knew better. It was everything he'd locked away for all these years, and he didn't want it. He wouldn't allow it. It made him feel like an animal again, wrong and violent and insane and drunk....

That was it.

It rang like a bell in him, low and urgent, swelling into everything. Echoing everywhere. No wonder he felt so off-kilter, so dangerously unbalanced. This woman made him feel *drunk*.

Nikolai forced a breath, then another.

Everything that had happened since she'd tripped in front of him flashed through his head, in the same random snatches of color and sound and scent he remembered from a thousand morning-afters. Her laughter, that sounded the way he thought joy must, though he'd no basis for comparison. The way she'd tripped and then fallen, straight into him, and hadn't had the sense to roll herself as he would have done, to break her fall. Her brilliant smile that cracked over her face so easily. Too easily.

No one had ever smiled at him like that. As if he was a real man. Even a good one.

But he knew what he was. He'd always known. His uncle's fists, worse after Ivan had left to fight their way to freedom one championship at a time. The things he'd done in the army. Veronika's calculated deception, even Ivan's more recent betrayal—these had only confirmed what Nikolai had always understood to be true about himself down deep into his core.

To think differently now, when he'd lost everything he had to lose and wanted nothing more than to shut himself off for good, was the worst kind of lie. Damaging. Dangerous. And he knew what happened when he allowed himself to become intoxicated. How many times would he have to prove that to himself? How many people would he hurt?

He was better off blank. Ice cold and gray, all the way through.

The day after Veronika left him, Nikolai had woken bruised and battered from another fight—or *fights*—he couldn't recall. He'd been shaky. Sick from the alcohol and sicker still with himself. Disgusted with the holes in his memory and worse, with all the things he *did* remember. The things that slid without context through his head, oily and barbed.

His fists against flesh. His bellow of rage. The crunch of wood beneath his foot, the shattering of pottery against the stone floor. Faces of strangers on the street, wary. Worried. Then angry. Alarmed.

*Blood on a fist*—and only some of it his. *Fear in those eyes*—never his. Nikolai was what grown men feared, what they crossed streets to avoid, but he hadn't felt fear himself in years. Not since he'd been a child.

Fear meant there was something left to lose.

That was the last time Nikolai had drunk a drop of alcohol and it was the last time he'd let himself lose control.

Until now.

He didn't understand this. He was not an impulsive man. He didn't pick up women, he *picked* them, carefully—and only when he was certain that whatever else they were, they were obedient and disposable.

When they posed no threat to him at all. Nikolai breathed in, out.

He'd survived wars. This was only a woman.

Nikolai looked at her then, memorizing her, like she was a code he needed to crack, instead of the bomb itself, poised to detonate.

She wore her dark black hair in a cloud of tight curls around her head, a tempting halo around her lovely, clever face, and he didn't want any part of this near-overpowering desire that surged in him, to bury his hands in the heavy thickness of it, to start the wild rush all over again. Her body was lithe and ripe with warm, mouthwatering curves that he'd already touched and tasted, so why did he feel as if it had all been rushed, as if it wasn't nearly enough?

He shouldn't have this longing to take his time, to really explore her. He shouldn't hunger for that lush, full mouth of hers again, or want to taste his way along that elegant neck for the simple pleasure of making her shiver. He shouldn't find it so impossible to look at her without imagining himself tracing lazy patterns across every square inch of the sweet brown perfection of her skin. With his mouth and then his hands, again and again until he *knew* her.

He'd asked her name, as if he'd needed it. He'd wanted her that much, and Nikolai knew better than to want. It could only bring him pain.

Vodka had been his one true love, and it had ruined him. It had let loose that monster in him, let it run amok. It had taken everything that his childhood and the army hadn't already divided between them and picked down to the bone. He'd known it in his sober moments, but he hadn't cared. Because vodka had warmed him, lent color and volume to the dark, silent prison of his life, made him imagine he could be something other than a six-foot-two column of glacial ice.

But he knew better than that now. He knew better than this.

Alicia's eyes fluttered open then, dark brown shot through with amber, almost too pretty to bear. He hated that he noticed, that he couldn't look away. She glanced around as if she'd forgotten where they were. Then she looked at him.

She didn't smile that outrageously beautiful smile of hers, and it made something hitch inside him, like a stitch in his side. As if he'd lost that, too.

She lifted one foot, shaking her head at the trousers that were still attached to her ankle, and the shoe she'd never removed. She reached down, picked up the tangle of her bright red shirt and lacy pink bra from the pile on the floor of the car, and sighed.

And Nikolai relaxed, because he was back on familiar ground.

Now came the demands, the negotiations, he thought cynically. The endless manipulations, which were the reason he'd started making any woman who wanted him agree to his rules before he touched her. Sign the appropriate documents, understand exactly how this would go before it started. Nikolai knew this particular dance well. It was why he normally didn't pick up women, let them into the sleek, muscular SUV that told them too much about his net worth, much less give them his address....

But instead of pouting prettily and pointedly, almost always the first transparent step in these situations, Alicia looked at him, let her head fall back and laughed.

# CHAPTER THREE

*THAT DAMNED LAUGH.*

Nikolai would rather be shot again, he decided in that electric moment as her laughter filled the car. He would rather take another knife or two to the gut. He didn't know what on earth he was supposed to do with laughter like that, when it sparkled in the air all around him and fell indiscriminately here and there, like a thousand unwelcome caresses all over his skin and something worse—much worse—deep beneath it.

He scowled.

"Never let it be said this wasn't classy," Alicia said, her lovely voice wry. "I suppose we'll always have that going for us."

There was no *we*. There was no *us*. Neither of those words were *disposable*. Alarms shrieked like air raid sirens inside of him, mixing with the aftereffects of that laugh.

"I thought you understood," he said abruptly, at his coldest and most cutting. "I don't—"

"Relax, Tin Man." Laughter still lurked in her voice. She tugged her trousers back up over her hips, then pulled her bra free of her shirt, shooting him a breezy smile that felt not unlike a blade to the stomach as she clipped it back into place. "I heard you the first time. No heart."

And then she ignored him, as if he wasn't vibrating

beside her with all of that darkness and icy intent. As if he wasn't Nikolai Korovin, feared and respected in equal measure all across the planet, in a thousand corporate boardrooms as well as the grim theaters of too many violent conflicts. As if he was the kind of man someone could simply *pick up* in a London club and then dismiss…

Except, of course, he was. Because she had. She'd done exactly that.

He'd let her.

Alicia fussed with her shirt before pulling it over her head, her black curls springing out of the opening in a joyful froth that made him actually ache to touch them. *Her*. He glared down at his hands as if they'd betrayed him.

When she looked at him again, her dark eyes were soft, undoing him as surely as if she really had eviscerated him with a hunting knife. He would have preferred the latter. She made it incalculably worse by reaching over and smoothing her warm hand over his cheek, offering him… comfort?

"You look like you've swallowed broken glass," she said. *Kindly.*

Very much as if she cared.

Nikolai didn't want what he couldn't have. It had been beaten out of him long ago. It was a simple, unassailable fact, like gravity. Like air.

Like light.

But he couldn't seem to stop himself from lifting his hand, tracing that tempting mouth of hers once more, watching the heat bloom again in her eyes.

*Just one night,* he told himself then. He couldn't help it. That smile of hers made him realize he was so tired of the cold, the dark. That he felt haunted by the things he'd lost, the wars he'd won, the battles he'd been fighting all his life. Just once, he *wanted*.

One night to explore this light of hers she shone so indiscriminately, he thought. Just one night to pretend he was something more than ice. A wise man didn't step onto a land mine when he could see it lying there in front of him, waiting to blow. But Nikolai had been through more hells than he could count. He could handle anything for a night. Even this. Even her.

*Just one night.*

"You should hold on," he heard himself say. He slid his hand around to cup the nape of her neck, and exulted in the shiver that moved over her at even so small a touch. As if she was his. That could never happen, he knew. But he'd allowed himself the night. He had every intention of making it a long one. "I'm only getting started."

*If only he really had been a wolf.*

Alicia scowled down at the desk in her office on Monday and tried valiantly to think of something—*anything*—other than Nikolai. And failed, as she'd been doing with alarming regularity since she'd sneaked away from his palatial penthouse in South Kensington early on Sunday morning.

If he'd really been a wolf, she'd likely be in hospital right now, recovering from being bitten in a lovely quiet coma or restful medicated haze, which would mean she'd be enjoying a much-needed holiday from the self-recriminating clamor inside her head.

*At least I wasn't drunk....*

Though if she was honest, some part of her almost wished she had been. *Almost.* As if that would be some kind of excuse when she knew from bitter experience that it wasn't.

The real problem was, she'd been perfectly aware of what she was doing on Saturday. She'd gone ahead and done it precisely *because* she hadn't been drunk. For no other reason than that she'd wanted him.

From her parents' back garden to a stranger in a car. She hadn't learned much of anything in all these years, had she? Given the chance, she'd gleefully act the promiscuous whore—drunk *or* sober.

That turned inside of her like bile, acidic and thick at the back of her throat.

"I think you must be a witch," he'd said at some point in those long, sleepless hours of too much pleasure, too hot and too addicting. He'd been sprawled out next to her, his rough voice no more than a growl in the dark of his cavernous bedroom.

A girl could get lost in a room like that, she'd thought. In a bed so wide. In a man like Nikolai, who had taken her over and over with a skill and a thoroughness and a sheer masculine prowess that made her wonder how she'd ever recover from it. *If* she would. But she hadn't wanted to think those things, not then. Not while it was still dark outside and they were cocooned on those soft sheets together, the world held at bay. There'd be time enough to work on forgetting, she'd thought. When it was over.

When it was morning.

She'd propped herself up on an elbow and looked down at him, his bold, hard face in shadows but those eyes of his as intense as ever.

"I'm not the driving force in this fairy tale," she'd said quietly. Then she'd dropped her gaze lower, past that hard mouth of his she now knew was a terrible, electric torment when he chose, and down to that astonishing torso of his laid out before her like a feast. "Red Riding Hood is a hapless little fool, isn't she? Always in the wrong place at the wrong time."

Alicia had meant that to come out light and breezy, but

it hadn't. It had felt intimate instead, somehow. Darker and deeper, and a different kind of ache inside. Not at all what she'd intended.

She'd felt the blue of his gaze like a touch.

Instead of losing herself there, she'd traced a lazy finger over the steel plates of his harshly honed chest. Devastatingly perfect. She moved from this scar to that tattoo, tracing each pucker of flesh, each white strip of long-ago agony, then smoothing her fingertip over the bright colors and Cyrillic letters that flowed everywhere else. Two kinds of marks, stamped permanently into his flesh. She'd been uncertain if she was fascinated or something else, something that made her mourn for all his body had suffered.

But it wasn't her place to ask.

"Bullet," he'd said quietly, when her fingers moved over a slightly raised and shiny patch of skin below his shoulder, as if she had asked after all. "I was in the army."

"For how long?"

"Too long."

She'd flicked a look at him, but had kept going, finding a long, narrow white scar that slashed across his taut abdomen and following the length of it, back and forth. So much violence boiled down to a thin white line etched into his hard, smooth flesh. It had made her hurt for him, but she still hadn't asked.

"Kitchen knife. My uncle." His voice had been little more than a rasp against the dark. She'd gone still, her fingers splayed across the scar in question. "He took his role as our guardian seriously," Nikolai had said, and his gruff voice had sounded almost amused, as if what he'd said was something other than awful. Alicia had chanced a glance at him, and saw a different truth in that wintry gaze, more vulnerable in the clasp of the dark than she'd imagined he knew. "He didn't like how I'd washed the dishes."

"Nikolai—" she'd begun, not knowing what she could possibly say, but spurred on by that torn look in his eyes.

He'd blinked, then frowned. "It was nothing."

But she'd known he was lying. And the fact that she'd had no choice but to let it pass, that this man wasn't hers to care for no matter how it felt as if he should have been, had rippled through her like actual, physical pain.

Alicia had moved on then to the tattoo of a wild beast rendered in a shocking sweep of bold color and dark black lines that wrapped around the left side of his body, from his shoulder all the way down to an inch or so above his sex. It was fierce and furious, all ferocious teeth and wicked claws, poised there as if ready to devour him.

As if, she'd thought, it already had.

"All of my sins," he'd said then, his voice far darker and rougher than before.

There'd been an almost-guarded look in his winter gaze when she'd glanced up at him, but she'd thought that was that same vulnerability again. And then he'd sucked in a harsh breath when she'd leaned over and pressed a kiss to the fearsome head of this creature that claimed him, as if she could wash away the things that had hurt him—uncles who wielded kitchen knives, whatever battles he'd fought in the army that had got him shot, all those shadows that lay heavy on his hard face. One kiss, then another, and she'd felt the coiling tension in him, the heat.

"Your sins are pretty," she'd whispered.

He'd muttered something ferocious in Russian as he'd hauled her mouth to his, then he'd pulled her astride him and surged into her with a dark fury and a deep hunger that had thrilled her all the way through, and she'd been lost in him all over again.

She was still lost.

"For God's sake, Alicia," she bit out, tired of the endless

cycle of her own thoughts, and her own appalling weakness. Her voice sounded loud in her small office. "You have work to do."

She had to snap out of this. Her desk was piled high after her two weeks abroad, her in-box was overflowing and she had a towering stack of messages indicating calls she needed to return now that she was back in the country. To say nothing of the report on the Latin American offices she'd visited while away that she had yet to put together, that Charlotte, her supervisor, expected her to present to the team later this week.

But she couldn't sink into her work the way she wanted, the way she usually could. There was that deep current of shame that flared inside of her, bright like some kind of cramp, reminding her of the last night she'd abandoned herself so completely....

At least this time, she remembered every last second of what she'd done. What *they'd* done. Surely that counted for something.

Her body still prickled now, here, as if electrified, every time she thought of him—and she couldn't seem to stop. Her nipples went hard and between her legs, she ran so hot it almost hurt, and it was such a deep betrayal of who she'd thought she'd become that it made her feel shaky.

Her thighs were still tender from the scrape of his hard jaw. There was a mark on the underside of one breast that he'd left deliberately, reminding her in that harsh, beautiful voice that *wolves bite, solnyshka*, making her laugh and squirm in reckless delight beneath him on that wide, masculine bed where she'd obviously *lost her mind*. Even her hips held memories of what she'd done, reminding her of her overwhelming response to him every now and again with a low, almost-pleasant ache that made her hate herself more every time she felt it.

She'd been hung over before. Ashamed of herself come the dawn. Sometimes that feeling had lingered for days as she'd promised herself that she'd stop partying so hard, knowing deep down that she wouldn't, and hadn't, until that last night in the back garden. But this wasn't *that*. This was worse.

She felt out of control. Knocked flat. Changed, utterly. A stranger to herself.

Alicia had been so sure the new identity she'd built over these past eight years was a fortress, completely impenetrable, impervious to attack. Hadn't she held Rosie at bay for ages? But one night with Nikolai had showed her that she was nothing but a glass house, precarious and fragile, and a single stone could bring it all crashing down. A single touch.

Not to mention, she hadn't even *thought* about protection that first time. He'd had to *put it in her hand*. Of all her many betrayals of herself that night, she thought that one was by far the most appalling. It made the shame that lived in her that much worse.

The only bright spot in all of this recrimination and regret was that her text to Rosie hadn't gone through. There'd been a big X next to it when she'd looked at her mobile that next morning. And when she'd arrived back at their flat on Sunday morning, Rosie had still been out.

Which meant that no one had any idea what Alicia had done.

"I wish I'd gone home when you did," Rosie had said with a sigh while they sat in their usual Sunday-afternoon café, paging lazily through the Sunday paper and poking at their plates of a traditional full English breakfast. "That place turned *absolutely mental* after hours, and I have to stop getting off with bankers who talk about the flipping property ladder like it's the most thrilling thing on the planet." Then she'd grinned that big grin of hers that meant she didn't regret a single thing, no matter what she said. "Maybe someday I'll actually follow your example."

"What fun would that be?" Alicia had asked lightly, any guilt she'd felt at lying by giant, glaring omission to her best friend drowned out by the sheer relief pouring through her.

Because if Rosie didn't know what she'd done, Alicia could pretend it had never happened.

There would be no discussing Nikolai, that SUV of his or what had happened in it, or that astonishing penthouse that she'd been entirely too gauche not to gape at, openly, when he'd brought her home. There would be no play-by-play description of those things he could do with such ease, that Alicia hadn't known could feel like that. There would certainly be no conversations about all of these confusing and pointless things she felt sloshing around inside of her when she thought about those moments he'd showed her his vulnerable side, as if a man whose last name she didn't know and hadn't asked was something more than a one-night stand.

And if there was no one to talk about it with, all of this urgency, this driving sense of loss, would disappear. *It had to*. Alicia would remain, outwardly, as solid and reliable and predictably boring as she'd become in these past years. An example. The same old Saint Alicia, polishing her halo.

And maybe someday, if she was well-behaved and lucky, she'd believe it again herself.

"Are you ready for the big meeting?"

Her supervisor's dry voice from the open doorway made Alicia jump guiltily in her chair, and it was much harder than it should have been to smile at Charlotte the way she usually did. She was sure what she'd done over her weekend was plastered all over her face. That Charlotte could *see* how filthy she really was, the way her father had. All her sins at a single glance, like that furious creature that bristled on Nikolai's chest.

"Meeting?" she echoed weakly.

"The new celebrity partnership?" Charlotte prompted her. At Alicia's blank look, she laughed. "We all have to show our faces in the conference hall in exactly five minutes, and Daniel delivered a new version of his official presidential lecture on tardiness last week. I wouldn't be late."

"I'll be right along," Alicia promised, and this time, managed a bit of a better smile.

She sighed heavily when Charlotte withdrew, feeling much too fragile. Hollow and raw, as if she was still fighting off that hangover she hadn't had. But she knew it was him. Nikolai. That much fire, that much wild heat, had to have a backlash. She shouldn't be surprised.

*This will fade,* she told herself, and she should know, shouldn't she? She'd had other things to forget. *It always does, eventually.*

But the current of self-loathing that wound through her then suggested otherwise.

This was not the end of the world. This was no more than a bit of backsliding into shameful behavior, and she wasn't very happy with herself for doing it, but it wouldn't happen again.

No one had walked in on her doing it. No one even knew. Everything was going to be fine.

Alicia blew out a shaky breath, closed down her computer, then made her way toward the big conference hall on the second floor, surprised to find the office already deserted. That could only mean that the celebrity charity in question was a particularly thrilling one. She racked her brain as she climbed the stairs, but she couldn't remember what the last memo had said about it or even if she'd read it.

She hated these meetings, always compulsory and always

about standard-waving, a little bit of morale-building, and most of all, PR. They were a waste of her time. Her duties involved the financial planning and off-site management of the charity's regional offices scattered across Latin America. Partnering with much bigger, much more well-known celebrity charities was more of a fundraising and publicity endeavor, which always made Daniel, their president, ecstatic—but didn't do much for Alicia.

She was glad she was a bit late, she thought as she hurried down the gleaming hallway on the second level. She could slip in, stand at the back, applaud loudly at something to catch Daniel's eye and prove she'd attended, then slip back out again and return to all that work on her messy desk.

Alicia silently eased open the heavy door at the rear of the hall. Down at the front, a man was talking confidently to the quiet, rapt room as she slipped inside.

At first she thought she was imagining it, given where her head had been all day.

And then it hit her. Hard.

She wasn't hearing things.

*She knew that voice.*

She'd know it anywhere. Her body certainly did.

Rough velvet. Russian. That scratch of whiskey, dark and powerful, commanding and sure.

*Nikolai.*

Her whole body went numb, nerveless. The door handle slipped from her hand, she jerked her head up to confirm what couldn't possibly be true, couldn't possibly be happening—

The heavy door slammed shut behind her with a terrific crash.

Every single head in the room swiveled toward her, as if she'd made her entrance in the glare of a bright, hot spotlight and to the tune of a boisterous marching band, complete with clashing cymbals.

But she only saw him.

Him. Nikolai. *Here.*

Once again, everything disappeared. There was only the fearsome blue of his beautiful eyes as they nailed her to the door behind her, slamming into her so hard she didn't know how she withstood it, how she wasn't on her knees from the force of it.

He was even more devastating than she'd let herself remember.

Still dressed all in black, today he wore an understated, elegant suit that made his lethal frame look consummately powerful rather than raw and dangerous, a clever distinction. And one that could only be made by expert tailoring to the tune of thousands upon thousands of pounds. The brutal force of him filled the room, filled her, and her body reacted as if they were still naked, still sprawled across his bed in a tangle of sheets and limbs. She felt too hot, almost feverish. His mouth was a harsh line, but she knew how it tasted and what it could do, and there was something dark and predatory in his eyes that made her tremble deep inside.

And remember. Dear God, what she remembered. What he'd done, how she'd screamed, what he'd promised and how he'd delivered, again and again and again....

It took her much too long to recollect where she was *now*.

Not in a club in Shoreditch this time, filled with drunken idiots who wouldn't recall what they did, much less what she did, but *in her office*. Surrounded by every single person she worked with, all of whom were staring at her.

Nikolai's gaze was so blue. So relentlessly, impossibly, mercilessly blue.

"I'm so sorry to interrupt," Alicia managed to murmur, hoping she sounded appropriately embarrassed and apologetic, the way anyone would after slamming that door—and not as utterly rocked to the core, as lit up with shock and horror, as she felt.

It took a superhuman effort to wrench her gaze away from the man who stood there glaring at her—who wasn't a figment of her overheated imagination, who had the same terrifying power over her from across a crowded room as he'd had in his bed, whom she'd never thought she'd see again, *ever*—and slink to an empty seat in the back row.

She would never know how she did it.

Down in the front of the room, a phalanx of assistants behind him and the screen above him announcing who he was in no uncertain terms, NIKOLAI KOROVIN OF THE KOROVIN FOUNDATION, she saw Nikolai blink. Once.

And then he kept talking as if Alicia hadn't interrupted him. As if he hadn't recognized her—as if Saturday night was no more than the product of her feverish imagination.

As if she didn't exist.

She'd never wished so fervently that she didn't. That she could simply disappear into the ether as if she'd never been, or sink into the hole in the ground she was sure his icy glare had dug beneath her.

What had she been thinking, to touch this man? To give herself to him so completely? Had she been drunk after all? Because today, here and now, he looked like nothing so much as a sharpened blade. Gorgeous and mesmerizing, but terrifying. That dark, ruthless power came off him in waves the way it had in the club, even stronger without the commotion of the music and the crowd, and this time, Alicia understood it.

This was who he was.

She *knew* who he was.

He was Nikolai Korovin. His brother was one of the most famous actors on the planet, which made Nikolai famous by virtue of his surname alone. Alicia knew his name like every other person in her field, thanks to his brilliant, inspired management of the Korovin Foundation since its creation two years ago. People whispered he was a harsh and demanding boss, but always fair, and the amount of money he'd already raised for the good causes the Korovin Foundation supported was staggering.

He was *Nikolai Korovin*, and he'd explored every part of her body with that hard, fascinating mouth. He'd held her in his arms and made her feel impossibly beautiful, and then he'd driven into her so hard, so deep, filling her so perfectly and driving her so out of her mind with pleasure, she had to bear down now to keep from reacting to the memory. He'd made her feel so wild with lust, so deliciously addicted to him, that she'd sobbed the last time she'd shattered into pieces all around him. *She knew how he tasted.* His mouth, his neck, the length of his proud sex. That angry, tattooed monster crouched on his chest. She knew what made him groan, fist his hands into her hair.

More than all of that, she knew how those bright eyes looked when he told her things she had the sense he didn't normally speak of to anyone. She knew too much.

He was Nikolai Korovin, and she didn't have to look over at Daniel's beaming face to understand what it meant that he was here. For Daniel as president, for making this happen. For the charity itself. A partnership with the Korovin Foundation was more than a publicity opportunity—it was a coup. It would take their relatively small charity with global ambitions and slam it straight into the big time, once and for all. And it went without saying that Nikolai Korovin, the legendary CEO of the Korovin Foundation and the person responsible for all its business decisions, needed to be kept happy for that to happen.

That look on his face when he'd seen her had been anything but happy.

Alicia had to force herself to sit still as the implications of this washed through her. She had betrayed herself completely and had a tawdry one-night stand. That was bad enough. But it turned out she'd done it with a man who could end her career.

Eight years ago she'd lost her father's respect and her own self-respect in the blur of a long night she couldn't even recall. Now she could lose her job.

Today. At the end of this meeting. Whenever Nikolai liked.

*When you decide to mess up your life, you really go for it,* she told herself, fighting back the panic, the prick of tears. *No simple messes for Alicia Teller! Better to go with total devastation!*

Alicia sat through the meeting in agony, expecting something to happen the moment it ended—lightning to strike, the world to come crashing to a halt, Nikolai to summon her to the front of the room and demand her termination at once—but nothing did. Nikolai didn't glance in her direction again. He and his many assistants merely swept from the hall like a sleek black cloud, followed by the still-beaming Daniel and all the rest of the upper level directors and managers.

Alicia told herself she was relieved. This had to be relief, this sharp thing in the pit of her stomach that made it hard to breathe, because nothing else made sense. She'd known he was dangerous the moment she'd met him, not that it had stopped her.

Now she knew exactly *how* dangerous.

She was an idiot. A soon-to-be-sacked idiot.

Her colleagues all grimaced in sympathy as they trooped

back downstairs. They thought the fact she'd slammed that door was embarrassing enough. Little did they know.

"Can't imagine having a man like that look at me the way he did you," one said in an undertone. "I think I'd have nightmares!"

"I believe I will," Alicia agreed.

She spent the rest of the afternoon torn between panic and dread. She attacked all the work on her desk, like a drowning woman grasping for something to hold. Every time her phone rang, her heart leaped in her chest. Every time she heard a noise outside her office door, she tensed, thinking she was finished.

Any minute now, she'd be called up to Daniel's office. She could see it spool out before her like a horror film. Daniel's secretary would message the salacious news to half the office even as Alicia walked to her doom. So not only would Alicia be dismissed from her job because of a tawdry one-night stand with a man most people would have recognized and she certainly should have—but everyone she worked with and respected would know it.

It would be as it had been that morning her father had woken her up and told her what he'd seen, what she'd done—but this time, far more people would know what kind of trollop she was. People she'd impressed with her work ethic over the years would now sit about imagining her naked. *Having sex. With Nikolai.* She felt sick even thinking about it.

"I warned you!" Charlotte said as she stuck her head through the doorway, making Alicia jump again. A quick, terrified glance told her that her supervisor looked…sympathetic. Not horribly embarrassed. Not scandalized in the least. "I told Daniel you were on a call that ran a bit long, so no worries there."

"Thank you." Alicia's voice sounded strained, but Charlotte didn't seem to notice.

"Nikolai Korovin is very intense, isn't he?" Charlotte shook her head. "The man has eyes like a laser beam!"

"I expect he doesn't get interrupted very often," Alicia said, fighting for calm. "I don't think he cares for it."

"Clearly not," Charlotte agreed. And then laughed.

And that was it. No request that Alicia pack up her things or don a scarlet letter. No summons to present herself in Daniel's office to be summarily dismissed for her sexually permissive behavior with the fiercely all-business CEO of their new celebrity partner foundation. Not even the faintest hint of a judgmental look.

But Alicia knew it was coming. She'd not only seen the way Nikolai had looked at her, but now that she knew that he was Nikolai *Korovin,* she was afraid she knew exactly what it meant.

He was utterly ruthless. About everything. The entire internet agreed.

It was only a matter of time until all hell broke loose, so she simply put her head down, kept off the internet because it only served to panic her more, and worked. She stayed long after everyone else had left. She stayed until she'd cleared her desk, because that way, when they tittered behind their hands and talked about how they'd never imagined her acting *that way,* at least they wouldn't be able to say she hadn't done her job.

Small comfort, indeed.

It was almost nine o'clock when she finished, and Alicia was completely drained. She shrugged into her coat and wrapped her scarf around her neck, wishing there was a suit of armor she could put on instead, some way to ward off what she was certain was coming. Dread sat heavy in her stomach, leaden and full, and there was nothing she could do about it but wait to see what Nikolai did. Go home, hole up on the couch with a takeaway and Rosie's usual happy chatter, try to ease this terrible anxiety with bad American television and wait to see what he'd do to her. Because he was Nikolai Korovin, and he could do whatever he liked.

And would. Of that, she had no doubt.

Alicia made her way out of the building, deciding the moment she stepped out into the cold, clear night that she should walk home instead of catching the bus. It was only thirty-five minutes or so at a brisk pace, and it might sort out her head. Tire her out. Maybe even allow her to sleep.

She tucked her hands into her pockets and started off, but had only made it down the front stairs to the pavement when she realized that the big black SUV pulled up to the curb wasn't parked there, but was idling.

A whisper of premonition tingled through her as she drew closer, then turned into a tumult when the back door cracked open before her.

Nikolai Korovin appeared from within the way she should have known he would, tall and thunderous and broadcasting that dark, brooding intensity of his. He didn't have to block her path. He simply closed the door behind him and stood there, taking over the whole neighborhood, darker than the sky above, and Alicia was as unable to move as if he'd pinned her to the ground himself.

She was caught securely in his too-knowing, too-blue gaze all over again, as if he held her in his hands, and the shiver of hungry need that teased down the length of her spine only added insult to injury. She despaired of herself.

If she respected herself at all, Alicia knew with that same old kick of shame in her gut, she wouldn't feel even that tiny little spark of something far too much like satisfaction that he was here. That he'd come for her. As if maybe he was as thrown by what had happened between them as she was...

"Hello, Alicia," Nikolai said, a dark lash in that rough voice of his, velvet and warning and so very Russian, smooth power and all of that danger in every taut line of his beautiful body. He looked fierce. Cold and furious. "Obviously, we need to talk."

# CHAPTER FOUR

FOR A MOMENT, Alicia wanted nothing more than to run.

To bolt down the dark street like some desperate animal of prey and hope that this particular predator had better things to do than follow.

Something passed between them then, a shimmer in the dark, and Alicia understood that he knew exactly what she was thinking. That he was picturing the same thing. The chase, the inevitable capture, and *then*...

Nikolai's eyes gleamed dangerously.

Alicia tilted up her chin, settled back on her heels and faced him, calling on every bit of courage and stamina at her disposal. She wasn't going to run. She might have done something she was ashamed of, but she hadn't done it alone. And this time she had to face it—she couldn't skulk off back to university and limit her time back home as she'd done for years until the Reddicks moved to the north.

"Well," she said briskly. "This is awkward."

His cold eyes blazed. He was so different tonight, she thought. A blade of a man gone near incandescent with that icy rage, a far cry from the man she'd thought she'd seen in those quieter moments—the one who had told her things that still lodged in her heart. The change should have terrified her. Instead, perversely, she felt that hunger shiver deeper into her, settling into a hard knot low in her belly, turning into a thick, sweet heat.

"This is not awkward," he replied, his voice deceptively mild. Alicia could see that ferocious look in his eyes, however, and wasn't fooled. "This is a quiet conversation on a deserted street."

"Perhaps the word loses something in translation?" she suggested, perhaps a shade too brightly, as if that was some defense against the chill of him.

*"Awkward,"* he bit out, his accent more pronounced than before and a fascinating pulse of temper in the hinge of his tight jaw, "was looking up in the middle of a business meeting today to see a woman I last laid eyes upon while I was making her come stare right back at me."

Alicia didn't want to think about the last time he'd made her come. She'd thought they were finished after all those long, heated hours. He'd taken that as a challenge. And he'd held her hips between his hands and licked into her with lazy intent, making her writhe against him and sob....

She swallowed, and wished he wasn't watching her. He saw far too much.

"You're looking at me as if I engineered this. I didn't." She eyed him warily, her hands deep in the pockets of her coat and curled into fists, which he couldn't possibly see. Though she had the strangest notion he could. "I thought the point of a one-night stand with no surnames exchanged was that this would never happen."

"Have you had a great many of them, then?"

Alicia pretended that question didn't hit her precisely where she was the most raw, and with a ringing blow.

"If you mean as many as you've had, certainly not." She shrugged when his dark brows rose in a kind of affronted astonishment. "There are no secrets on the internet. Surely you, of all people, must know that. And it's a bit late to tally up our numbers and draw unflattering conclusions, don't you think? The damage is well and truly done."

"That damage," Nikolai said, that rough voice of his too tough, too cold, and that look on his hard face merciless, "is what I'm here to discuss."

Alicia didn't want to lose her job. She didn't want to know what kind of pressure Nikolai was prepared to put on her, what threats he was about to issue. She wanted this to go away again—to be the deep, dark secret that no one ever knew but her.

And it still could be, no matter how pitiless he looked in that moment.

"Why don't we simply blank each other?" she asked, once again a touch too brightly—which she could see didn't fool him at all. If anything, it called attention to her nervousness. "Isn't that the traditional method of handling situations like this?"

He shook his head, his eyes looking smoky in the dark, his mouth a resolute line.

"I do not mix business and pleasure," he said, with a finality that felt like a kick in the stomach. "I do not *mix* at all. The women I sleep with do not infiltrate my life. They appear in carefully orchestrated places of my choosing. They do not ambush me at work. Ever."

Alicia decided that later—much later, when she knew how this ended and could breathe without thinking she might burst into panicked, frustrated tears—she would think about the fact that a man like Nikolai had so many women that he'd developed *policies* to handle them all. *Later.* Right now, she had to fight back, or surrender here and now and lose everything.

"I assure you," she said, as if she had her own set of violated policies and was considering them as she met his gaze, "I feel the same way."

Nikolai shifted, and then suddenly there was no distance between them at all. His hands were on her neck, his thumbs at her jaw, tipping her head back to look up at him. Alicia should have felt attacked, threatened. She should have leaped for safety. Screamed. *Something.*

But instead, everything inside of her went still. And hot.

"I am not here to concern myself with your feelings," he told her in that rough velvet whisper. That fascinating mouth was grim again, but she could almost touch it with hers, if she dared. She didn't. "I am here to eliminate this problem as swiftly and as painlessly as possible."

But his hands were on her. Just as they'd been in the club when he'd told her to run. And she wondered if he was as conflicted as she was, and as deeply. What it would take to see that guarded look on his face again, that vulnerable cast to his beautiful mouth.

"You really are the gift that keeps on giving, Nikolai," she managed to say, retreating to a sarcastic tone, hoping the bite of it might protect her. She even smiled, thinly. "I've never felt happier about my reckless, irresponsible choices."

He let out a short laugh, and whatever expression that was on his hard face then—oddly taut and expectant, dark and hot—was like a flame inside of her. His hands were strong and like brands against her skin. His thumbs moved gently, lazily, as if stroking her jaw of their own accord.

"I don't like sharp women with smart mouths, Alicia," he told her, harsh and low, and every word was a caress against her skin, her sex, as if he was using those long fingers deep in her heat. "I like them sweet. Soft. Yielding and obedient and easily dismissed."

That same electricity crackled between them even here on the cold street, a bright coil that wound tight inside of her, making her feel mad with it. Too close to an explosion she knew she couldn't allow.

"What luck," she said, sharp and smart and nothing like soft at all. "I believe there's a sex shop in the next street, filled with exactly the kind of plastic dolls you prefer. Shall I point you in the right direction?"

He let go of her as if she'd burned him. And she recognized that dark heat in his gaze, the way it changed his expression, the things it did to that mouth.

"Get in the car, Alicia," he ordered her darkly. "I have an aversion to discussing my private life on a public street, deserted or not."

It was her turn to laugh, in disbelief.

"You have to be crazy if you think I'm getting back in that thing," she told him. "I'd rather get down on my hands and knees and crawl across a bed of nails, thank you."

She knew it was a mistake almost before the words left her mouth, and that sudden wolfish look on his face nearly undid her. It was impossible, then, not to picture herself down on her hands and knees, crawling toward that ravenous heat in his winter eyes she could remember too well, and could see right there before her now.

"I wasn't thinking about sex at present," he said coolly, and even though she could see from that fire in his gaze that he'd imagined much the same thing she had, she felt slapped. Shamed anew. "Why? Were you?"

It was time to go, Alicia realized then. It had been time to go the moment she'd seen that SUV idling at the curb. Before this thing got any worse—and she had no doubt at all that it would.

"It was lovely to finally meet you properly, Mr. Korovin," she said crisply. She put a faint emphasis on the word *properly,* and he blinked, looking almost…abashed? But that was impossible. "I'm sure your partnership with the charity will be a huge boost for us, and I'm as grateful as anyone else. And now I'm going home, where I will continue to actively pretend none of this ever happened. I can only hope you'll do the same."

"You didn't tell me you worked for a children's charity."

She didn't know what she'd expected him to say, but it wasn't that, with that sting of accusation. She eyed him warily. "Neither did you."

"Did you know who I was, Alicia?" Nikolai's face was so hard, his gaze so cold. She felt the chill suddenly, cutting into her. "You stumbled into my arms. Then you stumbled into that conference room today. Convenient." His eyes raked over her, as if looking for evidence that she'd planned this nightmare. "Your next stumble had best not involve any tabloid magazines or tell-all interviews. You won't like how I respond."

But she couldn't believe he truly thought that, she realized when the initial shock of it passed. She'd been in that bed with him. She knew better. Which meant he was lashing out, seeing what would hurt her. *Eliminating problems,* as he'd said he would.

"There's no need to draw out this torture," she told him, proud of how calm she sounded. "If you want me sacked, we both know you can do it easily. Daniel would have the entire staff turn cartwheels down the length of the Mall if he thought that would please you. Firing me will be a snap." She squared her shoulders as if she might have to sustain a blow. As if she already had. "If that's what you plan to do, I certainly can't stop you."

He stared at her for a long moment. A car raced past on the street beside them and in the distance she could hear the rush of traffic on the main road. Her breath was coming hard and fast, like she was fighting whole battles in her head while he only stood there, still and watchful.

"You're a distraction, Alicia," he told her then, something like regret in his voice. "I can't pretend otherwise."

"Of course you can," she retorted, fighting to keep calm. "All people do is pretend. I pretended to be the sort of woman—" She didn't want to announce exactly what she'd been pretending for eight years, not to him, so she frowned instead. "Just ignore me and I'll return the favor. It will be easy."

"I am not the actor in the family."

"I didn't ask you to play *King Lear*," she threw at him, panicked and exasperated in equal measure. "I only asked you to ignore me. How difficult can that possibly be? A man like you must have that down to a science."

"What an impression you have of me," Nikolai said after a moment, his voice silken, his eyes narrow. "I treated you very well, Alicia. Have you forgot so soon? You wept out your gratitude, when you weren't screaming my name."

She didn't need the reminder. She didn't need the heat of it, the wild pulse in her chest, between her legs.

"I was referring to your wealth and status," Alicia said, very distinctly. "Your position. The fact you have armies of assistants to make sure no one can approach you without your permission. Not your…"

"Particular talents?" His voice was mild enough as he finished the thought for her. The effect his words had on her, inside her, was not.

But then he leaned back against the side of his car, as if he was perfectly relaxed. Even his face changed, and she went still again, because there was something far more predatory about him in this moment than there had been before. It scraped the air thin.

"I have a better solution," he said, in the confident and commanding tone she recognized from the conference room. "I don't need to fire you, necessarily. It will serve my purposes far better to use this situation to my advantage."

Alicia could only shake her head, looking for clues on

that face of his that gave nothing away. "I don't know what that means."

"It means, Alicia," he said almost softly, a wolf's dangerous smile in those winter eyes if not on that hard mouth, "that I need a date."

He could use this, Nikolai thought, while Alicia stared up at him as if he'd said that last sentence in Russian instead of English. He could use her.

A problem well managed could become a tool. And every tool could be a weapon, in the right hands. Why not Alicia?

He'd expected her to want more than Saturday night—they always did. And the sex they'd had had been...troubling. He'd known it while it was happening. He'd known it in between, when he'd found himself talking of things he never, ever talked about. He'd known it when he'd opened his eyes to watch her tiptoe from his room on Sunday morning, and had discovered he wanted her to stay.

He knew it now, remembering her sweet, hot mouth against his tattoo as if she'd blessed that snarling representation of the monster in him. As if she'd made it sacred, somehow. The moment he'd seen her, he'd expected she would try to leverage that, take it from him somehow. He'd planned to make it clear to her she had to go—before she could try.

But she claimed she wanted to ignore him. He should have been thrilled.

He told himself he was.

"I'm sorry." Her voice was carefully blank when she finally spoke, to match the expression on her face. "Did you say you needed a *date?*"

"I did." It occurred to him that he was enjoying himself, for the first time since he'd looked up and seen her standing in that conference room, in clear violation of all his rules. "There is a Christmas ball in Prague that I must attend in a few weeks, and it will go much more smoothly with a woman on my arm."

These things were always better with a date, it was true. It didn't matter who it was. The presence of any date at his side would repel most of the vulturelike women who always circled him like he was fresh meat laid out in the hot sun, allowing Nikolai to concentrate on business. And in the case of this particular charity ball, on Veronika—who had only this morning confirmed that she and her lover would attend.

Because Nikolai had realized, as he looked at her in the light of the streetlamps and thought strategy instead of containment, that Alicia could very well turn out to be the best weapon yet in his dirty little war.

"I'm certain there are hordes of women who would love nothing more than to fill that opening for you," she said, with none of the deference or courtesy he was used to from his subordinates and dates alike. There was no reason on earth he should find that intriguing. "Perhaps one of your many assistants has a sign-up sheet? A call list? Maybe even an audition process to weed out the lucky winner from the multitudes?"

He'd told her he liked sweet and biddable, and he did. But he liked this, too. He liked the way she talked to him, as if it hadn't occurred to her that she should fear him like everyone else did. It made him want to lick her until all of that tartness melted all over him, and he didn't want to examine that particular urge any closer.

"Something like that," he said. "But it's all very tedious. All I want is a pretty dress, a polite smile. I don't have time for the games."

"Or the person, apparently," she said, her voice dry. "I'm

sure that's very rewarding for whichever pretty dress you choose. But what does this have to do with me?"

Nikolai smiled, adrenaline moving through him the way it always did before a tactical strike. Before another win.

"You want nothing to do with me." His voice was a silken threat in the cold night. "Or so you claim."

"You're right," she said, but her voice caught. "I don't."

"Then it's perfect," he said. "It's only a handful of weeks until the ball. We'll allow ourselves to be photographed on a few dates. The world will think I'm smitten, as I am very rarely seen with the same woman more than once. More specifically, my ex-wife will think the same. And as she has always greatly enjoyed her fantasy that she is the only woman to have any power over me, and has never been one to resist a confrontation, it will put her right where I want her."

She stared at him. "And where is that, exactly?"

"Veronika and I need to have a conversation," Nikolai said with cool dismissal. "Hopefully, our last. The idea that I might have moved on will expedite that, I think."

"How tempting," she said after a moment, her voice as arid as that look in her eyes. "I've always aspired to be cold-bloodedly used to make another woman jealous, of course. It's truly every girl's dream. But I think I'll pass."

"This has nothing to do with jealousy," he said impatiently. "The only thing left between Veronika and me is spite. If that. I'm sure you'll see it yourself at the ball."

"Even more appealing. But still—no."

"Your whole office saw me stare at you today." He shrugged when her eyes narrowed. "They could hardly miss it. How much of a leap will it be for them to imagine that was the beginning of an infatuation?"

"But they won't have to make that leap." Her eyes were

glittering again. "I've declined your lovely offer and we're going to ignore each other."

"I don't think so." He watched her take that in. Knew she didn't like it. Found he didn't much care if she was happy about it, so long as she did it. "I'm going to take an interest in you, Alicia. Didn't you know? Everybody loves a romance."

"They won't believe it." Her voice sounded thick, as if the idea of it horrified her, and he was perverse enough to take that as a challenge. "They won't believe someone like you could get infatuated at all, much less with me."

He smiled. "They will. And more to the point, so will Veronika."

And he could kill two birds with one stone. He could dig into this attraction, the unacceptable intoxication this woman made him feel, and in so doing, strip away its power over him. Make certain he never again felt the need to unburden himself in such a shockingly uncharacteristic manner to a total stranger. At the same time, he could use Veronika's smug certainty about her place in his life against her. It was perfect.

Alicia stared back at him, so hard he thought he could hear her mind racing.

"Why bring any of this into the office at all?" she asked, sounding frustrated. Panicked, even. "If you want me to go to this ball, fine. I'll do it, but I don't see why anyone needs to know about it but us. No unlikely romance necessary."

"And how will that work?" he asked mildly. "When pictures of us at that ball show up in all the papers, and they will, it will look as if we were keeping our relationship a secret. As if we were hiding something. Think of the gossip then."

"You said you're not an actor," she said. "Yet this seems like a very elaborate bit of theater."

"I told you, you're a distraction," he replied, almost gently. He wanted to show her what he meant. To bury his face in that crook of her neck. To make her quiver for him the way he knew he could. Only the fact he wanted it too much kept him from it. "I don't allow distractions, Alicia. I neutralize them or I use them for my own ends."

"I don't want to be in any papers." Her voice was low, her eyes intense on his. It took him a moment to realize she was panicked. A better man might not have enjoyed that. "I don't want *pictures* of me out there, and certainly not with you."

"There's a certain liberty in having no choices, Alicia," he told her, not sure why it bothered him that she was so opposed to a picture *with him*. It made his voice harsher. "It makes life very simple. Do what I tell you to do, or look for a new job."

Nikolai didn't think that was the first moment it had occurred to her that he held all the power here, but it was no doubt when she realized he had every intention of using it as he pleased. He saw it on her face. In her remarkable eyes.

And he couldn't help but touch her again then, sliding his hand over her cheek as he'd done before. He felt the sweet heat of her where his fingertips touched her hairline, the chill of her soft skin beneath his palm. And that wild heat that was only theirs, sparking wild, charging through him.

Making him almost wish he was a different man.

She wore a thick black coat against the cold, a bright red scarf looped around her elegant neck. Her ink-black curls were pulled back from her face with a scrap of brightly patterned fabric, and he knew that beneath it she was dressed in even more colors, bright colors. Emerald greens and chocolate browns. She was so bright it made his head spin, even here in the dark. It made him achingly hard.

*She is nothing more than an instrument,* he told himself.

*Another weapon for your arsenal. And soon enough, this intoxication will fade into nothing.*

"Please," she whispered, and he wished he were the kind of man who could care. Who could soothe her. But he wasn't, no matter what he told her in the dark. "You don't understand. I don't want to lose my job, but I can't do this."

"You can," Nikolai told her. "And you will." He felt more in control than he had since she'd slammed into him at the edge of that dance floor, and he refused to give that up again. He wouldn't. "I'll be the one infatuated, Alicia. You need only surrender."

She shook her head, but she didn't pull her face from his grasp, and he knew what that meant even if she didn't. He knew what surrender looked like, and he smiled.

"Feel free to refuse me at first," he told Alicia then, his voice the only soft thing about him, as if he was a sweet and gentle lover and these words were the poetry he'd told her he didn't write. As if he was someone else. Maybe it would help her to think so. "Resist me, if you can. That will only make it look better."

"I won't do it," Alicia told him, hearing how unsteady her voice was and hating that he heard it, too. Hating all of this. "I won't play along."

"You will," he said in that implacable way that made something inside her turn over and shiver, while that half smile played with the corner of his hard mouth as if he knew something she didn't. "Or I'll have you sacked so fast it will make your head spin. And don't mistake sexual attraction for mercy, Alicia. I don't have any."

"Of course not," she bit out, as afraid that she would burst into tears right there as she was that she would nestle further into his hand, both impulses terrible and overwhelming at once. "You're the big, bad wolf. Fangs and teeth. I get the picture. I still won't do it."

She wrenched herself away from the terrible beguilement of his touch then, and ran down the street the way she should have at the start, panic biting at her heels as if she thought he might chase her.

He didn't—but then, he didn't have to chase her personally. His words did that for him. They haunted her as she tossed and turned in her sleepless bed that night. They moved over her like an itch she couldn't scratch. Like a lash against her skin, leaving the kind of scars he wore in their wake. Kitchen knives and bullets.

*Do what I tell you to do.*

Alicia was appalled at herself. He could say terrible things, propose to use her in some sick battle with his ex-wife, and still, she wanted him. He was mean and surly and perfectly happy to threaten her—and she wanted him. She lay awake in her bed and shivered when she thought about that last, simple touch, his hand hot despite the chill of the night air, holding her face so gently, making everything inside her run together and turn into honey.

Because that fool inside of her wanted that touch to mean something more. Wanted this attraction between them to have more to do with that vulnerability he'd shown her than the sex they'd had.

Wanted Saturday night to be different from that terrible night eight years ago.

*He wants to use you, nothing more,* she reminded herself for the millionth time, punching at her pillow in exhausted despair. *It means nothing more than that.*

But Alicia couldn't have pictures of herself in the tabloids. Not at all, and certainly not in the company of a man who might have been called a playboy, had he been less formidable. Not that it mattered what they called him—her father would know exactly what he was. Too wealthy, too hard. Too obvious. A man like that wanted women for one thing only, and her father would know it.

He would think she was back to old tricks. She knew he would.

Alicia shuddered, her face pressed into her pillow. She could *see* that awful look on her father's face that hideous morning as if he stood in front of her the way he'd done then.

"He is a *married man*. You know his wife, his children," her father had whispered, looking as deeply horrified as Alicia had felt.

"Dad," she'd managed to say, though her head had pounded and her mouth had been like sand. "Dad, I don't know what happened.... It's all—I don't remember—"

"I know what happened," he'd retorted, disgust plain in his voice and all across his face. "I saw you, spread-eagled on the grass with a *married man,* our *neighbor*—"

"Dad—" she'd tried again, tears in her voice and her eyes, afraid she might be sick.

"The way you dress, the way you flaunt yourself." He'd shaken his head, condemnation and that deep disgust written all over him. "I knew you dressed like a common whore, Alicia, but I never thought you'd *act* like one."

She couldn't go through that again, she thought then, staring in mute despair at her ceiling. She wouldn't go through it again, no matter how *infatuated* Nikolai pretended he was. No matter what.

He was going to have to fire her, she decided. She would call his bluff.

"No," she said, very firmly, when a coworker ran up to her the following day as she fixed herself a midmorning cup of tea and breathlessly asked if she'd *heard*. "Heard what?"

But she had a terrible suspicion she could guess. Ruthless and efficient, that was Nikolai.

"Nikolai Korovin *expressly* asked after you at the meeting this morning!" the excitable Melanie from the PR team whispered in that way of hers that alerted the entire office and most of the surrounding neighborhood, her eyes wide and pale cheeks red with the thrill of it all. "He *grilled* the team about you! Do you think that means he…?"

She couldn't finish that sentence, Alicia noted darkly. It was too much for Melanie. The very idea of Nikolai Korovin's interest—his *infatuation*—made the girl practically crumple into a shivering heap at Alicia's feet.

"I imagine he's the kind of man who keeps an annotated enemies list within arm's reach and several elaborate revenge plots at the ready," Alicia said as calmly as possible, dumping as much cold water on this fire of his as she could, even though she suspected it wouldn't do any good. "He certainly doesn't *like* me, Melanie."

The other woman didn't looked particularly convinced, no doubt because Alicia's explanation flew in the face of the grand romance she'd already concocted in her head. Just as Nikolai had predicted.

"No, thank you," Alicia told the emissary from his army of assistants two days after that, who walked up to Alicia as she stood in the open plan part of the office with every eye trained on her and asked if she might want to join them all for a meal after work?

"Mr. Korovin wanted me to tell you that it's a restaurant in Soho he thinks you'd quite enjoy," the woman persisted, her smile never dropping from her lips. "One of his favorites in London. And his treat, of course."

Alicia's heart hammered in her chest so hard she wondered for a panicked moment if she was having some kind of heart attack. Then she remembered how many people were watching her, much too avidly, and forced a polite smile in return.

"I'm still catching up from my trip," she lied. "I'll have to work late again, I'm afraid. But please do thank Mr. Korovin for thinking of me."

Somehow, that last part didn't choke her.

By the end of that week, the fact that ruthless and somewhat terrifying billionaire Nikolai Korovin had *taken an interest* in Alicia was the only thing anyone in the office seemed able to talk about, and he'd accomplished it without lowering himself to speak to her directly. She felt hunted, trapped, and she hadn't even seen him since that night on the street.

He was diabolical.

"I believe Nikolai Korovin wants to *date* you, Alicia," Charlotte said as they sat in her office on Friday morning, going over the presentation for their team meeting later that afternoon. She grinned widely when Alicia looked at her. "I don't know whether to be excited or a bit overwhelmed at the idea of someone like him dating a normal person."

"This is so embarrassing," Alicia said weakly, which was perhaps the first honest thing she'd said on the topic all week. "I honestly don't know why he's doing this."

"Love works in mysterious ways," Charlotte singsonged, making Alicia groan.

*Everybody loves a romance,* he'd said in that cold, cynical voice of his. Damn him.

"This is a man who could date anyone in the world, and has done," Alicia said, trying to sound lighter, breezier, than she felt. "Why on earth should a man like that want to date *me?*"

"You didn't drop at his feet on command, obviously," Charlotte said with a shrug. Only because he hadn't issued that particular command that night, Alicia thought sourly, fighting to keep her expression neutral. "Men like Nikolai Korovin are used to having anything they desire the moment they desire it. Ergo, they desire most what they can't have."

Alicia hadn't been so happy to see the end of a work week in years. She hated him, she told herself that weekend, again and again and again, until she could almost pretend that she really did. That it was that simple.

"I hate him," she told Rosie, taking out her feelings on the sad little boil-in-the-bag chicken curry they'd made for Sunday dinner with a violent jab of her fork. It had been two blessed Nikolai-free days. She couldn't bear the thought of what tomorrow might bring. "He's incredibly unprofessional. He's made the whole office into a circus! Nothing but gossip about him and me, all day every day!"

Rosie eyed Alicia from her side of the sofa, her knees pulled up beneath her and her blond hair piled haphazardly on her head.

"Maybe he likes you."

"No. He does not. This is some kind of sick game he's playing for his own amusement. That's the kind of man he is."

"No kind of man goes to all that trouble," her friend said slowly. "Not for a game. He really could simply like you, Alicia. In his own terrifyingly wealthy sort of way, I mean."

"He doesn't like *me,* Rosie," Alicia retorted, with too much heat, but she couldn't stop it. "The women he likes come with their own *Vogue* covers."

But she could see that Rosie was conjuring up Cinderella stories in her head, like everyone else, as Nikolai had known they would. Alicia felt so furious, so desperate and so trapped, that she shook with it. She felt his manipulation like a touch, like he was sitting right there next to her, that big body of his deceptively lazy, running his amused fingers up and down her spine.

*You wish you were anything as uncomplicated as furious,* a little voice taunted her, deep inside.

"Maybe you should play along," Rosie said then, and she grinned wide. "It's not going to be a drink down at the pub on a date with the likes of him, is it? He's the sort who has *mistresses,* not *girlfriends.* He could fly you to Paris for dinner. He could whisk you off to some private island. Or one of those great hulking yachts they always have."

"He could ruin my reputation," Alicia countered, and yet despite herself, wondered what being Nikolai's *mistress* would entail—what sort of lover he would be, what kind of sensual demands he would make if he had more than one night to make them. All of that lethal heat and all the time in the world… How could anyone survive it? She shoved the treacherous thoughts aside. "He could make things very difficult for me at work."

"Only because they'll all be seething with jealousy," Rosie said with a dismissive sniff. "And your reputation could use a little ruining."

Because she couldn't imagine what it was like to *actually* be ruined, Alicia knew. To have gone and ruined herself so carelessly, so irrevocably. She couldn't know what it was like to see that disgust in her own father's eyes whenever he looked at her. To feel it in her own gut, like a cancer.

Rosie smiled again, wickedly. "And I think Nikolai Korovin sounds like the kind of man who knows his way around a ruining."

Alicia only stabbed her chicken again. Harder. And then scowled at the television as if she saw anything at all but Nikolai, wherever she looked.

# CHAPTER FIVE

ALICIA WAS RUNNING a file up to Charlotte's office the following week when she finally ran into him, larger than life, sauntering down the stairs in the otherwise-empty stairwell as if he hadn't a care in the world.

The shock of it—the force and clamor that was Nikolai—hit her as hard as it had at the club. As it had outside the office building that night. Making her feel restless in her own skin. Electric.

*Furious,* she told herself sternly.

He saw her instantly and smiled, that tug in the corner of his hard mouth that made her insides turn to water no matter how much she wished it didn't. No matter how much she wanted to be immune to it. To him.

Because whatever she was, whatever this *thing* was that made her so aware of him, she certainly wasn't immune.

And Nikolai knew it.

He moved like water, smooth and inexorable. He seemed bigger than he actually was, as if he was so powerful he couldn't be contained and so expanded to fit—and to effortlessly dominate—any and all available space. Even an ordinary stairwell. Today he wore another absurdly well-fitting suit in his usual black, this one a rapturous love letter to his lean, muscled, dangerous form. He looked sinfully handsome, ruthless and cool, wealthy beyond imagining, and it infuriated her. So deeply it hurt.

Alicia told herself that was all it did.

"This is harassment," she informed him as she marched up the stairs, her heels clicking hard against each step, her tone as brisk as her spine was straight.

"No," he said, his gaze on hers. "It isn't."

Alicia stopped moving only when she'd reached the step above him, enjoying the fact it put her on eye level with him, for once. Even if those eyes were far too blue, bright and laughing at her, that winter cold moving in her, heating her from within.

*She hated him.*

God, how she wished she could hate him.

"It most certainly is," she corrected him with a bit of his own frostiness. "And I hate to break this to you when you've gone ahead and made your pretend infatuation so public, but it's actually quite easy to resist you."

"Is it?" He shouldn't sound so amused. So indulgent.

She would have scowled at him, but thought he would read that as weakness. Instead, she tilted up her chin and tried to project the kind of tough, cool competence she wished she felt as she called his bluff to his face.

"I'm not going to take part in your little bit of revenge theater no matter how much time you spend feeding the office gossip mill," she told him. Tough. Calm. Cool. "If you want to have me fired because you took me home from a club of your own free will, go right ahead." She let that sit there for a moment, then angled her head ever so slightly closer to his, for emphasis. "I didn't do anything wrong, I'm not afraid of you and I'd advise you try to communicate with your ex-wife through more traditional channels."

Nikolai simply…shifted position.

He moved with a primal grace that robbed her of speech,

pivoting without seeming to do so much as breathe. All Alicia knew was that she was facing him one moment and the next her back was up against the wall. As if he'd *willed* her to let him cage her there, his hands flat against the smooth wall on either side of her face.

He hadn't laid so much as a single finger upon her. He didn't now. He leaned in.

Much too close, and her body reacted as if he'd plugged her into the nearest socket. The white-hot light of this shocking heat between them pulsed through her, making her gasp. Her body betrayed her in a shivering flush, sensation scraping through her, making her skin pull taut, her breasts feel suddenly full and that wet, hot hunger punch its way into her belly before settling down between her legs. Where it stayed, a wild and greedy need, and all of it his. *His.*

As if she was, too.

"What the hell are you doing?" But it was no more than a whisper, and it gave her away as surely as that treacherous ache inside of her that Alicia was sure he could sense, somehow.

"I am a man possessed," Nikolai murmured, his mouth so close to hers she felt the pull of it, the ache, roll through her like a flash of pain, despite the hint of laughter she could hear in his voice. "Infatuated. Just as I promised you."

"I can see why your brother is the famous actor while you storm about, growling at other rich men and demanding their money." But her voice was little more than a breath, completely insubstantial, and she had to dig her fingers into the folder she carried to keep from touching that glorious chest that was right there in front of her, taunting her. "Because you're not terribly convincing, and by the way, I'm fairly certain this counts as stalking."

"Those are very strong words, Alicia." He didn't sound

concerned. Nikolai rested his considerable, sleek weight on his hands and surrounded her. Hemmed her in. Let his body remind her of all those things she wanted to forget. *Needed* to forget. "Harassment. Stalking."

"Strong, yes." She could feel her pulse in her throat, a frantic staccato. "And also accurate."

Alicia felt more than heard his small laugh against the tender skin of her neck, and she knew he saw the goose bumps that prickled there when he lifted that knowing gaze to hers.

"This is the first time I've seen you inside this office since you walked into the conference hall." Nikolai didn't move back. He gave her no room to breathe. If she tried to twist away, to escape him the way she wanted to do, she would have to brush up against him—and she didn't dare do that. She couldn't trust herself. Not when he smelled like winter. Not when she had the alarming urge to bury her face in his chest. "I haven't followed you around making suggestive comments. I extended a single invitation to you, Alicia. I didn't even do it myself. And you declined it without any repercussions at all."

"Says the man who has me pinned up against a wall."

"I'm not touching you," Nikolai pointed out, that dangerously lazy gleam in his bright gaze. "I'm not restraining you in any way. I could, of course." That gleam grew hotter, making her toes curl inside her shoes, making that need inside her rage into a wildfire. Making her despair of herself. "All you have to do is ask."

"I want you to stop this," she managed to get out, desperate to fight off the maelstrom he'd unleashed in her, the images carnal and tempting that chased through her head and made her much too aware of how weak she was.

How perilously close to compounding the error she'd already made with this man, right here in her office. In the *stairwell*. Every inch of her the whore her father had called her.

"Which *this?*" He sounded impossibly male, then. Insufferably smug, as if he knew exactly how close she was to capitulation. "Be specific."

She shifted then, and it was agonizing. He was *right there,* and she knew she couldn't allow herself to touch him, not even by accident—but she was terribly afraid she wasn't going to be able to help herself. How could she fight herself *and* him?

"I'd rather be sacked right now than have to put up with this," she whispered fiercely.

He laughed again then, and she wished that sound didn't get to her. She wished she could simply ignore it and him along with it. But it made him that much more beautiful, like a perfect sunset over a rugged mountain, and it made something inside of her ignite no matter how much she wished it didn't.

"You and I both know I could prove you a liar." He dropped his head slightly, and inhaled, as if pulling the scent of her skin deep into his lungs, and that fire in her began to pulse, greedy and insistent. Her nipples pressed against the soft fabric of her dress, and she was terrified he'd see it. Terrified he'd *know*. "How long do you think it would take, *solnyshka?* One second? Two? How long before you wrap yourself around me and beg?"

Of course he knew. Hadn't that long night with him taught her anything?

Alicia stiffened, panic like a drumbeat inside of her, but it only seemed to make that fire in her burn hotter. Nikolai moved even closer, somehow, though that shouldn't have been possible, and he was so big, so powerful, that it was as if nothing existed except the breadth of his shoulders. He surrounded her, and there was a part of her way down deep that wasn't at all conflicted. That simply exulted in it. In him.

But that was the part that had started all this. The part that had looked up into his face in that dark club and surrendered, there and then. She couldn't succumb to his version of dark magic again. She had too much to lose.

"You don't understand," she said hurriedly, almost desperately. "This is—you are—" She pulled in a breath. "I'm afraid—"

But she couldn't tell Nikolai Korovin the things she feared. She couldn't say them out loud, and anyway, this was only a bitter little game to him. The ways she hated herself, the ways she'd let herself down, the way she'd destroyed her relationship with her father—he didn't need to know about any of that.

She couldn't understand why she had the strange urge to tell him anyway, when she'd never told a soul.

It seemed to take him a very long time to pull his head back far enough to look her in the eyes, to study her too-hot face. Even through her agitation, she could see him grow somber as he watched her. Darker. He pushed back from the wall, letting his hands drop to his sides, and Alicia told herself that was exactly what she'd wanted.

"Good," he said quietly, an expression she couldn't read on his hard face. "You should be afraid of me. You should have been afraid that night."

She scowled at him, not caring anymore what he read into it.

"For God's sake," she snapped, not liking that look on his face and not at all sure why it bothered her so much and so deeply. "I'm not afraid of *you*."

That sat there between them, telling him things she should have kept to herself, and the expression on his face made her think of that moment in his bed, suddenly. When he'd talked of kitchen knives and sins and she'd kissed his tattoo, as if she could kiss it all away. As if he was wounded.

"I thought you liked the fact that I *don't* want you," she said after a moment, when all he did was stare at her, in a manner she might have called haunted if it was someone other than Nikolai. "Why are you so determined to prove otherwise?"

"You mistake me." His voice was silky then, but there was a dark kick beneath it, and it shivered over her skin like a caress. "I know you want me. I still want you. I told you this was a distraction." He stuck his hands in his pockets, shifting back on his heels, and his expression grew cooler. More distant. Assessing her. "It's your disinterest in having any kind of connection to me, your horror at the very idea, that makes the rest of this possible."

"And by that do you mean keeping my job?" she asked, ignoring his talk of who wanted who, because she didn't dare let herself think about it. She couldn't go there, or who knew what would become of her? "Or the twisted game you feel you need to play with your ex-wife?"

Nikolai only stared back at her, his face a study in ice. Impassive and cool.

"Let me guess," she said tightly. "You only want what you can't have."

"But you don't qualify, Alicia," he said, in that dangerously soft way of his that was like a seismic event inside of her, and she had to fight to hide the aftershocks. "I've already had you."

"That was a mistake," she retorted, and she wanted to play it down. Laugh, smile. But his eyes flashed and she knew she'd sounded too dark. Too close to *hurt*. "There won't be a repeat."

"You don't want to challenge me to prove you wrong."

His winter eyes probed hers, moved over her face, saw things she didn't want to share. "Or perhaps you do."

That last was a low growl. Wolf again, not man, and she wasn't sure she could survive it without imploding. Without betraying herself all over again, and there was no *wild night* to lose herself in, not here in this chilly stairwell. No pounding music, no shouting crowd. She felt the danger in him, the profound sensual threat, like heat all around her, seducing her without a single word or touch. She could smell that scent that was only his, the faint smoke and crisp slap of winter. She felt the strength of him, that lethal power, and her fingers ached to explore it again, every last lean muscle, until he groaned beneath her hands.

And she *wanted*.

Suddenly, and with every last cell in her body, Alicia wanted to be someone else. Someone free of her past, free to throw herself heedlessly into all of this wondrous fire and not care if it swallowed her whole. Someone who could do what she liked with this man without bringing her whole world down around her all over again.

Someone very much like the person she'd seemed to think she was the night she'd met him.

But she couldn't. And Nikolai still didn't touch her, which almost made it worse.

"It's time to move into the public phase of this arrangement," he told her in that distant way again, as if this was a planned meeting in the stairwell to calmly discuss the calendar of events that would lead to her downfall. "We'll start with dinner tomorrow night. There are things we need to discuss."

"What a lovely invitation—"

"It's not a request."

She studied him for a moment, all that ice and steel. "I'm otherwise engaged."

"Cancel."

"And if I refuse?"

Nikolai's smile turned dangerous. Her stomach contracted hard at the sight, and the ache of it sank low, turning molten and making her despair of herself anew.

It was that easy. *She* was that easy.

"You can try to run from me if you like." He looked intrigued at the prospect, and something dark and sensual twisted through her, leaving marks. "But I should give you fair warning—I'll find you. And you might not like the mood I'm in when I do."

"Fine," she made herself say, because she couldn't think of an alternate plan, certainly not while he stood there in front of her with a look on his face that told her he'd love to spend more time convincing her. She couldn't have that. And she certainly didn't want him to pursue her through the streets of London, to run her to ground like some mutinous fox, which she had no doubt he would do.... Did she? "Tomorrow night we'll suffer through the date from hell. That sounds delightful. Where do you want me to meet you?"

He reached out then and she braced herself, but he only wrapped a sprig of her curls around his finger, gave them a tug that was very nearly gentle, then let his hand drop, an odd cast to his fierce, proud mouth as he did it.

There was no reason at all that should pierce her heart.

"Don't try to top from the bottom, Alicia," he said, laughter in his brilliant gaze for a moment before it chilled into something much harder. More ruthless. "I'll let you know what I want tomorrow. And you'll do it. Because I really will have you fired if you don't, and despite this entertaining display of bravado, I think you know it."

And there it was.

She didn't want to lose her job—which meant she'd have to figure out how to survive losing her father all over again, once there were pictures to prove once more that she was nothing but a whore. And if there was a tiny spark inside of her, because some foolish part of her wished this wasn't all a game, that it wasn't all for show, that she was the kind of person men didn't use, she did her best to ignore it.

"I don't want to do this." Her voice was small, but still firm, and she thought she'd be proud, later, that she kept her head high. Even in defeat. "Any of it."

"I know you don't," Nikolai said, whole winters in his voice, in his beautiful eyes, so blue she wanted to cry. And there was a flash of something there, bright for a moment and then gone, as if this was more of a struggle for him than it seemed. It scared her, how much she wanted to believe that. "But you will."

Alicia sat where Nikolai had put her, at the corner of the dark wood table that stretched across a significant length of the great two-story room that was the center of his apartment, all low-slung modern couches and soaring windows. Nikolai could read her stiff tension in the way she sat, the way she held her lips too tight, the precise, angry movements of her hands.

His staff had served a five-star dinner that she'd barely touched. Nikolai hadn't spoken a word, and she hadn't broken the silence. Now she was pushing her dessert around on her plate, and he was well aware that her agitation level had skyrocketed even higher than before.

Bastard that he was, that amused him. He lounged in his seat, at the head of the table with her at his right, and studied her. He would figure her out. He would solve the mystery of this woman and when he did, lose interest in her. It was inevitable.

But he hadn't anticipated he would enjoy the process quite this much.

"You're a terrible date," he told her, and her dark eyes flashed when they met his. Then, after a moment, she rolled them. *At* him.

No one else would dare.

"Thank you," she said in that dry way that made him want her beneath him, right there on the table. He had to yank himself back under control, and it was significantly harder than it should have been. *Focus,* he ordered himself. "I can see why you're considered such a catch."

"This is an excellent opportunity to discuss my expectations," Nikolai said, as if her fearless defiance didn't make him want to lick his way into the heat of her, to make her writhe and sob in his hands. And he would, he promised himself, as soon as they came to an understanding. "Dating me comes with a number of requirements, Alicia. Making appropriate dinner conversation is only one of them."

"You're perfectly capable of making conversation," she pointed out in the same dry tone. "In fact, you're doing it right now, though I don't know if it qualifies as 'appropriate.'" She considered him for a moment, a small smile that he didn't like, yet found he wanted to taste, flirting with her full lips. "I suspected there must be some kind of application process and I'm delighted I'm right, but I'm not dating you. This isn't real." Her gaze turned hard on his. "This is blackmail."

"Call it whatever you like," he said, with a careless shrug. "The result is the same."

"Blackmail," she repeated, very distinctly. "I think you'll find that's what it's called when you force someone into doing something they don't want to do by holding something else over their head."

Nikolai could see all of that temper in her dark gaze, the flash of it when she couldn't hide her feelings. She wore a sleeveless wool top tonight in a deep aubergine shade, with a neck that drooped down low and left her smooth, toned arms on display, looking soft and sweet in the candlelight. But most important, he could see every time she tensed, every time she forced herself to relax, written up and down the lean, elegant shape of those arms and all across her slender frame. Like now, when she forced her shoulders back and down, then smiled at him as if she wasn't agitated at all.

She didn't know, yet, that he could read her body the way others read words on a page. But she would learn, and he would greatly enjoy teaching her. First, though, they had business to take care of. If it alarmed him that he had to remind himself of business before pleasure for the first time in living memory, he ignored it.

"There is a confidentiality agreement that you'll need to sign," he told her, dismissing her talk of blackmail, which he could see she didn't like. "Beyond that, I have only standard expectations. Don't venture out into public unless you're prepared to be photographed, as terrible pictures of you could lead to negative coverage of me, which is unacceptable. I'll let you know what pleases me—"

"If you mention a single thing about altering my appearance to suit your tastes, whatever those might be," she said almost conversationally, though there was murder in her eyes, "I will stab you with this fork. I'm not dating you, Nikolai. I'm acquiescing to your bizarre demands because I want to keep my job, but we're not reenacting some sick little version *My Fair Lady*. I don't care about pleasing you."

Nikolai was definitely enjoying himself. Especially when he saw that little shiver move through her, and knew they were both thinking about all the ways she could please him. All the ways she had. He smiled slightly.

"Is that a passive-aggressive demand that I compliment your looks?" he asked silkily. "I had no idea you were so insecure, Alicia. I'd have thought the fact that I had my mouth on every inch of that gorgeous body of yours would have told you my feelings on that topic in no uncertain terms. Though I'm happy to repeat myself."

"I may stab you with this fork anyway." She met his gaze then and smiled. But he could see that her breathing had quickened. He knew arousal when he saw it. When he'd already tasted it. All of that heat and need, sweet against her dark skin. "Fair warning."

"You can always try."

She considered that for a moment, then sat back against her chair, inclining her head slightly as if she held the power here and was granting him permission to carry on.

"Don't ever keep me waiting," Nikolai said, continuing as if she hadn't interrupted him. "Anywhere. For any reason. My time is more valuable than yours."

Her eyes narrowed at that, but she didn't speak. Perhaps she was learning, he thought—but he hoped not. He really hoped not. He wanted her conquered, not coerced. He wanted to do it himself, step by delectable step.

"Don't challenge my authority. In your case, I'll allow some leeway because I find that smart mouth of yours amusing, but only a little leeway, Alicia, and never in public. Your role is as an ornament. I won't tolerate disrespect or disobedience. And I will tell you what you are to me, explicitly—never imagine yourself anything else. I can't stress that enough."

The silence between them then felt tighter. Hotter. Breathless, as if the great room had shrunk down until there was nothing but the two of them and the gently flickering candles. And her eyes were big and dark and he realized he could no longer read the way she looked at him.

"You're aware that this is a conversation about dating you *for show,* not working for you as one of your many interchangeable subordinates at the Korovin Foundation," she said after a moment. "Aren't you?"

"The roles aren't dissimilar."

He stretched his legs out in front of him and lounged even lower in the chair.

"Is this your usual first date checklist, then?"

Her gaze swept over him, and he had no idea what she saw. It surprised him how much he wanted to know.

He nodded, never taking his gaze from hers. "More or less."

"You actually ask a woman to dinner and then present her with this list." She sounded dubious, and something else he wasn't sure he recognized. "Before or after you order starters? And what if she says no? Do you stand up and walk out? Leave her with the bill for her temerity?"

"No one has ever said no." He felt that fire between them reach higher, pull tighter. He could see it on her face. "And I don't take women to dinner without a signed confidentiality agreement. Or anywhere else."

Alicia tapped a finger against her lips for a moment, and he wanted to suck that finger into his own mouth almost more than he wanted his next breath. Need raked through him, raw and hungry.

"You brought me here that night," she pointed out, her tone light, as if there was no tension between them at all. "I certainly didn't sign anything."

Nikolai almost smiled. "You are an anomaly."

"Lucky me," she murmured, faint and dry, and there was no reason that should have worked through him like a match against flint. He didn't like anomalies. He shouldn't have to keep telling himself that.

"If you've absorbed the initial requirements," he said, watching her intently now, "we can move on."

"There are more? The mind boggles."

She was mocking him, he was sure of it. He could see the light of it bright in her eyes and in that wicked twist of her lips, and for some reason, he didn't mind it.

"Sex," he said, and liked the way she froze, for the slightest instant, before concealing her reaction. He had to shift in his seat to hide his.

"You don't really have rules for sex with your girlfriends, Nikolai," she said softly. Imploring him. "Please tell me you're joking."

"I think of this as setting clear boundaries," he told her, leaning forward and smiling when she shivered and sat back. "It prevents undue confusion down the line."

"Undue confusion is what relationships are all about," Alicia said, shaking her head. Her dark eyes searched his, then dropped to her lap. "I rather think that might be the whole point."

"I don't have relationships." He waited until her eyes were on him again, until that tension between them pulled taut and that electric charge was on high, humming through them both. "I have sex. A lot of it. I'll make you come so many times your head will spin, which you already know is no idle boast, but in return, I require two things."

Nikolai watched her swallow almost convulsively, but she didn't look away. She didn't even blink. And he didn't quite know why he felt that like a victory.

"Access and obedience," he said, very distinctly, and was rewarded with the faintest tremor across those lips, down that slender frame. "When I want you, I want you—I don't want a negotiation. Just do what I tell you to do."

He could hear every shift in her breathing. The catch, the slow release. It took every bit of self-control he possessed to wait. To keep his distance. To let her look away for a moment and collect herself, then turn that dark gaze back on him.

"I want to be very clear." She leaned forward, putting her elbows on the table and keeping her eyes trained on him. "What you're telling me, Nikolai, is that every woman pictured on your arm in every single photograph of you online has agreed to all of these *requirements*. All of them."

He wanted to taste her, a violent cut of need, but he didn't. He waited.

"Of course," he said.

And Alicia laughed.

Silvery and musical, just as he remembered. It poured out of her and deep into him, and for a moment he was stunned by it. As if everything disappeared into the sound of it, the way she tipped back her head and let it light up the room. As if she'd hit him from behind and taken him down to the ground without his feeling a single blow.

That laughter rolled into places frozen so solid he'd forgotten they existed at all. It pierced him straight through to a core he hadn't known he had. And it was worse now than it had been that first night. It cut deeper. He was terribly afraid it had made him bleed.

"Laugh as much as you like," he said stiffly when she subsided, and was sitting back in her chair, wiping at her too-bright eyes. "But none of this is negotiable."

"Nikolai," she said, and that clutched at him too, because he'd never heard anyone speak his name like that. So warm, with all of that laughter still moving through her voice. It was almost as if she spoke to someone else entirely, as if it wasn't his name at all—but she looked directly at him, those dark eyes dancing, and he felt as if she'd shot him. He wished she had. He knew how to handle a bullet wound. "I'll play this game of yours. But I'm not going to do any of that."

He was so tense he thought he might simply snap into pieces, but he couldn't seem to move. Her laughter sneaked inside him, messing him up and making even his breathing feel impossibly changed. He hated it.

So he couldn't imagine why he wanted to hear it again, with an intensity that very nearly hurt.

"That's not one of your options," he told her, his voice the roughest he'd ever heard it.

But she was smiling at him, gently, and looked wholly uncowed by his tone.

"If I were you, Nikolai," she said, "I'd start asking myself why I'm so incapable of interacting with other people that I come up with ridiculous rules and regulations to govern things that are supposed to come naturally. That are *better* when they do."

"Because I am a monster," he said. He didn't plan it. It simply came out of his mouth and he did nothing to prevent it. She stopped smiling. Even the brightness in her eyes dimmed. "I've never been anything else. These rules and regulations aren't ridiculous, Alicia. They're necessary."

"Do they make you feel safe?" she asked with a certain quiet kindness he found deeply alarming, as if she knew things she couldn't possibly guess at, much less *know*.

But this was familiar ground even so. He'd had this same conversation with his brother, time and again. He recognized the happy, delusional world she'd come from that let her ask a question like that, and he knew the real world, cynical and bleak. He recognized himself again.

It was a relief, cold and sharp.

"Safety is a delusion," he told her curtly, "and not one I've ever shared. Some of us live our whole lives without succumbing to that particular opiate."

She frowned at him. "Surely when you were a child—"

"I was never a child." He pushed back from the table and rose to his feet. "Not in the way you mean."

She only watched him, still frowning, as he crossed his

arms over his chest, and she didn't move so much as a muscle when he glared down at her. She didn't shrink back the way she should. She looked at him as if he didn't scare her at all, and it ate at him. It made him want to show her how bad he really was—but he couldn't start down that road. He had no idea where it would lead.

"Why do you think my uncle tried to keep me in line with a kitchen knife? It wasn't an accident. He knew what I was."

"Your parents—"

"Died in a fire with seventy others when I was barely five years old," he told her coldly. "I don't remember them. But I doubt they would have liked what I've become. This isn't a bid for sympathy." He shrugged. "It's a truth I accepted a long time ago. Even my own brother believes it, and this after years of being the only one alive who thought I could be any different. I can't." He couldn't look away from her dark eyes, that frown, from the odd and wholly novel notion that she wanted to fight *for* him that opened up a hollow in his chest. "I won't."

"Your brother is an idiot." Her voice was fierce, as if she was prepared to defend him against Ivan—and even against himself, and he had no idea what to do with that. "Because while families always have some kind of tension, Nikolai, monsters do not exist. No matter what an uncle who holds a knife on a child tells you. No matter what we like to tell ourselves."

"I'm glad you think so." Nikolai wasn't sure he could handle the way she looked at him then, as if she hurt for him. He wasn't sure he knew how. "Soft, breakable creatures like you *should* believe there's nothing terrible out there in the dark. But I know better."

# CHAPTER SIX

THAT WAS *PAIN* on his face.

In those searing eyes of his. In the rough scrape of his voice. It was like a dark stain that spilled out from deep inside of him, as if he was torn apart far beneath his strong, icy surface. *Ravaged*, it dawned on her, as surely as if that ferocious thing on his chest rent him to pieces where he stood.

Alicia felt it claw at her, too.

"I'm neither soft nor breakable, Nikolai." She kept her voice steady and her gaze on his, because she thought he needed to see that he hadn't rocked her with that heartbreakingly stark confession, even if he had. "Or as naive as you seem to believe."

"There are four or five ways I could kill you from here." His voice was like gravel. "With my thumb."

Alicia believed him, the way she'd believed he'd be good in bed when he'd told her he was, with a very similar matter-of-fact certainty. It occurred to her that there were any number of ways a man could be talented with his body—with his clever hands for pleasure, with his thumb for something more violent—and Nikolai Korovin clearly knew every one of them. She thought she ought to be frightened by that.

What was wrong with her that she wasn't?

"Please don't," she said briskly, as if she couldn't feel the sting of those claws, as if she didn't see that thick blackness all around him.

Nikolai stared at her. He stood so still, as if he expected he might need to bolt in any direction, and he held himself as if he expected an attack at any moment. As if he expected *she* might be the attacker.

Alicia thought of his coldness tonight, that bone-deep chill that should have hurt, so much harsher than the gruff, darkly amusing man she'd taken by surprise in that club. Who'd surprised her in return. She thought about what little he'd told her of his uncle meant for the boy he must have been—what he must have had to live through. She thought about a man who believed his own brother thought so little of him, and who accepted it as his due. She thought of his lists of rules that he obviously took very seriously indeed, designed to keep even the most intimate people in his life at bay.

*I am a monster,* he'd said, and she could see that he believed it.

But she didn't. She couldn't.

She ached for him. In a way she was very much afraid—with that little thrill of dark foreboding that prodded at her no matter how she tried to ignore it—would be the end of her. But she couldn't seem to make it stop.

"Nikolai," she said when she couldn't stand it any longer—when she wanted to reach over and touch him, soothe him, and knew she couldn't let herself do that, that *he* wouldn't let her do that anyway, "if you were truly a monster, you would simply *be* one. You wouldn't announce it. You wouldn't know how."

A different expression moved across his face then, the way it had once before in the dark, and tonight it broke her heart. That flash of a vulnerability so deep, so intense. And then she watched him pack it away, cover it in ice, turn it hard and cold.

"There are other things I could do with my thumb," he said, his voice the rough velvet she knew best. Seductive. Demanding. "That wouldn't kill you, necessarily, though you might beg for it before I was done."

But she knew what he was doing. She understood it, and it made her chest hurt.

"Sex is easier to accept than comfort," she said quietly, watching his face as she said it. He looked glacial. Remote. And yet that heat inside of him burned, she could feel it. "You can pretend it's not comfort at all. Just sex."

"I like sex, Alicia." His voice was a harsh lash through the room, so vicious she almost flinched. "I thought I made that clear our first night together. Over and over again."

He wanted to prove he was the monster he said he was. He wanted to prove that he was exactly as bad, as terrifying, as he claimed he was. Capable of killing with nothing more than his thumb. She looked at that cold, set face of his and she could see that he believed it. More—that he simply accepted that this was who he was.

And she found that so terribly sad it almost crippled her.

She got up and went to him without consciously deciding to move. He didn't appear to react, and yet she had the impression he steeled himself at her approach, as if she was as dangerous to him as he was to her. But she couldn't let herself think about that stunning possibility.

Nikolai watched her draw near, his expression even colder. Harder. Alicia tilted her head back and looked into his extraordinary eyes, darker now than usual as he stared back at her with a kind of defiance, as if he was prepared to fight her until she saw him as he saw himself.

Until she called him a monster, too.

"Do you want to know what I think?" she asked.

"I'm certain I don't."

It was a rough scrape of sound, grim and low, but she thought she saw a kind of hunger in his eyes that had nothing to do with his sexual prowess and everything to do with that flash of vulnerability she almost thought she'd imagined, and she kept going.

"I think you hide behind all these rules and boundaries, Nikolai." She felt the air in the room go electric, but she couldn't seem to stop herself. "If you tell yourself you're a monster, if you insist upon it and act upon it, you make it true. It's a self-fulfilling prophecy."

And she would know all about that, wouldn't she? Hadn't she spent eight long years doing exactly that herself? That unexpected insight was like a kick in the stomach, but she ignored it, pushing it aside to look at later.

"Believe me," she said then, more fiercely than she'd intended. "I know."

His hands shot out and took her by the shoulders, then pulled her toward him, toward his hard face that was even more lethal, even more fierce than usual. His touch against her bare arms burned, and made her want nothing more than to melt into him. It was too hot. Too dark.

And he was close then, so powerful and furious. *So close.* Winter and need, fire and longing. The air was thick with it. It made her lungs ache.

"Why don't you have the good sense to be afraid of me?" he said in an undertone, as if the words were torn from that deep, black part of him. "What is the matter with you? Why do you *laugh* when anyone else would cry?"

"I don't see any monsters when I look at you, Nikolai," she replied, winning the fight to keep her tone light, her gaze on his, no matter how ravaged he looked. How undone. Or how churned up she felt inside. "I only see a man. I see you."

His hands tightened around her shoulders for a brief

instant, and then he let her go. Abruptly, as if he'd wanted to do the opposite.

As if he couldn't trust himself any more than she could.

"You don't want to play with this particular fire," he warned her, his expression fierce and dark, his gaze drilling holes into her. "It won't simply burn you—it will swallow you whole. That's not a self-fulfilling prophecy. It's an inevitability."

Alicia didn't know what seared through her then, shocking and dark, thrilling to the idea of it. Of truly losing herself in him, in that fire neither one of them could control, despite the fact there was still that panicked part of her— that part of her that wished she'd gone home and done her laundry that night and never met him—that wanted anything but that. And he saw it. All of it.

She had no idea what was happening to her, or how to stop it, or why she had the breathless sense that it was already much too late.

"Get your coat," he growled at her. "I'll take you home."

Alicia blinked, surprised to find that she was unsteady on her own feet. And Nikolai was dark and menacing, watching her as if no detail was too small to escape his notice. As if he could see all those things inside of her, the fire and the need. That dark urge to demand he throw whatever he had at her, that she could take it, that she understood him—

*Of course you don't understand him,* she chided herself. *How could you?*

"That's unnecessary," she said into the tense silence, stiffly, and had to clear the roughness from her voice with a cough.

She straightened her top, smoothed her hands down the sides of her trousers, then stopped when she realized she was fidgeting and he'd no doubt read the anxiety that betrayed the way he did everything else.

"You don't have to take me home," she said when he didn't respond. When he only watched her, his expression brooding and his blue eyes cold. She frowned at him. "This night has been intense enough, I think. I'll get a taxi."

The ride across London—in the backseat of Nikolai's SUV with him taking up too much of the seat beside her because he'd informed her a taxi was not an option—was much like sitting on simmering coals, waiting for the fire to burst free.

Not exactly comfortable, Alicia thought crossly. And as the fever of what had happened between them in his penthouse faded with every mile they traveled, she realized he'd been right to warn her.

She felt scorched through. Blackened around the edges and much too close to simply going up in flames herself, until she very much feared there'd be nothing left of her. A few ashes, scattered here and there.

Had she really stood there thinking she wanted more of this? Anything he had to give, in fact? What *was* the matter with her?

But then she thought of that bleak look in his beautiful eyes, that terrible certainty in his voice when he'd told her what a monster he was, and she was afraid she knew all too well what was wrong with her.

"You can go," she told him, not bothering to hide the tension in her voice as they stood outside the door that led into her building in a narrow alcove stuck between two darkened shops.

Nikolai had walked her to the door without a word, that winter fire roaring all around them both, and now stood close beside her in the chilly December night. Too close beside her. Alicia needed to get inside, lock her doors, take a very long soak in the bath—*something* to sort her head out before she lost whatever remained of her sanity, if not something far worse than that. *She needed him to go.* She dug for her keys in her bag without looking at him, not trusting herself to look away again if she did.

"I'm fine from here. I don't need an escort."

He didn't respond. He plucked the keys from her hand when she pulled them out, and then opened the door with no hesitation whatsoever, waving her inside with a hint of edgy impatience.

It would not be wise to let him in. That was perfectly clear to her.

"Nikolai," she began, and his gaze slammed into her, making her gulp down whatever she might have said.

"I understand that you need to fight me on everything," he said, his accent thicker than usual. "If I wanted to psychoanalyze you the way you did me, I'd say I suspect it makes you feel powerful to poke at me. But I wouldn't get too comfortable with that if I were you."

"I wasn't psychoanalyzing you!" she cried, but he brushed it off as if she hadn't spoken.

"But you should ask yourself something." He put his hand on her arm and hauled her into the building, sent the door slamming shut with the back of his shoulder and then held her there in the narrow hall. "Exactly what do you think might happen if you get what you seem to want and I lose control?"

"I don't want—"

"There are reasons men control themselves," he told her, his face in hers, and she should have been intimidated. She should have been terrified. And instead, all she felt was that greedy pulse of need roll through her. That impossible kick of this jagged-edged joy he brought out in her no matter what she thought she *ought* to feel. "Especially men like me, who stand like wolves in the dark corners of more than just London clubs. You should think about what those reasons are. There are far worse things than a list of demands."

"Like your attempts to intimidate me?" she countered, trying to find her footing when she was so off balance she suspected she might have toppled over without him there to hold her up.

"Why don't you laugh it off?" he asked softly, more a taunt than a question, and she had the wild thought that this might be Nikolai at his most dangerous. Soft and deadly and much too close. His gaze brushed over her face, leaving ice and fire wherever it touched. "No? Is this not funny anymore?"

"Nikolai." His name felt unwieldy against her tongue, or perhaps that was the look in his eyes, spelling out her sure doom in all of that ferocious blue. "I'm not trying to make you lose control."

"Oh, I think you are." He smiled, though it was almost feral and it scraped over her, through her. "But you should make very, very sure that you're prepared to handle the consequences if you succeed. Do you think you are? Right here in this hallway, with a draft under the door and the street a step away? Do you think you're ready for that?"

"Stop threatening me," she bit out at him, but it was a ragged whisper, and he could see into her too easily.

"I don't make threats, Alicia." He leaned in closer and nipped at her neck, shocking her. Making her go up in flames. And flinch—or was that simply an electric charge? "You should think of that, too."

And then he stepped away and jerked his head in an unspoken demand that she lead him up the stairs. And Alicia was so unsteady, so chaotic inside, so unable to process all the things that had happened tonight—what he'd said, what she'd felt, that deep ache inside of her, that fire that never did anything but burn hotter—that she simply marched up the stairs to the flat she shared with Rosie on the top floor without a word of protest.

He didn't ask if she wanted him inside when they reached her door, he simply strode in behind her as if he owned the place, and the insanity of it—of *Nikolai Korovin* standing there *in her home*—was so excruciating it was like pain.

"I don't want you here," she told him as he shut her door behind him, the sound of the latch engaging and locking him inside with her too loud in her ears. "I didn't invite you in."

"I didn't ask."

He was still dressed in black, and that very darkness made him seem bigger and more lethal as he walked inside, his cold gaze moving over the cheerful clutter that was everywhere. Bright paperbacks shoved haphazardly onto groaning shelves, photographs in colorful frames littering every surface, walls painted happy colors and filled with framed prints of famous art from around the world. Alicia tensed, expecting Rosie to pad into view at any moment, but the continuing stretch of silence suggested she was out. *Thank God.*

"It's messy," she said, aware she sounded defensive. "We never quite get around to cleaning it as we should. Of course, we also don't have a household staff."

"It looks like real people live here," he replied, frowning at one of Rosie's abandoned knitting projects, and it took her a moment to understand that this, too, was a terribly sad thing to say.

That ache in her deepened. Expanded. Hurt.

Alicia tossed her keys on the table in the hall, her coat over the chair, and then followed Nikolai warily as he melted in and out of the rooms of the flat like a shadow.

"What are you looking for?" she asked after a few minutes of this.

"There must be a reason you're suicidally incapable of recognizing your own peril when you see it," he said, his eyes moving from place to place, object to object, taking everything in. Cataloging it, she thought. Examining every photograph the way he did every dish left in the sink, every pair of shoes kicked aside in the hall, and the spine of every book piled on the overstuffed bookshelves. "Perhaps there are environmental factors at play."

He moved past the kitchen off to the right and stood at the far end of the hall that cut down the middle of the flat, where the bedrooms were.

"And what would those be, do you think?" she asked, her voice tart—which felt like a vast improvement. Or was perhaps a response to what had sounded like the faintest hint of that dark humor of his. It was absurd how much she craved more of it. "Fearlessness tucked away in the walls like asbestos?"

Nikolai didn't answer her, he only sent one of those simmering looks arrowing her way down the hallway, as effective from a few feet away as it was up close. And almost as devastating.

Alicia blew out a breath when he opened the door to her bedroom, the aftershocks of that winter-blue look shifting into something else again. A kind of nervous anticipation. He looked inside for a long moment, and her heart raced. She wished, suddenly, that she'd had the presence of mind to prevent this. She didn't like the fact that he knew, now, that she favored all those silly, self-indulgent throw pillows, piled so high on her bed, shouting out how soft and breakable she really was. They felt like proof, somehow—and when he looked back at her it was hard to stand still. To keep from offering some kind of explanation.

"A four-poster bed." It could have been an innocent comment. An observation. But the way he looked at her made her knees feel weak. "Intriguing."

Alicia thought she understood then, and somehow, that eased the relentless pulse of panic inside.

"Let me guess." She leaned her hip against the wall and watched him. "The faster you puzzle me out, the less you think you'll have to worry about losing this control of yours."

"I don't like mysteries."

"Will it make you feel safe to solve whatever mystery you think I am, Nikolai? Is that what this is?"

The look he gave her then did more than simply *hurt*. It ripped straight down into the center of her, tearing everything she was in two, and there was nothing she could do but stand there and take it.

"I'm not the one who believes in safety, Alicia," he said softly. "It's nothing more than a fairy tale to me. I never had it. I wouldn't recognize it." His expression was hard and bleak. Almost challenging. "The next time you tally up my scars, keep a special count of those I got when I was under the age of twelve. That knife was only one among many that drew my blood. My uncle used the back of his hand if I was lucky." His beautiful mouth twisted, and her heart dropped to her feet. "But I was never very lucky."

He stood taller then. Almost defiant. And it tore at her. She felt her eyes heat in a way that spelled imminent tears and knew she couldn't let herself cry for this hard, damaged man. Not where he could see it. She knew somehow that he would never forgive her.

"Don't waste your pity on me." His voice was cold, telling her she'd been right. No sympathy allowed. No compassion. He sounded almost insulted when he continued, as if whatever he saw on her face was a slap. "Eventually,

I learned how to fight back, and I became more of a monster than my uncle ever could have been."

"We're all monsters," she told him, her voice harsh because she knew he wouldn't accept anything softer. Hoping against hope he'd never know about that great tear inside of her that she could feel with every breath she took, rending her further and further apart. "Some of us actually behave like monsters, in fact, rather than suffer through the monstrous actions of others. No one escapes their past unscathed."

"What would you know about it, Alicia?" His gaze was cold, his tone a stinging lash. "What past misdeeds could possibly haunt you while you're tucked up in your virginal little bedroom, laughing your way through your cheery, happy life? What blood do you imagine is on your hands?"

And so she told him.

Alicia had never told a soul before, and yet she told Nikolai as easily as if she'd shared the story a thousand times. Every detail she could remember and all the ones she couldn't, that her father had filled in for her that awful morning. All of her shame, her despicable actions, her unforgivable behavior, without garnishment or pretense. As if that tear in her turned her inside out, splayed there before him.

And when she was finished, she was so light-headed she thought she might sag straight down to the floor, or double over where she stood.

"Everyone has ghosts," she managed to say, crossing her arms over her chest to keep herself upright.

Nikolai turned away from her bedroom door and moved toward her, thrusting his hands into the pockets of his trousers as he did. It made him look more dangerous, not less. It drew her attention to the wide strength of his shoulders, the long, lethal lines of his powerful frame. It made her wonder how anyone could have hurt him so badly when he'd been small that he'd felt he needed to transform himself into so sharp, so deadly a weapon. It made her feel bruised to the core that he'd no doubt look at her now the way her father had....

His eyes burned as they bored into hers, and he let out one of those low laughs that made her stomach tense.

"That doesn't sound like any ghost," he said, his voice dark and sure. "It sounds like an older man who took advantage of a young girl too drunk to fight him off."

Alicia jolted cold, then flashed hot, as he turned her entire life on end that easily. She swayed where she stood.

"No," she said, feeling desperate, as some great wave of terror or emotion or *something* rolled toward her. "My father said—"

"Your father should have known better than to speak to you like that." Nikolai scowled at her. "News flash, Alicia. Men who aren't predators prefer to have sex with women who are capable of participating."

Her head was spinning. Her stomach twisted, and for a panicked moment she thought she might be sick. She felt his words—so matter-of-fact, as if there could be no other interpretation of that night, much less the one that she'd held so close all these years—wash through her, like a quiet and devastating tsunami right there in her own hallway.

"What's his name?" Nikolai asked, in that soft, lethal way of his that lifted the hairs at the back of her neck. "The man who did these things to you? Does he still live next door to your parents?"

He was the first person she'd told. And the only one to defend her.

Alicia couldn't understand how she was still standing upright.

"That doesn't sound like a question a monster would ask," she whispered.

"You don't know what I'd do to him," he replied, that dark gleam in his gaze.

And he looked at her like she was important, not filthy. Not a whore. Like what had happened had been done to *her,* and hadn't been something *she'd* done.

Like it wasn't her fault after all.

She couldn't breathe.

His gaze shifted from hers to a spot down at the other end of the flat behind her, and she heard the jingling of keys in the hall outside. She felt as if she moved through sticky syrup, as if her body didn't understand what to do any longer, and turned around just as Rosie pushed her way inside.

Rosie sang out her usual hello, slinging her bags to the floor. Nikolai stepped closer to Alicia's back, then reached around to flatten his hand against the waistband of her trousers before pulling her into his bold heat. Holding her to his chest as if they were lovers. Claiming her.

"What...?" Alicia whispered, the sizzle of that unexpected touch combining with the hard punch of the revolution he'd caused inside of her, making her knees feel weak.

"I told you we were taking this public," he replied, his voice a low rumble pitched only to her that made her shiver helplessly against him. "Now we have."

Rosie's head snapped up at the sound of his voice. Her mouth made a perfect, round O as if the devil himself stood there behind Alicia in the hall, no doubt staring her down with those cold winter eyes of his. And then she dropped the bottle of wine she'd been holding in her free hand, smashing it into a thousand pieces all over the hall floor.

Which was precisely how Alicia felt.

Nikolai stared out at the wet and blustery London night on the other side of his penthouse's windows while he waited for the video conference with Los Angeles to begin. His office was reflected in the glass, done in imposing blacks and burgundies, every part of it carefully calculated to trumpet his wealth and power without him having to say a word to whoever walked in. The expensive view out of all the windows said it for him. The modern masterpieces on the walls repeated it, even louder.

It was the sort of thing he'd used to take such pleasure in. The application of his wealth and power to the most innocuous of interactions, the leverage it always afforded him. War games without a body count. It had been his favorite sport for years.

But now he thought only of the one person who seemed as unimpressed with these trappings of wealth and fame as she did with the danger he was well aware he represented. Hell, *exuded*. And instead of regaining his equilibrium the more time he spent with Alicia, instead of losing this intense and distracting interest in her the more he learned about her, he was getting worse.

Much worse. Incomprehensibly worse. And Nikolai knew too well what it felt like to spiral. He knew what obsession tasted like. *He knew.*

She was a latter-day version of his favorite drink, sharp and deadly. And he was still nothing but a drunk where she was concerned.

He'd ordered himself not to hunt down the man who had violated her, though he knew it would be easy. Too easy. The work of a single phone call, an internet search.

*You are not her protector,* he told himself over and over. *This is not your vengeance to take.*

He'd sparred for hours with his security team in his private gym, throwing them to the floor one after the next, punching and kicking and flipping. He'd swum endless laps in his pool. He'd run through the streets of London in the darkest hours of the night, the slap of the December weather harsh against his face, until his lungs burned and his legs shook.

Nothing made the slightest bit of difference. Nothing helped.

She'd all but pushed him out her front door that night, past her gaping flatmate and the wine soaking into her floorboards, her eyes stormy and dark, and he'd let her.

"Rosie calls me *Saint Alicia* and I *like* it," she'd whispered fiercely to him, shoving him into the narrow hall outside her flat. She'd been scolding him, he'd realized. He wasn't sure he'd ever experienced it before. His uncle had preferred to use his belt. "It's better than some other things I've been called. But you looming around the flat will be the end of that."

"Why?" he'd asked lazily, those broken, jagged things moving around inside of him, making him want things he couldn't name. Making him want to hurt anyone who'd dared hurt her, like she was his. "I like saints. I'm Russian."

"Please," she'd scoffed. "You have 'corruptor of innocents' written all over you."

"Then we are both lucky, are we not, that neither one of us is innocent," he'd said, and had enjoyed the heat that had flashed through her eyes, chasing out the dark.

But by the next morning, she'd built her walls back up, and higher than before. He hadn't liked that at all, though he'd told himself it didn't matter. It shouldn't matter. He told himself that again, now.

It was the end result he needed to focus on: Veronika. The truth about Stefan at long last, and the loose thread she represented snipped off for good. Whatever he suffered on the way to that goal would be worth it, and in any case, Alicia would soon be nothing but a memory. One more instrument he'd use as he needed, then set aside.

He needed to remember that. There was only a week left

before the ball. Nikolai could handle anything for one last week, surely. He'd certainly handled worse.

But she was under his skin, he knew, no matter how many times he told himself otherwise. No matter how fervently he pretended she wasn't.

And she kept clawing her way deeper, like a wound that wouldn't scar over and become one more thing he'd survived.

He'd picked her up to take her to the Tate Modern on the opening night of some desperately chic exhibit, which he'd known would be teeming with London's snooty art world devotees and their assorted parasites and photographers. It wasn't the kind of place a man took a woman he kept around only for sex. Taking a woman to a highly intellectual and conceptual art exhibit suggested he might actually have an interest in her thoughts.

It was a perfect place for them to be "accidentally spotted," in other words. Nikolai hadn't wanted to dig too deeply into his actual level of interest in what went on inside her head. He hadn't wanted to confront himself.

Alicia had swung open the door to her flat and taken his breath that easily. She'd worn a skimpy red dress that showed off her perfect breasts and clung to her curves in mouthwatering ways he would have enjoyed on any woman, and deeply appreciated on her—and yet he'd had the foreign urge to demand she hide all of her lush beauty away from the undeserving public. That she keep it for him alone. He'd been so startled—and appalled—at his line of thought that he'd merely stood there, silent and grim, and stared at her as if she'd gone for his jugular with one of her wickedly high shoes.

Alicia had taken in the black sweater with the high collar he wore over dark trousers that, he'd been aware, made him look more like a commando than an appropriately urbane date to a highly anticipated London art exhibit.

Not that commandos wore cashmere, in his experience.

"Have you become some kind of spy?" she'd asked him, in that dry way that might as well have been her hands on his sex. His body hadn't been at all conflicted about how he should figure her out. It had known exactly what it wanted.

When it came to Alicia, he'd realized, it always did.

"You must be confusing me for the character my brother plays in movies," he'd told her dismissively, and had fought to keep himself from simply leaning forward and pressing his mouth to that tempting hollow between her breasts, then licking his way over each creamy brown swell until he'd made them both delirious and hot. He'd almost been able to taste her from where he stood in the doorway.

Alicia had pulled on her coat from the nearby chair and swept her bag into her hand. She hadn't even been looking at him as she stepped out into the hall and turned to lock her door behind her.

"Your brother plays you in his Jonas Dark films," she'd replied in that crisp way of hers that made his skin feel tight against his bones. "A disaffected kind of James Bond character, stretched too thin on the edge of what's left of his humanity, yet called to act the hero despite himself."

Nikolai had stared at her when she'd turned to face him, and she'd stared back, that awareness and a wary need moving across her expressive face, no doubt reflecting his own. Making him wish—

But he'd known he had to stop. He'd known better from the first with her, hadn't he? He should have let her fall to the floor in that club. He'd known it even as he'd caught her.

"I'm no hero, Alicia," he'd said, sounding like sandpaper and furious that she'd pushed him off balance again. Hadn't he warned her what would happen? Was that what she wanted? She didn't know what she was asking—but he did. "Surely you know this better than anyone."

She'd looked at him for a long moment, her dark gaze shrewd, seeing things he'd always wanted nothing more than to hide.

"Maybe not," she'd said. "But what do you think would happen if you found out you were wrong?"

And then she'd turned and started down the stairs toward the street, as if she hadn't left the shell of him behind her, hollow and unsettled.

Again.

Nikolai saw his own reflection in his office windows now, and it was like he was someone else. He was losing control and he couldn't seem to stop it. He was as edgy and paranoid and dark as he'd been in those brutal days after he'd quit drinking. Worse, perhaps.

Because these things that raged in him, massive and uncontrollable and hot like acid, were symptoms of a great thaw he knew he couldn't allow. A thaw she was making hotter by the day, risking everything. Oceans rose when glaciers melted; mountains fell.

He'd destroy her, he knew. It was only a matter of time.

If he was the man she seemed to think he was, the man he sometimes wished he was when she looked at him with all of those things he couldn't name in her lovely dark eyes, he'd leave her alone. Play the hero she'd suggested he could be and put her out of harm's way.

But Nikolai knew he'd never been any kind of hero. Not even by mistake.

# CHAPTER SEVEN

NIKOLAI HADN'T HEARD his family nickname in such a long time that when he did, he assumed he'd imagined it.

He frowned at the sleek and oversize computer display in front of him, realizing that he'd barely paid attention to the video conference, which was unlike him. Stranger still, no one remained on his screen but his brother.

Nikolai wasn't sure which was more troubling, his inattention during a business meeting or the fact he'd imagined he'd heard Ivan speak his—

"Kolya?"

That time there was no mistaking it. Ivan was the only person alive who had ever used that name, very rarely at that, and Nikolai was looking right at him as he said it from the comfort of his Malibu house a world away.

It was the first time he'd spoken directly to Nikolai in more than two years.

Nikolai stared. Ivan was still Ivan. Dark eyes narrowed beneath the dark hair they shared, the battered face he'd earned in all of those mixed martial arts rings, clothes that quietly proclaimed him Hollywood royalty, every inch of him the action hero at his ease.

Nikolai would have preferred it if Ivan had fallen into obvious disrepair after turning his back on his only brother so cavalierly. Instead, it appeared that betrayal and delusion suited him.

That, Nikolai reflected darkly, and the woman who'd caused this rift between them in the first place, no doubt.

"What's the matter with you?" Ivan asked in Russian, frowning into his camera. "You've been staring off into space for the past fifteen minutes."

Nikolai chose not to investigate the things that churned in him, dark and heavy, at the way Ivan managed to convey the worry, the disappointment and that particular wariness that had always characterized the way he looked at Nikolai, talked to him, in two simple sentences after so much silence. And yet there was a part of him that wanted nothing more than to simply take this as a gift, take his brother back in whatever way Ivan was offering himself....

But he couldn't let himself go there. Ivan's silence had been a favor to him, surely. He knew where it led, and he wanted nothing to do with that particular prison any longer.

"I'm reeling from shock," he said. "The mighty Ivan Korovin has condescended to address me directly. I imagine I ought to feel festive on such a momentous occasion." He eyed Ivan coolly, and without the faintest hint of *festive*. "I appreciate the show of concern, of course."

Nikolai could have modified his tone, the sardonic slap of it. Instead, he kept his face expressionless, his gaze trained on his brother through the screen. *Your brother is an idiot,* Alicia had said, so emphatically. It felt like encouragement, like her kind hand against his cheek even when she wasn't in the room.

But he didn't want to think about Alicia. She didn't know what he'd done to deserve the things his brother thought of him. And unlike her confession of the sins of others, Nikolai really had done each and every thing Ivan thought he had.

Ivan's mouth flattened and his dark eyes flashed with his familiar temper.

"Two years," he said in that gruff way of his, his long-suffering older brother voice, "and that's what you have to say to me, Nikolai? Why am I not surprised that you've learned nothing in all this time?"

"That's an excellent question," Nikolai replied, his voice so cold he could feel the chill of it in his own chest. "If you wanted me to learn something you should have provided some kind of lesson plan. Picked out the appropriate hair shirts for me to wear, outlined the confessions you expected me to make and at what intervals. But you chose instead to disappear, the way you always do." He shrugged, only spurred on by the flash of guilt and fury he knew too well on his brother's face. "Forgive me if I am not weeping with joy that you've remembered I exist, with as much warning as when you decided to forget it." He paused, then if possible, got icier. *"Brother."*

"Nikolai—"

"You come and you go, Vanya," he said then, giving that darkness in him free rein. Letting it take him over. Not caring that it wasn't fair—what was *fair?* What had ever been *fair?* "You make a thousand promises and you break them all. I stopped depending on you when I was a child. Talk to me or don't talk to me. What is it to me?"

Ivan's face was dark with that same complicated fury—his guilt that he'd left Nikolai years before to fight, his frustrated anger that Nikolai had turned out so relentlessly feral despite the fact he'd rescued him, eventually; even his sadness that this was who they were, these two hard and dangerous men—and Nikolai was still enough his younger brother to read every nuance of that. And to take a kind of pleasure in the fact that despite the passage of all this time, Ivan was not indifferent.

Which, he was aware, meant he wasn't, either.

"One of these days, little brother, we're going to fight this out," Ivan warned him, shoving his hands through his dark hair the way he'd no doubt like to shove them around Nikolai's neck and would have, had this conversation taken place in person. Nikolai felt himself shift into high alert, readying for battle automatically. "No holds barred, the way we should have done two years ago. And when I crush you into the ground, and I will, this conversation will be one of the many things you'll apologize for."

"Is that another promise?" Nikolai asked pointedly, and was rewarded when Ivan winced. "I understand this is your pet fantasy and always has been. And you could no doubt win a fight in any ring, to entertain a crowd. But outside the ring? In real life with real stakes?" Nikolai shook his head. "You'd be lucky to stay alive long enough to beg for mercy."

"Why don't you fly to California and test that theory?" Ivan suggested, his expression turning thunderous. "Or is it easier to say these things when there are computer screens and whole continents to hide behind?"

"You would follow the rules, Vanya," Nikolai said with a certain grim impatience. "You would fight fair, show mercy. This is who you are." He shrugged, everything inside of him feeling too sharp, too jagged. "It will be your downfall."

"Mercy isn't weakness," Ivan growled.

"Only good men, decent men, have the luxury of dispensing it," Nikolai retorted, ignoring the way his brother stared at him. "I wouldn't make that kind of mistake. You might put me on the ground, but I'd sink a knife in you on my way back up. You should remember that while you're issuing threats. I don't fight fair. I fight to survive."

They stared at each other for an uncomfortable moment. Ivan settled back in his chair, crossing his strong arms over his massive chest, and Nikolai sat still and watchful, like the sentry he'd once been.

"Is this about your new woman?" Ivan asked. Nikolai didn't betray his surprise by so much as a twitch of his eyelid, much less a reply. Ivan sighed. "I've seen the papers."

"So I gather."

Ivan studied him for another moment. "She's not your usual type."

"By which you mean vapid and/or mercenary, I presume," Nikolai said coldly. He almost laughed. "No, she's not. But you of all people should know better than to believe the things you read."

Ivan's gaze on his became curiously intent.

"Tabloid games don't always lead where you think they will, brother. You know that."

It was Nikolai's turn to sigh. "And how is your favorite tabloid game gone wrong?" he asked. "Your wife now, if I'm not mistaken. Or so I read in the company newsletter."

"Miranda is fine," Ivan said shortly, and then looked uncomfortable, that guilty look flashing through his dark eyes again. "It was a very private ceremony. No one but the man who married us."

"I understand completely," Nikolai murmured smoothly. "It might have been awkward to have to explain why your only living family member, the acting CEO of your foundation, was not invited to a larger wedding. It might have tarnished your image, which, of course, would cost us all money. Can't have that."

"She's my family, Kolya." Ivan's voice was a hard rumble, his jaw set in that belligerent way of his that meant he was ready to fight. Here and now.

And that really shouldn't have felt like one of his brother's trademark punches, a sledgehammer to the side of the head. It shouldn't have surprised him that Ivan considered that woman his family when he'd so easily turned his back on his only actual blood relation. Or that he was prepared to fight Nikolai—again—to defend her.

And yet he felt leveled. Laid out flat, no air in his lungs.

"Congratulations," he ground out. Dark and bitter. Painful. "I hope your new family proves less disappointing than the original version you were so happy to discard."

Ivan wasn't the only one who could land a blow.

Nikolai watched him look away from the screen, and rub one of his big hands over his hard face. He even heard the breath that Ivan took, then blew out, and knew his brother was struggling to remain calm. That should have felt like a victory.

"I know you feel that I abandoned you," Ivan said after a moment, in his own, painful way. "That everyone did, but in my case, over and over, when you were the most vulnerable. I will always wish I could change that."

Nikolai couldn't take any more of this. Ice floes were cracking apart inside of him, turning into so much water and flooding him, drowning him—and he couldn't allow this to happen. He didn't know where it was heading, or what would be left of him when he melted completely. He only knew it wouldn't be pretty. For anyone. He'd always known that. The closest he'd ever been to *melted* was drunk, and that had only ever ended in blood and regret.

"It's only been two years, Ivan." He tried to pull himself back together, to remember who he was, or at least pretend well enough to end this conversation. "I haven't suddenly developed a host of tender emotions you need to concern yourself with trampling."

"You have emotions, Nikolai. You just can't handle them," Ivan corrected him curtly, a knife sliding in neat and hard. Deep enough to hit bone. His eyes were black and intense, and they slammed into Nikolai from across the globe with all of his considerable power. "You never learned how to have them, much less process them, so your first response when you feel something is to attack. Always."

"Apparently things *have* changed," Nikolai shot back with icy fury. "I wasn't aware you'd followed your wife's example and become no better than a tabloid reporter, making up little fantasies and selling them as fact. I hope the tips of the trade you get in bed are worth the loss of self-respect."

"Yes, Nikolai," Ivan bit out, short and hard. "Exactly like that."

Nikolai muttered dark things under his breath, fighting to keep that flood inside of him under control. Not wanting to think about what his brother had said, or why it seemed to echo in him, louder and louder. Why he had Alicia's voice in his head again, talking about sex and comfort in that maddeningly intuitive way of hers, as if she knew, too, the ways he reacted when he didn't know how to feel.

Did he ever know how to feel?

And Ivan only settled back in his chair, crossing his arms over his chest, and watched Nikolai fall apart.

"I'm the thing that goes bump in the night," Nikolai said through his teeth after a moment or two. "You know this. I've never pretended to be anything else."

"Because our uncle told you so?" Ivan scoffed. "Surely you must realize by now that he was in love with our mother in his own sick way. He hated us both for representing the choice she made, but you—" He shook his head. "Your only sin was in resembling her more than I did."

Nikolai couldn't let that in. He couldn't let it land. Because it was nothing but misdirection and psychological inference when he knew the truth. He'd learned it the hard way, hadn't he?

"I know what I am," he gritted out.

"You like it." Ivan's gaze was hard. No traces of any guilt now. "I think it comforts you to imagine you're an irredeemable monster, unfit for any kind of decent life."

*You make it true,* Alicia had told him, her dark eyes filled with soft, clear things he hadn't known how to define. *It's a self-fulfilling prophecy.*

"You think it yourself," Nikolai reminded Ivan tightly. "Or did I misunderstand your parting words two years ago?"

"If I thought that," Ivan rumbled at him, "I wouldn't think you could do better than this, would I? But you don't want to accept that, Nikolai, because if you did, you'd have to take responsibility for your actions." He held Nikolai's gaze. "Like a man."

*I only see a man,* Alicia had told him, her dark gaze serious. *I see you.*

But that wasn't what Nikolai saw. Not in the mirror, not in Alicia's pretty eyes, not in his brother's face now. He saw the past.

He saw the truth.

He'd been nine years old. Ivan had been off winning martial arts tournaments already, and Nikolai had borne the brunt of one of his uncle's drunken rages, as usual.

He'd been lucky the teeth he'd lost were only the last of his milk teeth.

"I can see it in you," his uncle had shouted at him, over and over again, fists flying. "It looks out of your eyes."

He'd towered over Nikolai's bed, Nikolai's blood on his hands and splattered across his graying white shirt. That was the part Nikolai always remembered so vividly, even now—that spray of red that air and time had turned brown, set deep in the grungy shirt that his uncle had never bothered to throw out. That he'd worn for years afterward, like a promise.

His uncle had always kept his promises. Every last one, every time, until his nephews grew big enough to make a few of their own.

"Soon there'll be nothing left," his uncle had warned him, his blue eyes, so much like Nikolai's, glittering. "That thing in you will be all you are."

Ivan hadn't come home for days. Nikolai had thought that his uncle had finally succeeded in killing him, that he'd been dying. By the time Ivan returned and had quietly, furiously, cleaned him up, Nikolai had changed.

He'd understood.

There was nothing good in him. If there had been, his uncle wouldn't have had to beat him so viciously, so consistently, the way he had since Nikolai had come to live with him at five years old.

It was his fault his uncle had no choice but to beat the bad things out.

It was his fault, or someone would have rescued him.

It was his fault, or it would stop. But it wouldn't stop, because that thing inside of him was a monster and eventually, he'd understood then, it would take him over. Wholly and completely.

And it had.

"Nikolai."

Maybe Ivan had been right to sever this connection, he thought now. What did they have between them besides terrible memories of those dark, bloody years? Of course Ivan hadn't protected him, no matter how Nikolai had prayed he might—he'd barely managed to protect himself.

And now he'd made himself a real family, without these shadows. Without all of that blood between them.

"Kolya—"

"I can't tell you how much I appreciate this brotherly talk," Nikolai said, his tone arctic. Because it was the only way he knew to protect Ivan. And if Nikolai could give that to him, he would, for every bruise and cut and broken bone that Ivan had stoically tended to across the years. "I've missed this. Truly."

And then he reached out and cut off the video connection before his brother could say another word. But not before he saw that same, familiar sadness in Ivan's eyes. He'd seen it all his life.

He knew it hurt Ivan that this was who Nikolai was. That nothing had changed, and nothing ever would.

Ivan was wrong. Nikolai *was* changing, and it wasn't for the better. It was a terrible thing, that flood inside him swelling and rising by the second, making all of that ice he'd wrapped himself in melt down much too quickly.

He was changing far more than he should.

Far more than was safe for anyone.

He knew he needed to stop it, he knew how, and yet he couldn't bring himself to do it. At his core, he was nothing but that twisted, evil thing who had earned his uncle's fists.

Because he wasn't ready to give her up. He had a week left, a week of that marvelous smile and the way she frowned at him without a scrap of fear, a week of that wild heat he needed to sample one more time before he went without it forever. He wanted every last second of it.

Even if it damned them both.

Alicia stood in a stunning hotel suite high above the city of Prague, watching it glow in the last of the late-December afternoon, a storybook kingdom brought to life before her. Snow covered the picturesque red rooftops and clung to the spires atop churches and castles, while the ancient River Vltava curved like a sweet silver ribbon through the heart of it. She listened as bells tolled out joyful melodies from every side, and reminded herself—again—that she wasn't the princess in this particular fairy tale, despite appearances to the contrary.

That Nikolai had told her the night he'd met her that it would end in teeth. And tears.

The charity Christmas ball was the following night, where he would have that conversation with his ex-wife at last, and after that it wouldn't matter how perfect Prague looked, how achingly lovely its cobbled streets or its famous bridges bristling with Gothic saints. It didn't matter how golden it seemed in the winter sunset, how fanciful, as if it belonged on a gilded page in an ancient manuscript. She would leave this city as she'd found it, and this agonizing charade would end. Nikolai would get what he wanted and she would get her life back.

She should want that, she knew. She should be thrilled.

If she stuck her head out her door she could hear the low rumble of Nikolai's voice from somewhere else in the great, ornate hotel suite he'd chosen, all golds and reds and plush Bohemian extravagance. He was on a call, taking care of business in that ruthless way of his. Because he didn't allow distractions—he'd told her so himself.

Not foreign cities that looked too enchanted to be real. Certainly not her.

And Alicia was in a room that was twice the size of her flat and a hundred times more lush, one deep breath away from losing herself completely to the things she was still afraid to let herself feel lest she simply explode across the floor like that bottle of wine, practicing her prettiest smile against the coming dark.

None of this was real, she reminded herself, tracing her finger across the cold glass of the window. None of this was hers.

In the end, none of it would matter.

The only thing that would remain of these strange

weeks were the pictures in the tabloids, stuck on the internet forever like her very own scarlet letter. There would be no record of the way she ached for him. There would be no evidence that she'd ever felt her heart tear open, or that long after he'd left that night, she'd cried into her mountain of frilly pillows for a scared little boy with bright blue eyes who'd never been lucky or safe. And for the girl she'd been eight years ago, who only Nikolai had ever tried to defend from an attack she couldn't even remember. No one would know if she healed or not, because no one would know she'd been hurt.

There would only be those pictures and the nonexistent relationship Nikolai had made sure they showed to the world, that she'd decided she no longer cared if her father knew about.

*Let him think what he likes,* she'd thought.

Alicia had taken the train out for his birthday dinner the previous week, and had sat with her sisters around the table in his favorite local restaurant, pretending everything was all right. The way she always pretended it was.

But not because she'd still been racked with shame, as she'd been for all those years. Instead, she'd realized as she'd watched her father *not* look at her and *not* acknowledge her and she understood at last what had actually happened to her, she'd been a great deal closer to furious.

"Will you have another drink, love?" her mother had asked her innocuously enough, but Alicia had been watching her father. She'd seen him wince at the very idea, as if another glass of wine would have Alicia doffing her clothes in the middle of the King's Arms. And all of that fury and pain and all of those terrible years fused inside of her. She'd been as unable to keep quiet as she'd been when she'd told Nikolai about this mess in the first place.

"No need to worry, Dad," she'd said brusquely. "I haven't

been anywhere close to drunk in years. Eight years to be precise. And would you like to know why?"

He'd stared at her, then looked around at the rest of the family, all of them gaping from him to Alicia and back.

"No need," he'd said sharply. "I'm already aware."

"I was so drunk I couldn't walk," she'd told him, finally. "I take full responsibility for that. My friends poured me into a taxi and it took me ages to make it up to the house from the lane. I didn't want to wake anyone, so I went into the garden and lay down to sleep beneath the stars."

"For God's sake, Alicia!" her father had rumbled. "This isn't the time or place to bring up this kind of—"

"I passed out," she'd retorted, and she'd been perfectly calm. Focused. "I can't remember a single thing about it because I was *unconscious*. And yet when you saw Mr. Reddick helping himself to your comatose daughter, the conclusion you reached was that I was a whore."

There'd been a long, highly charged silence.

"He tried it on with me, too," her older sister had declared at last, thumping her drink down on the tabletop. "Vile pervert."

"I always thought he wasn't right," her other sister had chimed in at almost the same moment. "Always staring up at our windows, peering through the hedge."

"I had no idea," her mother had said urgently then, reaching over and taking hold of Alicia's hand, squeezing it tightly in hers. Then she'd frowned at her husband. "Bernard, you should be ashamed of yourself! Douglas Reddick was a menace to every woman in the village!"

And much later, after they'd all talked themselves blue and teary while her father had sat there quietly, and Douglas Reddick's sins had been thoroughly documented, her father had hugged her goodbye for the first time in nearly a decade. His form of an apology, she supposed.

And much as she'd wanted to rail at him further, she hadn't. Alicia had felt that great big knot she'd carried around inside of her begin to loosen, and she'd let it, because she'd wanted her father back more than she'd wanted to be angry.

She'd have that to carry with her out of her fake relationship. And surely that was something. Only she would know who had helped her stand up for herself eight years later. Only she would remember the things he'd changed in her when this was over. When the smoke cleared.

That was, if the smoke didn't choke her first.

"It's not even real," Alicia had blurted out one night, after a quarter hour of listening to Rosie rhapsodize about what a wedding to a man like Nikolai Korovin might entail, all while sitting on the couch surrounded by her favorite romance novels and the remains of a box of chocolates.

"What do you mean?"

"I mean, it's not real, Rosie. It's for show."

Alicia had regretted that she'd said anything the instant she'd said it. There'd been an odd, twisting thing inside of her that wanted to keep the sordid facts to herself. That hadn't wanted anyone else to know that when it came down to it, Nikolai Korovin needed an ulterior motive and a list of requirements to consider taking her out on a fake date.

Not that she was bitter.

"You're so cynical," Rosie had said with a sigh. "But I'll have you know I'm optimistic enough for the both of us." She'd handed Alicia a particularly well-worn romance novel, with a pointed look. "I know you sneak this off my shelf all the time. I also know that this tough, skeptical little shell of yours is an act."

"It's not an act," Alicia had retorted.

But she'd also taken the book.

If she'd stayed up too late some nights, crouched over

her laptop with her door locked tight, looking through all the photos of the two of them together online, she'd never admit it. If she'd paused to marvel over the way the tabloids managed to find pictures that told outright lies—that showed Nikolai gazing down at her with something that looked like his own, rusty version of affection, for example, or showed him scowling with what looked like bristling protectiveness at a photographer who ventured too close, she'd kept that to herself, too. Because if she'd dared speak of it, she might betray herself—she might show how very much she preferred the tabloid romance she read about to what she knew to be the reality.

And then there was Nikolai.

"Kiss me," he'd ordered her a few days before they'd had to leave for Prague, in that commanding tone better suited to tense corporate negotiations than a bright little café in his posh neighborhood on a Tuesday morning. She'd frowned at him and he'd stared back at her, ruthless and severe. "It will set the scene."

He'd been different these past few days, she'd thought as she'd looked at him over their coffees. Less approachable than he'd been before, which beggared belief, given his usual level of aloofness. He'd been much tenser. Darker. The fact that she'd been capable of discerning the differences between the various gradations of his glacial cold might have worried her, if she'd had any further to fall where this man was concerned.

"What scene?" she'd asked calmly, as if the idea of kissing him hadn't made her whole body tremble with that ever-present longing, that thrill of heat and flame. "There's a wall between us and the street. No one can see us, much less photograph us."

"We live in a digital age, Alicia," he'd said icily. "There are mobile phones everywhere."

Alicia had looked very pointedly at the people at the two other tables in their hidden nook, neither of whom had been wielding a mobile. Then she'd returned her attention to her steaming latte and sipped at it, pretending not to notice that Nikolai had continued to stare at her in that brooding, almost-fierce way.

"They took pictures of us walking here," she'd pointed out when the silence stretched too thin, his gaze was burning into her like hot coals and she'd worried she might break, into too many pieces to repair. "Mission accomplished."

Because nothing screamed *contented domesticity* like an early-morning stroll to a coffee place from Nikolai's penthouse, presumably after another long and intimate night. That was the story the tabloids would run with, he'd informed her in his clipped, matter-of-fact way, and it was guaranteed to drive his ex-wife crazy. Most of Nikolai's women, it went without saying—though her coworkers lined up to say the like daily—were there to pose silently beside him at events and disappear afterward, not stroll anywhere with him as if he *liked* them.

She'd been surprised to discover she was scowling. And then again when he'd stood up abruptly, smoothing down his suit jacket despite the fact it was far too well made to require smoothing of any kind. He'd stared at her, hard, then jerked his head toward the front of the café in a clear and peremptory command before storming that way himself.

Alicia had hated herself for it, but she'd smiled sheepishly at the other patrons in the tiny alcove, who'd eyed Nikolai's little display askance, and then she'd followed him.

He stood in the biting cold outside, muttering darkly into his mobile. Alicia had walked to stand next to him, wondering if she'd lost her spine when she'd felt that giant ripping thing move through her in her flat that night, as if she'd traded it for some clarity about what had happened to her eight years ago. Because she certainly hadn't used it since. She hadn't been using it that morning, certainly. The old, spined Alicia would have let Nikolai storm off as he chose, while she'd sat and merrily finished her latte.

Or so she'd wanted to believe.

Nikolai had slid his phone into a pocket and then turned that winter gaze on her, and Alicia had done her best to show him the effortlessly polite—if tough and slightly cynical—mask she'd tried so hard to wear during what he'd called *the public phase of this arrangement.* Yet something in the way he'd stared down at her that gray morning, that grim mouth of his a flat line, had made it impossible.

"Nikolai…" But she hadn't known what she'd meant to say.

He'd reached over to take her chin in his leather-gloved hand, and she'd shivered though she wasn't cold at all.

"There are paparazzi halfway down the block," he'd muttered. "We must bait the trap, *solnyshka.*"

And then he'd leaned down and pressed a very hard, very serious, shockingly swift kiss against her lips.

Bold and hot. As devastating as it was a clear and deliberate brand of his ownership. His possession.

It had blown her up. Made a mockery of any attempts she'd thought she'd been making toward politeness, because that kiss had been anything but, surging through her like lightning. Burning her into nothing but smoldering need, right there on the street in the cold.

She'd have fallen down, had he not had those hard fingers on her chin. He'd looked at her for a long moment that had felt far too intimate for a public street so early in the morning, and then he'd released her.

And she'd had the sinking feeling that he knew exactly

what he'd done to her. Exactly how she felt. That this was all a part of his game. His plan.

"Let me guess what that word means," she'd said after a moment, trying to sound tough but failing, miserably. She'd been stripped down to nothing, achingly vulnerable, and she'd heard it clear as day in her voice. There'd been every reason to suppose he'd read it as easily on her face. "Is it Russian for gullible little fool, quick to leap into bed with a convenient stranger and happy to sell out her principles and her self-respect for any old photo opportunity—"

"Little sun," he'd bit out, his own gaze haunted. Tormented. He'd stared at her so hard she'd been afraid she'd bear the marks of it. She'd only been distantly aware that she trembled, that it had nothing to do with the temperature. He'd raised his hand again, brushed his fingers across her lips, and she'd had to bite back something she'd been terribly afraid was a sob. "Your smile could light up this city like a nuclear reactor. It's a weapon. And yet you throw it around as if it's nothing more dangerous than candy."

Here, now, staring out at the loveliest city she'd ever seen, as night fell and the lights blazed golden against the dark, Alicia could still feel those words as if he'd seared them into her skin.

And she knew it would be one more thing that she'd carry with her on the other side of this. One more thing only she would ever know had happened. Had been real. Had mattered, it seemed, if only for a moment.

She blinked back that prickly heat behind her eyes, and when they cleared, saw Nikolai in the entrance to her room. No more than a dark shape behind her in the window's reflection. As if he, too, was already disappearing, turning into another memory right before her eyes.

She didn't turn. She didn't dare. She didn't know what she'd do.

"We leave in an hour," he said.

Alicia didn't trust herself to speak, and so merely nodded.

And she could feel that harshly beautiful kiss against her mouth again, like all the things she couldn't allow herself to say, all the things she knew she'd never forget as long as she lived.

Nikolai hesitated in the doorway, and she held her breath, but then he simply turned and melted away, gone as silently as he'd come.

She dressed efficiently and quickly in a sleek sheath made of a shimmery green that made her feel like a mermaid. It was strapless with a V between her breasts, slicked down to her waist, then ended in a breezy swell at her knees. It had been hanging in her room when she'd arrived, next to a floor-length sweep of sequined royal blue that was clearly for the more formal ball tomorrow night. And accessories for both laid out on a nearby bureau. She slid her feet into the appropriate shoes, each one a delicate, sensual triumph. Then she picked up the cunning little evening bag, the green of the dress with blues mixed in.

*He's bought and paid for you, hasn't he?* she asked herself as she walked down the long hall toward the suite's main room, trying to summon her temper. Her sense of outrage. Any of that motivating almost-hate she'd tried to feel for him back in the beginning. *There are words to describe arrangements like this, aren't there? Especially if you're foolish enough to sleep with him....*

But she knew that the sad truth was that she was going to do this, whether she managed to work herself into a state or not. She was going to wear the fine clothes he'd bought her and dance to his tune, quite literally, because she no longer had the strength to fight it. To fight him.

To fight her own traitorous heart.

And time was running out. By Monday it would be as if she'd dreamed all of this. She imagined that in two months' time or so, when she was living her normal life and was done sorting out whatever Nikolai fallout there might be, she'd feel as if she had.

A thought that should have made her happy and instead was like a huge, black hole inside of her, yawning and deep. She ignored it, because she didn't know what else to do as she walked into the lounge. Nikolai stood in front of the flat-screen television, frowning at the financial report, but turned almost before she cleared the entryway, as if he'd sensed her.

She told herself she hardly noticed anymore how beautiful he was. How gorgeously lethal in another fine suit.

Nikolai roamed toward her, his long strides eating up the luxurious carpet beneath his feet, the tall, dark, brooding perfection of him bold and elegant in the middle of so much overstated opulence. Columns wrapped in gold. Frescoed ceilings. And his gaze was as bright as the winter sky, as if he made it daylight again when he looked at her.

There was no possibility that she would survive this in anything like one piece. None at all.

*You can fall to pieces next week,* she told herself firmly. It would be Christmas. She'd hole up in her parents' house as planned, stuff herself with holiday treats and too much mulled wine, and pretend none of this had ever happened. That *he* hadn't happened to her.

That she hadn't done this to herself.

"Are you ready?" he asked.

"Define ready." She tried to keep her voice light. Amused. Because anything else would lead them to places she didn't want to go, because she doubted she'd come back from them intact. "Ready to attend your exciting whirl of corporate events? Certainly. Ready to be used in my capacity as weapon of choice, aimed directly at your ex-wife's face?" She even smiled then, and it felt almost like the real thing. "I find I'm as ready for *that* as I ever was."

"Then I suppose we should both be grateful that there will be no need for weaponry tonight," he said, in that way of his that insinuated itself down the length of her back, like a sliver of ice. The rest of her body heated at once, inside and out, his brand of winter like a fire in her, still. "This is only a tedious dinner. An opportunity to make the donors feel especially appreciated before we ask them for more money tomorrow."

When he drew close, he reached over to a nearby incidental table and picked up a long, flat box. He held it out to her without a word, his expression serious. She stared at it until he grew impatient, and then he simply cracked open the box himself and pulled out a shimmering necklace. It was asymmetrical and bold, featuring unusually shaped clusters of blue and green gems set in a thick rope that nonetheless managed to appear light. Fun. As fanciful, in its way, as this golden city they stood in.

The very things this man was not.

"I would have taken you for the black diamond sort," Alicia said, her eyes on the necklace instead of him, because it was the prettiest thing she'd seen and yet she knew it would pale next to his stark beauty. "Or other very, very dark jewels. Heavy chunks of hematite. Brooding rubies the color of burgundy wine."

"That would be predictable," he said, a reproving note in his low voice, the hint of that dark humor mixed in with it, making her wish. *Want.*

He slid the necklace into place, cool against her heated skin, his fingers like naked flame. She couldn't help the sigh that escaped her lips, and her eyes flew to his, finally, to find him watching her with that lazy, knowing intensity in his gaze that had been her undoing from the start.

He reached around to the nape of her neck, taking his time fastening the necklace, letting his fingertips dance and tease her skin beneath the cloud of her curls, then smoothing over her collarbone. He adjusted it on her neck, making sure it fell as he wanted it, one end stretched down toward the upper swell of one breast.

Alicia didn't know if he was teasing her or tearing her apart. She could no longer tell the difference.

When he caught her gaze again, neither one of them was breathing normally, and the room around them felt hot and close.

"Come," he said, and she could hear it in his voice. That fire. That need. That tornado that spiraled between them, more and more out of control the longer this went on, and more likely to wreck them both with every second.

*And it would,* she thought. *Soon.*

Just as he'd warned her.

# CHAPTER EIGHT

A GOLD-MIRRORED LIFT delivered them with hushed and elegant efficiency into the brightly lit foyer of the presidential suite in one of Prague's finest hotels, filled with the kind of people who were not required to announce their wealth and consequence because everything they did, said and wore did it for them. Emphatically.

These were Nikolai's people. Alicia kept her polite smile at the ready as Nikolai steered her through the crowd. This was his world, no matter how he looked at her when they were in private. No matter what stories she'd told herself, she was no more than a tourist, due to turn straight back into a pumpkin the moment the weekend was over. And then stay that way, this strange interlude nothing more than a gilt-edged memory.

She could almost feel the heavy stalk beginning to form, like a brand-new knot in her stomach.

Nikolai pulled her aside after they'd made a slow circuit through the monied clusters of guests, into a small seating area near the farthest windows. Outside, in the dark, she could see the magnificence of Prague Castle, thrusting bright and proud against the night. And inside, Nikolai looked down at her, unsmiling, in that way of his that made everything inside of her squeeze tight, then melt.

"I told you this would be remarkably boring, did I not?"

"Perhaps for you," she replied, smiling. "I keep wondering if the American cattle baron is going to break into song at the piano, and if so, if that very angry-looking German banker will haul off and hit him."

His blue eyes gleamed, and she felt the warmth of it all over, even deep inside where that knot curled tight in her gut, a warning she couldn't seem to heed.

"These are not the sort of people who fight with their hands," Nikolai said, the suggestion of laughter in his gaze, on his mouth, lurking in that rough velvet voice of his. "They prefer to go to war with their checkbooks."

"That sounds a bit dry." She pressed her wineglass to her lips and sipped, but was aware of nothing but Nikolai. "Surely throwing a few punches is more exciting than writing checks?"

"Not at all." His lips tugged in one corner. "A fistfight can only be so satisfying. Bruises heal. Fight with money, and whole companies can be leveled, thousands of lives ruined, entire fortunes destroyed in the course of an afternoon." That smile deepened, became slightly mocking. "This also requires a much longer recovery period than a couple of bruises."

Alicia searched his face, wondering if she was seeing what she wanted to see—or if there really was a softening there, a kind of warmth, that made that wide rip in her feel like a vast canyon and her heart beat hard like a drum.

He reached over and traced one of the clever shapes that made up the necklace he'd given her, almost lazily, but Alicia felt the burn of it as if he was touching her directly. His gaze found hers, and she knew they both wished he was.

It swelled between them, bright and hot and more complicated now, that electric connection that had shocked her in that club. It was so much deeper tonight. It poured into every part of her, changing her as it went, making her realize she didn't care what the consequences were any longer. They'd be worth it. Anything would be worth it if it meant she could touch him again.

She couldn't find the words to tell him that, so she smiled instead, letting it all flow out of her. Like a weapon, he'd said. Like candy.

*Like love.*

Nikolai jerked almost imperceptibly, as if he saw what she thought, what she felt, written all over her. As if she'd said it out loud when she hardly dared think it.

"Alicia—" he began, his tone deeper than usual, urgent and thick, and all of her confusion and wariness rolled into the place where she'd torn in two, then swelled into that ache, making it bloom, making her realize she finally knew what it was....

But then the energy in the suite all around them shifted. Dramatically. There was a moment of shocked silence, then an excited buzz of whispering.

Nikolai's gaze left hers and cut to the entryway, and then, without seeming to move at all, he froze solid. She watched him do it, saw him turn from flesh and blood to ice in a single breath.

It was the first time he'd scared her.

Alicia turned to see the crowd parting before a graceful woman in a deceptively simple black dress, flanked by two security guards. She was cool and aristocratic as she walked into the room, smiling and exchanging greetings with the people she passed. Her dark red hair was swept back into an elegant chignon, she wore no adornment besides a hint of diamonds at her ears and the sparkle of the ring on her hand, and still, she captivated the room.

And had turned Nikolai to stone.

Alicia recognized her at once, of course.

"Isn't that...?"

"My brother's wife. Yes."

Nikolai's tone was brutal. Alicia flicked a worried glance at him, then looked back to the party.

Miranda Sweet, wife of the legendary Ivan Korovin and easily identifiable to anyone with access to Rosie's unapologetic subscription to celebrity magazines, swept through the assembled collection of donors with ease. She said a word or two here, laughed there and only faltered when her gaze fell on Nikolai. But she recovered almost instantly, squaring her shoulders and waving off her security detail, and made her way toward him.

She stopped when she was a few feet away. Keeping a safe distance, Alicia thought, her eyes narrowing. Miranda Sweet was prettier in person, and taller, and the way she looked at Nikolai was painful.

While Nikolai might as well have been a glacier.

Alicia could have choked on the thick, black tension that rose between the two of them, so harsh it made her ears ring. So intense she glanced around to see if anyone else had noticed, but Miranda's security guards had blocked them off from prying eyes.

When she looked back, Nikolai and his brother's wife were still locked in their silent battle. Alicia moved closer to Nikolai's side, battling the urge to step in front of him and protect him from this threat, however unlikely the source.

Then, very deliberately, Nikolai dropped his gaze. Alicia followed it to the small swell of Miranda's belly, almost entirely concealed by her dress. Alicia never would have seen it. She doubted anyone was supposed to see it.

When Nikolai raised his gaze to his sister-in-law's again, his eyes were raw and cold. Alicia saw Miranda swallow. Hard. Nervously, even.

Another terrible moment passed.

Then Miranda inclined her head slightly. "Nikolai."

"Miranda," he replied, in the same tone, so crisp and hard and civil it hurt.

Miranda glanced at Alicia, then back at Nikolai, and something moved across her face.

*Fear,* Alicia thought, confused. *She's* afraid *of him.*

Miranda hid it almost immediately, though her hand moved to brush against her belly, her ring catching the light. She dropped her hand when she saw Nikolai glance at it.

"He misses you," she said after a moment, obvious conflict and a deep sadness Alicia didn't understand in her voice. "You broke his heart."

"Are you his emissary?"

"Hardly." Miranda looked at Nikolai as if she expected a reply, but he was nothing but ice. "He would never admit that. He'd hate that I said anything."

"Then why did you?" Cold and hard, and Alicia thought it must hurt him to sound like that. To be that terribly frigid.

Miranda nodded again, a sharp jerk of her head. Her gaze moved to Alicia for a moment, as if she wanted to say something, but thought better of it. And then she turned and walked away without another word, her smile in place as if it had never left her.

While Alicia stood next to Nikolai and hurt for him, hard and deep, and all the things he didn't—couldn't—say.

"I take it you weren't expecting her," she said after a while, still watching Miranda Sweet work the party, marveling at how carefree she looked when she'd left a wind chill and subzero temperatures in her wake.

"I should have." Nikolai's gaze was trained on the crowd, dark and stormy. "She often makes appearances at high-level donor events when Ivan is held up somewhere else. It helps bring that little bit of Hollywood sparkle."

He sounded as if he was reporting on something he'd read a long time ago, distant and emotionless, but Alicia knew better. She felt the waves of that bitter chill coming off him, like arctic winds. This was Nikolai in pain. She could feel it inside her own chest, like a vise.

"A bit of a chilly reunion, I couldn't help but notice."

Nikolai shifted. "She believes I tried to ruin her relationship with Ivan."

Alicia frowned up at him. "Why would she think that?"

It took Nikolai a breath to look down, to meet her eyes. When he did, his gaze was the coldest she'd ever seen it, and her heart lurched in her chest.

"Because I did."

She blinked, but didn't otherwise move. "Why?"

A great black shadow fell over him then, leaving him hollow at the eyes and that hard mouth of his too grim. *Grief,* she thought. And something very much like shame, only sharper. Colder.

"Why do I do anything?" he asked softly. Terribly. "Because happiness looks like the enemy to me. When I see it I try to kill it."

Alicia only stared at him, stricken. Nikolai's mouth tugged in one corner, a self-deprecating almost smile that this time was nothing but dark and painful. Total devastation in that one small curve.

"You should be afraid of me, Alicia," he said, and the bleak finality in his voice broke her in two. "I keep warning you."

He turned back to the crowd.

And Alicia followed an instinct she didn't fully understand, that had something to do with that deep ache, that wide-open canyon in her chest she didn't think would ever go away, and the proud, still way he stood next to her, ruthlessly rigid and straight, as if bracing himself for another blow.

Like that brave boy he must have been a lifetime ago, who was never safe. Or lucky. Who had given up all hope.

She couldn't bear it.

Alicia reached over and slid her hand into his, as if it belonged there. As if they fitted together like a puzzle, and she was clicking the last piece into place.

She felt him flinch, but then, slowly—almost cautiously—his long fingers closed over hers.

And then she held on to him with all of her might.

Nikolai hadn't expected Alicia to be quite so good at this, to fill her role so seamlessly tonight, as if she'd been born to play the part of his hostess. As if she belonged right there at his side, the limb he hadn't realized he'd been missing all along, instead of merely the tool he'd planned to use and then discard.

He stood across the room, watching from a distance as she charmed the two men she'd thought might break into a fight earlier. She was like a brilliant sunbeam in the middle of this dark and cold winter's night, outshining his wealthiest donors in all their finery even here, in a luxurious hotel suite in a city renowned for its gleaming, golden, incomparable light.

Nikolai had never seen her equal. He never would again.

She'd held on to his hand. *To him.* Almost ferociously, as if she'd sensed how close he'd been to disappearing right where he stood and had been determined to stand as his anchor. And so she had.

Nikolai couldn't concentrate on his duties tonight the way he usually did, with that single-minded focus that was his trademark. He couldn't think too much about the fact that Ivan had a child on the way, no matter the vows they'd made as angry young men that they would never inflict the uncertain Korovin temper on more innocent children.

He couldn't think of anything but that press of Alicia's palm against his, the tangling of their fingers as if they belonged fused together like that, the surprising strength of her grip.

As if they were a united front no matter the approaching threat—Miranda, the pregnancy Ivan had failed to mention, the donors who wanted to be celebrated and catered to no matter what quiet heartbreaks might occur in their midst, even the ravaged wastes of his own frigid remains of a soul.

She'd held his hand as if she was ready to fight at his side however she could and that simple gesture had humbled him so profoundly that he didn't know how he'd remained upright. How he hadn't sunk to his knees and promised her anything she wanted, anything at all, if she would only do that again.

If she would choose him, support him. Defend him. Protect him.

If she would treat him like a man, not a wild animal in need of a cage. If she would keep treating him like that. Like he really could be redeemed.

As if she hadn't the smallest doubt.

Because if he wasn't the irredeemable monster he'd always believed—if both she and Ivan had been right all along—then he could choose. He could choose the press of her slender fingers against his, a shining bright light to cut through a lifetime of dark. Warmth instead of cold. Sun instead of ice. *He could choose.*

Nikolai had never imagined that was possible. He'd stopped wanting what he couldn't have. He'd stopped *wanting*.

Alicia made him believe he could be the man he might have been, if only for a moment. She made him regret, more deeply than he ever had before, that he was so empty. That he couldn't give her anything in return.

*Except,* a voice inside him whispered, *her freedom from this.*

From him. From this dirty little war he'd forced her to fight.

Nikolai nearly shuddered where he stood. He kept his eyes trained on Alicia, who looked over her shoulder as if she felt the weight of his stare and then smiled at him as if he really was that man.

As if she'd never seen anything else.

That swift taste of her on a gray and frigid London street had led only to cold showers and a gnawing need inside of him these past few days, much too close to pain. Nikolai didn't care anymore that he hardly recognized himself. That he was drowning in this flood she'd let loose in him. That he was almost thawed through and beyond control, the very thing he'd feared the most for the whole of his life.

He wanted Alicia more. There was only this one last weekend before everything went back to normal. Before he had his answer from Veronika. And then there was absolutely no rational reason he should ever spend another moment in her company.

He'd intended to have her here, in every way he could. To glut himself on her as if that could take the place of all her mysteries he'd failed to solve, the sweet intoxication that was Alicia that he'd never quite sobered up from. He'd intended to make this weekend count.

But she'd let him imagine that he was a better man, or could be. He'd glimpsed himself as she saw him for a brief, brilliant moment, and that changed everything.

*You have to let her go,* that voice told him, more forcefully. *Now, before it's too late.*

He imagined that was his conscience talking. No wonder he didn't recognize it.

Nikolai took her back to their hotel when the dinner

finally ground to a halt not long after midnight. They stood outside her bedroom and he studied her lovely face, committing it to memory.

Letting her go.

"Nikolai?" Even her voice was pretty. Husky and sweet. "What's the matter?"

He kissed her softly, once, on that very hand that had held his with such surprising strength and incapacitating kindness. It wasn't what he wanted. It wasn't enough. But it would be something to take with him, like a single match against the night.

"You don't need to be here," he said quietly, quickly, because he wasn't sure he'd do it at all if he didn't do it fast. "Veronika will seek me out whether you're with me or not. I'll have the plane ready for you in the morning."

"What are you talking about?" Her voice was small. It shook. "I thought we had a very specific plan. Didn't we?"

"You're free, Alicia." He ground out the words. "Of this game, this blackmail. Of me."

"But—" She reached out to him, but he caught her hand before she could touch him, because he couldn't trust himself. Not with her. "What if I don't particularly want to be free?"

Under any other circumstances, he wouldn't have hesitated. But this was Alicia. She'd comforted him, protected him, when anyone else would have walked away.

When everyone else had.

It wasn't a small gesture to him, the way she'd held his hand like that. It was everything. He had to honor that, if nothing else.

"I know you don't," Nikolai said. He released her hand, and she curled it into a fist. Fierce and fearless until the end. That was his Alicia. "But you deserve it. You deserve better."

And then he'd left her there outside her room without another word, because a good man never would have put her in this position in the first place, blackmailed her and threatened her, forced her into this charade for his own sordid ends.

Because he knew it was the right thing to do, and for her, he'd make himself do it, no matter how little he liked it.

"But I love you," Alicia whispered, knowing he was already gone.

That he'd already melted into the shadows, disappeared down the hall, and that chances were, he wouldn't want to hear that anyway.

She stood there in that hall for a long time, outside the door to her bedroom in a mermaid dress and lovely, precarious heels he'd chosen for her, and told herself she wasn't falling apart.

*She was fine.*

She was in love with a man who had walked away from her, leaving her with nothing but a teasing hint of heat on the back of her hand and that awful finality in his rough, dark voice, but Alicia told herself she was absolutely, perfectly *fine*.

Eventually, she moved inside her room and dutifully shut the door. She pulled off the dress he'd chosen for her and the necklace he'd put around her neck himself, taking extra care with both of them as she put them back with the rest of the things she'd leave behind her here.

And maybe her heart along with them.

She tried not to think about that stunned, almost-shattered look in his beautiful eyes when she'd grabbed his hand. The way his strong fingers had wrapped around hers, then held her tight, as if he'd never wanted to let her go. She tried not to torture herself with the way he'd looked at her across the dinner table afterward, over the sounds of merriment and too much wine, that faint smile in the corner of his austere mouth.

But she couldn't think of anything else.

Alicia changed into the old T-shirt she wore to sleep in, washed soft and cozy over the years, and then she methodically washed her face and cleaned her teeth. She climbed into the palatial bed set high on a dais that made her feel she was perched on a stage, and then she glared fiercely at that book Rosie had given her without seeing a single well-loved sentence.

The truth was, she'd fallen in love when she'd fallen into him at that club.

It had been that sudden, that irrevocable. That deeply, utterly mad. The long, hot, darkly exciting and surprisingly emotional night that had followed had only cemented it. And when he'd let her see those glimpses of his vulnerable side, even hidden away in all that ice and bitter snow, she'd felt it like a deep tear inside of her because she hadn't wanted to accept what she already knew somewhere inside.

Alicia let out a sigh and tossed the paperback aside, sinking back against the soft feather pillows and scowling at the billowing canopy far above her.

She wasn't the too-drunk girl she'd been at twenty-one any longer—and in fact, she'd never been the shameful creature she'd thought she was. Had she tripped and fallen into any other man on that dance floor that night, she would have offered him her embarrassed apologies and then gone straight home to sort out her laundry and carry on living her quiet little life.

But it had been Nikolai.

The fact was, she'd kicked and screamed and moaned about the way he'd forced her into this—but he hadn't. She could have complained. Daniel was a CEO with grand plans for the charity, but he wasn't an ogre. He wouldn't have simply let her go without a discussion; he might not have let her go at all. And when it came down to it, she hadn't even fought too hard against this mad little plan of Nikolai's, had she?

On some level, she'd wanted all of those tabloid pictures with their suggestive captions, because her fascination with him outweighed her shame. And more, because they proved it was real. That the night no one knew about, that she'd tried so hard to make disappear, had really, truly happened.

She'd tasted him in that shiny black SUV, and she'd loved every moment of his bold possession. She'd explored every inch of his beautiful body in that wide bed of his. She'd kissed his scars and even the monster he wore on his chest like a warning. And he'd made her sob and moan and surge against him as if she'd never get enough of him, and then they'd collapsed against each other to sleep in a great tangle, as if they weren't two separate people at all.

All of that had happened. All of it was real.

*All of this is real,* she thought.

Alicia picked up the paperback romance again, flipping through the well-worn pages to her favorite scene, which she'd read so many times before she was sure she could quote it. She scanned it again now.

*Love can't hinge on an outcome. If it does, it isn't love at all*, the heroine said directly to the man she loved when all was lost. When he had already given up, and she loved him too much to let him. When she was willing to fight for him in the only way she could, even if that meant she had to fight every last demon in his head herself. *Love is risk and hope and a terrible vulnerability. And it's worth it. I promise.*

"You either love him or you don't, Alicia," she told herself then, a hushed whisper in her quiet room.

And she did.

Then she took a deep breath to gather her courage, swung out of the high bed and went to prove it.

Nikolai sat by the fire in the crimson master bedroom that dominated the far corner of the hotel suite, staring at the flames as they crackled and danced along the grate.

He wished this wasn't the longest night of the year, with all of that extra darkness to lead him into temptation, like one more cosmic joke at his expense. He wished he could take some kind of pride in the uncharacteristic decision he'd made instead of sitting here like he needed to act as his own guard, as if a single moment of inattention would have him clawing at her door like an animal.

He wished most of all that this terrible thaw inside of him wasn't an open invitation for his demons to crawl out and fill every extra, elongated hour with their same old familiar poison.

He shifted in the plush velvet armchair and let the heat of the fire play over his skin, wishing it could warm him inside, where too many dark things lurked tonight, with their sharp teeth and too many scenes from his past.

He hated Prague, happy little jewel of a city that it was, filled to the top of every last spire with all the joyful promises of a better life even the Iron Curtain had failed to stamp out. Anywhere east of Zurich he began to feel the bitter chill of Mother Russia breathing down his neck, her snow-covered nails digging into his back as if she might drag him back home at any moment.

It was far too easy to imagine himself there, struggling to make it through another vicious winter with no end, dreamless and broken and half-mad. Feral to the bone. In his uncle's bleak home in Nizhny Novgorod. In corrupt, polluted, snowbound Moscow with the equally corrupt and polluted Veronika, when he'd been in the military and had thought, for a time, it might save him from himself.

Or, even sadder in retrospect, that Veronika might.

Being in Prague was too much like being back there. Nikolai was too close to the raw and out-of-control creature he'd been then, careening between the intense extremes that were all he'd ever known. Either losing himself in violence or numbing himself however he could. One or the other, since the age of five.

He could feel that old version of him right beneath his skin, making him restless. On edge.

Then again, perhaps it wasn't Prague at all. Perhaps it was the woman on the other side of this hotel suite even now, with her dark eyes that saw more of him than anyone else ever had and that carnal distraction of a mouth.

He was in trouble. He knew it.

This was the kind of night that called for a bottle of something deliberately incapacitating, but he couldn't allow himself the escape. He couldn't numb this away. He couldn't slam it into oblivion. He had to sit in it and wait for morning.

Nikolai scowled at the fire while his demons danced on, bold and sickening and much too close, tugging him back into his dirty past as if he'd never left it behind.

As if he never would.

A scant second before Alicia appeared in his door, he sensed her approach, his gaze snapping to meet hers as she paused on the threshold.

He almost thought she was another one of his demons, but even as it crossed his mind, he knew better. Alicia was too alive, that light of hers beaming into his room as if she'd switched on the lamps, sending all of those things that tortured him in the dark diving for the shadows.

She'd changed out of her formal attire and was standing

there in nothing but an oversized wide-necked T-shirt—a pink color, of course—that slid down her arm to bare her shoulder and the upper slope of one breast. Her curls stood around her head in abandon, and her feet were bare.

Nikolai's throat went dry. The rest of him went hard.

"It's below zero tonight," he barked at her, rude and belligerent. *Desperate.* "You shouldn't be walking around like that unless you've decided to court your own death, in which case, I can tell you that there are far quicker ways to go."

The last time he'd used a tone like that on a woman, she'd turned and run from him, sobbing. But this was Alicia. His strong, fearless Alicia, and she only laughed that laugh of hers that made him want to believe in magic.

When he looked at her, he thought he might.

"I've come to your room wearing almost nothing and your first reaction is to talk about the weather and death," she said in that dry way of hers, and God help him, this woman was worse than all his demons put together. More powerful by far. "Very romantic, indeed. My heart is aglow."

Nikolai stood up then, as if that would ward her off. He didn't know which was worse. That she was standing there with so much of her lush brown skin on display, her lithe and supple legs, that shoulder, even the hint of her thighs—naked and smooth and far too tempting. Or that teasing tone she used, so dry and amused, that set off brushfires inside him.

His body felt as if it was someone else's, unwieldy and strange. He wished he hadn't stripped down to no more than his exercise trousers, low on his hips, the better to while away a sleepless night at war with himself.

There was too much bare flesh in the room now. Too many possibilities. He could only deny himself so much....

He scowled at her, and she laughed again.

"Relax," she said, in that calm, easy way that simultaneously soothed and inflamed him. "*I'm* seducing *you,* Nikolai. You don't have to do anything but surrender."

"You are not seducing me," he told her, all cold command, and she ignored it completely and started toward him as if he hadn't spoken. As if he hadn't said something similar to her what seemed like a lifetime ago. "And I am certainly not surrendering."

"Not yet, no," she agreed, smiling. "But the night is young."

"Alicia." He didn't back away when she roamed even closer, not even when he could see her nipples poking against the thin material of her shirt and had to fight to keep himself from leaning down and sucking them into his mouth, right then and there. "This is the first time in my life I've ever done the right thing deliberately. Some respect, I beg you."

Her smile changed, making his chest feel tight though he didn't know what it meant.

"Tell me what the right thing is," she said softly, not teasing him any longer, and she was within arm's reach now. Warm and soft. *Right there.* "Because I think you and I are using different definitions."

"It's leaving you alone," he said, feeling the stirrings of a kind of panic he thought he'd excised from himself when he was still a child. "The way I should have done from the start."

She eased closer, her scent teasing his nose, cocoa butter and a hint of sugar, sweet and rich and *Alicia*. He was so hard it bordered on agony, and the way she looked up at him made his heart begin to hit at him, erratic and intense, like it wanted to knock him down. Like it wouldn't take much to succeed.

"You vowed you didn't want to sleep with me again," he reminded her, almost savagely. "Repeatedly."

"I'm a woman possessed," she told him, her voice husky and low, washing over him and into him. "Infatuated, even."

He remembered when he'd said those same words to her in that far-off stairwell, when her scent had had much the same effect on him. Her dark eyes had been so wide and anxious, and yet all of that heat had been there behind it, electric and captivating. Impossible to ignore. Just as she was.

Tonight, there was only heat, so much of it he burned at the sight. And he wanted her so badly he was afraid he shook with it. So badly he cared less and less with every passing second if he did.

"I've never had the slightest inclination to behave the way a good man might," he began, throwing the words at her.

"That simply isn't true."

"Of course it is. I keep telling you, I—"

"You've dedicated your life to doing good, Nikolai," she said, cutting him off, her voice firm. "You run a foundation that funds a tremendous amount of charity work. Specifically, children's charities."

"I'm certain bands of activists would occupy me personally if they could pin me down to a single residence or office." He glared at her, his voice so derisive it almost hurt, but he knew he wasn't talking to her so much as the demons in all the corners of the room, dancing there in his peripheral vision. "I take money from the rich and make it into more money. I am the problem."

"Like Robin Hood, then? Who was, as everyone knows, a great villain. Evil to the very core."

"If Robin Hood were a soulless venture capitalist, perhaps," Nikolai retorted, but there was that brilliant heat inside of him, that terrible thaw, and he was on the verge of something he didn't want to face. He wasn't sure he could.

Alicia shook her head, frowning at him as if he was hurting her. He didn't understand that—this was him *not* hurting her. This was him *trying*. Why was he not surprised that he couldn't do that right, either?

"You help people," she said in that same firm, deliberate way, her gaze holding his. "The things you do and the choices you make *help people*. Nikolai, you do the right thing *every single day*."

He didn't know what that iron band was that crushed his chest, holding him tight, making everything seem to contract around him.

"You say that," he growled at her, or possibly it was even a howl, torn from that heart he'd abandoned years ago, "but there is blood on my hands, Alicia. More blood than you can possibly imagine."

She stepped even closer, then picked up his much larger hands in hers. He felt a kind of rumbling, a far-off quake, and even though he knew there was nothing but disaster heading toward him, even though he suspected it would destroy him and her and possibly the whole of the city they stood in, the world, the stars above, he let her.

And he watched, fascinated beyond measure and something like terrified, that tight, hard circle around him pulling tighter and tighter, as she turned each hand over, one by one, and pressed a kiss into the center of each.

The way she'd done for the creature on his chest, that she'd called *pretty*.

She looked up at him again, and her dark eyes were different. Warm in a way he'd never seen before. Sweet and something like admiring. Filled with that light that made him feel simultaneously scraped hollow and carved new.

Shining as if whatever she saw was beautiful.

"I don't see any blood," she said, distinct and direct, her gaze fast to his. "I only see you. I've never seen anything but you."

And everything simply...ended.

Nikolai shattered. He broke. All of that ice, every last glacier, swept away in the flood, the heat, the roaring inferno stretching high into the night, until he was nothing but raw and wild and *that look* she gave him took up the world.

And replaced it with fire. Fire and heat and all of the things he'd locked away for all those bleak and terrible reasons. Color and light, flesh and blood. Rage and need and all of that hunger, all of that pain, all of that sorrow and grief, loss and tragedy. His parents, taken so young. His brother, who should never have had to fight so hard. The uncle who should have cared for them. The army that had broken him down and then built him into his own worst nightmare. Veronika's lies and Stefan's sweet, infant body cradled in his arms, like hope. Every emotion he'd vowed he didn't have, roaring back into him, filling him up, tearing him into something new and unrecognizable.

"You have to stop this," he said, but when it left his mouth it was near to a shout, furious and loud and she didn't even flinch. "You can't be *kind* to a man like me! You don't know what you've done!"

"Nikolai," she said, without looking away from him, without hiding from the catastrophic storm that was happening right there in front of her, without letting go of his hands for an instant or dropping her warm gaze, "I can't be anything else. That's what *you* deserve."

And he surrendered.

For the first time in his life, Nikolai Korovin stopped fighting.

# CHAPTER NINE

NIKOLAI DROPPED TO his knees, right there in front of her

For a moment he looked ravaged. Untethered and lost, and then he slid his arms around her hips, making Alicia's heart fall out of her chest, her breath deserting her in a rush. She could feel the storm all around them, pouring out of him, enveloping them both. His hard face became stark, sensual. Fierce.

It all led here. Now. To that look in his beautiful eyes that made her own fill with tears. A fledging kind of joy, pale and fragile.

*Hope.*

And she loved him. She thought she understood him. So when that light in his eyes turned to need, she was with him. It roared in her too, setting them both alight.

He pulled up the hem of her T-shirt with a strong, urgent hand that shook slightly, baring her to his view, making her quiver in return. And that fire that was always in her, always his, turned molten and rolled through her, making her heavy and needy and almost scared by the intensity of this. Of him. Of these things she felt, storming inside of her.

Her legs shook, and he kissed her once, high on her thigh. She could feel the curve of his lips, that rare smile, and it went through her like a lightning bolt, burning her straight down to the soles of her feet where they pressed into the thick carpet.

And then slowly, so slowly, he peeled her panties down her legs, then tossed them aside.

Alicia heard a harsh sort of panting, and realized it was her.

*"Solnyshka,"* he said, in that marvelous voice of his, darker and harsher than ever, and it thrilled her, making her feel like the sun he thought she was, too bright and hot to bear. "I think you'd better hold on."

He wrapped one strong arm around her bottom and the back of her thighs, and then, using his shoulder to knock her leg up and out of his way, he leaned forward and pressed his mouth against her heat.

And then he licked into her.

It was white-hot ecstasy. Carnal lightning. It seared through her, almost like pain, making her shudder against him and cry out his name. She fisted her hands in his hair, his arms were tight around her to keep her from falling, and she simply went limp against his mouth.

His wicked, fascinating, demanding mouth.

She detonated. Her licked her straight over the edge, and she thought she screamed, lost in a searingly hot, shuddering place where there was nothing left but him and these things he did to her, this wild magic that was only his. *Theirs.*

"Too fast," he rumbled, from far away, but everything was dizzy, confused, and it took her a long breath, then another, to remember who she was. And where.

And then another to understand that he'd flipped them around to spread her out on the deep rug in front of the fire.

"Nikolai," she said, or thought she did, but she lost whatever half-formed thought that might have been, because he was taking up where he'd left off.

He used his mouth again, and his hands. He stroked deep into her core, throwing her straight back into that inferno as if she'd never found release. Soon she was writhing against him, exulting in how he held her so easily, with such confident mastery, and used his tongue, his teeth, even that smile again, like sensual weapons.

Alicia arched up against him, into him. Her hands dug at the carpet below her, and his mouth was an impossible fire, driving her wild all over again, driving her higher and higher, until he sucked hard on the very center of her heat and she exploded all around him once again.

When she came back to herself this time, he was helping her up, letting her stumble against him and laughing as he pulled her T-shirt over her head, then muttering something as he took her breasts in his hands. He tested their weight, groaned out his approval, and then pulled each hard, dark nipple into his mouth.

Lighting the fire in her all over again. Making her burn.

He picked her up and carried her to the bed, following her down and stretching out beside her, sleek and powerful, tattooed and dangerous. He'd rid himself of his trousers at some point and there was nothing between them then.

Only skin and heat. Only the two of them, at last.

For a while, it was enough. They explored each other as if this was the first time, this taut delight, this delicious heat. Alicia traced the bright-colored shapes and lines that made up his monster with her tongue, pressed kisses over his heart, hearing it thunder beneath her. Nikolai stroked his big hands down the length of her back, testing each and every one of her curves as he worshipped every part of her equally.

He didn't speak. And Alicia kissed him, again and again, as if that could say it for her, the word she dared not say, but could show him. With her mouth, her hands. Her kiss, her smile.

They teased the flames, built them slowly, making up for all those lost weeks since the last time they'd touched like this. Until suddenly, it was too much. They were both out of breath and the fire had turned into something darker, more desperate. Hotter by far.

Nikolai reached for the table near his bed and then rolled a condom down his hard length, his eyes glittering on hers, and Alicia almost felt as if he was stroking her that way, so determined and sure. She could feel his touch inside of her, stoking those flames. Making her wild with smoke and heat and need.

Alicia couldn't wait, as desperate to have him inside her again as if she hadn't already found her own pleasure, twice. As if this was new.

Because it felt that way, she thought. It felt completely different from what had gone before, and she knew why. She might have fallen hard for him the night she met him, but she loved the man she knew. The man who had saved her from a prison of shame. This man, who looked at her as if she was a miracle. This man, who she believed might be one himself.

"Kiss me," she ordered him, straddling his lap, pressing herself against his delicious hardness, torturing them both.

He took her face in his hands and then her mouth with a dark, thrilling kiss, making her moan against him. He tasted like the winter night and a little bit like her, and the kick of it rocketed through her, sensations building and burning and boiling her down until she was nothing but his.

*His.*

The world was his powerful body, his masterful kiss, his strong arms around her that anchored her to him. And she loved him. She loved him with every kiss, every taste. She couldn't get close enough. She knew she never would.

He lifted her higher, up on her knees so she knelt astride him, then held her there. He took her nipple into his mouth again, the sharp pull of it like an electric charge directly into her sex, while his wicked fingers played with the other. Alicia shuddered uncontrollably in his arms, but he held her still, taking his time.

And all the while the hardest part of him was just beneath her, just out of reach.

"Please..." she whispered frantically. "Nikolai, *please*..."

"Unlike you," he said in a voice she hardly recognized, it was so thick with desire, with need, with this mighty storm that had taken hold of them both, "I occasionally obey."

He shifted then, taking her hips in his hands, and then he thrust up into her in a single deep stroke, possessive and sure.

*At last.*

And for a moment, they simply stared at each other. Marveling in that slick, sweet, perfect fit. Nikolai smiled, and she'd never seen his blue eyes so clear. So warm.

Alicia moved her hips, and his breath hissed out into a curse. And then she simply pleased them both.

She moved on him sinuously, sweetly. She bent forward to taste the strong line of his neck, salt and fire. She made love to him with every part of her, worshipping him with everything she had. She couldn't say the words, not to a man like Nikolai, not yet, but she could show him.

And she did.

Until they were both shuddering and desperate.

Until he'd stopped speaking English.

Until he rolled her over and drove into her with all of his dark intensity, all of that battle-charged skill and precision. She exulted beneath him, meeting every thrust, filled with that ache, that wide-open rift he'd torn into her, that only this—only he—could ever soothe.

And when he sent her spinning off into that wild magic for the third time, he came with her, holding her as if he loved her too, that miraculous smile all over his beautiful face.

*At last*, she thought.

"You're in love with him, aren't you?"

Alicia had been so lost in her own head, in Nikolai, that she hadn't heard the door to the women's lounge open. It took her a moment to realize that the woman standing next to her at the long counter was speaking to her.

And another moment for what she'd said to penetrate.

*Veronika.*

The moment stretched out, silent and tense.

Alicia could hear the sounds of the ball, muffled through the lounge's walls. The music from the band and the dull roar of all those well-dressed, elegant people, dancing and eating and making merry in their polite way. She'd almost forgotten that *this* was the reason she was here at all. This woman watching her with that calculating gleam in her eyes, as if she knew things about Alicia that Alicia did not.

There was nothing hard or evil-looking about Veronika, as Alicia had half expected from what little Nikolai had said of her. Her hair cascaded down her back in a tumble of platinum waves. She wore a copper gown that made her slender figure look lithe and supple. Aside from the way she looked at Alicia, she was the picture of a certain kind of smooth, curated, very nearly ageless beauty. The kind that, amongst other things, cost a tremendous amount to maintain and was therefore an advertising campaign in itself.

Alicia told herself there was no need for anxiety. She was wearing that bold, gorgeous blue dress, alive with sequins, that had been waiting for her in her room. It clung to her from the top of one shoulder to the floor, highlighting all of her curves, sparkling with every breath, and until this moment she'd felt beautiful in it. Nikolai had smiled that sexy wolf's smile when he saw her in it, and they'd been late coming here tonight. Very late.

Standing with him in this castle-turned-hotel, dressed for a ball in a gorgeous gown with the man she loved, she'd felt as if she might be the princess in their odd little fairy tale after all.

She'd let herself forget.

"Tell me that you're not so foolish," Veronika said then, breaking the uncomfortable silence. She sounded almost… sympathetic? It put Alicia's teeth on edge. "Tell me you're smart enough to see his little games for what they are."

It was amazing how closely this woman's voice resembled the ones in her head, Alicia thought then. It was almost funny, though she was terribly afraid that if she tried to laugh, she'd sob instead. She was still too raw from last night's intensity. A bit too fragile from a day spent in the aftermath of such a great storm.

She wasn't ready for this—whatever this was.

"If you want to speak to Nikolai," she said when she was certain her tone would be perfectly even, almost blandly polite, "he's in the ballroom. Would you like me to show you?"

"You must have asked yourself why he chose you," Veronika said conversationally, as if this was a chat between friends. She leaned closer to the mirror to inspect her lipstick, then turned to face Alicia. "Look at you. So wholesome. So *real*. A charity worker, of all things. Not his usual type, are you?"

She didn't actually *tell* Alicia to compare the two of them. She didn't have to, as Alicia was well aware that all of Nikolai's previous women had been some version of the one who stood in front of her now. Slender like whippets, ruthlessly so. Immaculately and almost uniformly manicured in precisely the same way, from their perfect hair to their tiny bodies and their extremely expensive clothes. The kind of women rich men always had on their arms, like interchangeable trophies, which was precisely how Nikolai treated them.

Hadn't Alicia told him no one would believe he was interested in her after that kind of parade?

"I can't say I have the slightest idea what his 'type' is," she lied to Veronika. "I've never paid it as much attention as you've seemed to do."

Veronika sighed, as if Alicia made her sad. "He's using you to tell a very specific story in the tabloids. You must know this."

Alicia told herself she didn't feel a chill trickle down her spine, that something raw didn't bloom deep within at that neat little synopsis of the past few weeks of her life. She told herself that while Veronika was partly right, she couldn't know about the rest of it. She couldn't have any idea about the things that truly mattered. The things that were only theirs.

"Or," she said, trying desperately not to sound defensive, not to give any of herself away, "Nikolai is a famous man, and the tabloids take pictures of him wherever he goes. No great conspiracy, no 'story.' I'm sorry to disappoint you."

But she was lying, of course, and Veronika shook her head.

"Who do you think was the mastermind behind Ivan Korovin's numerous career changes—from fighter to Hollywood leading man to philanthropist?" she asked, a razor's edge beneath her seemingly casual tone, the trace of Russian in her voice not nearly as appealing as Nikolai's. "What about Nikolai himself? A soldier, then a security specialist, now a CEO—how do you think he manages to sell these new versions of himself, one after the next?"

"I don't see—"

"Nikolai is a very talented manipulator," Veronika said, with that sympathetic note in her voice that grated more each time Alicia heard it. "He can make you believe anything he wants you to believe." Her gaze moved over Alicia, and then she smiled. Sadly. "He can make you fall in love, if that's what he needs from you."

Alicia stared back at her, at this woman who *smiled* as she listed off all of Alicia's worst fears, and knew that she should have walked away from this conversation the moment it started. The moment she'd realized who Veronika was. Nothing good could come of this. She could already feel that dark hopelessness curling inside of her, ready to suck her in....

But her pride wouldn't let her leave without putting up some kind of fight—without making it clear, somehow, that Veronika hadn't got to her. Even if she had.

"You'll forgive me," she said, holding the other woman's gaze, "if I don't rush to take your advice to heart. I'm afraid the spiteful ex makes for a bit of a questionable source, don't you think?"

She was congratulating herself as she turned for the door. What mattered was that she loved Nikolai, and what she'd seen in him last night and today. What she knew to be true. Not the doubts and fears and possible outright lies this woman—

"Do you even know what this is about?"

Alicia told herself not to turn back around. Not to cede her tiny little bit of higher ground—

But her feet wouldn't listen. They stopped moving of their own accord. She stood there, her hand on the door, and ordered herself to walk through it.

Instead, like a fool, she turned around.

"I try not to involve myself in other people's relationships, past or present," she said pointedly, as if the fact she hadn't left wasn't evidence of surrender. As if the other woman wasn't aware of it. "As it's none of my affair."

"He didn't tell you."

Veronika was enjoying herself now, clearly. She'd dropped the sympathy routine and was now watching Alicia the way a cobra might, when it was poised to strike.

*Leave,* Alicia ordered herself desperately. *Now.*

Because she knew that whatever Veronika was about to say, she didn't want to hear it.

"Of course he didn't tell you." Veronika picked up her jeweled clutch and sauntered toward Alicia. "I told you, he's very manipulative. This is how he operates."

Alicia felt much too hot, her pulse was so frantic it was almost distracting, and there was a weight in her stomach that felt like concrete, pinning her to the ground where she stood. Making it impossible to move, to run, to escape whatever blow she could feel coming.

She could only stare at Veronika, and wait.

The other woman drew close, never taking her intent gaze from Alicia's.

"Nikolai wants to know if my son is his," she said.

It was like the ground had been taken out from under her, Alicia thought. Like she'd been dropped into a deep, black hole. She almost couldn't grasp all the things that swirled in her then, each more painful than the next.

*Not here,* she thought, fighting to keep her reaction to herself, and failing, if that malicious gleam in Veronika's eyes was any indication. *You can't deal with this here!*

She would have given anything not to ask the next question, not to give this woman that satisfaction, but she couldn't help herself. She couldn't stop. None of this had ever been real, and she needed to accept that, once and for all. None of this had ever been—nor ever would be—hers.

No matter how badly she wished otherwise. No matter how deeply, how terribly, how irrevocably she loved him.

"Is he?" she asked, hating herself. Betraying herself. "Is your son Nikolai's?"

And Veronika smiled.

Nikolai saw Alicia from the other side of the ballroom, a flash of shimmering blue and that particular walk of hers that he would know across whole cities.

He felt it like a touch. Like she could reach him simply by entering the same room.

*Mine,* he thought, and that band around his chest clutched hard, but he was almost used to it now. It meant this woman and her smile were his. It meant that odd sensation, almost a dizziness, that he found he didn't mind at all when he looked at her.

It meant this strange new springtime inside of him, this odd thaw.

At some point last night, it had occurred to him that he might survive this, after all.

Nikolai had lost track of how many times they'd come together in the night, the storm in him howling itself out with each touch, each taste of her impossible sweetness. All of her light, his. To bathe in as he pleased.

And in the morning, she'd still been there. He couldn't remember the last time any woman had slept in his bed, and he remembered too well that the first time, Alicia had sneaked away with the dawn.

Daylight was a different animal. Hushed, he thought. Something like sacred. He'd washed every inch of her delectable body in the steamy shower, learning her with his eyes as well as his greedy hands. Then he'd slowly lost his mind when she'd knelt before him on the thick rug outside the glass enclosure, taking him into her mouth until he'd groaned out his pleasure to the fogged-up mirrors.

He didn't think he'd ever get enough of her.

She curled her feet beneath her when she sat on the sofa beside him. Her favorite television program was so embarrassing, she'd claimed, that she refused to name it. She was addicted to cinnamon and licked up every last bit of it from the pastries they'd had at breakfast, surreptitiously wetting her fingertip and pressing it against the crumbs until they were gone. She read a great many books, preferred tea first thing in the morning but coffee later, and could talk, at length, about architecture and why she thought that if she had it to do over again, she might study it at university.

And that was only today. One day of learning her, and he'd barely scratched the surface. Nikolai thought that maybe, this time, he wouldn't have to settle for what he could get. This time, he might let himself want…everything. Especially the things he'd thought for so long he couldn't have, that she handed him so sweetly, so unreservedly, as if they were already his.

*Mine,* he thought again, in a kind of astonishment that it might be true. That it was even possible. *She's mine.*

Alicia disappeared in the jostling crowd, and when she reappeared she'd almost reached him. Nikolai frowned. She was holding herself strangely, and there was a certain fullness in her eyes, as if she were about—

But then he saw the woman who walked behind her, that vicious little smile on her cold lips and victory in her gaze, and his blood ran cold.

Like ice in his veins and this time, it hurt. It burned as he froze.

"*Privyet,* Nikolai," Veronika purred triumphantly when the two of them finally reached him. As sure of herself as she'd ever been. And as callous. "Look who I discovered. Such a coincidence, no?"

This, he thought, was why he had no business anywhere near a bright creature like Alicia. He'd destroy her without even meaning to do it. He'd already started.

*This is who you are,* he reminded himself bitterly, and it was worse because he'd let himself believe otherwise. He'd fallen for the lie that he could ever be anything but the monster he was. It only took a glance at Veronika, that emblem of the bad choices he'd made and with whom, to make him see that painful truth.

"Alicia. Look at me."

And when she did, when she finally raised her gaze to his, he understood. It went off inside him like a grenade, shredding him into strips, and that was only the tiniest fraction of the pain, the torment, he saw in Alicia's lovely brown eyes.

Dulled with the pain of whatever Veronika had said to her.

He'd done this. He'd put her in harm's way. He was responsible.

Nikolai had been tested last night. He'd had the opportunity to do the right thing, to imagine himself a good man and then act like one, and he'd failed. Utterly.

All of his demons were right.

Nikolai moved swiftly then, a cold clarity sweeping through him like a wind. He ordered Veronika to make herself scarce, told her he'd come find her later and that she'd better have the answer he wanted, and he did it in Russian so Alicia wouldn't hear the particularly descriptive words he used to get his point across.

"No need," Veronika said, also in Russian, looking satisfied and cruel. He wanted to wring her neck. "I had the test done long ago. You're not the father. Do you want to know who is?" She'd smiled at Nikolai's frigid glare. "I'll have the paperwork sent to your attorney."

"Do that," Nikolai growled, and if there was a flash of pain at another small hope snuffed out, he ignored it. He'd see to it that Stefan was taken care of no matter what, and right now, he had other things to worry about.

He forgot Veronika the moment he looked away. He took Alicia's arm and he led her toward the door, amazed that she let him touch her. When they got to the great foyer, he let her go so he could pull his mobile from his tuxedo jacket and send a quick, terse text to his personal assistant.

"Whatever you're about to say, don't," he told her when she started to speak, not sure he could keep the riot of self-hatred at bay just then. She pressed her lips together and scowled fiercely at the floor, and his self-loathing turned black.

*Your first response when you feel something is to attack,* Ivan had said. But Nikolai had no idea how to stop. And for the first time since he was a boy, he realized that that sinking feeling in him was fear.

He slipped his mobile back in his pocket, and guided her toward the front of the hotel, not stopping until they'd reached the glass doors that led out through the colonnaded entrance into the December night. Above them, the palatial stairs soared toward the former palace's grand facade, but this entranceway was more private. And it was where his people would meet them and take her away from him. Take her somewhere—anywhere she was safe.

Finally, he let himself look at her again.

She was hugging herself, her arms bare and tight over her body. There was misery in her dark eyes, her full lips trembled, and he'd done this. He'd hurt her. Veronika had hurt *him,* and he'd been well nigh indestructible. Why had he imagined she wouldn't do her damage to something as bright and clean as Alicia, simply to prove she could? She'd probably been sharpening her talons since the first picture hit the tabloids.

This was entirely his fault.

"Your ex-wife is an interesting woman," Alicia said.

"She's malicious and cruel, and those are her better qualities," Nikolai bit out. "What did she say to you?"

"It doesn't matter what she said." There was a torn, thick sound in her voice, and she tilted back her chin as if she was trying to be brave. He hated himself. "Everyone has secrets. God knows, I kept mine for long enough."

"Alicia—"

"I know what it's like to disappoint people, Nikolai," she said fiercely. "I know what it's like to become someone the people you love won't look at anymore, whether you've earned it or not."

He almost laughed. "You can't possibly understand the kind of life I've led. I dreamed about a father who would care about me at all, even one who shunned me for imagined sins."

"Congratulations," she threw at him. "Your pain wins. But a secret is still a—"

"Secrets?" He frowned at her, but then he understood, and the sound he let out then was far too painful to be a laugh. "She told you about Stefan."

And it killed him that Alicia smiled then, for all it was a pale shadow of her usual brightness. That she gave him that kind of gift when he could see how much she hurt.

"Is that his name?"

"He's not mine," he said harshly. "That's what she told me back there. And it's not a surprise. I wanted to be sure."

"But you wanted him to be yours," Alicia said, reading him as she always did, and he felt that band around his chest pull so tight it hurt to breathe, nearly cutting him in half.

"You want to make me a better man than I am," he told her then, losing his grip on that darkness inside of him. "And I want to believe it more than you can imagine. But it's a lie."

"Nikolai—"

"The truth is, even if Stefan was my son, he'd be better off without me." It was almost as if he was angry—as if this was his temper. But he knew it was worse than that. It was that twisted, charred, leftover thing she'd coaxed out of its cave. It was what remained of his heart, and she had to *see*. She had to *know*. "I was drunk most of the five years I thought I was his father. And now I'm—" He shook his head. *"This."*

"You're what?" Her dark eyes were glassy. "Sober?"

He felt that hard and low, like a kick to the gut. He didn't know what was happening to him, what she'd done. He only knew he had to remove her from this—get her to a minimum safe distance where he could never hurt her again, not even by mistake.

"Seeing Veronika made things perfectly clear to me," he told her. "All I will ever do is drag you down until I've stolen everything. Until I've ruined you. I can promise you that." He wanted to touch her, but he wouldn't. He couldn't risk it. "I would rather be without you than subject you to this—this sick, twisted horror show."

He was too close to her, so close he could hear that quick, indrawn breath, so close he could smell that scent of hers that drove him wild, even now.

He was no better than an animal.

Alicia looked at him for a long moment. "Are you still in love with her?" she asked.

"Do I *love* her?" Nikolai echoed in disbelief. "What the hell is *love*, Alicia?"

His voice was too loud. He heard it bouncing back at

him from the polished marble floors, saw Alicia straighten
her back as if she needed to stand tall against it. He hated
public scenes and yet he couldn't stop. He rubbed his hands
over his face to keep himself from punching the hard stone
wall. It would only be pain, and it would fade. And he would
still be right here. He would still be him.

"Veronika made me feel numb," he said instead, not realizing the truth of it until he said it out loud. Something
seemed to break open in him then, some kind of painful
knotted box he'd been holding on to for much too long. "She
was an anesthetic. And I thought that was better than being
alone." He glared at her. "And she didn't love me either, if
that's your next question. I was her way out of a dead-end
life, and she took it."

"I think that however she's capable of it, she does love
you," Alicia argued softly. "Or she wouldn't want so badly
to hurt you."

"Yes," he said, his voice grim. "Exactly. That is the kind
of love I inspire. A vile loathing that time only exacerbates.
A hatred so great she needed to hunt you down and take it
out on you. Such are my gifts." He prowled toward Alicia
then, not even knowing what he did until she'd backed up
against one of the marble columns.

But he didn't stop. He couldn't stop.

"I was told I loved my parents," he said, the words flooding from him, as dark and harsh as the place they'd lived
inside him all this time. "But I can't remember them, so
how would I know? And I love my brother, if that's what
it's called." He looked around, but he didn't see anything
but the past. And the demons who jeered at him from all
of those old, familiar shadows. "Ivan feels a sense of guilt
and obligation to me because he got out first, and I let him
feel it because I envy him for escaping so quickly while

I stayed there and rotted. And then I made it my singular goal to ruin the only happiness he'd ever known."

He'd thought he was empty before, but now he knew. This was even worse. This was unbearable, and yet he had no choice but to bear it.

"That's a great brotherly love, isn't it?"

"Nikolai," she said thickly, and she'd lost the battle with her tears. They streaked down her pretty face, each one an accusation, each one another knife in his side. "You aren't responsible for what happened to you as a child. With all the work you do, you can't truly believe otherwise. You *survived,* Nikolai. That's what matters."

And once again, he wanted to believe her. He wanted to be that man she was called to defend. He wanted to be anything other than *this*.

"I've never felt anything like these things I feel for you," he told her then, raw and harsh, so harsh it hurt him, too, and then she started to shake, and that hurt him even more. "That light of yours. The way you look at me—the way you *see* me." He reached out as if to touch her face, but dropped his hand back to his side. "I knew it that first night. I was *happy* when you walked into that conference room, and it terrified me, because do you know what I do with *happy?*"

"You do not kill it," she told him fiercely. "You try, and you fail. Happiness isn't an enemy, Nikolai. You can't beat it up. It won't fight back, and eventually, if you let it, it wins."

"I will suck you dry, tear you down, take everything until nothing remains." He moved closer, so outside himself that he was almost glad that he was so loud, that he was acting like this so she could see with her own eyes what kind of man he was. "Do I love you, Alicia? Is that what this is? This charred and twisted thing that will only bring you pain?"

"I love you," she said quietly. Clearly and distinctly, her

eyes on his. Without a single quaver in her voice. Without so much as a blink. Then she shifted, moved closer. "I love you, Nikolai."

Nikolai stilled. Inside and out. And those words hung in him like stained glass, that light of hers making them glow and shine in a cascade of colors he'd never known existed before.

He thought he almost hated her for that. He told himself he'd rather not know.

He leaned in until her mouth was close enough to kiss, and his voice dropped low. Savage. "Why would you do something so appallingly self-destructive?"

"Because, you idiot," she said calmly, not backing away from him, not looking even slightly intimidated. "*I love you.* There's always a risk when you give someone your heart. They might crush it. But that's no reason not to do it."

He felt as if he was falling, though he wasn't. He only wished he was. He leaned toward her, propping his hands on either side of her head as he had once before, then lowering his forehead until he rested it against hers.

And for a moment he simply breathed her in, letting his eyes fall shut, letting her scent and her warmth surround him.

He felt her hands come up to hold on to him, digging in at his hips with that strong grip that had already undone him once before, and he felt a long shudder work through him.

"This is the part where you run for cover, Alicia," he whispered fiercely. "I told you why I couldn't lose control. Now you know."

He heard her sigh. She tipped back her head, then lifted her hands up to take his face between them. When he opened his eyes, what he saw in her gaze made him shake.

"This is where you save yourself," he ground out at her.

She smiled at him, though more tears spilled from her eyes. She held him as if she had no intention of letting him go. She looked at him as if he was precious. Even now. "And then who saves you?"

# CHAPTER TEN

NIKOLAI'S HANDS SLIPPED from the marble column behind her, his arms came around her, and he held her so tightly, so closely, that Alicia wasn't sure she could breathe.

And she didn't care.

He held her like that for a long time.

A member of the hotel staff came over to quietly inquire if all was well, and she waved him away. A trio of black-suited people who could only be part of Nikolai's pack of assistants appeared, and she frowned at them until they backed off.

And outside, in the courtyard of the former palace, it began to snow.

Nikolai let out a long, shaky breath and lifted his head. He kissed her, so soft and so sweet it made her smile.

"If I had a heart, I would give it to you," he said then, very seriously. "But I don't."

She shook her head at him, and kissed him back, losing herself in that for a long time. His eyes were haunted, and she loved him so much she didn't know if she wanted to laugh or cry or scream—it seemed too big to contain.

And he loved her, too. He'd as much as said so. He just didn't know what that meant.

So Alicia would have to show him. Step by step, smile by smile, laugh by laugh, until he got it. Starting now.

"You have a heart, Nikolai," she told him gently, smiling up at that beautifully hard face, that perfectly austere mouth, her would-be Tin Man. "It's just been broken into so many pieces, and so long ago, you never learned how to use it properly."

"You're the only one who thinks so," he said softly.

She reached out and laid her hand on his chest, never looking away from him.

"I can feel it. It's right here. I promise."

"And I suppose you happen to know how one goes about putting back together a critically underused heart, no doubt fallen into disrepair after all these years," he muttered, but his hands were moving slow and sweet up her back and then down her arms to take her hands in his.

"I have a few ideas," she agreed. "And your heart is not a junked-out car left by the side of a road somewhere, Nikolai. It's real and it's beating and you've been using it all along."

He looked over his shoulder then, as if he'd only then remembered where they were. One of his assistants appeared from around the corner as if she'd been watching all along, and he nodded at her, but didn't move. Then he looked out the glass doors, at the snow falling into the golden-lit courtyard and starting to gather on the ground.

"I hate snow," he said.

"Merry Christmas to you, too, Ebenezer Scrooge," Alicia said dryly. She slid an arm around his waist and looked outside. "It's beautiful. A fairy tale," she said, smiling at him, "just as you promised me in the beginning."

"I think you're confused." But she saw that smile of his.

It started in his eyes, made them gleam. "I promised you fangs. And tears. Both of which I've delivered, in spades."

"There are no wolves in a story involving ball gowns, Nikolai. I believe that's a rule."

"Which fairy tale is this again? The ones I remember involved very few ball gowns, and far more darkness." His mouth moved into that crooked curve she adored, but his eyes were serious when they met hers. "I don't know how to be a normal man, Alicia. Much less a good one." His smile faded. "And I certainly don't know how to be anything like good for you."

Alicia smiled at him again, wondering how she'd never known that the point of a heart was to break. Because only then could it grow. And swell big enough to hold the things she felt for Nikolai.

"Let's start with normal and work from there," she managed to say. "Come to Christmas at my parents' house. Sit down. Eat a huge Christmas dinner. Make small talk with my family." She grinned. "I think you'll do fine."

He looked at her, that fine mouth of his close again to grim.

"I don't know if I can be what you want," he said. "I don't know—"

"I want you," she said. She shook her head when he started to speak. "And all you have to do is love me. As best you can, Nikolai. For as long as you're able. And I'll promise to do the same."

It was like a vow. It hung there between them, hushed and huge, with only the falling snow and the dark Prague night as witness.

He looked at her for a long time, and then he leaned down and kissed her the way he had on that London street. Hard and demanding, hot and sure, making her his.

"I can do that," he said, when he lifted his head, a thousand brand-new promises in his eyes, and she believed every one. "I can try."

Nikolai stood facing his brother on a deep blue July afternoon. The California sky arched above them, cloudless and clear, while out beyond them the Pacific Ocean rolled smooth and gleaming all the way to the horizon.

"Are you ready?" Ivan barked in gruff Russian. He wore his game face, the one he'd used in the ring, fierce and focused and meant to be terrifying.

Nikolai only smiled.

"Is this the intimidating trash talk portion of the afternoon?" he asked coolly. "Because I didn't sign up to be bored to death, Vanya. I thought this was a fight."

Ivan eyed him.

"You insist on writing checks you can't cash, little brother," he said. "And sadly for you, I am the bank."

They both crouched down into position, studying each other, looking for tells—

Until a sharp wail cut through the air, and Ivan broke his stance to look back toward his Malibu house and the figures who'd walked out from the great glass doors and were heading their way.

Nikolai did a leg sweep without pausing to think about it, and had the great satisfaction of taking Ivan down to the ground.

"You must never break your concentration, brother," he drawled, patronizingly, while Ivan lay sprawled out before him. "Surely, as an undefeated world champion, you should know this."

Ivan's dark eyes promised retribution even as he jack-knifed up and onto his feet.

"Enjoy that, Kolya. It will be your last and only victory."

And then he grinned and slapped Nikolai on the back, throwing an arm over his shoulders as they started toward the house and the two women who walked to meet them.

Nikolai watched Alicia, that smile of hers brighter even than a California summer and her lovely voice on the wind, that kick of laughter and cleverness audible even when he couldn't hear the words.

"You owe him an apology," she'd told him. It had been January, and they'd been tucked up in that frilly pink bedroom of hers that he found equal parts absurd and endearing. Though he did enjoy her four-poster bed. "He's your brother. Miranda is afraid of you, and she still risked telling you how hurt he was."

He'd taken her advice, stilted and uncertain.

And now, Nikolai thought as he drew close to her with his brother at his side, he was learning how to build things, not destroy them. He was learning how to trust.

The baby in Miranda's arm wailed again, and both women immediately made a cooing sort of sound that Nikolai had never heard Alicia make before his plane had landed in Los Angeles. Beside him, Ivan shook his head. And then reached over to pluck the baby from his wife's arms.

"Naturally, Ivan has the magic touch," Miranda said to Alicia with a roll of her eyes, as the crying miraculously stopped.

"How annoying," Alicia replied, her lips twitching.

Nikolai stared down at the tiny pink thing that looked even smaller and more delicate in Ivan's big grip.

"Another generation of Korovins," he said. He caught Miranda looking at him as he spoke, and thought her smile was slightly warmer than the last time. Progress. He returned his attention to Ivan and the baby. "I don't think you thought this through, brother."

"It's terrible, I know," Ivan agreed. He leaned close and

kissed his daughter's soft forehead, contentment radiating from him. "A disaster waiting to happen."

Nikolai smiled. "Only if she fights like you."

Later, after he and Ivan spent a happy few hours throwing each other around and each claiming victory, he found Alicia out on the balcony that wrapped around their suite of rooms. He walked up behind her silently, watching the breeze dance through the cloud of her black curls, admiring the short and flirty dress she wore in a bright shade of canary yellow, showing off all of those toned brown limbs he wanted wrapped around him.

Now. Always.

She gasped when he picked her up, but she was already smiling when he turned her in his arms. As if she could read his mind—and he often believed she could—she hooked her legs around his waist and let him hold her there, both of them smiling at the immediate burst of heat. The fire that only grew higher and hotter between them.

"Move in with me," he said, and her smile widened. "Live with me."

"Here in Malibu in this stunning house?" she asked, teasing him. "I accept. I've always wanted to be a Hollywood star. Or at least adjacent to one."

"The offer is for rain and cold, London and me," he said. He shifted her higher, held her closer.

"This is a very difficult decision," she said, but her eyes were dancing. "Are you sure you don't want to come live with me and Rosie instead? She's stopped shrieking and dropping things when you walk in rooms. And she did predict that the night we met would be momentous. She's a prophet, really."

"Move in with me," he said again, and nipped at her neck, her perfect mouth. He thought of that look on his brother's face, that deep pleasure, that peace. "Marry me, someday. When it's right. Make babies with me. I want to live this life of yours, where everything is multicolored and happiness wins."

And then he said the words, because he finally knew what they meant. She'd promised him he had a heart, and she'd taught it how to beat. He could feel it now, pounding hard.

"I love you, Alicia."

She smiled at him then as if he'd given her the world, when Nikolai knew it was the other way around. She'd lit him up, set him free. She'd given him back his brother, broke him out of that cold, dark prison that had been his life. She was so bright she'd nearly blinded him, all those beautiful colors and all of them his to share, if he liked. If he let her.

"Is that a yes?" He pulled back to look at her. "It's okay if you don't—"

"Yes," she said through her smile. "Yes to everything. Always yes."

She'd loved him when he was nothing more than a monster, and she'd made him a man.

*Love* hardly covered it. But it was a start.

"Look at you," she whispered, her dark eyes shining. She smoothed her hands over his shoulder, plucking at the T-shirt she'd bought him and made him wear. He'd enjoyed the negotiation. "Put the man in a blue shirt and he changes his whole life."

She laughed, and as ever, it stopped the world.

"No, *solnyshka*," Nikolai murmured, his mouth against hers so he could feel that smile, taste the magic of her laughter, the miracle of the heart she'd made beat again in him, hot and alive and real. "That was you."

* * * * *